Tinay
the
Warrior Princess

Tinay
the
Warrior Princess

The Initiation

To Paige may this be the beginning of a new adventure

[signature] 2019

Sonya Roy

Copyright © 2015 by Sonya Roy.

Library of Congress Control Number:		2014922182
ISBN:	Hardcover	978-1-5035-2711-9
	Softcover	978-1-5035-2713-3
	eBook	978-1-5035-2712-6

Cover photo by Sonya Roy.

All rights reserved. No part of this book may be reproduced or transmitted in any form or by any means, electronic or mechanical, including photocopying, recording, or by any information storage and retrieval system, without permission in writing from the copyright owner.

This is a work of fiction. Names, characters, places and incidents either are the product of the author's imagination or are used fictitiously, and any resemblance to any actual persons, living or dead, events, or locales is entirely coincidental.

Any people depicted in stock imagery provided by Thinkstock are models, and such images are being used for illustrative purposes only.
Certain stock imagery © Thinkstock.

Print information available on the last page.

Rev. date: 12/12/2014

You can contact the author through multi media:
 www.TinayTheWarriorPrincess.com
 Facebook
 www.facebook.com/sonya.roy.author
 Twitter
 @RoySonyaroy

To order additional copies of this book, contact:
Xlibris
1-888-795-4274
www.Xlibris.com
Orders@Xlibris.com
701834

Contents

Acknowledgment 9

Chapter 1: Mani the Storyteller 11
Chapter 2: The Story of Tinay.. 18
Chapter 3: Departure for Os... 29
Chapter 4: The Lithil... 47
Chapter 5: Space Travel.. 59
Chapter 6: Os... 75
Chapter 7: Essay.. 98
Chapter 8: The Pyramid.. 118
Chapter 9: Kaplara.. 128
Chapter 10: The Tournament 144
Chapter 11: The Celebration... 156
Chapter 12: The History of Atlanteus 171
Chapter 13: The Seven Temples 186
Chapter 14: The Gifts of the Fairies 198
Chapter 15: The Centaur 208
Chapter 16: The Guardian.. 224
Chapter 17: The Third Eye... 243
Chapter 18: The Crown.. 267
Chapter 19: Loni... 281
Chapter 20: The Return Home... 294
Chapter 21: The Birthday... 308

Dedication

To my father who initiated me to legends and started me on my quest for knowledge.

Acknowledgment

I want to thank Heavenly Father for the inspiration, guidance and his gift of writing, for allowing me to create such an incredible story. Without Him, this enterprise would not be possible. It is with his Spirit that this story came together.

I want to thank my son, Ben, who inspired me to create this story, without him I would have never become a writer.

To Danni my undying Love aand Friendship,m oney (duh! What money!) Her supoport and enthousism help make this book a reality. These were the only lines she didn't corect for repetition, repetition, repetion. Making sure ? That ; the punctuality was perfect=taking from her nowledge and education. She make sure spelling and gramar was just right. She wanted the reader to be hooked (I appologize in advance for all of you who will get hurt in the process) So that the reader could enjoy the story she loved so much. Danielle, I hope our collaboration and complicity will last forever. In order for that to happen I will make sure that I write until my dying breath, Hugs and Kisses. For those of you reading this and have no sense of humor just skip this and go strait to the story....

I want to thank my daughters, Kaylun and Audrey, for their constant demands for new bedtime stories. They keep me inspired and keep the creative juice flowing. They are my personal critics and always expect nothing less than the best.

I want to thank Allan MacLeod for his help and advice. It was a blessing to have his support.

To Joelle, Catou, Isa, Susan, Rachel, Lindsay, Dorial, Jan, Shirley, Vivian, Tammy, my dear friends who have been there for me when I needed them the most. Their gift of friendship and love gave me strength to overcome obstacles and bloom into the woman I am today.

A great thanks to Lindsay who helped make the publishing process a smooth and easy one.

Chapter 1

MANI THE STORYTELLER

The long day was hard on her feet. Saturday was always the busiest day of the week. Students came in looking for books, parents stopped in with their children. Today was an exceptionally bright and sunny day, and people walking in the sun would come in to browse in her shop.

The shop was a fair size, but it looked much smaller with all of the clutter it had collected throughout the years. Mani could never say "no" to a new book coming to her store. She wanted to be able to say she had at least one print of each book. She had special sections for her collections. One wall was covered with ancient scrolls enclosed in a special glass tank. Only people who had a proven love for books and knew how to manipulate the scrolls could enter. The scrolls were so delicate that they needed special attention and care. One could not just go in and tear one open; they were irreplaceable, and therefore of great value.

Mani looked at the glass cell. These books were her pride and joy. They were her heritage. Before there were books, there were scrolls, and she had most of them here. Despite her efforts, some scrolls had been lost forever. As a safety measure, she had them all printed by hand into leather-covered books. It took many years of hard work, but it was something she was very proud of. She hated to deny anyone access to the scrolls and their gift of knowledge, so this way anyone could read, learn and share their knowledge without any harm coming to the scrolls. She walked past the section of history and myth; stories that had intertwined so much that the truth seemed lost through time.

She picked up the oldest, most ragged-looking book she could find and opened it.

"Oh my," she exclaimed. "My handwriting was terrible when I first started."

Over the years she had developed beautiful calligraphy, but her earliest attempts were sketchy and bold. She put the book back, after all, there was hardly any time left for her to daydream. She had to prepare for her story night. It was her favorite thing to do; to bring the books she loved so much back to life in her own store.

Tonight she had to choose carefully because she had to impress and please an older crowd, the 12 to 15 year olds. "Hum," she thought, "hardly old enough to know the tribute of life, yet too young for a magical story. I think I have just the one." She walked past the center of her bookstore and headed for an alcove in the back. Opening up a glassed-in room, the countryside in the distance presented a beautiful cliff and below, the crashing waves of the sea. This was the perfect backdrop for any story. The changing moods of the sky, the ever-changing scenery, the passing of seasons, and the bright colored flowers. Each of these had inspired her to create wonderful stories year after year. Her life had a life of its own. She was merely following a path that seemed to have been drawn from the dawn of time.

Mani started out by buying an old house far out in the country and fixing it. She then bought acres and acres of land to make sure the forest would remain to inspire her, for the lake and the ocean to remain peaceful and quiet until she would bring back the ancient soldiers, fairies, and magician.

She then completed the task of reuniting the scrolls. What an adventure this was! Then she worked with her best friends to transcribe them. This was tedious work because some of the scrolls were in such poor condition that once they were opened they would crack and fall apart. When this happened, the scroll would lay open until the transcription was completed. Once, before the glass cell was created, someone opened the door and the wind blew the pieces of the scrolls, making them gently float in the air. It took weeks just to put the scrolls back on the table in the proper order.

That's the day the glass cell arrived. Yes, she learned from her mistakes over the years. Just like the story room she started with chairs. She thought this was the most convenient arrangement; it provided more seating space and allowed for listeners to look at her and concentrate on her words. Boy, was she wrong! Instead, the chairs turned out to be a distraction. No one, it seemed, could sit still long enough for her to get through her introduction. Her friends told her she didn't need that many chairs anyway. Who would come all the way from the city to hear her stories? Adults had better uses for their time. But Mani thought differently. People were so busy with their life. They needed magic and needed to find a reason, a quest, for their everyday life. Those who needed it would come.

As the years passed, she replaced the chairs with cushions, large and soft, some made of silk, and some made of suede. Each had a different feel to it, and each capturing the scent of the incense she burned throughout the day. For the more formal clients, she had couches all around the room. It turned out to be a blessing for breast-feeding mothers, and grandparents that felt too old to sit on the floor. Indeed, people from all ages and societies had come to listen to her tell the stories. Her story time had become so popular that she had to hire employees to run the store for her while she read to her mesmerized clients. She had a talent for keeping crowds hanging on her every word. She knew when she was good by the glitter in their eyes and how their jaws dropped and stayed open. It was a thrill she couldn't compare to anything else she ever did!

She started out with a morning story time from the children's books she sold.

Soon she had to do two readings a day to answer the demand, but she kept her evenings to herself to paint canvases, which illustrated the stories she would tell next.

Saturday nights had become a special project of hers. She wanted to reach out to the teenagers, but they were at school all day, so she had to come up with a new way to get them to read and, in turn, come to shop in her store. She didn't just want to sell a book every week, she wanted them to be hooked for life. So she started multiple series of stories. "Yes, Mani, old girl, you did the trick there," she said to herself.

She was very proud of one accomplishment: she had made a series of paintings of the old stories in the scrolls and gave them life. She never thought anyone else would be interested in the scroll mythology, but this had proven to be inspirational and uplifting; the ultimate fight between good and evil.

The leather-bound books were unique because they were a special order she transcribed herself and, to keep the magic alive, each book had a spirit of its own because they were written from her verbal recollections of story time. None of them were exactly the same. She told the stories so many times that she could quote half of the scrolls by heart. But, by writing the book from the recording she made from her story time, she personalized them so much to her audience that this kept them interested. It didn't seem to matter that the books were expensive, the demand grew and grew until her original pupils started to bring their own children to story time and wanted to immortalize their experience in their own private book. She had hooked them, all right. Now she had a full-time support staff, each of whom had gorgeous handwriting to do this task for her. Over the years, she had delegated many of her obligations to others, all except one. The illustrations were hers and hers alone. It was through her eyes that the different worlds were to be seen. After all these years, she was still the backbone of her stories. She also wrote one copy of the story and the book was raffled to the participants of story time.

Tonight, she would start a new group. People had signed up in advance not knowing what she would tell. "Inspiration is a gift, it cannot be commanded in advance," she would say. Nevertheless, her class was always full. Tonight, however, she had a special treat for them. She would tell the story of Tinay, the fourteen-year-old daughter of Lilay and Tamael, a young girl in search of her identity, stuck on the desert planet of Sasgorg. "Yes, that will be a good series," she said as she pulled the paintings from their enclave. She hung them up all over the room.

The room was round and extremely high so she could hang dozens of paintings, none of which were the same size.

She had told this story many times over the years and it was her favorite, and the one she had the most illustrations for. As she was hanging the pictures, the reflection of the sun off the wall turned a deep orange. With a little bit of imagination you could see the wall burning into a bright fire. "Oh!" she said. "It's almost time. They'll be here soon." At the same moment, a young girl walked in.

"Mani," she said, "you know I'm supposed to do this for you. If mother saw you perched up there, she would be mad at both of us!"

Mani tenderly looked at her granddaughter. Her heart warmed instantly. Alayana was tall with luxurious brown hair that had a touch of red flaming through it. She was slender and muscular, not at all the type one would expect to love books and work in a library.

Alayana saw the deep look of her grandmother and knew what she was thinking. "I am not giving up sports, Mani, but I'm not giving up magic and fairies either." She loved her grand-mother so much. She had given her hours of pleasure in this room and she wanted nothing more than to learn the craft and to one day take over the shop.

Mani said, "Your mother is too serious. She needs to lighten up a bit. I may be old, but I'm still in great shape. I may not do sports but I'm still active in a healthy body . . ."

They both finished together, ". . . and a healthy mind."

"That's right, young lady," said Mani. "And both of mine are functioning quite well. Besides, this story is my favorite. I want to prepare it alone."

"Oh!" Alayana said. "Are you telling Tinay's story?"

"Yes, I am." Mani smiled knowing it had always been her daughter and granddaughter's favorite.

"I couldn't wait to be fourteen to finally hear it and picture myself doing what she did." Alayana had heard the story a few times before but, the heroine being fourteen, she couldn't wait to see herself doing what Tinay had done.

"Yes, I thought it would be a great present for your birthday. It will take a few weeks to tell the story and I should be finished for your birthday, dear," Mani said, smiling.

"But if I sit in, who will look after the store?" Alayana asked.

"Your mother is coming to help me. I guess it's our present to you," said Mani.

"Oh, thank you, Mani!" She jumped and hugged Mani so hard, Mani thought for a second she was going to suffocate.

Alayana ran off to her room on the third floor and got her own cushion. It seemed small now, but when she was younger she would lay on it and close her eyes and see the story play in her head. Each time she heard Tinay's story, normally once every 4 years, she saw new things. But one things was always constant -- the heroine, Tinay, looked like her. Sometimes she felt it was her. This was going to be the best birthday ever!

Once downstairs, Mani turned to face the mirror. She didn't look like herself anymore. When Mani closed her eyes, she could see her hair, still lightly brown with touches of red floating through it, slightly wavy and bouncy. Her face was soft, and she was lean and slim. But now that her eyes were opened, she saw an old lady with long, white, straight but soft hair, braided on each side of her face. Her skin was still soft, but she had wrinkles around her mouth and eyes. Her body still moved softly, but she was no longer lean and slim. She had a little belly rounded off by four pregnancies. She was trying to hide it under a loose dress, but she knew better. She walked around in sandals and a veil usually covered her hair. She smiled as she remembered that in her husband eyes, she always looked twenty-five.

She was startled from her daydreaming by a knock at the door. She went over to open it. It was her daughter Lyauria. "Hello, darling. How was your day?"

Lyauria was a beautiful woman, very much like Alayana. "Very good, Mother." Lyauria hugged and kissed her mother. "The patients are numerous and sometimes I'm afraid I won't be able to cure them, but in the end it works out alright."

Mani was proud of her daughter.

Lyauria took her jacket off. She was an excellent doctor and she remained caring and loving to her own children even though she was always so busy. "Is everything ready?" Lyauria asked.

Just as Mani was about to answer, a voice came from the stairs. "Yes, everything is set up. We're just waiting for our guests to come in." Alayana had a bounce in her step, as if there was an invisible rope making her jump.

"Oh, Mother, you told her already?" asked Lyauria.

"Sorry," said Mani. "I wanted to wait, but I just couldn't." Again a knock on the door interrupted. "Ah! Here are our guests. You best settle in, Alayana, or else they'll take the best seats in the house."

Mani walked towards the door and opened it. It was Marcus with his mother, Andrea. "Welcome. Please find a seat." Mani stayed at the door breathing in the fresh evening air. She filled her lungs and breathed deeply. More cars were pulling up to the house. She waved at them. Yes, tonight would be good!

Chapter 2

THE STORY OF TINAY

Mani closed the door behind her. Everyone was there. This was a great night to start Tinay's story.

Mani slowly walked back to the circular room, and looked around. She had children here that had been her pupils for more than ten years now. Some of them had, with time, started to bring their own cushions and they settled into their favorite spots. All of them were lying on their backs looking at the high wall, to see the different paintings ornamenting it. Mani could already see the twinkle in some of the parents' eyes. They remembered, yes, they did.

Mani sat down on a cushion on the wooden stage by the window. She always started sitting down, but when the action was rising she would walk around and act out the scenes. Some would look at her intensely, but others would look at her paintings and imagine themselves there. Others, like Alayana, would simply close their eyes and create their own magical world. The room was full. She looked around one more time and saw a few new faces. They had a "deer caught in the headlights of a fast-moving vehicle" look; not too sure what would happen next.

John was sitting squarely on his cushion, not yet comfortable with the floor. He was fifteen-years-old and felt he should sit on the couch, but the couch seats were reserved, and there was no room for him there.

Brett, on the other hand, sat staring at Mani. He heard she could do magic and that she was able to cast a spell on you from the first words she spoke. He was twelve years old. This was his first time and he couldn't wait.

Marcus was lying down comfortably on his cushion and waiting for the magic to start. No one could tell a story like Mani could, he thought. Mani took a deep breath and exhaled; she was ready. She turned down the room's light and turned on the spotlight to one of the paintings. She walked to her seat, then she stopped and looked around. Near her cushion were a projector and a laser effect console and other device controls, such as smoke, sound effects, room temperature. There was even mist, which could be created to help create the right mood for the story. There was a time when storytellers only had their voice to keep a crowd interested. For a week day performance, she would dress up, have puppets, and use paintings. But she wanted the teenagers to feel like they were taken seriously by her. It was still the same idea of magic, fascination, and sending them to another world, just with a different tool.

She might lose the respect of other storytellers, but she went the unusual way and created for them their own world; and it worked. They were here to listen to her and not out there on the streets. She walked slowly to her seat and began.

"Welcome to all of you, welcome. I recognize some faces and see some that are new. I am here to present the story of Tinay, the warrior Princess." She slowly pointed her finger at the central painting on the wall. A painting was brightly lit up of a demure-looking woman, wearing a long dress fitted at her waist and long, tight sleeves. She was a grown woman wearing her hair just like Mani, but her hair was a rich brown with red and blond highlights. She wore a crown and a cape. In her hands rested a sword with a blade that started off three inches wide at the handle and grew like wings to nine inches, then shrank back to a fine point of two inches. The blade was a brilliant metal. The handle was covered with leather and the pommel was shaped like a heart. A small gust of wind made her hair float around her face, her cape hung suspended in the air, and mist covered her feet. Her crown was made of fine linen, and leaves of metal, not gold or silver, but something else that reflected the color of her surroundings. There was an aura about her, a soft green glow. Her eyes shined gently in the suspended light. If eyes were truly the mirror to the soul, then her eyes were like deep space with millions of stars and galaxies. Intelligence and cunning resided there as did love and compassion.

This was such a contrast to the sword. Why would such a gentle, loving creature need to carry a sword? Even though the tip rested on the ground, it was obvious it could be put to deadly use in an instant. Determination was in her stance; yes, she looked magical.

Marcus had caught a glimpse of this woman before and now that he could directly stare at her, time suspended itself. She was beautiful and strong, yet delicate. She had all the qualities of a good heroine. Softly Mani began.

* * * * *

"It was not so long ago that Tinay, the warrior Princess, lived among us. Her rise to power was a quest for knowledge, truth and justice. To understand how she became the woman you see in this painting you must know she had a much simpler beginning. She was born in the 40,000 year of our Lord Atlanti, who first invented the calendar. She was born to a miner by the name of Tamael and an artisan mother, Lilay. They lived on Sasgorg." She lit up another painting from the wall, a desert planet where the sand was white and the rock was black. The sky took on shades of deep purple at night and transformed into a light lilac during the day. There were five mountains on Sasgorg. Ecumel was the mountain of the north where Tinay lived in a cave. To the east was Landel where the top was a flat enough surface to land the transport ship. To the west sat Zuel, a vast chain of mountains with a central peak. The west side of the mountain was covered with small grottos which all inter-linked each other. Directly south of Ecumel, but in between Zuel and Landel, was Ardel. Ardel was the tallest peak of them all. Its black rock was shattered, jagged and dangerous to climb, but at its peak was where the most beautiful sunrise could be seen. Finally, to the south of

Ardel, was Galgamel a majestic volcano, asleep for thousands of years. Tinay grew up quickly to become an intelligent and perspicacious child. She loved to play strategy games with her father and challenged her mother to enigmas and puzzles. She loved to take things apart and discover how they worked. She learned most of what she knew about plants and herbs from her mother. There was not very much growing outside on the planet, but some very resilient plants grew on the mountains, and inside the caves of Zuel were the most fantastic arrangements of plants and flowers. It took a hard day at the caves to collect the specimens they needed but, Tinay grew up loving her planet. Some of the merchants of the planet Os who visited the planet never stayed long, for it was too hot and dry for their taste. There were few travelers in this far region of space, since a nearby star had gone nova about the year 37,846 of our lord Atlanti. Luckily it was a twin sun solar system. The star had burned the surface of all habitable planets for light years around.

Tinay grew up alone with her pet ferret, Draco. He was white, furry and had two grey lines of hair on his forehead that made him look like a dragon. Seven years ago, Raphael, Tinay's brother, was born to her family. Together, they grew up and, in the last few months, Tinay had become his guide through their daily meditation. The cave where they lived was decorated by their mother, a very prodigious artisan who worked the rock in every spare minute she had to make it the most beautiful thing anyone had ever seen. Flowers and exotic birds and animals danced all around the cavern walls.

The entrance to the cave had three doors to prevent the sand from penetrating the cavern and to cut down the wind's power to transport small rocks into their home. The first door was small and to the left, covered by a thick canvas. Then there was a narrow passage leading to a wooden door at the far right. The passage was anciently decorated with the story of Atlanti and one would not walk briskly to the second door, but admire the history of their people. Then, again, a long, narrow hallway lead to the final door, which was in the center and ornamented by beads suspended on a string. The story of Atlanti and his people leaving earth for the stars was depicted there. Even though Tinay had lived there for all her fourteen years of life, she loved to run her hand along the rock surface and remember the story her mother would often tell her. She walked up and down those hallways many times, but never got tired of the story. What a great adventure that had been! Tinay pushed aside the beads to make her way into the kitchen area where her mother was preparing dinner. She worked slowly lately; she was pregnant with her third child and, somehow, that child was very demanding of her. It was to be a girl, her mother had said. Tinay remembered her mother had a great intuition for such things and did not question her mother on how she could be so sure about that. Her brother, Raphael, was stealing half the beans her mother managed to clean up.

"Raphael, it's time for your meditation," Tinay said.

Her mother looked up and smiled. It wasn't time at all, but it was the only way she could finish supper on time.

Raphael looked up at his mother and asked, "Oh, Mum, must I? It's so boring, that stuff."

"Yes, you must," she said, kissing him on the forehead. "It is time for you to start learning the ways of our people. And your father will be most impressed."

As if she had pronounced magic words, Raphael leaped to his feet and ran toward the stairs circling down the back of the cave, yelling. "Well, Tinay what are you waiting for?"

"I'm coming, Raphael."

Tinay passed by her mother and hugged her. She, too, was granted a kiss on the forehead. She grabbed a basket full of trinkets and followed her brother down the stairs.

Down the second flight of stairs was their bedroom. Another flight of stairs led down to the lower level where plants grew and their well was. Above them, at the very top of the wall, a crystal pyramid intensified any light and sent it to the center of the mountain, which allowed the plants to grow.

Raphael was lying on his back on the cushion staring at the crystal dangling from the cavern wall. It was like staring at the night sky in the middle of the day. The reflection of the sun on the crystal made a clear bright light shine throughout the whole cavern.

Tinay grabbed a cushion and sat beside her brother and put the basket beside her.

"All right, now close your eyes and start telling me what you are doing," she said.

"I start to breathe from my stomach and send the air through my whole body. Then I slowly move the air to the top of my lungs and exhale from the stomach and then I exhale whatever is left from my lungs," Raphael said.

"Right. Do it slowly. Take the time to see the air circulating through your body; view its energy moving through you; see it coming in as white and pure and exhale all that is dark and impure."

"I exhale what again?" Raphael always forgot this part.

"You exhale your fear, your anxiety, and your ambivalence. Steady yourself. You want the air to cleanse your body and heal yourself."

"But I'm not hurt," said Raphael.

"Not now, you're not, but if you were to control your pain after being hurt, this is what you would do. Pain is all in your head and it takes over your brain and makes you react on survival mode. If you can control your pain, then you have full control of your thoughts. It takes a lot of mental discipline to do so."

"All right. The air is moving through me and it's filling up my body with light. Then I make a bubble of gold around me -"

"No, not yet. You forgot the seven temples." Tinay chided him.

"Oh, right, sorry."

"Not to worry, you are new at this. Okay, the first temple is on top of your pelvis; it's red. Try to see its energy."

"Is it okay if I picture something?"

"Yeah."

"Can you help me?"

"Yeah," Tinay deposited a red apple on her brother. "Picture the apple in your mind and see the energy radiate from it."

"Okay, it's glowing red . . ."

"Good. Now try to spin the apple on itself and see the energy intensify."

"Okay, I think I got it," said Raphael. Unbeknownst to him, his sister, Tinay, knew he did because she could see the apple gently lift itself from her brother's body and spin on itself.

"You're doing well." Tinay reached for his head with her left hand and with her right, gently deposited an orange on his stomach, "Now try to see the orange without stopping the spinning apple."

"Okay, I feel the orange."

"No, don't feel it. You must see it." Tinay closed her eyes and helped her brother picture the orange in his mind.

"Eh! Get out! I didn't ask for your help," Raphael yelled.

"Okay, come down or you'll lose the apple. Now the orange must have an aura also."

"I'm working on it. This is really hard." Indeed, it was hard; it had taken her many years to master all seven temples.

"All right, what do you see?" asked Tinay.

"I see the orange spinning on itself. I'm doing it, Tinay, I'm doing it!"

"Good, good work." Tinay could see the orange slowly lift itself from her brother's body and spin, "Let's try the sun next." Tinay deposited a yellow crystal with rays coming out of it on his sternum. "You must try to focus the energy of the sun. Can you see it?"

"No, not yet. What color is that one again?"

"It's yellow, very bright yellow, like the sun at midday."

"All right, here it goes." Raphael could feel the pointy ray of the sun resting against his chest. He had looked at it often enough but was unsure how it would look once the energy was harvested in it.

"Raph, you must continue to breathe. If you don't breathe you'll have no energy to focus."

"Right, right."

"And don't forget the apple and the orange."

"Right, this is hard." Raphael felt warm and tired. This was a very demanding exercise; he didn't know he was levitating the apple and the orange while his concentration was elsewhere.

"Maybe it's enough for tonight?"

"No, I want to try," said Raphael

"All right, do you want my help then?" asked Tinay.

"Yeah, ok, but just a little bit."

"Yes, just a little bit." Tinay was breathing at the same speed as her brother and joined her thoughts with his and together they lifted the sun gently and made it spin.

"Oh, it's beautiful," said Raphael.

"Yes, it is. You should see the fifth temple, it's my favorite."

"What is the fifth temple?"

"All in good time, Raph. All in good time."

She surrounded him with a golden cloak and left him to meditate on what he could see. She remembered being this age when she started meditation. She thought it was a waste of time. Now she couldn't have a good day unless she started it with meditation on mount Zuel.

Tinay went back up the stairs to the kitchen to see if her mother needed help. She found the kitchen empty except for a pot on the fire slowly cooking vegetable soup. The sweet aroma filled the kitchen. She loved her mother's soup; it was so comforting after a long day in the desert. Tinay's father would be home soon. Where could her mother have gone?

She looked into the room by the stairs. It was her parent's room where they laid their tools. All of her mother's tools were resting in their place. She tip-toed to the next room and saw her mother sleeping in her bed, her hand resting on her large belly. The baby was due in a month, in the fall. She went over to the table and started to set the plates for supper when her father walked in. "Hel . . ."

"Shh," she said. "Mom's asleep and Raph is meditating."

"Okay then," he said, hardly whispering, and walked over to her and kissed her on the forehead. "How was your day?" asked Tamael as he continued to the storage room and deposited his tools.

"I went to Zuel this morning and meditated there until Draco came back for breakfast. Then we went to the caves and found some raspberries and ate the hard dough mom had prepared. I collected more samples of medicinal herbs for my book like mom asked and returned home about an hour ago."

Tamael headed down the stairs, "Hmm." Tamael looked at Raphael, who was lying on his cushion. "I thought you said he was meditating." The fruits were back on his body and his head was tilted sideways. It was obvious that Raphael was no longer meditating but was fast asleep.

"Well, he was." Tinay was embarrassed. She knew how much it offended her father to find them sleeping through a mental exercise. "It's difficult for him. He just turned seven, Pa. You're not mad are you?"

"No, but he has many steps to take to get where we need him to be, and sleeping in the middle of his exercise is displaying very poor mental discipline."

Tamael walked over to the water pool and drew out a large vase filled with water, which was warm because of the reflecting crystal. He quickly washed his arms and face and went over to Raphael. He lightly put his hands on both sides of his son's head and gently put his forehead on Raphael's forehead to see his dream. Raphael was in the mine with his father picking up the crystals for them to sell.

Tamael gently replaced the image and addressed Raphael directly in his dream, "Son, you will not be working the mines like I did all those years. You have a new future ahead of you."

Raphael knew his father had entered his mind, "Hello, father. What future is that?"

"You will become a farmer. A time will come when we must leave this place and become more then we are. Our exile is coming to an end."

"Exile?" Raphael asked.

"Yes, we will soon return to a better climate and leave Sasgorg," said Tamael.

"I love it here, Pa. Why do we have to leave?

"Because it is time for us to take the place that is ours in this world."

"So we'll be farmers?"

"Yes, for a time, you will."

"What of the caste? How will we change our caste?"

"That is for me to worry about and for your mother to comfort. Time for supper. Wiggle your toes. Feel the current of life coming back to your legs. Wiggle your fingers..."

Meanwhile, Tinay watched the strange scene. Her father was squatting on the ground. He was a tall man and to see him so close to the ground made him look like a stooped old man.

She saw her little brother start to stir and she knew that he would soon awake from his slumber. Her father let go of Raphael's head and slowly straightened himself. He was majestic when seated on the ground, always a peaceful look on his face, his balance never wavering. He was able to achieve a deep meditative state in an instant. Raphael got up and waited for his father to open his eyes and jumped in his arms. This was his favorite moment of the day.

Tamael hugged him long and hard; he loved his son and missed every moment he was away from him. He also knew of the long tribulation coming up ahead and was not certain how prepared he was to face them. He had been away for twenty years. This was a long time for anyone, even for him.

He walked up the stairs with Raphael in his arms and embraced Tinay on his way up and said, "You do better next time and make sure he completes the exercise properly."

Hmm, she thought. It was not like her father to be so lenient. Something was amiss and she couldn't tell what it was, but her parents had grown more serious and stern over the last three years. Since the announcement of the pregnancy, her mother's face became somber. She remembered how happy her mother was when she announced her pregnancy of Raphael. Tinay was confused and did not understand the whole picture. There was more than what was being said, so she did her best to obey and help her parents. Her father whispered in her mind, "We'll tell you more soon." Tinay continued to prepare the dinner table while her father went to wake up his wife. He woke her the same way he had his son, gently putting his hands on each side of his wife's head. He noticed her wrinkled forehead and lowered his head and slightly touched his wife. A sharp pain immediately filled his brain. He let go of his wife head and grabbed his own. He muffled his scream and lowered himself to the ground. Slowly, his wife awoke.

"Oh no! I'm sorry, I was having another nightmare and I felt someone else trying to intrude," said Lilay apologetically.

"Someone else?" asked Tamael.

"Yes, my mother has been trying to track us down. It's not safe here anymore, we'll have to move soon." said Lilay.

"How could she find us so fast?" asked Tamael.

"Fast? What do you mean fast? We've been here for twenty years!" said Lilay with a hint of irony in her voice.

"Right, but she's been closing in on you since you got pregnant."

"Each pregnancy helped her. She knew that I would be drained when I got pregnant again. It was only a matter of time," said Lilay.

"I still think we should wait until she actually locates us and then depart. That way there's a chance for us to be one step ahead. We won't compromise the alliance," said Tamael. He was now the one with a frown on his brow. The pain his wife could inflict was terrible when one was unprepared to face it.

"Yes, I know. I'm just so tired." Lilay whispered so she would not attract the attention of her children in the next room.

"Tinay must do her initiation before we go anywhere. She turned fourteen eleven months ago. She should be taken to the caves now," insisted Tamael.

"You know it's not up to me to send her, she has to be called. Besides, that would mean she must disobey us and climb mount Ardel. If she doesn't take the climb when the baby is born, I'll try to send her that way. Meanwhile, we must plan for our move. You must go to Os before long."

Tamael interrupted Lilay and said, "Actually, we'll have to contact Ohuru. I'm finished: the orb for the council is ready."

Inside, Lilay was enthusiastic, and yet fear came over her. This would mean they were finished mining. This would also mean her beloved husband had to leave Sasgorg and go sell the last of the crystal to Os, a far distant planet of trade. In the same trip, for the safety of her young, Raphael was to be dropped at Essay, the farming planet, to learn new skills and be left behind as an apprentice. It was the only way to ensure the survival of her lineage and keep it safe from her mother. Once the baby was born, they would leave behind the life of loneliness and solitude for a more social life. But still more prevalent was the fear of being recognized and delivered to the authorities. Tamael was a brave man, but would he be able to defeat an entire army even with the alliance?

Just then she noticed her husband's sweaty brow and wiped it off with her hand. Tamael looked up at her and smiled. His wife's touch was filled with grace and love. It could cure any ailments he suffered. She had been mastering her potions for the last twenty years and never needed much healing to be done other than pulled muscles and sunburn. It was comforting that she had not lost her touch after so long. The time away from the alliance could have gone awry if they had not such strong mental and physical discipline. He was proud to be her husband. They both got up and went to the kitchen.

Chapter 3

DEPARTURE FOR OS

Tamael and Lilay both entered the kitchen holding hands together. Tinay looked up and smiled, "I'm glad you had some rest Mom. Dinner is ready, and, as usual, your timing is perfect."

"Thank you," said Lilay. "Let's hope that my soup will be as perfect as you say."

"Let's eat," yelled Raphael.

"Let's not forget to say grace," said Tamael, raising his left hand toward Raphael and holding on to his beautiful wife's soft hand. Raphael grabbed his father's and sister's hand. Tinay took her mother's and they completed a circle around the table.

"Dear Overseer, Father of all, grant us the blessing of peace and see that my family remains safe over time. Dear ancestors, see to it that our strength is preserved and that our knowledge is not lost. Dear Mother Goddess, see to it that my wife and children are guarded in my absence and be fruitful in your blessing to our table. We are thankful for all of our blessings, our health and our house. Bless this meal we are about to have and bless this family which is about to eat it. Argor."

Tamael lowered his head and seemed to continue on in his mind, while the rest of the family replied "Argor."

The family sat at the table and began eating the soup and sharing the bread. Raphael filled in his Pa on how much progress he made with the sun in his meditation, "You should have seen it, Pa. It was fantastic. There was the sun, but then they were stars and they were woven in the sky and looked like they moved together. It was like water flowing down; everything was fluid and majestic. My whole body was as if it was made out of stars and I was very light and it floated just above me. It was great."

Tamael raised his eyebrow and looked at Tinay to see how much of this she had done.

Tinay recognized the inquisitive look her father gave her and answered before he asked, "It wasn't me. I tried to help him and he told me to butt out. When he did ask for my help, all I did was align the sun with the orange and the apple and I left him protected by the golden cloak. The rest he did for himself."

"Well," Tamael said, turning over to his son, "I'm impressed, although I did find you asleep down there. Nonetheless, I'm impressed with your progress. That's awesome work. Really, either your sister is an incredible teacher or you are exceptionally gifted. . ."

"Or both," said Lilay. She did not want to interrupt this great moment for her family. To achieve the step of self-awareness was hard work and to be just seven years old and accomplish this was a moment to be celebrated. "Let's have a dessert."

"Yahoo! Hooray!" Raphael exclaimed. "Can we have your strawberry mix, Mom?"

"I can't see why not. After you're done, Tinay, please go downstairs and fetch me strawberries."

"All of them, mother?" Tinay asked.

"Yes, this is a great occasion. We must celebrate."

Tinay was happy because strawberries were a special treat. They had medical purposes and were not to be eaten. She grabbed a basket and ran down the stairs to the strawberry patch. They were nice and red, perfect for picking. Living in the desert meant she had a very frugal life. She knew that no matter what was bothering her parents, they were still trying to do something special because of Raphael's immense progress.

"Raphael," Tamael said, "I am still amazed by your progress. Are you sure no one else has helped you?"

Suddenly Raphael looked sheepish "Well, no one directly."

Tamael didn't like the sound of his answer, "And what does that mean?"

Raphael wanted to disappear. He did not want the strawberries taken away, but most of all, he didn't want his father disappointed in him, "Um, well I was in my golden bubble and I saw a man . . ."

"What!" Lilay dropped the clay pot she held in her arms onto the floor. Sugar spilled everywhere. "What did you say?"

"Um, well, you see, ah . . ." Now Raphael knew he was in trouble. He never saw his mother turn that shade of red before, "He said he was a relative and . . ."

His mother took hold of the counter and Tamael reached out to her and grabbed her before she fell to the ground. Raphael was very scared and started to sob, "I'm sorry. He said he wanted to help me because very soon I would need all my strength and the faster and the better I could master the principles, the better off this whole family would be," Raphael sobbed harder, "I wanted to do my part. Mother works so hard every day in the hydroponics bay and Pa is gone all day to the caves and even Tinay has to help gather the herbs and flowers Mom needs. I just wanted to be prepared when my turn came to help."

"All right," said Tamael. "Maybe we're overreacting."

At that moment Tinay came up the stairs. She laughed when she saw her mother seated on the floor in a pile of sugar, but the scene was no longer funny when she realized her dad seemed too preoccupied to finish lifting her mother up and that her brother was crying. She started to worry. "What do you mean, overreacting? Mom, are you all right?" Tinay asked as she moved toward her.

"She's fine," said Tamael.

"Yes, I'm fine," said Lilay. "It's just that your brother is full of surprises tonight."

"Yeah? Like what?" Tinay turned to her brother, not knowing whether she should be mad at him or glad that everything was fine.

"I met Alzabar in my meditation. He's the one that helped me with the cosmos thing," Raphael grinned widely.

"ALZABAR!" Both her mother and father turned green.

"Are you sure it was him?" asked his mom.

"Well, how should I know? I never met him before. That's just whom he said he was. He looked kind and loving. I didn't think he was lying. Why would he lie to me?" answered Raphael, wiping his tears. He didn't like to cry in front of his sister; he wanted to think he was strong.

"Is someone going to enlighten me? Who is Alzabar and what's the big deal?" Tinay was confused.

"Alzabar was my father," said Lilay. "He died a long time ago and has not been seen or heard for a long time. I find it strange that he would present himself to you, Raphael."

"Wow! Cool!" said Raphael. "Well, if he's my papili, what's the problem? He wouldn't want to hurt me."

Suddenly Tinay started to feel stones in the pit of her stomach, "No, maybe not him, but Mami would love to get her hands on you." She knew her grandmother had somehow been turned to evil and she was to always protect herself against her in any type of mental exercise she could do. That's why she never left her brother's side unless he was wrapped in the golden cocoon.

"Wait, it can't be a lie," said Tamael, recovering his wits. "The spirits can't lie."

"Um," Lilay said. "They can't lie to those who know them, but Raph is hardly able to remember the shade of the aura, never mind knowing if someone is lying to him."

"Yes, maybe so," said Tamael, "but spirits gamble a lot not knowing this."

As he was saying this, Lilay disappeared into her room and came back with an old frame in her arms.

"Here, is this who you saw?" Lilay handed Raphael the old picture frame.

"Yes! That's him. That's the man!" Raphael felt better knowing that if his mother had a picture of the man, he couldn't be that bad.

"Well, it's Alzabar all right. Now the question is, why he decided to show himself to you and why now."

Tamael circled around the kitchen. Tinay stood at the top of the stairs with the strawberries wondering if she would get to eat them after all. "Um, mom?" she asked.

Her mother lifted her head and looked at her wondering what else could be happening when she saw Tinay disconcerted, "Oh! Sorry, honey. Let's clean this mess up and get these strawberries ready."

Lilay moved towards her daughter and grabbed her by the arm. On their way to the counter, she mumbled to herself, "What does he want? Why is he coming out now? I don't want to move before the baby is born. What are we supposed to think of this?"

Raphael wiggled. He had more to say and although he felt a little better that he wasn't in so much trouble anymore he was wondering if he should tell them everything now.

"Raphael," said Tamael, "what is it? What is bothering you?"

"Well, Alzabar told me he was my protector and he would see to it I remained safe and he would help me advance in my search. He also said he would contact Mom. He said he didn't know why she would marry you, a miner. He said you should have been of an order better than that.... What did he mean, Daddy?"

"Um. . ." Tamael hated it when this discussion came up. For the good of his family, he lied to his son. "Your mother is an artisan and, therefore, she would be living in an artistic community surrounded by other artists. Instead, she fell in love with me and married below her caste, dragging her children with her. So, you see, this is why I have been working so hard. You can become a farmer and go a caste higher. Normally one can only go up one link of the chain per lifetime, but because your mother was an artisan, I was able to negotiate your legal entry into the Farmer strata. It is a great honor and that's why you will not be working at the mine with me. It's also why, after my next and final trip to sell the crystals, we will be moving into the artisan strata on Kyr. It's a beautiful place."

Raphael was not about to interrupt his pa, but if they were to live on Kyr and he was to be a farmer, where was he going to farm? Kyr was for artisans.

"Um… Pa? Where am I going to live?"

"Yes, well, you will have to be living on Essay and . . ."

"What? What do you mean? I'm only seven years old! How can I be on my own?"

Now Raphael was extremely afraid. His mom came close to him and held him in her arms, "Honey, I think that's why Alzabar is coming to help you. He will be there for you, beside you, and your dad can keep in touch by telepathy, so you'll be fine." She could feel Raphael's tears fall from his eyes as he sobbed quietly in her arms.

Suddenly, Tinay came back to reality. "Hang on a minute. So you and Pa are moving to Kyr and Raph is moving to Essay. Where am I going?"

Lilay tried to comfort Raphael and sighed, "We are planning on moving, but it won't happen until the baby is born and your dad has finished harvesting the crystals."

"But the baby is due in a month, Mom," Tinay was getting nervous.

"Yes, and I have harvested the last piece of crystal from the caves. I'll go on my trip and sell the crystals, have enough money to buy the artisan house on Kyr and then Raph will work on his apprenticeship on Essay. We will visit, but he'll have to be there for a long time until he's ready and accomplished. As for you, Tinay, we've been waiting to see if you would find your calling, but so far, we're still waiting. There's still the option that you will continue what your mother has done."

"And how am I supposed to know what my calling is?" Tinay asked.

"You just need to be inspired," said Tamael. "You've been a great learner; you've helped gather and mix herbs for your mother, but you've not yet created anything on your own to be accepted in the artisan community."

"Okay, I can do this. I just never felt a need before. I can create something, I'm sure I can." Tinay assured herself.

"There's no pressure, honey. There are still a few months. You'll be fine." Tamael tried to be reassuring, but he wasn't sure if he sounded convincing enough.

"Mom, what do you think I could do?" asked Tinay.

"Well, I've seen how you often paint the sand with your fingers. Maybe you could paint on canvas and see if you like it."

"Canvas? Where am I going to find a canvas?" Tinay wanted this to work, she needed this to work.

"Well, we can take an old robe and stretch it onto a canvas," said Tamael.

"I can make some paint out of sand and some of our powder supplies," added Lilay.

"Your supplies? You are willing to give me your precious supplies for a canvas? But it took us so many seasons to prepare them all. Mother, are you sure?"

"Yes, Tinay. I'm not going to give you everything, but I'll give you enough to paint a canvas and then, when your dad comes back from his trip, he'll bring you some paint and real canvas. We'll work it out, honey." Lilay was improvising now. She knew the truth, but she could not reveal it all at once; there was enough shocking news being delivered for one night. In time, all would make sense, but for now, she wanted to reassure her children and make sure they slept quietly for the night.

"Now, how about those strawberries?" she asked with a fake smile. Everyone returned the favor with a mild smile as she moved towards the kitchen. She had broken the small bowl of sugar, but luckily there was enough left to create the desert, mostly made of squashed strawberries coated with sugar and mixed with milk.

She quickly made a batch while Tinay cleaned up the floor and Tamael cleared the table. She poured the dessert into bowls and walked back to the table. She looked at her family and realized how little time was left for all of them to be safe together. Soon enough, her mother would come looking for her or one of her children and the only way to protect them all was to separate them before they could be identified. She wanted peace to last just a little longer. She, too, had her own fears: a new home, new neighbors, and new rules. It was going to require some adjustment that her quiet life in the desert didn't prepare her for.

For the rest of the meal, they ate in silence. After supper, they prepared for bed and had one last prayer. Tamael lead them in prayer, "Dear Overseer, Father of all, grant us the blessing of peace and see that my family remains safe over time. Dear ancestors, see to it that our strength is preserved and that our knowledge is not lost. Dear Mother Goddess, see to it that my wife and children are guarded in my absence and are fruitful in their activities. We are thankful for all of our blessings, our health and our house. Guide us in our new challenge and guide this family, which is about to embark in a new adventure. Argor."

Tamael lowered his head and seemed to continue on in his mind, while the rest of the family replied "Argor."

The next morning things were quiet. The only sound that could be heard was the radio repeating its calling message over and over again. "Calling Ohuru of the space ship Armada for transport from Sasgorg, please reply . . . Calling Ohuru of the space ship Armada for transport from Sasgorg, please reply . . . Calling Ohuru of the space ship Armada for transport from Sasgorg, please reply . . ."

"How long has Pa been calling?" Tinay asked.

"Since five a.m. this morning," said Lilay. She looked tired and had baggy puffy eyes.

"Are you alright, Mom?" Tinay asked.

"Yes, I just didn't sleep very well last night and your dad decided to leave as soon as possible to be able to be back on time to prepare for the baby."

"Calling Ohuru of space ship Armada for transport from Sasgorg, please reply. . ."

Tinay decided to stay quiet and prepare breakfast.

"Calling Ohuru of space ship Armada for transport from Sasgorg, please reply. . ."

"This is Armada. Caller ID, please?"

Ohuru always liked the official version of things. Tamael scrambled to find the codes.

"Um, code 9649632, planet Sasgorg, one passenger plus non lethal cargo."

The metallic voice replied, "Destination of cargo, weight of cargo, and method of payment?"

Tamael hated this protocol. "Destination, Os. Merchant port, Osmos. Weight of merchandise, five kilos. Method of payment, as usual."

The metallic voice crackled through the speaker again, "Hello, old fool. You know, after all these years, you think you would know the protocol."

"Never mind, Ohuru. I have a pressing matter and I must leave as soon as possible."

"Yeah, well, I figured you would be calling me soon so I arranged to travel in your direction. We'll be in for lunch. Any chance you can feed two of us?" Ohuru asked.

"Two? What do you mean 'two'? Who is with you?" Tamael never liked surprises, and in view of the recent events, he liked them even less.

"Since you're not a merchant, I thought I would bring a fellow who could help you negotiate and get a better deal for your money."

Tamael knew better than to argue; this was a sound idea. If he really cared about the crystals, it would be a great idea to make more money. But even if Ohuru was safe to talk to, anyone else listening to the subspace transmission might see more then he wished.

"Hello? Sasgorg, are you there? Stupid machine, infernal. . ."

"I'm here Armada. Glad you thought of it first, it will save us a stop. We'll be ready for your arrival. I'll meet you at Landel at noon."

"10-04, old goose. See ya soon!"

"Roger out." Tamael shifted his eyes to Lilay. "Well, I guess there will be guests for us to feed at lunch. Think you could conjure up something nice?"

"Tamael, this is not what we had planned," Lilay said. "You're not to attract any attention to yourself, it's . . ."

"Lilay, will you be able to manage food for two extra people?" Tamael said, cutting her short.

"Yes, of course. I'll work on it." Tamael was right. It was better to keep quiet for now with the children around.

Tamael went to pack his bags for his journey and Lilay got busy in the kitchen. Raphael was also packing his bags; he was going to go with his dad for this trip and it would be his last chance to spend time with him for a while. Tinay was left with nothing to do. She went to her mother and asked if she could help.

"No, dear, I'm fine. I'm just adding a bit more vegetables, that's all. I'll try to lay down for a nap shortly."

Tinay went over to her father and asked the same question.

Tamael was almost ready, "Actually, no. I'm almost done and I'm on my way to help your brother finish up. I was wondering if you would prepare water gourds for our guests, and go to meet them at the platform."

"Oh, sure, I could do that," Tinay said and went over to the squash and started carving them. Time always passed by faster when there was something to do. Soon enough, it was 11:00am and time for her walk through the desert to mount Landel. It was not a long walk, but it was tedious in the sand, so she often let her ferret, Draco ride on her shoulder, as she did today. Since most guests never came prepared for the weather, she carried bundles of clothes to protect their skin, head and eyes against the sun. Her father had built a small shed for those waiting for anyone landing. She sat and got her binoculars out and started looking for herbs or plants she might not already have in her collection. Her mother had explained to her that the planets in this system were very productive and fertile before the sun went nova. Sasgorg had a particularly wide and vast registry of plants that could heal the sick, comfort the wounded and fight off bacteria and infections. Now she understood why her mother had collected all those seeds; it was for replanting once they moved. How long had her mother known they would relocate? They never had much and got by with very little but she thought it was because of the desert; there was nothing here. Now she realized that with very little, you could leave in a hurry and not miss much of your previous life. Draco burrowed under the bench.

Draco had been a great help in locating plants, his nose being much more sensitive to changes in the air. She looked beneath her and, in the shadow of the shed, something new had grown. The desert was unkind to any vegetation, but with a little bit of shade, usually from a rock, the most resilient plants would find a way to grow. She would bring them back to the cave where they could grow freely and reproduce. Tinay heard a loud noise. She delicately put the seedling in her pouch and looked up. A flyer was coming down. No, maybe it was a small ship. She knew it was the same one that she had seen twice already, but now that she had grown older, the ship seemed smaller. She waited for the ship to land and for the hatch door to open.

She recognized Ohuru right away. He was without a doubt the best mechanic-space-flyer-inventor she'd ever heard off. Not very many people had a ship to fly and if the ship needed a new part, it was up to Ohuru to repair it or, more often, create it. He would get a lot of deep space assignments and get very little chance to meet anyone; his caste was slowly becoming extinct. The emperor tried to revive deep space exploration, but the number of ships available made it hard for anyone to join. Nonetheless, Ohuru had been able to train a few recruits and revive the caste.

Ohuru was tall and very thin. His face was long and his features seemed a bit out of proportion. He had a long thin chin, a large nose that covered two thirds of his face and long skinny ears. His eyes were large and protruded from his face. He had very little hair on the top of his head. Despite his strange features, he looked friendly and amicable. The young merchant that followed him was unlike most merchants. He was lean and muscular, not fat and tubby. He was not much older than her. What use would her father have of such a boy? *Pa might as well bring me to do the exchange for him. He can't have that much experience.* She left the hut and walked towards them.

"Welcome to Sasgorg," she said. "I have clothes, tunics, and head covers so you don't get burnt on our way back."

"I always forget how cold space is compared to your planet," said Ohuru.

"You can change in the hut," said Tinay, pointing to the shed.

"I'll take the blue, my favorite colour. You don't mind, Atleos, do you?" asked Ohuru.

"No, of course not. I thank our host for the generosity she's demonstrating," said the boy as he turned to Tinay and bowed. "I will keep the orange cloak for myself. Go change, Master Ohuru, and I'll wait here until you're done."

Tinay was confused. Atleos was not fat, but suddenly he looked much older. She bowed back to him and said, "I'm afraid you'll have to cover yourself right away or else the sun will give you heat stroke." She approached him, gave him the orange tunic, which was too big, and took out the shawl from the pile of clothes and asked, "May I?"

Atleos was surprised to find someone wearing so many clothes in this terrible heat. "Yes, of course. I have no idea how to put one on."

"I'll help you," said Tinay, as she covered his head and most of his face.

"Why wear so much clothes if it's so hot here?"

"Well," Tinay answered, "first off, the sun will burn your skin if it does not get covered. Next, the blends of cotton from which your tunic is made will help your body breath unlike the space suit you're wearing. Finally, the many layers isolate you from the heat and protect you from the cold of the desert at night. It also helps keep your body moisture from evaporating. It's the best way to dress if you live or stop by here for a visit."

"I see."

Ohuru came back out of the hut. He looked like a Meji, a priest from the capital.

"Well," Ohuru said, "your turn boy. Tinay, my dear, I think that I should buy this tunic from your mother. It's really comfortable and fits me perfectly."

"She made it especially for you, Ohuru," said Tinay. "I'm surprised you can tie a turban so fashionably without any help."

"Sasgorg is not the only planet I visit that is hot and dry, but it's the only place that is this generous and welcoming," said Ohuru, hugging Tinay.

Atleos came out and looked like a clown; the gown she had picked was for an experienced merchant who weighed at least 300 pounds, not for a slender young man. The gown was too short and did not cover his legs properly. This could be a problem for the walk back if the wind picked up. The sand, whipping against his legs, would injure him. She took her belt off. She did not really need it, but Atleos was definitely in need of some assistance. She wrapped the belt around his hips and overlapped the excess tunic over it. The walk back to the house was a challenge for Ohuru. He loved his friend Tamael, but why he chose to mine on this forsaken piece of stone, he could not understand. Atleos seemed to do just fine and was speaking with Tinay, or at least he was trying.

"So tell me, who else lives here?" he asked.

"What do you mean?"

"Well, this is a large planet and there's room for many people. Who else lives here?" Atleos asked again.

"There are very little resources on Sasgorg and the mining is very limited. My father obtained the whole planet for mining purposes. No one else wanted to come here and live frugally the way we have for the last twenty years . . ."

"Twenty years! Your family has been mining this desert for twenty years!" Atleos said with disbelief.

"Yes, my father has harvested the last of the Alenor crystal. This will be his last shipment."

"Alenor crystal! Ohuru, you knew this?" Atleos turned around to see his commander.

"Yes, this is the only thing to be harvested on this rock. So for twenty years now, Tamael has been one of the very few miners in this quadrant of the galaxy to be able to harvest it and sell it to the Metropole using my transport." Ohuru had to stop talking because his throat hurt.

"Well, this will be a very profitable barter, I must say. I was not prepared for such a product." Atleos turned back to Ohuru. "What quality are we looking at?"

Ohuru waved his hand in front of him. He could not utter another word; his throat was on fire from the drying heat of the desert and the coarse sand stuck in his throat.

"Perfect," said Tinay. She was proud her father had the best crystal in the galaxy. After all, there was a reason why they were here for this, or so she had been told over the years. Her smile disappeared. No, maybe that was the only place they could go and her parents had made a twenty-year-long sacrifice to be able to protect them.

Atleos started talking to himself, "Wow! Perfect! I heard of a miner who could extract them, but usually the crystals were fragmented and impure. Perfect, that'll be a totally different . . ."

"Here we are," said Tinay.

"Where are we exactly?" asked Atleos.

"Home, of course," said Tinay with a look of incredulity in her eyes.

Atleos stared straight ahead at mountain Ecumel and could not see any hint of a house. Surely a man as rich as Tamael would be able to build a huge home. Incredulously, he looked again and still could not see anything.

"Atleos," said Ohuru in a rough voice, "it's inside the mountain. They must protect themselves from the sand and the sun."

"Ah, I see," said Atleos. No, he didn't see anything, but it did make sense. Everything was bare here. Tinay lead them through the mountain and to the canvas door.

"Welcome," she said with a proud smile.

Atleos walked behind Ohuru. Ohuru didn't pay any attention to the decorative walls, but Atleos could not help but marvel at the beauty and the amount of work that was displayed here. He stopped in his tracks and stared at the images and signs on the wall.

"It's the history of Atlanti and his departure from Earth to space and how they stopped returning once they found out the Conquistador almost annihilated the Maya. They saved those who wanted to be saved and left Earth for the last time. It explains that the propulsor orbiting around Earth, which helped deep space ships jump to a speed ten times faster than light, was destroyed shortly after the last voyage took place. By then any hopes of seeing Atlantis emerge from the water was in vain. They could not take the chance that the Spaniard had developed the technology to travel in space and locate where the Atlantis survivors now lived. After the destruction and death they left behind on the South American continent, it was their last chance for peace following the submersion of Atlantis." Tinay felt proud she had finally found someone else who was as intrigued as she was by this history.

Atleos was mesmerized by the quality of the work. Ohuru had spoken of an artisan, but he didn't mentioned how good she was. Surely, he thought, for an artisan to marry below her caste she must have been a poor artist. The more he learned about Tamael and his family, the more he was impressed. Tinay led him through the corridor into the kitchen.

Ohuru drank the water as if he had been in the desert for weeks. Lilay approached Atleos with a large smile on her face and offered him water. Apparently, if Atleos was a merchant, he must be a busy one to never get a chance to get fat.

"Here, have some water," Lilay offered. "I'll look for a more appropriate tunic for you; this one is obviously too big."

"I dare say, way too big." Tamael, unlike his wife, could not contain his laughter. "Young man, you look absolutely ridiculous." Everyone started laughing.

Lilay returned with a smaller tunic. "This is one of my husband's," she said. "It's not nearly as nice, but it's clean. Oh no, your leg!"

Atleos had an aching in his shin, but he didn't know why. Now that Lilay mentioned it, he did feel a burning sensation.

"Don't move, I know exactly what to do," said Tinay and she ran downstairs to mix some ingredients together. When she returned, she had a yellow-green paste. "Here, let's put that on your burnt leg. It'll heal without a scar."

Atleos couldn't believe the short amount of time it took for his leg to sunburn. It hurt, but the paste was soothing.

When Ohuru finally stopped drinking water he said, "My apologies everyone. My need for water surpassed my etiquette savoir faire. Tamael, let me introduce to you to Atleos from the Merchant guilds. He will help you make a fortune. Atleos, this is Tamael, his wife, Lilay the artisan, and their children, Tinay, and Raphael, the future farmer."

Tinay had thought so; even Ohuru knew of this plan to make Raphael a farmer.

Ohuru continued, "It was on our last trip when Raphael was only two years old that we brought him to the Farmer's guild and they decided that Raphael would be mentored by Merdaine. It was quite a successful trip, if I may say so."

"Yes, it was," said Tamael. "Let's hope that this trip will be just as fortunate. Ohuru, we will need your help to move from this planet after I return from our business trip. Will you still be available?"

"Yes, of course," Ohuru said. "Atleos' quest is unique and requires me to travel a lot; a bit of rest will be welcome."

"What is your quest for, Atleos?" Lilay asked.

"Oh, nothing important, really." Atleos felt uncomfortable answering such questions.

"It's all right," Ohuru said. "You're among friends, and Tamael, on his previous trip, has met a lot of people and something tells me he might be able to guide us."

"What is it?" Tamael asked.

"I have spent all my heritage trying to find a healer," Atleos explained. "My brother is in need of one."

"A Healer? There was one I knew a long time ago. She had come to help my father when a mine collapsed. We might be able to find one," said Tamael.

"Yes, well, easier said than done. All of the healers have gone into hiding for the last 27 years, ever since the insurrection. They will not trust just anyone," said Lilay.

"Right . . ." said Tamael, pausing for a moment. He knew the healer well, for she was a descendant of the same lineage as his wife. It would be a great risk to bring her out of hiding until the time had come, but he also had dealt with many merchants over the last 20 years, and he had never met a man from the class of Os that wasn't fat. Atleos was not who he pretended to be, that Tamael knew for certain. "We'll try anyway."

"Tamael, you can't go gallivanting around the galaxy when the baby is due in less than a month," said Lilay. There was a hint of authority in her voice that surprised everyone in the room, except for Tamael. He continued, unfazed, "I will not go gallivanting, I will simply make a few short stops on the way back. If Atleos is as good as he says he is I should be able to sell my crystal faster. The time I save in bartering I'll use in searching. We'll be back in one week's time."

"I don't like this," said Lilay.

"I know, I know." Tamael grew impatient with her. The strain his family had been under for so long was starting to show. "Please, my love, I will not miss the birth of my child. We'll be back in time. Don't worry." He got up and embraced her.

"I'm sorry. I haven't slept much lately and this pregnancy is harder than the last ones."

"Yes, I know, my love," whispered Tamael. "Well, let's eat before we go."

For the first time in front of strangers, Tinay saw her father do the blessing:

"Dear Overseer, Father of all, grant us the blessing of peace and see that my family remains safe over time. Dear ancestors, see to it that our strength is preserved and that our knowledge is not lost. Dear Mother Goddess, see to it that my wife and children are guarded in my absence and be fruitful in your blessing to our table. We are thankful for our blessings, our health, and our house. Grant your love to the friends at our table and let them be welcome to us as family. Bless this meal we are about to eat and bless this family who are about to eat it. . ."

Then, most surprisingly, Atleos added, "Bless the order of the Malatar and grant them wisdom in this time of peril. Argor."

Tamael smiled as the rest of the family replied, "Argor."

After lunch, the family and guests walked to the ship on mount Landel. This time, Ohuru brought a large supply of water for the forty-five minute trek. The sun was just past its zenith, making it extremely hot on the surface of Sasgorg. Lilay was tired, and the strain on her back from the baby was already making her fall behind.

Come on, old girl, she told herself, *almost there.* They arrived at Landel as the high wind spit sand in her face. Atleos was not a man to complain, but he could feel the pain of his burns again. He slowed down and waited for Lilay to catch up.

"Atleos, what's wrong?" asked Lilay.

"My legs are on fire. I can feel the sand in the burnt skin."

"Tinay has packed some of the paste for you. She can wash your wound and apply some more before you leave," said Lilay.

"No, I'm sure I can to it," said Atleos, who didn't want anyone too close to his skin.

"I insist. She will look after you before you leave. Tinay, you must bandage Atleos' leg before he leaves." Lilay had to yell to be heard.

All right, Mother, Tinay answered in telepathy, not wanting to swallow a mouth full of sand in the reply.

At the ship, Atleos could not wear his combination suit because of the burns on his leg. Tinay approached him with water and the paste. Atleos grounded his teeth as he thought to himself, *I'm getting looked after by a kid. Why couldn't the mother help me?*

"All right, Atleos. I'll wash the sand from your wound, reapply the paste and cover your leg with a bandage. That's the best I can do." Tinay shook her head. The burn was a bad one.

"Where did you learn to do this anyway?" asked Atleos.

"I read the books my mother wrote on the medicinal qualities of plants and I learned how to mix and apply them from the books."

The water was meant to cool his leg, but it only brought more pain. Atleos never realized how much pain a sunburn could produce.

Tinay slowly applied the paste and wrapped his leg in the bandage she had found in the first aid kit.

"There, that should do it." Tinay stood up with a wide grin on her face. She was quite satisfied with her work, and Atleos had to admit, he felt much better.

Ohuru embraced Lilay and wished her peace on her journeys. Lilay replied, "May the wisdom of the ancestors guide you."

Lilay hugged her son, then her husband. They kissed and murmured to each other. She checked once more on Atleos and said, "May the wisdom of the ancestors guide you."

Tinay hugged her father as hard as she could and told him, "May health and strength accompany you."

Tamael whispered something back to her and went to his seat.

"Well, little brother," said Tinay, "once again you get to fly into space and I get to stay home. May health and strength accompany you."

Raphael hugged her again, "I hope I'll see you soon. I love you, sister!" and he ran to his seat.

Tinay and Lilay exited the ship and went in the hut to protect them from the sand as the ship took off. They saw the ship rise into the air and suddenly drop hard onto the plateau as the motor sputtered. A shockwave traveled through ground and felt like a seismic shock.

Lilay and Tinay fell to the ground.

"Well," Tamael said sarcastically, "we're off to a good start."

"Ah, don't worry. The hydraulic converter jammed. Your planet dries up all of the lubricant. I forgot to adjust it, that's all. Here we go again," replied Ohuru.

Again, the ship slowly lifted off from the ground and departed in the sky. Lilay and Tinay watched the ship until it disappeared, then walked back to the cave.

Chapter 4

THE LITHIL

After their long walk back, Tinay felt tired. She started to clean the table while her mother stretched her back.

"Oh," Lilay said, "this baby is getting heavier by the day."

"It's okay, Mom. I'll clean up and prepare supper for us."

"All right. I'll prepare a canvas for you. At least I can do that sitting down." Lilay went to her room with the tools and put herself to work.

Tinay finished her work and went to join her mother in the tool room. As she walked in she said, "I didn't know it would take . . ." and realized her mother was asleep at the bench with a canvas almost completed. *Hmm,* she thought, *maybe I better stay quiet for a while.* She slowly exited the room. *Now, what should I do?*

She walked over to the niche and started climbing the steep ladder. She looked around. Suddenly a seismic tremor occurred and she fell down the ladder. She ran to the entrance of the cave and looked around. She saw smoke rising in the horizon. *Oh no!* she thought.

Tinay ran back inside and found her mother, bewildered, "What's going on?" Lilay asked.

"I saw some smoke coming out of Galgamel," said Tinay.

"The volcano is waking up?"

"That's what it looks like. Why now, Mother?"

"It's probably from Ohuru's shockwave. It must have cracked the cap of the mountain. Leave it for now. Tomorrow, if there's still some smoke coming out, we'll investigate."

They settled uneasily at the table and ate their supper. Shortly after, they went to bed.

The next day was like all the rest on Sasgorg; sunny with a little wind. Tinay used the peace and quiet to meditate. She didn't need the apple or the orange anymore; she could form her own mental images. First, she focused on breathing. Secondly, she concentrated on the energy. Thirdly, she concentrated on the red energy over the pelvic area. The orange energy on top of her stomach was next. Then, finally, she saw the sun on top of her sternum.

She had progressed farther than Raphael in her extra seven years of training. She could master the green belt around her chest and the blue crystal at her throat. She had been working on the next temple, the third eye, but she could not open it. She had been stuck here for three years now, and, once again, she was unable to open it. She didn't know what this temple meant, but she knew it was important. Her parents spent two hours a day meditating at this temple, therefore, it must be important for her to do this also. Frustrated, she got up and went in search of food.

Her mother was up, yet Lilay was nowhere to be found. Tinay grabbed an apple and walked outside. She found her mother sitting on a bench, looking through binoculars, staring at the south.

"Mom?"

"Yes?" Lilay was quiet.

"Is the volcano just disturbed or is it reopening again?"

"I don't know. I can't really see, but there is a cloud forming on top of Galgamel. That means there's water at the surface of the sand. It's going to rain, Tinay." Lilay deposited her binoculars with a large smile on her face. "Do you know what this means?"

"No, not really." Tinay wondered why this made her mother so happy.

"The plants in the cave live on the moisture trapped there, but if it rains, all the seeds that have lain dormant in the sand will sprout, which means we might find new varieties of plants." Lilay was ecstatic, "I'll prepare some hard bread and we'll pack our bags and be ready to go out hunting for herbs shortly."

Tinay felt the excitement coming from her mother and couldn't wait. She looked towards the volcano and saw a small cloud formation, but for the most part, the mountain Ardel blocked the view.

Two days went by and there was still no rain, but now it was possible to see that the cloud formation had grown bigger. Tinay's mother no longer had a smile on her face.

"What's wrong, Mother? It'll rain eventually, we just need to be patient."

"Patience I have, it's water that I'm worried about. The level of water in the well has gone down nine inches. We must find the leak and close it."

"How are we going to do that, Mother?"

"We will use the last of the explosive from your father's equipment and close down the volcano. With the water source covered, it won't evaporate any longer and we'll be fine."

"That easy, eh?" Tinay was not convinced the plan would work.

"We have to try or else our water might get contaminated."

"But, Mother, it's such a long ways from here. What about you?"

"We'll start traveling after supper and get a head start. Help me pack our equipment and we'll be there on time."

Tinay knew better than to argue. She went and prepared her backpack when all of a sudden, a giant "Crack!" was heard and the storm gave way. "It's finally raining, Mother," Tinay said smiling.

"Well, let's go. It's a full day's walk to Galgamel. We'll have to start now and arrive there later tonight. Tomorrow we'll repair the cave-in and save our water supply."

Tinay gathered up most of the equipment so her mother wouldn't have to carry much, put Draco in her pouch, and left the cave. The walk was uneventful; they didn't get wet until they reached the south side of Ardel. There, they rested and had supper. Afterwards, they continued to Galgamel. They arrived late and went to sleep.

The next day, they located the breach and could immediately see what the problem was. The seismic tremor had caused the side of the mountain to crack, and now water flowed on top of the ground instead of under it.

"Mother, how do you suppose we'll fix this?"

"We'll have to make a lake. Once the lake is full of water, the water will continue to flow inside the mountain."

"What?" Tinay could not believe what her mother just said. Make a lake!

"Just joking, Tinay," her mother said. "All we need to do is take away the rocks that are diverting the water and then cover up the hole. Get the pickaxes out."

They both started to hammer at the rock, which was crystallized volcanic rock. This was not an easy task. Finally the piece gave way and Lilay pushed it outward just long enough to jam the pickaxe in to keep the rock from falling back in.

"There, that should do it until your father returns. Now let's patch the hole up." As Lilay said this, she took a large quantity of clay from her pouch. "The sun will cook it in place and the hole will be covered."

"Ingenious, Mom! Good thinking." Tinay was amazed. She knew her mother could be creative, but this was impressive.

"We'll start making our way back tomorrow."

"In the daylight, Mother? Are you sure you can do it?" Tinay started to notice her mother's wobble and aching back.

"Yes, but we'll only make it to Ardel. Tomorrow, I want to see if we can find new plants on the way back."

So it was decided. They would get to hunt for herbs and plants after all.

The next morning the sky was clear on top of Galgamel. Most of the clouds were resting on the south side of Ardel and kept its sides humid.

"Perfect," said Lilay. "We'll climb Ardel tomorrow and gather everything we can find. En route!"

As they traveled back to Ardel, their trek was slow. Lilay wobbled quietly while Tinay chased after Draco left and right, collecting every herb she could find. By evening they had reached Ardel, tired and in need of rest.

"Be careful, Tinay. The rocks are still slippery. By tomorrow, everything will start to dry up. That means we'll have to work quickly."

After a meager dinner of vegetables and fruit, they went to sleep.

The harsh sun woke them early the next morning. Lilay gathered her things and told Tinay to hurry up, "There's not much time. The sun will dry up everything. We only have a couple of hours left to gather what we can."

Tinay suddenly had a strange thought, "Mom, if we're leaving Sasgorg soon, why do we need to keep collecting plants and herbs?"

"Because some plants that grow here only grew on Earth and the star that went nova destroyed most of the plants from Earth. Most people left and did not know the medical uses for them. No one thought of saving them from extinction. We may need these plants soon and they will be good for trade. We must prepare as much as we can."

"All right then, let's go," said Tinay.

For an hour, they carefully climbed Ardel. Tinay had left everything behind at the camp and was gathering what she could when she saw a plant she had never seen before.

"Tinay," yelled her mother. "Tinay, come here."

Tinay worried that Lilay might be hurt and hurried to her mother's side. "What is it, Mother?"

"Ah! A contraction." Lilay's face contorted with pain.

"Oh, Mom. You over-exerted yourself. You must rest."

"No, darling. They started after I fell to the ground in Landel. I kept dismissing them until now. This is a warning. Exhausted or not, I have to go back home and rest."

"All right Mother, let's go now then." Tinay wanted her mother to be safe. She looked extremely tired and needed rest.

They gathered up their things and left for the cave. As Tinay looked up once more at Ardel, she saw an herb she thought she recognized. "Mother, give me the binoculars, please."

"Oh, honey. They're packed. Come on, let's go."

"Mother, please. This might help you."

Lilay was too tired to fight with her daughter and searched for the binoculars. "Here they are."

Tinay adjusted the binoculars and found what had attracted her attention before. "Chamomile, Mother. It's chamomile."

Lilay knew the benefit of chamomile and could use some in the next few days. Chamomile was hard to grow in the cave and a resilient strand like this one would do better than what she had at home.

"Listen, I must get home. If the labor stops, then you can come and get it tomorrow."

"But it'll be too late. By tomorrow, the strand will have dried up."

"Maybe not. It's in the shade; it'll survive a day longer. Come, let's go," Lilay was anxious to return home and try to stop the labor. *It's too soon,* she thought, *too soon.*

The regular half a day walk transformed itself into a one-day trek. Lilay often needed to sit and rest. She had three more contractions that day and, by nightfall, they had finally arrived home. Tinay prepared a bath for Lilay. Tinay prepared some food for her mother and herself, and afterward, they both had a well-deserved rest.

The next day, Lilay woke up relaxed and somewhat relieved that the contractions had stopped over night. Tinay was up at dawn and was preparing to return to Ardel to gather the chamomile for her mother. Chamomile would help stop the contractions and delay labor.

"Mother, I prepared some food for you so you don't over exert yourself. Rest as much as you can until I get back tonight. Alone, the journey will be short. I've packed some food for myself and I'm on my way."

Lilay looked at her daughter and saw a determined young woman. *Oh, she's going to the caves!* Lilay thought. *She'll sense her calling today.* A wave of emotion entered her body and she felt the baby move. *Yes,* she thought, *you feel it too.* She knew now that her daughter was finally fulfilling her calling and she was proud.

"Don't worry, dear," she said. "Everything will be fine. Now go and come back quickly." She hugged her daughter, kissed her forehead and added, "Oh, take some extra water for the plants. They need to have their roots watered. Grab a crystal to put with the plants to refresh them in your bag."

"Ok." Tinay quickly put more water in the pouch and grabbed an extra crystal and left the house.

She walked quickly as the sun rose higher in the sky. She was not used to walking so fast. Usually as she walked, she looked at the beauty around her, but today she wanted to hurry before the chamomile dried. She arrived at Ardel at 10:00 a.m. and started to climb. The rocks were jagged and climbing was no easy task. Slowly, she made her way to a cliff and, from there, she searched for her first plant. She spotted one just a little higher. She picked it and continued her task until she saw the plant from the previous day. It was something she never hoped for; she recognized the plant. It was lilith, a powerful anti-labor plant that could trick the body into thinking it no longer needed to contract. That's exactly what she needed to stop her mother's pain. She climbed up and reached out to gently remove the lithil. As she reached for the water to wet the roots, the rock beneath her gave way and she fell ten meters onto another ledge. Tinay hit her head and fell unconscious.

As Lilay rested at home, she felt a quiver all over her body. She was alert and listening for anything. She had felt this sensation before when her husband had been hurt in one of his excavations. She didn't want to exert herself walking to the mountain to find out what was wrong. She decided for the next best thing: an astral voyage, a voyage of the soul. She did those when she needed to contact Mamili but lately, with her mother trying to access her dreams and sub consciousness to get her to reveal where she was hiding, Lilay didn't dare attempt an astral voyage. But she had to make sure Tinay was fine.

She was an experienced traveler, so it didn't take her long to start her voyage to Ardel. This way of traveling was much faster. She didn't feel the heat or the weight of her baby. She was light and free.

Looking everywhere, Lilay was about to give up when she saw Tinay's bag on the ledge. There her daughter was, unconscious in the sun. Tinay needed to wake up as her skin was already starting to sunburn. The sun was at its zenith and Tinay needed to cover up and be in the shade. Lilay lowered herself to the ledge and slowly hovered on top of Tinay, concentrating the energy in Tinay's feeling center.

Tinay could feel a warming sensation on her chest and started to move. "Oh, my head," she said. Her voice echoed and sounded raucous. She was parched. She looked around and saw her water pouch a few meters to the left. She tried to get up and suddenly felt a horrible pain in her ankle. The she heard her mother's voice.

You sprained your ankle and cannot make the journey back. You must find shelter and wait for me.

Tinay felt disoriented and too weak to use telepathy. She simply said, "It's no use for you to come and help me. We'll be both stranded here and you'll have the baby. Mother, I found some lithil. It'll help you, but you must stay and rest. I'll find a way back at night fall." As she said this, she started to wrap her ankle in a cloth so she could walk on it without putting too much pressure. As she did so she saw that the ledge was in fact an entrance to a cave.

"You see, Mother, I'll hide in here."

Then her mother, under pain of a new contraction said, *I can't stay, I'll be back later.*

Tinay collected her things and entered the cave. She sat down and gave water to Draco and her seedling to make sure they would survive. Then, as her eyes got used to the dark, she noticed it wasn't just a cave she was in, it had carvings on the walls. Her mother had taught her how to read the symbols and writing that was on the walls. She slowly walked inside the cave and, just as her own garden was lit by crystals incrusted in the walls, so was this cave.

"Um, this is very strange. Whoever built our cave must have built this one, too." She decided this was the best discovery she had ever made and started to read.

The wall told a completely different story than the one in her cave. It told about Atlantis and its rise to power in the Atlantic Ocean. It told about how the Atlanteans mastered the power of the crystal and managed to create weapons for themselves. They used the weapons to terminate the trade industry and make the other races slaves. Before this, Atlantis had been a proud nation that had colonies on many continents and shared its advances in agriculture and herding with the settlers. They built cities and temples to honor the Goddess and the Overseer. The God of the moon and the Sun combined together, and with the help of the elements of the world, they gave life. The balance lasted a long time until a greedy emperor decided to overthrow the temple Meji and take control of Atlantean politics and religion. He misinterpreted the signs and the religious book and asked for blood sacrifices to appease the Gods. Their power and knowledge had been used to destroy instead of to build.

In the year 24,000 of our lord Atlanti, a cataclysm occurred when the authorities tried to tap into the core of the planet for plasma energy. An enormous tsunami destroyed many ports. The tectonic plates had been destabilized and needed to readjust themselves. In the year 26,000, a second tsunami raised Atlantis fifty-seven meters out of the ocean. They thought they were safe, but scientists soon realized that the continent was even more unstable and that another seismic shock would submerge Atlantis forever. There were many studies conducted over the centuries and, as time passed, the people started to feel comfortable and lost their trust in the scientific movement that was trying to save what was left of their way of life.

A small group of individuals started to look to the sky for answers. They knew the earth would be irreparably damaged and would need a long time to heal. Apotheleme, a re-known scientist, discovered that once Atlantis sank beneath the ocean, the water on Earth would rise one hundred meters high and create tsunamis that would cover most of the earth. There wouldn't be enough time to evacuate everyone unless this was done in advance. Everything would be destroyed. Life as they knew it would have to start all over again. To save the achievements that were done on Earth from the sea, the Atlanteans had to bring them into space, or else all would be lost to the sea.

A secret society had been created under the order of the knight Temlamar, the protector of truth. The religious order had been saved from corruption and they had organized themselves genetically to have children every seven years starting at the age of twenty-one. Four children would be born from a fairy and a knight; three daughters and a son. The son would automatically join the knight order while the daughters would organize a trinity to rule over the land. Generation after generation, the mother's lineage would continue. As all the children would inherit the crown, there were never any fights for power. To choose which lineage would inherit the trinity crown, all of the children had to possess the gifts and be a virgin until their elevation. Since there was only one boy for every three girls, it limited the number of complete trinities. The sacred rite of elevation remained sacred and was not divulged on the wall.

The caste system had been put aside and a new order had been established. The new order had guilds. Children, as they reached the age of fourteen, would answer to their calling and be an apprentice for seven years. At twenty-one, they would become a productive member of society.

A new society had been created and a new balance had been obtained. There hadn't been many followers. The Atlanteans thought that it would be easy to relocate to a new planet. With all of the stars in the galaxy, they believed there had to be another habitable planet out there. Their belief was that if the power was administered by a trinity, it would be harder to corrupt. Each would have a special gift from the fairies: a healer, a storyteller and a medium. With their combined gifts, they healed their society and created a new culture of equality and balance. The storyteller retained the history and the lineage of her clan. She was the holder of prophecies and the revealer of truth. With her gift, she was the one who interpreted the vision of the medium. The medium received communication from the ancestors and had visions of the future. She unveiled the future of communities on uncertain worlds and prevented any misuse of power.

Almost 2,000 years after the last cataclysm, the vessels to travel into space were not yet filled with all that was to be taken from Earth when Earth started to shake again. All that was part of the society had been called to board the ship. An elder and his sect stayed behind to continue the story on Earth. Their sacrifice was immense because once the ship departed and the third cataclysm occurred, the axis of the Earth shifted and created an ice age that covered most of the earth. All technology was lost and only information told by word of mouth survived. They passed on the tradition orally until they were once again visited by the Order millenniums later.

The Order left the earth and traveled many light years across space. They finally reached Sasgorg and established themselves there. They built temples and homes in the pyramids. The structures were primitive but sufficient to protect them from nature's wrath. They lived happily and grew. But peace did not last. It was foretold that one of two suns was going to go nova. The signs were all around them: a once fruitful jungle was transformed into a semi-desert climate. Sasgorg was being burnt by its own sun. In the year 37,846 of our lord Atlanti, the star went nova. It had been 9,846 years since they had last immigrated. By then, rudimentary ships had been built to move the population from the home planet, a population that had reached millions. Scientists did try to contain the damage but were unable to restore enough life to support an entire society. Research missions had been conducted and different planets had been found to be suitable for colonization. The Meji Order was to protect the fairies, and many gave up their lives without completing their obligation of providing children. By the time the star went nova, only four royal houses of the fairies were complete and ready to inherit the throne. Each was given a chance to supervise a planet.

The planet Essay was fertile and was found to have the best soil of all the planets visited. The farmer's guild would relocate there. By then, many branches of fairies from the Royal House of Aya had been deemed suitable for the throne. To eliminate any disputes, one was appointed by the Meji to administer the planet, Essay, while the others were to help the governing fairies by overlooking smaller areas.

The planet Os, a mild-tempered planet covered mostly by water, was transformed into a business planet where all of the exchanges were done in ports. Many islands remained unexplored and still had wild forests growing on them. The guild of merchants inhabited very little of the planet, preferring to stay close to the ports to negotiate deals and exchanges. Another trinity was left to govern this planet.

The Order established itself in the capital on a planet called Ara. This planet was where the order had its temple: the Meji. Also co-inhabiting with them were the fairies, joining their gifts for the greater good.

On the planet of Kyr, a beautiful temperate planet full of resources, lived the Artisans. They created the beauty and the art for rest of the communities. Atlantis had once been a great civilization, devoted to beauty, art and science. They could not leave this behind, no matter what. Once again, another trinity was left behind.

In order to keep each community administered equally, the Administrator traveled from one planet to another from his planet Isis. The law and administration of justice was, first and foremost, dealt with by the administrator at an equal measure throughout the galaxy. Each trinity reported to their mother who reported the trinity to the Ancestor, the Overseer and the Goddess. The trinity was free to live where they pleased and, once a year would convene at the council on Ara to update their files and report any problems. The council was able to keep in touch telepathically and, therefore, if an emergency arose there was no delay in gathering.

The guild of miners, named El, was composed of nomads that traveled from planet to planet, scavenging what metals they could find to help rebuild Atlantis. They had their own space station orbiting Os, but never settled anywhere. In payment for their sacrifice, they were given the privilege to live where they chose after their life commitment was complete.

The last guild was that of the engineers, architects, mechanics and inventors. They were called the Guild of Us. They worked closely with the miners and were independent of each other. They were often called to service other planets, most often researching the capabilities of new metals which had been found. They were given a ship and were based out of Os.

Os, which became the center for the new empire, reunited the merchants, miners and engineers. It quickly became too crowded and, as the Empire had, it too, expanded its boundary to many different star systems, along with the guilds of Us and El.

In expanding its realm, Atlantis relied heavily on the services of the administrator to keep it united. There was peace and balance again in the world.

Tinay stopped reading. "Wow! That's amazing. I wonder why Mother never told me any of this." Tinay was getting ready to exit the chamber when another seismic tremor shook the base of the mountain and a cave-in occurred.

Chapter 5

SPACE TRAVEL

Ohuru might have felt confident in his spacecraft, but Atleos wasn't. Atleos had just begun traveling into space. He was using his merchant's license as an excuse to find what he was really looking for: a healer. Healers had been imprisoned twenty-seven years ago by the evil Paletis. She wanted to reign over the amalgamation of all the guilds with her husband, Tameris, and in order to do so she had to destroy the power of the Trinity. She deployed many plots, but each time a fairy was hurt or dying, a Healer would come and cure them. So Paletis employed drastic measures to kill the Healers. Those she wasn't powerful enough to kill, she imprisoned. Some Healers, extremely few, survived and went into hiding. Paletis had discovered a poison that the healers could not cure. No one knew what she used to create the potion, but it was impossible for them to find the key to heal their friends. One by one, the Healers had fallen sick and died a slow and painful death.

Paletis had an insatiable appetite for power and wanted to reunite the guilds under one single leader. It was against all that the guilds had worked for. Since the departure of the survivors of Atlantis from

Earth many millennia before, they had worked to undo the caste system and to open the door of each guild to the most able and willing people. Paletis, in her supremacy, had ordered that the caste system be reinforced. But one could, in a lifetime, buy his children their way into another caste. The money, of course, went to Paletis. She used it to build a new space station that would facilitate travel through space to Earth in a fraction of the time it took now. She wanted to invade primitive Earth and take advantage of the un-evolved species that humans had become. To them, Paletis would be a goddess and would be treated with the rank she thought she deserved.

What Paletis didn't count on was that the scientists would be reluctant to help her in her quest for power. Many decided to die rather than help her become the supreme leader. Many scientists died under her iron fist and she had to wait for a new generation of scientists to grow up and embrace her will. This way of life started to change though. Justice was ignored, and equality of the guilds had been dismissed by a stroke of her hand. Scientists had only started to make progress at this time. In her attempt to assert herself, she had destroyed many brilliant minds. Although she prevented the passing of knowledge of the old ways, she also prevented the passing of knowledge about space travel and technology.

Paletis' efforts had numerous flaws. Her master plan was evolving at a much slower pace then she hoped, giving a chance for a resistance to prepare to counter her plan. Atleos knew that the resistance had a master plan to undo the evil of Paletis, but it was taking so long he was afraid it wouldn't be fast enough. The resistance had reunited fairies in order to bring forth the ascension of Xinayra and Aznebar, but Paletis found out about the meeting and managed to poison them all. All of their guest, the fairies and the guest of honor, except three, were poisoned. Some died, but many of them were frozen. Not all scientists had joined forces with Paletis, and they worked to help the remainder of the fairies find a cure, but they only found cryogenics. The potion slowed the poisonous effects, but completely froze the individual. The rest of the surviving fairies were hard at work finding a cure that would restore the balance of life on each planet.

Atleos went to the cargo bay where the bulk of his effects were stored. Looking into a sarcophagus, he made sure that the cryogenic process was still functioning.

"Smooth sailing, indeed," he thought. "What kind of ship have I got us into, Ben?"

He looked in the glass and watched as a young man sleeping peacefully.

"I wonder, Ben, do you dream?" Atleos asked, knowing Ben would not answer.

"Who's Ben?" Raphael asked.

Startled, Atleos gasped and quickly turned around, "What are you doing here? This is my private cargo bay. You have no business here!" Atleos could hardly control his anger. He wasn't mad at the child for being curious, but at himself for letting the child spy on him so easily. The success of his mission relied on him being undetected, and if a child found the sarcophagus, what would his dad say?

"I was just bored. I saw you leave and I thought it was okay for me to follow you. I didn't mean to scare you." Raphael assured Atleos.

"You startled me, but I was not afraid."

Raphael had a gift to see the aura of people, a rare gift his father had told him. He knew that Atleos was lying.

"What are you trying to hide?"

"Nothing, I'm hiding nothing."

"You're lying!" Raphael left the cargo bay as fast as he could and ran to his father in the main control room. The endless grey corridors seemed to stretch and extend themselves in a never-ending maze.

True to his nature, Raphael had been careless when he followed Atleos and had not made any effort to remember if he had turned left or right, and how many floors down he had gone. His heart pumped faster. Not only was Atleos lying, but he was trying to hide something. Raphael felt the weariness of his father. At first, Raphael thought it had to do with his father leaving him on a planet and moving away from the cave, but now Raphael thought maybe his father felt danger and this was it. Raphael felt a hand on his shoulder. He screamed and passed out.

Tamael heard the scream and recognized his son's voice. He turned to a screen and ordered the computer to locate Raphael.

"Raphael is located on deck ten, section B," it replied.

"Ohuru, I'm going to check on Raph. Keep an eye on the monitor." Tamael hurried out of the room.

"He should be okay. Atleos is with him," Ohuru yelled as Tamael ran out of the room.

Tamael started to run. He knew Paletis well and he also knew she had spies everywhere. Maybe Atleos was not a merchant or a member of any guild but a well-trained spy. He could not lose his son, not after all this waiting and the oppression that Paletis was putting on the people. His son was part of the key to undo Paletis and Tameris. The turbo lift was slower than usual, or so it seemed. The short minutes it took for Tamael to get there seemed like eternity.

The door opened and Tamael ran towards section B. As he turned the corner, he saw Atleos about to pour a liquid into Raphael's mouth.

"Nooooo!" he screamed and let a dagger fly out of his hand. It cut through the water gourd and planted itself in the center of Atleos' hand. Atleos let out a scream.

"What have you done? Who are you? What do you want from us? Answer me!" Tamael demanded.

Atleos was surprised. He remembered how Tamael had prayed to the Overseer. This was not unusual for an older person to do, but Atleos had the feeling that nobody was who they seemed. Now he was scared. He wasn't scared for himself but for Ben. Ben was his only hope. He didn't know what to say.

"Answer me!" Tamael roared.

Raphael woke up and opened his eyes. The poor child had never been afraid of anything before in his life, and he didn't like the feeling. He was even more embarrassed that he had passed out. He felt like a wimp.

"Father, Atleos is lying. Don't believe him," Raphael said groggily.

"Are you going to be okay, Raph?" Tamael asked worriedly.

"Yes, Pa. I just feel a little lightheaded, that's all."

"Why did you try to poison my son?" Tamael stared accusingly at Atleos.

"Poison? I wasn't trying to poison him. I was trying to wake him with water."

"Son?" Tamael turned to Raphael, waiting.

"He's telling the truth, Pa."

"All right then, let's go to the command center. You and Ohuru have some explaining to do."

Atleos got up on his feet and held his hand. His shins still burned and now his hand throbbed because of the knife still planted in the middle of it.

"My hand," Atleos said weakly.

"Later. I want to know who you are first."

Atleos was in shock. He had never seen such ability at knife-throwing and there was no way a simple miner was that good. That kind of skill required a lot of practice and some knowledge, and the blade was perfect. Wherever Tamael had gotten this knife was not a common marketplace on Os.

Tamael grabbed Raphael in his arms and pushed the button for the turbo lift. The doors opened and off they went to the control room.

"What was all the ruckus about?" Ohuru asked.

"You tell me," Tamael replied. "I want to know who Atleos really is, why he's lying, why he's on this ship, and where do your loyalties lie, Ohuru."

"What?" Ohuru was baffled by the sudden change in Tamael's attitude. He was now much more commanding and certain of himself, more so than on the previous three trips to Os that they had flown together. "I'm not hiding anything from you. I am, and always will be, your servant. I swore loyalties to you and your family twenty years ago, and I will stand by my word. I fail to see how Atleos traveling with us is a problem."

"Atleos is hiding something in his cargo bay," said Raphael.

"Hiding? Why do you say he's hiding anything? Atleos, what are you hiding?" Ohuru started to sweat. Atleos had come highly recommended and he was traveling the same path as Tamael. Ohuru saw no harm in killing two birds with one stone, but he certainly didn't want to betray Tamael or for anyone to get hurt.

Atleos looked at the floor. The pain in his hand was making it hard to concentrate. Sweating profusely, he had no idea what to say, but he knew they could tell if he was lying. There was no other choice, but to tell the truth. Atleos took a deep breath and started to explain, "I may be called Atleos, but that is not my real name. I am disguised as a merchant to travel easily from one planet to another. I was taught the ways of barter and exchange to facilitate my hiding and reaffirm my position in this role. My real mission is to try to find a healer to find an antidote to the poison that plagues the fairies. The poison is so effective it has not been changed in the last twenty-seven years. I have one of the guests from the ascending ceremony of Xinayra and Aznebar. If we can cure him, then we can cure everyone who has been put in cryogenics and re-establish the balance in the Order."

"Who?" Tamael asked.

"Who? What?" Atleos asked, not sure what the question meant.

"What ascending ceremony did you say he was a guest from?" Tamael asked.

"Xinayra and Aznebar."

"He's telling the truth, Pa," Raphael said.

Atleos was relieved that he was able to tell so little. There was still a chance to accomplish his mission and protect Ben as he had sworn he would do.

"A merchant would not have been entrusted with such a task only a Meji could do." Tamael was still suspicious.

Atleos was surprised by Tamael's knowledge.

"Hmm, well you see. . ." Atleos started.

"Don't lie!" shouted Raphael.

"It's all right, son. I think we're on the same side," said Tamael. "Very well, you search for the Healer and we'll keep your secret. Is there anything else we should know?"

"No. If I say anymore, you would have to die," Atleos had a certainty in his voice that sent a chill down of Ohuru's neck.

Why did I ever get involved with the resistance? he thought.

Because it was the right thing to do, answered Tamael with a smile. "Now, we should look after your hand and give me back my knife." Tamael broke the connection.

"No problem. Where did you learn to throw like that?" Atleos asked.

"If I told you, I would have to kill you," answered Tamael.

Atleos smiled. Okay, so Tamael knew there was more to his story than he was saying, but he would leave it at that for now.

Tamael had often hurt himself with knives and knew what he had to do, but it didn't mean he was skilled in the art of suturing.

"It will probably leave a scar. Sorry about that," Tamael said.

"Yeah, it's okay, as long as I can still use it." Atleos tried bending his fingers and felt a stinging sensation.

"You will, but not for now. I'll bandage it up to prevent infection." Tamael moved to get bandages.

"Very well."

"What is in the cargo hold, Atleos?" Tamael asked.

"If I told you...."

"Sorry, that won't work, you can keep your name to yourself, but I need to know what is in the cargo hold."

"Just a guest for the ceremony. I'm entrusted to protect him and to find a cure. He's the only one they wanted to part with, but he's the guinea pig."

"Very well. What Healer are you searching for?" asked Tamael.

"I am not sure..."

"He's lying again, Pa!" Raphael was in the room reading a book, but had not seemed to pay attention.

"That boy is good!" Atleos said.

Pride crept into Tamael's voice, "So good that no lie will get past him. He's been well trained."

Atleos started to wonder what else Tamael had trained his son to do.

"I'm looking for Kaplara from the Order of the Blue Eagle. She might be on Os hiding in the forest."

"Kaplara? Isn't she a bit old for this?"

"She's seventy-seven years old, but she is still alive. The important thing is she's one of the few elders still alive that could provide an antidote to the poison," Atleos explained. "She's been researching for years now. She was close to a solution. I have to have faith in her. She's our last hope."

Ohuru raised his eyebrows. "There are more healers then you think, Atleos, or more than you were told. In this time of precariousness, one is only told enough to succeed in his mission. It's only the success of all the missions that makes the over-all goal achievable. You only know part of the truth. I'll help you find Kaplara."

"Thank you." Atleos was relieved. Maybe it was destiny that the two of them took this trip together after all.

Ohuru returned to the main deck while Atleos and Tamael walked to cargo bay two and Atleos showed the sarcophagus to Tamael.

"Nice piece of technology," Tamael said in wonderment.

Raphael peeked inside and asked, "Is he dead?"

"No, we caught him in the early stage of the poison and, therefore, he's relatively healthy. But he would die if he was released from his slumber. If I can find a cure for him, a lot more people will be freed from their sarcophaguses and join the resistance."

Tamael frowned. "The resistance? I would be careful who you say that to, boy. Paletis would pay good money to have that type of information."

"Yes," Atleos blushed. He had to be more careful about what he said.

"Well, let's go eat something. It will make it easier to think." Tamael went over to the computer station. His voice sounded out of a microphone on the main deck, "Ohuru?"

"Yes, Tamael, what is it?" Ohuru replied.

"I'm heading over to the canteen and preparing us something to eat. Care to join us?"

"Yes, I'm starting to get hungry, too. Be right over." Ohuru was pleased he didn't have to eat his own food for once. It was not such a bad idea to travel with guests.

He put the ship on auto-pilot, had one last look at his dials and left for the canteen.

Raphael watched his father prepare dinner. "What are you making, Pa?"

"Salad and fruits. We have to eat what won't keep first, and then we will eat our rations. They don't taste so bad, but they do tend to get boring after a while." Tamael looked out the window. They were traveling slower than he expected.

Ohuru walked in the room with a large smile on his face. He whistled a song Tamael had never heard before.

"Why are we traveling so slowly, Ohuru?" Tamael asked.

"Because the imperial guard is looking for good engineers. If we go to light speed, we might attract too much attention or I might lose my life and my engines to Paletis. I've got light speed if we need to evade them, but otherwise, it's regular speed for everything." Ohuru explained.

"It's just that Lilay is due to give birth soon and I want to be back for it." Genuine concern showed in Tamael's eyes.

"There's plenty of time. I figure that with Atleos to help in the negotiations, you'll be done in no time and we can make a little visit to El to visit your old friends," Ohuru grinned.

"Really, you mean that?" Tamael was excited.

"Yes," Ohuru laughed at the delight that showed on Tamael's face. "Atleos is quite the merchant for his young age. A little too fast when negotiating when he becomes attached to something. But in your case, everything should be fine."

"Attached? What do you mean attached?" Tamael was confused.

Ohuru turned to Atleos. "Atleos, show Tamael your ring."

Atleos blushed. He knew he had done a poor deal on this exchange and he was not proud of it, but the ring was so beautiful he had to have it. To his vexation, the other merchants had identified his desire and had refused to lower the price anymore. Atleos showed Tamael his finger.

"Hmm, interesting. A snake biting its own tail. What do you suppose this means?" asked Tamael.

"I don't know. I just fell in love with it." Atleos explained.

"It's an ancient ouroboros. It means eternal struggle and infinity," said Ohuru.

"Well, it's sad that it means nothing to you, but it is beautiful," agreed Tamael.

Raphael had not been paying attention to the conversation. He stared at the fruits, not realizing how hungry he was. Now that he was waiting to be served, he was famished.

Tamael divided the salad and the fruits into bowls and handed each traveler a stick with meat on it.

"What is that?" asked Atleos

"Dried lizard, full of protein. It's good, you'll see," Tamael explained.

Atleos started to think that the ration he had been eating for some days had tasted really good! He looked at the meat and felt his stomach churn. Maybe he would stick to salad and fruit tonight. Tamael sat down and took a large bite out of the lizard meat.

"Father!" Raphael could not believe his eyes, "We didn't say our prayer!"

"Yes, about that, Raph. I'm afraid you're going to have to pray in your head while I prepare the food and be ready to eat once you are being served. Praying is an old custom that is not looked upon well in the world that Paletis has created. To pray out loud would be to betray yourself and to endanger those you are with."

"Who's Paletis?" Raphael asked.

"She's the queen of all the planets that the guilds have settled on," Tamael explained. "She's mean and evil and wants to control everyone. No one really knows how she got that way, but they know, now that she has tasted power and greed, she has become consumed by it, and there's no way out. She has created a web of lies so that no one could find the truth. The resistance that was created by her tyranny was actually working to bring about her demise, but she was too powerful. The resistance needs the help of the surviving Healers to find a remedy to the poison she has created. Then, with the power of all the surviving fairies, they will beat her at her own game."

"Why is this so hard, Father?" Raphael asked, curious.

Tamael sighed, "Because Paletis was a fairy herself; a Medium. She can see the future. Whatever she has seen has led her astray and now she can't find her way back. The resistance is hoping that if enough fairies are brought back, they would be able to overcome her strength and bring her down."

"Since she's a Medium, she often knows of the plots to assassinate her and escapes them all," said Atleos.

"How is the resistance ever going to beat her?" Raphael kept digging.

"By keeping the plan a secret until the last minute. If she captures anyone, she will only be able to defeat one part of the plan and won't know how many more agents are involved with the whole plan," said Ohuru.

"Which makes for a very lonely existence. Everybody must always be kept separated from one another, but the plan has been successful so far," said Atleos.

Raphael's eyes widened. "Wow! So you're a member of the resistance, Atleos?"

Atleos chuckled, "Well, since I can't lie to you, it's useless to say I'm not. Let's just say that anyone who is helping the resistance or associating with the resistance is considered a traitor and is condemned to death if found. It's important to keep my secret, otherwise Ohuru and your father will get hurt in the process also."

Raphael started to weigh the events of the day. He was filled with excitement. Atleos was a member of the resistance, remotely, but still associated with the resistance. This was great.

"Pa, where do you stand?" Raphael looked at his father.

"I stand by the original order of Nazar." Tamael knew what the next question would be.

"Who is Nazar?"

Tamael knew that he wouldn't be able to get out of answering these questions. "He's the original member of the Order that helped our descendants from Atlantis escape Earth. Nazar believed that everyone who was born equal and knowledgeable should be available to everyone. He wanted each individual to contribute to society and be given a chance to be what he wanted in life without being confined to a caste. Each profession came to be regarded with respect, and each had an important value to bring to society. Society could not survive unless each member worked his best in his field. Nazar created equality and distributed the power to those who would use it to better the Order. He created a system that divided the power and made it insignificant, so that no one would want to abuse it."

"So what happened? Why is Paletis so hungry for power?" asked Raphael.

"No one really knows exactly what took place, and that is why it's so hard to get to her. Her powers turned evil. It's not the first time this has happened, but it's the first time no one can prevent her from overthrowing the Order. It's still a mystery, son. To be able to survive Paletis' rule, we must shroud ourselves in mist and clouds, so she cannot see us and find our true purpose."

"No more praying, then," said Raphael.

"No more praying." Tamael smiled. He loved his son. It was going to be painful to leave him behind in Essay, but he had no choice. In the window, Tamael stared at Us floating by in the sky. They were getting closer to their goal.

Ohuru decided to orbit around Us for the night. He needed to sleep and hated to leave the autopilot on for long. Everyone called it a night and went to their separate quarters.

Tamael was putting Raphael to sleep when he noticed that Raph was frowning.

"What is it, Raph?"

"I've been wondering, what if I say something I'm not supposed to say?"

"When?"

"When I get to Essay."

"You'll be safe on Essay. You'll be staying with a friend of mine. He'll continue to teach you, like I have. He'll teach you new things about farming the land and caring for animals. Actually, I have a book you can read tomorrow. I think you'll like it. It will give you information about what you will do during the next few years. You'll get the chance to try a bit of everything. It'll be fun and time will fly by without you even noticing it. You'll see."

"Maybe the day will go by fast, but when I go to bed at night, you'll feel so far away." Raphael's eyes filled with tears. He would miss his whole family. He already missed his mother and, strangely enough, his sister, too.

"You'll be fine, Raph. You know we love you. I'll try to find excuses to come and visit you as much as I can. Your mother is going to be busy with the new baby and your sister will begin her own apprenticing, but Tinay will come to visit you when the time is right."

"What is she going to be?"

"An artist, a painter, a sculptor, a seamstress and a creative artisan."

"Did you have to buy into that caste as well?"

"No, your mother is an artisan, so it's not a problem for your sister to follow your mom."

"Oh, I see. Why can't I become an artisan like Mother?"

"Well, there's time for you to decide. The next seven years will help you decide if you want to be a farmer or if, at fourteen years of age, you want to be a miner. Maybe by then things will have changed enough for you to be able to do whatever your heart desires."

"What about my knife training?" Raphael desperately wanted to learn how to throw knives.

"Ah, that. Merdaine will be able to help you, but you will have to do your chores during the day first. He'll help you if you help him. Understand?"

"Yes, I do. I wish you were the one teaching me."

"I can't, but I wouldn't worry if I were you. Merdaine is quite a capable individual. You'll see."

"All right, Pa, good-night."

The night was short-lived for Ohuru. He only slept five hours a night before waking up rested and ready to tackle another day at the command of his ship. The ship was nearing Essay by the time everyone else woke up.

"Tamael, you'll prepare your famous breakfast for us?" Ohuru asked.

Tamael was still stretching and yawning. "Yes, I guess I can. Do you have yogurt and eggs?"

"Yes, my friend. I've been hiding them from Atleos for a while now, counting on you to cook it for me. I've been looking forward to this for about five years now."

Tamael and Raphael headed for the canteen,

"Where are we, Father?" asked Raphael.

"Just entered the orbit of Essay."

"Oh, I thought I was going to spend more time with you guys." Raphael was disappointed.

"You are, son. We are not ready to stop here, yet. Our first stop has to be Os. Now, sit down for breakfast. You have a lot of work ahead of you today." Tamael pushed a bowl towards his son.

"What do you mean?" Raphael wanted to know what he would be doing.

"I want you to read about what you'll be learning on Essay. I've got a book your mother prepared for you."

"Great, it'll help pass the time that way." Raphael loved to learn.

"Breakfast is served!"

They all sat down and ate a beautiful breakfast as pleasing for the eyes as for the stomach. A fresh scent of vanilla floated in the air, the hydroponic bay produced beautifully ripe strawberries and bananas. Ohuru couldn't have asked for a more perfect way to start the day, or, in his case, continue it.

Raphael settled down in a corner of the canteen where he could see the stars. The next star system they would come to would be Os. Then they would finally get to walk on the ground and explore the markets. Raphael could not wait to see the merchants and their tables full of goods. He wanted to sense the clothes, the food, the colors, the smell, and even the taste. What an adventure this would be!

He opened the book his father had given him. There was too much writing for his taste. His mother had been kind enough to include a few drawings. His apprenticing would be divided by the seasons. Each year, for seven years, he would learn how to cultivate many plants. First he would study each plant, and then he would prepare the seedlings and replant them where they were needed. In some cases, he would learn how to harvest their products and store them in a suitable facility for food, seeds, and transport to other planets. Each winter he would settle and learn how to play a musical instrument of his choice.

Music! he thought. *Nobody ever mentioned I had to learn a musical instrument! This ordeal might not be so bad after all.*

In his first year, he would learn about grains and cereals. The second year was devoted to vegetables and fruits. The third year was devoted to animals like horses, cows, pigs, and chickens. The fourth year would be dedicated to growing spices and herbs. The fifth year, he would help replant forests of different trees. The sixth year, he would devote to growing flowers. His final year's project would be to build a garden for a retired member of society. This was to be functional and yet beautiful. The Order placed a great deal of importance to beauty in the life of its citizens and it was important for people to grow up surrounded by beauty. Through all this time, he would learn to hunt and feed himself.

There wasn't mention of knives in this book. Raphael walked over to the com link and hailed his father.

"Pa, are you there?" he asked.

"Yes, son, what is it?"

"What about knives?"

Tamael shook his head, there was not going to be an easy way out of this one, "Hang on, I'm coming."

Tamael joined his son on the canteen deck and sat down beside him.

"What are you so obsessed about?" Tamael sighed.

"I would love to learn about knives. I like the hand-to-hand combat techniques, but the knives are so much better. I want to know more."

"Unfortunately, you know everything I know. Now you just need to practice, a lot."

"Am I going to have any time to do any of this with Merdaine?"

"Yes, he'll allow it. He'll teach you how to use a najar, a wooden stick, to do your work-outs. And then he'll take you hunting with a bow and a crossbow. You'll have plenty to learn."

"Like how to fertilize flowers?" Raphael said.

"It's part of growing up. You don't always do exactly what you want."

"Tinay didn't have to do any growing up until now."

"Yes, she did. She helped your mother grow the herbs, plants, vegetables, and fruits for our survival. She had to learn a great deal. She just never left home, that's all."

"Then why couldn't I just stay at home with Mother and learn?"

"Because we're moving to a new planet and we won't have to do everything by ourselves anymore. Your mother will have to start working as an artist. I'll be the one busy taking care of the house. It's my turn to help. And I can't really teach you about gardening since I have to learn that for myself. Do you understand?"

"I don't want to leave you and Ma. I miss her already."

"Once you are on Essay, you will be so busy you will only have time for us in your prayers at night and you'll sleep quickly because of exhaustion. You'll see. Don't be worried. To prepare for things you know nothing about, let life take its course. I will be visiting you lots. After all, who else could teach you how to handle a sword?"

"Swords? Really, Pa?"

"Yes, but it's not really part of your program with Merdaine so it will be extra work."

"That's alright, I can do it. You know I can."

"Yes, I believe you will do great things. You simply need to learn to take it one day at a time."

"Thanks, Pa!"

Tamael hugged his son, holding back tears. He, too, would miss his son. The only way he could protect his family was to divide it into space under the cover of false names. For Tinay's and Raphael's protection, they were never called by their real names. That way, Paletis could never search for their souls and interrogate them. Because the future was so uncertain, Tamael was trying to restrain his own anxiety and give strength to his son, whom he loved so much. A single tear escaped his eye and flowed gently down his cheek. He kissed his son's head and looked outside. There was Os, resembling a large cloud, covered by oceans, rivers and lakes. Another day had gone by, and it was time for Tamael to prepare yet another meal.

Ohuru's voice came over the intercom, "We're orbiting Os, but it's too late for any business today. Let's eat and get a good head start tomorrow. What's on the menu, Tamael?"

"I found some salted bacon I can prepare with some vermicelli. What say you?"

"Sounds good. Much better than the ration that Atleos has been preparing." Ohuru grimaced.

Tamael smiled. "When was the last time you cooked your own meal, Ohuru?"

"Hey, now, I cook all the time when I'm alone. All this traveling leaves little time for restaurants and entertaining, you know."

"Okay, Ohuru, don't be so hard on yourself," said Atleos as he walked to the canteen. "Tamael, do you need a hand for this feast?"

"Sure." Tamael got up and quickly wiped the tear from his face. He went over to the counter and started to prepare another meal.

Raphael stayed behind by the window. He had seen the reflection of his father in the window and he had seen the tear. Even though it was his duty to go to Essay, and he understood the importance of moving up in the caste system, he wondered how his father, who seemed to love him so much, could leave him behind. He, too, had a silent tear running down his cheek.

It's because I love so much that I'm doing this, Raph. I'm doing it for love.

Raphael smiled and looked at his father's reflection in the window, and saw his father watching him. Yes, his father loved him. This he knew for sure.

Chapter 6

Os

The sun shone brightly on Os as clouds floated across the sky. Amos stared up into the sky. He wondered when his friend would show up. They were due sometime today. Amos rubbed his large belly. He wondered if he should have another muffin. Looking back at his table he saw very few remnants of what had been set before him an hour ago. There was a muffin left, but five had already gone missing. He rubbed his belly once more, "No, I better resist temptation."

"Yes, if you can call it that."

Startled, Amos turned around and saw Tamael standing at the door.

"Come in, come in. I was waiting for you!"

"Ha ha, Amos! You've gained weight. You're looking great. I'm sure Ohuru would pay much money to get your cook on his ship." Tamael gave a big hug to Amos, hardly able to walk around him.

"Ohuru cannot have her. She would have to divorce me before I would let her cook for anyone else."

Ohuru, Raphael and Atleos walked in behind Tamael. Raphael was happy to see his father so happy. He smiled from his soul.

"Where are my manners? Welcome, Ohuru. Who's this you have with you?"

"This is my new partner, Atleos. He's here to help bargain for some of my rare finds." Ohuru replied.

"Rare finds? I might be interested in that. Atleos, welcome to my humble home." Amos moved toward Atleos and hugged him, making Atleos feel minuscule. Amos laughed from deep within his belly. "You're just a beginner, but you'll get there. The pleasure of making a good deal is always accompanied with a thirst for celebration. The fatter you get, the better you demonstrate your ability to barter. You'll see."

"Is it healthy to be this fat?" Raphael spurted out.

"Oh! Now that hurts, son. Who are you?"

"I'm sorry, I just meant, you're really big and . . . um . . . Pa?"

"This is my son, Raphael. You'll have to excuse him, he hasn't been introduced to a lot of people," chuckled Tamael, slightly embarrassed.

"Ha ha! It's alright, son. My size is exponentially the measure of my success."

"Wow, you must be very successful then." Raphael stared in awe.

Loud laughter filled the room, "I guess kids call them as they see them."

Amos was proud that he was as large as he was, indeed, a mark of his success, as were the clothes he wore. He was dressed in a light blue tunic and a dark blue jacket with a large light blue and marine striped scarf that hung over his shoulders. His belt that held it all together was made of satin and matched the ensemble. Atleos looked around, curious to find what a house of such a well-known merchant really looked like. The best word to describe it, he thought, was eclectic. Nothing had a rhyme or a reason, making Amos' home decidedly interesting. There was a mix of not only cultures but also of races: sculptures, tapestry, tapas, and paintings. Not an inch of the walls were empty.

"Atleos, I see you are a connoisseur of art. Only an initiate could appreciate the measure of this room."

"Yes, sir. How long has it taken you to amass such riches?"

"Actually, most of the articles displayed in this room are gifts I received from friends I bartered for. I'm a traditional dressmaker. I dress entire ceremonies at once: weddings, baptism, confirmation, or simply reverence day. It took me a while to figure out a lucrative venue, but I found that I was getting many compliments for the way I dressed. People liked my traditional gowns and tunics, and my wife looks sublime in those dresses. They bring her exquisite beauty into perspective."

"Where is your wife, Amos?" Tamael asked.

"She stays at home much these days. She knows I have little time to offer her when I'm at work. I now have employees to supervise and I'm still the one in charge of creation. I'm a very busy man."

"But they all look alike!" said Raphael. "What kind of creation can you do if they all look alike?"

"Raph!" Tamael was starting to think he would have been better off to leave Raphael on Essay instead of bringing him here.

"It's alright, my friend, no worries. Raphael, only the clothing stays traditionally the same, thus the word 'tradition'. I make little variances depending on a person's height, eye and hair color, and depending on the ceremony he is attending. From time to time, I have been known to create for other species a variance of their own traditional outfits. Now you ask why I have such a broad collection of artifacts. Most of them are gifts from satisfied customers who received praise about their clothing. Sometimes there's more than money in my business. It's part of my business to encourage trading and sales. So I give away presents from our local artisans."

"Why not give your clothing?"

"Ah! The secret of my success lies in two things. No one else sells traditional clothing. Over the years some have tried, thinking there was enough of a market for two of us, but I build my clientele and a strong reputation by myself and people always come to me."

"And the second?" Raphael asked.

"The second rule is I never give away any of my clothing. You want it, you buy it."

The guests could not help but laugh. Amos had discovered the road to riches by simply never giving away the very product he sold.

"Wise indeed, Amos," said Atleos.

"You're still young, son. Find one thing that you can sell better than anyone else and just concentrate on that. Make sure there will always be a demand for it and just go for the top." Amos was proud of his success. He had never taken on an apprentice because of the lack of time he had to offer. But times were changing; maybe he should take an apprentice.

"Who trained you, Atleos?"

"I was trained at the school of the merchants on Anarbel on the system of the three moons of Marion."

"What a secluded area of space for you to learn. With whom did you apprentice then?"

"I'm afraid my parents could only afford to promote me from their engineer guild."

"Caste."

"What?"

"Caste, not guild. Guilds no longer exist. To call it a guild might bring unwanted ears to you."

"Sorry, caste. There was no money for me to begin my apprenticing anywhere, so I joined Ohuru and …"

"Ohuru is a very good engineer. He has done well in the past trading his inventions, but without proper training, you will be mediocre at best, son. You must learn the trade properly."

"What do you suggest, Master Amos?" asked Tamael.

"I'm lonely. New blood and new ideas might be what I need. My wife has been taking time at home to work on her art. She makes wonderful tapas. The island is situated in the meridional southern forest. The trees she needs grow near my property on Isifilmos. She's keeping very busy."

"She still makes time for your lunch. That has to take her quite some time to prepare," said Tamael, muffling his laughter.

"She only prepares breakfast. I encourage the local merchant to give me food for the rest of the day," Amos rubbed his stomach, "but it's never as good as hers. Speaking of food, anyone hungry?"

Ohuru turned around and looked at the table. For him, there was enough food there to last him a week, but he wondered if there was enough there to sustain Amos until lunch.

"I ate already. I was contemplating maybe another muffin. Please, sit down and eat," Amos invited.

The four guests decided to join in on the feast. Tamael loved the fruits grown on Isifilmos; they had a special bite to them.

Raphael leaned towards his father and asked, "Pa, what is a tapa?"

"It's a paper-like cloth made from tapa bark or similar bark. It's a very lovely piece of art that can be used as a carpet, poncho or belt."

"You know, Raphael," Amos said between bites, "my wife is one of the very few artisans that can work the bark to be so soft that my clients order her works of art to wear for special ceremonies. It's very exquisite."

"I see" said Raphael, looking around to find an example.

"Look here," said Amos rolling from side to side in an attempt to get up. "This is a prime example of her work." Amos pointed at a tapestry made in a collection of geometric forms all lined up with one another consisting of four different colors. "My wife created a process to soften most barks growing on our island so her tapas are multi-colored, and she is very creative in attaching different pieces together. Her art is greatly appreciated around here."

"Lovely. I like it," said Raphael.

"She would be pleased to hear you say that. I'll pass on the message when I get home. So, Atleos, what do you say? Would you care to join me and become my apprentice?"

"It would be an honor to learn from you."

"Why do I sense a 'but' coming?"

"No 'but'. When do I start?" Atleos smiled.

Tamael was surprised by Atleos' reaction. If he knew how busy Amos would keep him, he would know how little time he would have to look for healers.

"I was thinking you could start in six weeks or so, when Tinay arrives."

"Tinay?"

"Yes, Tamael's daughter. Have you not met?" Amos knew what the answer was.

"Yes, of course, but I wasn't aware she was coming here."

"Yes, she is to train with my wife. She will start to study the art of water. I'm very glad to have her among us."

"I'm afraid that would be too much of a burden for you. I couldn't accept."

"It's alright. Tinay will stay with us for only a year, and then she'll leave for Essay. You, on the other hand, can stay much longer, if you wish."

"I don't know what to say." Atleos looked at Tamael with pleading eyes. His secret identity would be jeopardized if he didn't accept, but it was vital for him to continue his search.

"I think that he is young and he would be wise to only commit himself to a year with you, Amos," said Tamael.

"Tamael is wise. Let's have you come with Tinay, and when the time for her to leave comes, then you will decide if you stay or move on."

"Very well, one year." Atleos felt he had made a mistake, but no matter how else he could have planned this, it could always come back as his cover up story. He had to protect his true identity and play the game as it was dealt to him.

The food was delicious and they emptied the table quickly. When they finished eating, Amos offered to tour the markets with them. Raphael was curious and wanted to see more of Amos' planet. He wanted to see the water, the lakes, and the ocean. Amos was close to a quiet quay only a short boat ride away, and he was part of a very affluent market. It was decided that Tamael would prepare to sell his products and take Raphael with him, and Ohuru would embark on a trek with Atleos to visit the market with Amos as a guide.

Amos got on the boat with Ohuru and Atleos and headed for the docks of Osmos. The water was calm and the sun kept shining. It was a beautiful day. The market was full of food, herbs, and spices. There's was a little of everything for everyone. Amos smiled as he headed for a shrimp display. Atleos looked around and was surprised to see only food at the market.

"Ohuru, did you notice that there's nothing but food here?"

"Yes, I have. What do you expect? It's lunch time for Amos."

"But we have just left the table," Atleos argued.

"We have indeed, but Amos was kind to let us eat his food and only took a muffin. We must, in turn, allow him to eat."

"Oh! I feel sick just looking at him."

"Ha ha! I can just imagine what you will look like when you get home after a year on Os, my friend." Ohuru patted Atleos' flat stomach. "If you appreciate your figure, I would have a picture taken of it before it's too late."

Ohuru followed Amos who was smacking his lips saying, "Those shrimps look scrumptious."

Atleos forced himself to follow his friends and restrained himself to only a skewer of absolutely delicious shrimps.

Tamael divided his Alenor crystal shards into smaller bags and tagged them as Raphael watched.

"What are you doing, Father?"

"Just like Amos suggested twenty years ago, I found a market for something extremely rare but indispensable, and that never goes out of fashion."

"What's that?"

"Alenor crystals."

"Yes, and. . ."

"They are excessively rare, son. I'm one of the few miners that have found them, so I sell them every five years to companies that need their water purified. I put them in bags for each planet I visit. They know I'm coming and have prepared their payments for me. Atleos won't have much negotiating to do."

"Why can't Amos negotiate for you? He's more experienced."

"Amos already negotiated contracts twenty years ago. He still makes money off of them. But each year I come back, a new price has to be settled on. Ohuru benefits from the exchange, too."

"How so?"

"He made the coupling needed to hide the crystals inside and help the crystals purify the energy."

"Why do the crystals need to be changed? Aren't they good forever?"

"No, not under the circumstance under which they are put. They erode and need to be recharged."

"Couldn't your clients do this on their own?"

"Yes, but they wouldn't need me anymore, would they?"

Raphael smiled. He liked to watch his cunning father. Raphael would accompany his father tomorrow and see how the bargaining went.

Amos, Ohuru and Atleos returned. Ohuru had eaten so much that his stomach bulged from his pants.

Tamael turned around to see his friends return. "What have we here?"

"The three fat men of Os. Ha ha!" answered Amos.

"At first, it was only a skewer of shrimps, but there was lobster, crab, rice, cakes. . . Oh, the cakes!" Ohuru said, delighted.

"The food was so good you couldn't say no. But they were wise not to tell you how much it cost until after you ate. Amos spent a lot of money. More than he had intended," Atleos said.

"Expensive?" Tamael asked.

"Ah, not that much. I had to celebrate a new apprentice and the return of friends. Your visit always brings joy to my heart, Tamael!" Amos grinned.

"And money to your pocket," added Raphael.

Amos burst out laughing. His large tummy shook and tears ran down his face. "Well said, my boy, well said."

"What about supper, Amos? I'm hungry after all this work," Tamael's stomach growled.

Ohuru laughed as Atleos ran for the washroom.

"I think it will only be you and me, along with your boy tonight, Tamael," grinned Amos. "What do you say?"

"It's a deal. Where should we go?" Tamael asked.

"There's a fantastic new restaurant just around the river bend and I was dying to try it."

"Should I bring any money?"

"Of course not. It's my treat, old friend. Besides, my ten percent from five years ago can still cover our supper tonight. Ha ha!"

The food was delicious and Tamael, more prudent, only ordered once and ate like a normal human being. Raphael didn't order anything. He simply tasted a sample of Amos' many dishes. Raphael could not believe his own eyes. No wonder Amos was fat.

Once they headed home, they found Ohuru sound asleep and Atleos still complaining about cramps. Amos gave him tea to soothe his stomach and headed for bed. Raphael slept with his father in the guest room. He could hear the buzzing of insects outside, and other strange noises. Compared to his planet, Os was noisy and busy, and he loved it.

By the time Atleos, Tamael and Raphael got up, Ohuru and Amos had already finished breakfast. Amos was fitting Ohuru for his new blue tunic.

"You know that a new tunic every five years isn't much. You should get two."

"No no. I only wear them when I land on a planet. It's not practical at all in space. One is enough."

"My powers of persuasion never worked well on you, Ohuru," Amos turned around. "What about you, Tamael? Need a tunic?"

"Yes, I may need a new one. Is it ready?"

"Yes, my friend, I have it in the back." Amos went to the back of the store and grabbed a purple tunic that was as light as air. "You will love the fabric, it breathes."

Tamael smiled. Amos could sell anything. He had perfected his art and his talent to read people's mind.

"Breathes? Let's see." Tamael grabbed the tunic and went into a change room.

"You look great. The purple accentuates your black hair, very distinguishing."

"Enough, Amos. You're not selling it to me. Remember, I already paid for this."

"Nevertheless, it's a work of art. But I have nothing for the child and your friend, Atleos. If I would have been warned. . ."

"I will not be going anywhere today and, therefore, will not need a new tunic. I will watch Raphael and stay close to the bathroom. Thank you very much." Atleos could hardly look at the food on the table.

"What? I want to go!" Raphael objected.

"No, maybe you better stay with Atleos. He might need help," said Tamael.

Raphael was clearly disappointed, but he obeyed his father.

"I'll make some more tea for you, Atleos. You'll be back on your feet in no time," said Amos as he left the room.

"As long as I don't eat any food for the rest of the week." Atleos turned green at the thought of food and his stomach made odd noises.

All Raphael could think of to summarize this experience in one word was, "Yeurk!"

Amos returned with the tea and helped Tamael fix his tunic. Amos was dressed in a fancy orange-colored tunic he had been preparing for ages. He loved being colorful. Most importantly, he wanted his delegation's clothing to match. Amos, Ohuru, and Tamael set out to the nearest water cleaning plant, leaving Atleos and Raphael to do as they pleased. They arrived at the plant just as the president of the corporation, accompanied by the administrator, landed on the pad.

"Welcome, Master Amos. Welcome to you, also, Tamael and Ohuru," the president greeted them.

"Thank you. Tamael is anxious to get to work while we discuss the arrangement our payment," Amos said as he shook the president's hand.

"I thought a friend of yours was doing the negotiation this year, Ohuru?" asked the administrator.

"Yes, but he is indisposed. He sends his deepest apologies." Ohuru bowed to the administrator, surprised to see him there.

"Hmm, I see. I had not expected to negotiate with you, Master Amos."

"I'm sure we can find an arrangement that will suit us all." Amos was perplexed.

"Very well. May I see the crystals?"

Tamael pulled out a large round disc of Alenor crystal, and several marble-sized Alenor crystals.

"What is this?"

"The disc will clean the impurity in the water and the marble will energize it. It's part of a new coupler Ohuru created," said Tamael, demonstrating the new coupling.

"I see. No doubt more money, Master Amos?"

"Indeed. Every new technology must get its just reward."

"Indeed," the administrator said.

Amos started to walk away from the landing pad into the president's office. He already knew what he would walk away with. This was just a game for him. He knew the administrator figured the price to be outrageous, but somehow, he was ready to pay to get the technology.

Tamael and Ohuru walked towards the plant. They exchanged the old coupling for the new ones, saving a tremendous amount of time. Tamael was careful to keep the spare parts and put them in a box he would bring to Ohuru's ship.

Ohuru knew well what he had to do. He changed the crystals from the old couplings to the new ones, knowing the crystals would be effective forever. It was only the metal in the couplings that compromised the efficiency of the crystals. They were quick at their task, as they didn't want anyone to come and start asking questions.

Once they were done replacing the old couplings, they went back to the ship. Tamael took all the filters out and saved the Alenor crystal discs and marbles in a safe box to use them later. Then he walked over to the main administration building.

He entered the room where Amos was. Amos had a large smile on his face. Business had gone extremely well, as usual.

"Here are the residual crystals, sir, if you care to inspect them."

"Let me see," said the president. "Well, as usual, you came just in time. These look pretty useless. Are you sure you cannot recycle them?"

"No, sir. They've been rendered useless with the erosion and would not work well for more than another month. They can be thrown out."

"Very well. You brought them in, you can take them out," Said the administrator.

Tamael was surprised. The previous president had always insisted on keeping everything they had paid for, no matter how useless it was.

"Yes, sir."

"My decision surprises you, miner?" asked the administrator.

"A little, sir." Tamael tried to act like an unimportant miner who had struck it rich. He disliked the head administrator to start with, but this one had a certain air about him that Tamael hated.

The president was looking off into the distance, detached from the whole conversation.

"Tameris, my father, has put me in charge," the administrator said, answering Tamael's unasked question.

Now Tamael was trying not to act surprised, but now knew why he disliked the young man so much. He was Paletis' son.

"I decided there was no need to keep useless things around. We pay you for a service, and very well, I might add," the administrator said as he turned to Amos, who bowed down, "and once that service is no longer required, we dispose of useless artifacts that are around."

"Very well, sir."

"My name is Titlis. I administer all the cleaning plants you are to visit today. The presidents of the plants are no longer in charge of bartering for any cleaning plant. Since Amos bartered directly with me for all the plants already, you will not see me again. I will send the payment home with him, and I expect you to continue your work."

"Of course, sir."

"I also asked for a guarantee that the product will provide at least seven years work this time, since the technology has improved and new material is being installed."

"Actually, sir, I cannot only guarantee seven, but eight years of service from this new product."

"Very well, then. At no extra charge?" demanded Titlis.

"Well, this is new information to me, I did not negotiate. . ." Amos was flustered. He had negotiated seven years, no more.

"It's alright, Amos. The power plants have been our main supporter for fifteen years now. We can afford to give a little from time to time."

"Be it noted I object, as your financial adviser, but if you must."

"I insist. Mr. President, it will be eight years before you see us again," said Titlis.

"Very well done. However, in eight years, we might not need you anymore. To have to depend on a sole individual is not wise. Engineers are starting to work on a purification model that might replace your hard-to-find crystal. Be aware, you will not have a buyer when you come back."

"Very well, my lord." Tamael bowed as low as he could and stayed there until Titlis left the room.

"We've done very well, Tamael," Amos congratulated.

"Maybe, but we'll discuss that later. Ohuru and I have a lot of work ahead of us. Are you capable of returning home without us?"

"Yes, I'll go prepare supper. Then visit with Atleos. Hopefully he feels a little better now."

"Very well. We'll join you at the end of the day."

Amos boarded a rented jet, carrying a large heavy box, and sailed home. He was proud. He knew that Tamael, or Ohuru, for that matter, cared little about the money, but he had bargained ten million golden leaves. He didn't have to work ever again. And yet he would continue working because his work pleased him so much. He always demanded his payment in the form of leaves, so that they could easily be stacked and exchanged or stored and hidden from thieves. He was surprised that Titlis had agreed so easily, but once he read his mind and understood his plan, Amos demanded more money. Titlis had a twisted mind that could only come from his father. He was a crooked administrator that liked profit more than any merchant Amos had ever met. Amos needed a plan, and he had time to think of one.

Tamael and Ohuru worked well into the afternoon replacing couplings at each water plant. Tamael's little pouch remained unused. What could he do with these fragments of Alenor's crystal? He couldn't just throw them away. He would put them aside until he figured out what he could do with them.

"That was the last of it," said Ohuru.

"Good. Let's go back to Amos' shop. I'm worried about him."

"What for?"

"He mentioned he did very well. He's never said that before."

"He must have done very well, indeed. Well, let's go!"

Tamael and Ohuru sailed home on Amos' ship. While Ohuru sailed, Tamael took out the Alenor crystals from the couplings. He could melt the couplings and Ohuru could sell them as metal on Us later on. Ohuru was the driver, mainly a taxi driver. He didn't make much money on his errands, so anything that could help Ohuru was always welcome.

Amos paced. It didn't matter that his clothes breathed, he was still hot and sweaty. He waited nervously for Tamael to get back. He had his seamstress make an outfit for Raphael and Atleos. Atleos, the poor fellow had been sick all morning.

"What are you doing, Atleos?" asked Raphael.

"I'm putting the cream your sister gave me on my shin. It seems to help," Atleos grunted.

"She's really good at that. She read all of Mother's books on potions and creams."

"I didn't realize how badly burnt my legs were, but they're getting better now."

"I wonder why your tunic is purple like Pa's."

"Who knows. I won't spit at the gift. These clothes are much more comfortable than the space uniform Ohuru provided for me."

"What's with Amos?"

"He's worried about your father taking so long."

"I'm not nervous. He's alright."

"Oh! And you know that because?" asked Atleos skeptically.

"Because I just know," Raphael said defensively. "He's my dad."

"Alright you two, stop it." Amos was no longer smiling. "Your dad is usually back by now. I don't understand."

"Here we are!" Tamael and Ohuru walked into the store sporting bags of food, "and we brought food with us."

"That was very thoughtful of you two, but there's food here."

"Really? Where?" Ohuru asked smiling.

Amos had been so worried that he had forgotten to prepare anything. "Oh my! What kind of host am I?"

"A troubled one, perhaps?" ventured Atleos.

"Troubled?" asked Tamael, now realizing that his host did not sport his usual smile, but instead had a frown.

"I must speak to you at once, Tamael."

Tamael and Amos went into a little office at the back and Amos confided what he had learned from Titlis mind.

"As I was negotiating, I found him to be too agreeable, and I found him unwise. He is, by nature, far more generous than any administrator I have ever met. But then I realized he had a hidden thought," Amos explained. "So I searched his mind and found his plan. He will have us robbed tonight and get his money back. The guards are on his father's payroll, and probably the ones doing the theft also. We need a plan, quickly."

"Very well. What have you got?"

"They know not of Raphael and Atleos, so I will hide Raphael and Atleos, and Ohuru will leave the store. Atleos will wear your clothing." Amos quickly explained the rest of the plan.

Tamael left the office with a grin on his face. He loved Amos because he was so cunning and brilliant. Tamael quickly took Raphael to the cellar, told him what was going to happen and that he must remain quiet for the plan to work. Raphael wished he could take part in the plan, but he agreed, nonetheless. During that time, Amos was fitting Atleos with Tamael's clothes and telling him and Ohuru what their share of the plan was. The plan was simple if executed properly, but Atleos was worried that someone might notice he was not, in fact, Tamael.

Amos reassured him, "Tamael was seen all over Os today installing couplings in this tunic and everyone knows I never sell the same tunic twice. They'll think you're Tamael, and that's all that matters. Now, be ready."

Tamael went back to the store and hid in the attic. He had his najar and was ready for a fight. He watched Amos follow his friends to the door, and give them a last piece of advice, "The best ale is found at Temos tavern. Tell him I sent you. Bye."

"Alright, will do," replied Ohuru as he and Atleos, disguised as Tamael, walked away.

Amos entered his home and locked it, as usual. Only a few hours passed before he heard noises coming from the back of the store. He ignored it and continued to count the gold leaves and deposit them in three boxes. He was almost done. He was sure they had been watching him count his gold leaves, to make sure they would not leave any behind.

Amos wondered how Tamael was faring up in the attic when he was hit on the back of the head. He closed his eyes and stayed immobile while the thieves turned the lights down. They took the boxes away and left by the back door. He heard Tamael leave and go after the culprits. Amos quickly got out of his fat suit that he wore daily. He looked at his belly thinking he had to be more careful, he was gaining weight, eating like a pig. He put on glasses and went to run after Tamael.

Tamael ran behind the thieves and marked the walls with a phosphorescent marker, hoping that Amos would be able to follow. The thieves stopped and entered a small door in the alley behind the market square. Tamael leaned in close to a window and looked on.

The thieves were already acting up between themselves.

"Why should we return it all? We should keep some for us," said the first thief, Anis.

"He will find out and have us killed," said the second, Teris.

"Chances are he'll have us killed once we have returned the payroll anyway. Anis is right, we should keep some for ourselves, to leave for our family," said the third, Iklis.

"Don't be so childish, Iklis. Titlis needs us more than you know. He has many projects he has not yet unveiled. But if we betray his trust he'll kill us for sure," said Teris.

"Maybe Teris is right," said Iklis.

Tamael looked over his shoulder and saw Amos running out of breath down the street.

"So much for keeping in shape, Amos," whispered Tamael.

"It's not that the last few years have been particularly kind to my stomach. Deception comes at a price."

"Very well. There are three of them. Are you sure you can do this?"

"Yes, I'll be fine. Besides, I owe one of them a hit on the head."

"We'll deliver more than that!"

Tamael and Amos casually walked in the door and surprised the thieves in their conversation.

"Who are you? What are you doing here?" asked Teris.

"We overheard your having some problems dividing some gold leaves."

"What we do here is no business of yours. Leave or…"

Tamael interrupted Anis, "Or what? Call the guards? Too many questions to answer, no?"

"We'll help you divide your profits equally, half for us and half for you. Doesn't that sound like a fair deal?" said Amos.

"Why should we share with you two?" asked Iklis.

"Ah! That is the question. Well, either we share, or we take it all!" Tamael grinned.

"Never!" Teris jumped up, brandishing an energy weapon, illegal on any of the guild planets.

Tamael looked at Amos nodded, "Very well, then, it's all ours."

Tamael and Amos hit the man's head and weapon as one with their najars. The other two thieves did not know what to do or what to think. Before they could react, they were each grabbed in a choke hold by Amos and Tamael.

"Well, boys, the ride is over. Your career as thieves ends here," Tamael said.

"Who are you?" asked Anis.

"I am the great Jim Smith," said Tamael.

"The pirate?"

"Yes, and this is the lord Miguel," Said Tamael, pointing at Amos.

"Oh!" Anis and Iklis were surprised. It was bad luck to be robbed of a treasure that did not belong to them, but it was an honor that it was done by the famous pirates of Mitiryl.

"Gentlemen, I'm afraid this will cost you your heads," Tamael said.

"What? Can't we make a deal?" asked Anis.

"Sorry, fellows. You've had your chance," and with a twist of Amos' hand, he broke Iklis' neck.

Tamael did the same to Anis and that was the end of the business arrangement they had entered. Tamael turned to Teris, who was slowly waking up.

"And for you, my lord, what shall your fate be?" Amos glanced at Teris, waiting for his answer.

"No, no, you can't just kill me!" shrieked Teris.

"Of course we can. You're a low-life scum and we're pirates. It's all in the family. Really, don't you agree?" Tamael asked.

"No. No, I really don't," argued Teris.

"Lord Miguel, what do you suggest?" Tamael turned to Amos.

"Well, we could count to five and see if he's still around."

"Great idea. One, two. . ."

Teris didn't consider if they were serious, he simply vanished.

"We don't have much time. We have to leave quickly," said Amos.

"I'll grab the big box. Put the contents of the small one in Ohuru's box, and let's run."

Tamael and Amos hurried through the shadows with their black outfits, false beards, and scars. Amos almost laughed, but stopped when he remembered he had killed a man tonight.

"Do you think we should have. . ." started Amos.

"Not now, Amos. Save your doubts for later when we're safe. You still have to wake up and call the guards."

"Right, forgot about that," said Amos.

During their night's excursion, Ohuru and Atleos had planned to make sure everyone saw them, so that everyone could testify that they were out of the house while the robbery occurred. They drank ale and wine and some sort of mixture that instantly gave Atleos a headache. When Ohuru started to argue with the people at the table next to them, Atleos wanted to be far away. Instead, he threw up on someone's girlfriend and that was enough to start a fight. Atleos was in no shape to box and acted his part quite well. Not only did his stomach turn upside down, but his eye was starting to swell shut. He landed on a patrol of the imperial guard and they all fell to the floor. All he could remember was being dragged outside. He could hear from a distance that Ohuru arguing that it was not his fault. He had to defend his companion.

"Ohuru, shut up," grumbled Atleos. "The guards do not care about me or you, for that matter. Let's go home, my friend."

"You two are going to jail. You can sober up and maybe face charges for assault," stated one of the guards.

"Assault? All I'm guilty of is being unable to contain my liquor. When I was last visiting Os, it was not a crime to vomit. Or has that changed?" asked Atleos.

"No, it's not a crime to vomit, but to be intoxicated in a public place is," argued the other guard.

"Well, our friend would be much more agreeable if you were just to bring us home," said Ohuru.

"Really? And who's your friend?" asked the guard.

"Amooou. . . Amour. . . Ampo. . ." Atleos stumbled on the name.

"Who?" asked the guard.

"Amos. He means to say Amos, the merchant," said Ohuru.

"Amos, the seller and maker of authentic tunics?" demanded the guard.

"Yes, the very same," said Ohuru.

"Very well. He is honest with me in his dealings. If indeed you are his friend, I will try to see if he'll have you," the guard hesitated.

The guard, with his subordinate, walked a very inebriated Atleos and Ohuru home to Amos.

"Amos, how do you live in this outfit?" asked Tamael, glancing at Amos' fat suit.

"It's part of the course. I'm used to it now, but Romanichel thought it was better if I actually wore real weights to leave creases behind and to slow me down a bit to better act the part," explained Amos.

"Yes, well, you better hurry and get back in the suit, my friend," said Tamael.

"Yuk! It's all sweaty. Usually I get to clean it up before getting back in there," Amos grimaced.

"Amos, no time..." Tamael pushed the suit towards Amos.

"Right."

Amos heard a familiar voice yell, "Our friend, Amos, is the greatest friend anyone could ever have."

"Quick! They're coming," said Tamael.

Amos squeezed back into his fat suit. The sweat, although gross, made it easier for him to slide into the suit. He sat back down on the couch where he had been hit and passed out.

Tamael looked at him and felt sorry for his friend. He would wake up with a terrible headache. He ran to the attic where he hid with the boxes of gold leaves, and waited.

There was a knock on the door, but no one stirred inside.

Ohuru yelled, "Amos, open up!"

Ohuru started to wonder if he had given enough time for the men to retrieve the leaves. If not, they were in big trouble. He shook off the guards and jumped to the window. Maybe he would have to spend the night in jail after all.

"There he is, asleep on the couch. Let me wake him," shouted Ohuru.

"You've woken half of this part of town already. That's enough." Anelis said, pulling Ohuru back.

"Well, then, why isn't our friend coming to the door?" questioned Atleos.

"Hmm, that is curious," said Anelis.

Anelis was a good man. He had been recruited to be part of the imperial guard and believed in his duty. He was one of the few guards not corrupted by the power and greed that Tameris offered. This was probably why he was still a corporal and not a staff sergeant.

"Do you think your friend might need help?" asked Anelis.

"If you ate what he ate, you'd need help too," blurted Atleos.

Anelis kicked the door in and ran to Amos to take his pulse.

"He's alive, but he has been hit on the head. Boris, get some water!" ordered Anelis.

Atleos fell to the ground and Ohuru ran towards Amos to check on him. Maybe the thieves had hit him harder than they should have.

"Ouch! That's going to leave a mark," Ohuru said.

Atleos, to the best of his abilities, got back to his feet and stumbled into the room.

Anelis spilled a jug of water over Amos' face, who woke startled.

"Don't hit me," he said, raising his hand to his face, looking scared. "Oh! My head!" He looked around. "My money! Where's my money?"

"Calm down, sir. What happened here?" Anelis asked.

"I was counting our money and…"

"What do you mean by 'my money is gone'? Who took it? They'll hear from me…." said Ohuru.

BANG! Atleos hit the floor.

Ohuru looked down at the unconscious Atleos, "That's going to leave a mark."

"Maybe, but at least we can talk now. What happened?" asked Anelis.

"I was counting our money. We each had a share of the gold leaves and I was separating it into boxes," explained Amos.

"Boxes? That's a strange place to keep gold leaves," Anelis raised his eyebrows.

"Yes, well, there were ten million worth and I don't have a wallet that big so…"

"Ten million?" Anelis was shocked.

"Yes, for all the couplings in the treatment centers on Os. We made a good deal and …"

"Why gold leaves for such a sum? That was imprudent." Anelis shook his head.

"My friends travel to many solar systems. They carry their money with them and so it is not practical for them to open an account at the merchant's bank. I was going to deposit my money tomorrow."

"Master Amos, I will say it again, it was imprudent of you and your friends. Who are they, may I ask?"

"Ah! Ohuru is in the blue outfit, and Tamael is in the purple. They've been working hard all day to install the couplings and they went out to celebrate our good fortune tonight. Ah, the thieves!" Amos moaned.

"Can you describe them to me?"

"No, I saw nothing. I was hit in the head and passed out!"

"Yes, judging by the looks of it, they almost killed you. What did they take?"

"Three boxes containing ten million gold leaves. They were in one hundred-leaf dominations."

"Well, actually, it was more like nine million, nine hundred and ninety-nine thousand, and five hundred. We took five hundred to celebrate tonight," blurted out Ohuru.

"I see," replied Anelis. "No wonder you're drunk. Master Ohuru, I can only try to help, but you're not giving much to go on. Do you know how they left?"

"I don't know. I was knocked out!"

"Right. I will call a team in and we'll do a search and see what we can find. Can you stay elsewhere for the night?" suggested Anelis.

"No, I don't think my friends can be moved tonight. I'll leave in the morning for Isifilmos and spend the week with my wife. Maybe she'll be able to heal my scar better than me."

"Very well, Master Amos, very well. We'll be back in a minute and start the investigation. We must also keep you awake."

"So it must be," said Amos.

Anelis and Boris left Amos' house and went to get some help to investigate this giant theft.

"Tamael, to the boat with the child, now!" Amos called out.

Amos was back to his senses. The night had almost gone as planned, but Atleos had to play his role a little longer.

"Tea for you, Atleos?" asked Amos.

"Yes, Master Amos. Tea would be fine."

Tamael left by the front door, while Ohuru carried their boxes and Raphael with them.

"Will you be fine here?" Ohuru asked.

"Yes, just be quiet when you return to Amos and help Atleos sober up. We don't want him talking too much."

"Yes, the boy can't hold his liquor," Ohuru said with a laugh.

Ohuru ran back swiftly and Tamael settled down to sleep. Tamael had killed before, and tonight he had to once more. Although he wished, just like his friend Amos, that he could have let them live.

Ohuru got back and jumped in the bath. He figured it was the best way to face another day. It was already five o'clock in the morning on Os, with a long day was ahead.

* * * * *

Slowly, one by one, the lights in the atrium came on. A general sigh was heard. Mani was done for the night. She had left her audience in suspense. Lilay was expecting the baby safely at home and Tinay was alone and stuck in a cave, but she had food and water. It was a good time to stop and go home.

"I'm sorry, everyone," Mani said, "but it is very late and time for all of you to go home before you fall asleep and miss some of my story while you sleep."

Brett had completely forgotten that he was in the atrium. He had been transported into space, a desert, and into the caves. He had smelled the humidity of the cave and the heat of the sun. To him the last few hours had been real. He could not believe how good Mani was. He walked over to her and shook her hand. "Thank you, thank you so much!" and walked away with his mother.

Mani knew not everyone was going to be as pleased as Brett. A few newcomers would want to know more. What else took place? What happened to Tamael? Who is Paletis? Why is she so bad when her descendants are so good?

John got up feeling like he had been dreaming. He, too, had become lost in the story, but he was now enthralled and wanted to know the end.

He walked over to Mani and demanded, "If you knew there wasn't enough time to tell the whole story, why did you start it in the first place? Now we'll never know what happens!"

Mani realized he was terribly upset. She smiled and said, "Don't worry. Your session has paid for the whole story no matter how long it takes. The story is free, only the refreshment cost money."

John was surprised; nothing was free in this world. What was the catch? He looked perplexed.

"Don't worry, John. I won't be asking for more money. I sell enough books to make a good living. This I do because I enjoy it so much."

Now John could not help but smile. This was a good thing; there were so few good things left in the world and he had found one. "Well," he said, "I guess I'll see you next week then. Same time?"

"Yes, same time, six p.m. next Saturday,"

Lyauria was helping the visitors retrieve their jackets and put their personal cushions away. Alayana looked at the clock and was surprised to find that it was already midnight. She had once again fallen under the spell of her grandmother. She loved Mani's stories, particularly the story of Tinay because Tinay had such a simple beginning, but became such an important person. It gave her hope that she, too, had a chance to change the world and make her mark in history. She didn't know yet how she would achieve this, but time would tell.

Slowly, the bookstore emptied and Mani finished replacing the cushions neatly. Another night and another story, but she had a great success to celebrate.

"Mom," Lyauria said, "everyone has left."

"Yes, dear. What did you think of tonight?" Mani asked.

"Judging by the crowd, I think you successfully hooked them up for a number of weeks. They won't want to miss a session. What do you think, Alayana?" asked Lyauria.

"I don't know about anyone else, but I was captured by the story. What will be incredible next week is getting us back into the same mood."

"Ah, yes," said Mani. "That is always a challenge. Our heroes are just in enough trouble for us to find out what has happened to them and yet not enough that anyone would lose any sleep over it. You see, you don't want people to worry too much. You want them to dream and find that the adventure continues on with them even after they have left."

"How so?" asked Alayana.

"You want them to be asking themselves the question 'What will happen next?' They'll imagine fifty or even one hundred variations about what will happen next, but if I'm good, only a few will guess what exactly took place the next morning."

"Do you think I will guess, Mani?"

"I don't know, sweetheart, I don't know. You will have to wait until next week for the rest of the story."

Mani and Alayana went to sleep on the third floor of the bookshop while Lyauria locked up and left for the city.

Chapter 7

ESSAY

The week passed slowly for Alayana. She loved summer vacation. She always came to the bookstore to help her grandmother and to read old books. She was now old enough to help, to really help. She sold old books, entered the records into the computer, and completed sales. She had become indispensable to the shop. She loved to read the new books because there was always so much to read. Of course, there were her favorites that she read again and again, but most often these were also the biggest ones. She also had to dust and vacuum the store which she hated, but it was part of the job and caused her to discover amazing things that she would have missed otherwise.

    She had developed a tactic to sell old books. Once she discovered something she really liked, she would display it in the window to attract new readers to the old book. It always worked.

    She wondered what she would do with her life. She wasn't sure she wanted to be a doctor like her mother, but she wasn't sure she had enough imagination to tell stories like her grandmother. Mani had told Alayana that many of the stories she told were already written down, but she also knew that some of the stories had actually been written down by Mani. The reason Mani was so good was because she created those worlds and didn't just talk about them, but made you feel like you were a part of that world.

Alayana hoped that she would have that gift also. To live here in this house and share the knowledge with unexpected patrons was what she dreamt of doing. She looked at Mani who was preparing for yet another adventure of the Pirates of Kilar. There were so many tales to choose from and so many children. How did she know which story to pick? Alayana was amazed.

Mani approached her. "So," she said, "what is going on in that head of yours, Alayana?"

"Just wondering if you ever picked the wrong book for one of your groups."

"Ah, you see, there's never a wrong book. It's all in the way the story is told. If you tell the story right, then everyone likes it. Everyone who walks through that door is looking for a get-away, a new adventure and a hero to identify with. If your customers can somehow identify with a character in the story they're sold, then they're happy. That's all they need -- one character."

"Is that why you always have so many characters in your stories?" asked Alayana.

"Yes, of course," replied Mani. "And the more the merrier! I best get ready for my session. Here comes my group now."

Mani walked toward the young children and bent down to hug them. Mani wasn't young anymore, but she always greeted her customers at their level and always had plenty of hugs to go around. There was a special quality about Mani that made everyone feel welcome. She made everyone feel special.

Alayana's eyes surveyed the crowd and, all of a sudden, she swore she heard music and the room lost its focus. There he was, the man of her dreams. *Well not a man yet,* she thought to herself, *but a valiant knight.* She had never felt this way before. She had seen boys many times at school, at the theater, and even here at the bookstore, but there was something special about him. She walked over to him and grabbed a book lying on the table as she walked by.

"Hello. Welcome to the Unicorn Bookstore. How can I help you?" She tried to sound professional, but she heard a tremor in her voice.

He stared at her for a moment before he replied. Maybe he hadn't heard the question. She asked again, "Sir, can I help you?"

"Oh yes, I'm sorry. I was lost somewhere. Uh, I'm looking for ..." He plucked his wallet out and pulled out an old business card, "Um, Verana Naguliar?"

"Ver. . . Oh, Mani! Everyone calls her Mani." Alayana turned around and was happy to find that Mani had already started her story, "I'm afraid she'll be busy for the next hour or so. Maybe I can help you?"

"Of course. I was looking forward to hearing the story of a princess and I had been told to come here and ask Mrs. Naguliar..."

"Mani." Alayana couldn't remember the last time her grandmother had used her proper name.

"Yes, Mani. She would have the story in the archives, I believe."

"There are a lot of princesses in the Mythology and History section. Do you perhaps, have a name you could give to work with?" Alayana made her way to the computers to prepare a search.

"Tinay, the warrior Princess," said the young man.

"Oh!"

"Is there a problem?"

"No, of course not. Tinay's story comes in seven volumes. Do you know which volume you were interested in?"

"No, I'm not sure. I might need to get all seven."

Alayana didn't want him to buy the books, especially not all seven at once. Then he would never be back, not a good business practice. *The more he comes back, the more he'll buy and then we'll make a regular customer out of him,* she thought. She knew she was lying to herself. She didn't care about selling him the books, she just wanted an excuse to see him again. *Quick, think quickly,* she said to herself.

"Um, miss?"

Bingo! Got it! Alayana thought.

"Oh, I'm sorry. I'm Alayana. I'm Mani's granddaughter and I help here during the summer time. And you are?"

"Jeremyah. Jeremyah Gozetar."

"Welcome. I was just thinking that before you buy the book, or the whole series, for that matter, you might want to hear it from Mani herself."

"What do you mean?" asked Jeremyah.

"Every Saturday Mani has a teenage group that gathers together at six p.m. She tells many stories, and last weekend, she started the story of Tinay."

"I see. Isn't it a long story to tell in one night?"

"Yes. The story goes on for a few weeks and gets told from beginning to end. Mani also has illustrations that she has never reproduced in any of her books, so the only way to see them is to be here next Saturday. If you want, I can lend you a copy of what was heard already and you could follow from there. At the end of the verbal recollection of the story, it will be for sale and you could buy that and have a unique experience to tell your children."

"I don't have any kids, I'm only 17."

"Of course, but with time. When you, or perhaps your friends, have children, you'll be able to share the magic together."

"How many weeks are we talking about?" Jeremyah asked

"I'm sorry. I have no idea. With Mani, no one ever knows. She'll try to keep us busy for at least the next four weeks."

"As long as the story is done by the end of August. I need to depart for Peru for September."

"Peru? What's there?"

"Is that going to help me acquire any books?" Jeremyah asked.

Alayana felt herself blush. She had never been this inquisitive before, but if he lived in Peru what was he doing here? More importantly, how were they going to continue to see each other? Not that they were going to see each other again. There she was, mind rambling.

"Um, no, of course not," she babbled. "I was just wondering. It's the first time, I believe, that we have had a referral from Peru. It's kind of far away."

"Yes, I don't live there, I just go to the academy. One of my teachers said that while I was here this summer I should check in here and find out more about Tinay."

"Well, I can sell you those books if you like, but Mani has a special touch. You'd be missing a lot."

"How much?"

"$20.00 a book."

"No, I meant for the story time."

"Oh, that's free. You only pay for refreshment and you can bring your own cushion."

"A cushion?"

"Yes, we sit on the ground and then…"

"The ground?"

"Why don't I show you and you can decide for yourself."

They walked over to the atrium and stopped at the entrance of the rounded door.

Jeremyah looked at the magical scenery: the forest, the sea, the plain, and the flowers. Soon he was listening to Mani tell the story....

Mani was up on the stage and had a wooden stake in her hands. She was fighting an invisible pirate.

Jeremyah turned around and asked, "Mani?"

"Yup, at her best…" Alayana stopped talking.

Jeremyah was hanging onto every word Mani uttered. He slowly slipped onto the couch, his eyes twinkling. Mani had once more worked her magic. In truth, it didn't matter if you were six or sixty years old, a good story was a good story and when you had the chance to hear it from Mani herself, well, it simply became alive and took over all your senses.

Alayana knew she would be seeing him again and was not afraid to walk away.

The hour flew by and Mani finished just in time for Alayana to bring cookies and milk for the guests. Mani was talking with some parents that were asking if she would do a birthday party and tell their children their favorite story.

"Of course. Have a time reserved for you by Alayana and make sure you tell her which book it is you want. It won't be a private session, but we will have decorations and a cake instead of cookies."

"Wonderful," said the mom as she walked away.

"Mani," Alayana interrupted, "someone is waiting to meet you."

"Of course, dear," said Mani.

Jeremyah stood in the corner looking at the pictures on the wall. There was one of the pirates, one of the boats, and another of the hero that had defeated the pirates. He wanted to see the paintings of Tinay.

"Mr. Gozetar, I would like to introduce you to Mani."

"It's an honor. Please call me Jeremyah."

"Well, Jeremyah, it's a pleasure to meet you. Did you enjoyed the story, or were you just waiting for me to finish?" Mani said with a twinkle in her eye and a grin on her face.

"As a matter of fact," said Jeremyah, "I enjoyed every word. It reminded me of my bedtime stories when I was a child, but none were ever told as lively. Thank you."

"You're welcome, young man. Now, what can I do for you?"

"I was sent here by Andremar. He gave me your card. I was searching for..."

"Who did you say?" asked Mani.

"Andremar, one of my teachers at the Academy."

"Are you from Peru then?"

"Yes, I study there, but I live close to the city. He said you had a certain book I should read."

"Yes, I remember Andremar quite well. I didn't know he was still teaching." Mani wondered what to make of Jeremyah. When she glanced at Alayana, she saw a young girl who stood staring through everything and nothing. Mani had never seen Alayana like this.

Alayana was concerned that her vision would never return to normal. She couldn't help but stare and she didn't care if he noticed. She just hoped that she was not going to be asked any questions because she had no idea what they were talking about. Not only was her vision impaired, so was her hearing.

Jeremyah stood there wondering what to say next, "Yes, Andremar is still teaching private sessions. I was told to look for the book of Tinay. I was wondering if you had a copy left that I could buy."

"Yes, but if you wait a couple more weeks, I'll be finished telling the story and you can have a fresh book."

"I was told about it by Alana."

"It's Alayana." Alayana frowned and could feel her forehead crease. He couldn't even remember her name.

"Alayana. Got it." Jeremyah blushed and lowered his eyes.

Mani was not blind and could see what was going on. "Maybe you would care to join us next Saturday at six p.m. and see for yourself. The stories are free. You just need to pay for refreshments."

"I was told that also. I was not sure I could commit."

"It's better to hear the story from a storyteller, but if you'd rather, there's always an extra copy I could sell you. You'll want the initial copy, I imagine?"

"Well, I could come next week, if you could provide me a tape of the first part I missed."

"Of course, we would be glad to help. Alayana, could you give me a copy of the tape, dear?" Mani was happy to help this Jeremyah, if he was referred by Andremar.

"Thank you," Jeremyah said. He bowed to them and left.

Alayana spluttered out, "Don't forget your cushion."

Jeremyah turned around and smiled, "I won't."

Mani grinned, "I guess we have a new customer."

All Alayana answered was, "Uh -huh," and walked away with a little bounce in her step that hadn't been there before.

If the former week had gone by slowly, now it passed at the speed of a snail. Alayana went about as usual, but she kept daydreaming about Jeremyah and couldn't wait to see him again.

Saturday finally arrived and she was eager to clean the Atrium so it would be ready for the evening. She baked delicious treats the night before for all the people who would attend, but she had Jeremyah especially in mind.

Her mother was the first to arrive and all three of them had supper together after the store closed.

It wasn't long before six p.m. came around and Mani went to greet her customers. They all arrived fairly quickly, and among them was Jeremyah.

"Good evening, Jeremyah. How are you?" asked Mani.

"Good, thank you." He showed her a little pillow, "I hope this will be enough."

"If not, I have spares. Go make yourself comfortable. I had a full class, but since you were sent by Andremar, I decided to allow you to come. Would you please pay Alayana before we start?"

"Class?" Jeremyah asked "I thought this was..."

"What am I saying?" said Mani interrupting, "I meant story time."

"Oh! Of course." Jeremyah bowed and walked over to the cash register.

Alayana came right away.

"I guess you're ready to pay?"

"Yes. It's the first time I've ever had to pay for something before receiving it."

"It'll be worth your while. Twenty dollars, please."

"What are you serving, caviar?" said Jeremyah sarcastically.

"No, but you are paying for the whole story. Same fee for everyone. How was the tape?"

"Good, but it wasn't the same as seeing her live, I'm sure."

"No, it's not. You'll get a full experience tonight," said Mani, smiling.

They walked over to the atrium and settled down. The pictures were already on the wall, patiently waiting.

Mani saw everyone seated and lowered the lights. "Let's start. Where were we?" A few hands rose up in the air. "Brett?" she asked.

"Tinay is stuck in a cave and Tamael and Amos killed the thieves and are about to escape."

"Yes, that's right," said Mani and continued the story.

*****

There were clouds in the sky and a light drizzle fell. The ground was wet as Anelis returned to Amos' store. He looked somber. He couldn't explain what had happened at Amos' house, but in view of the recent news, he was perplexed. His sergeant had been attacked by pirates the night before and they were seen carrying boxes. It would seem his investigation had taken a new turn. If the information from Teris was right, the pirates had broken into Amos' store, stolen the leaves, probably meant to kill him, and made away with their treasure. On their way, they met Teris and the two guards, Anis and Iklis, but what happened next was unclear. It was unlikely that the pirates would decide to kill them. The pirates must have been offended, for they already had their money. They could have gotten away. Teris was not telling the whole truth. But it was the pirates' signature, a broken neck, and the fear in Teris' eyes that convinced Anelis there was some truth to the story. The hard part was to tell Amos that his money was gone and that in the event that Anelis would have a lucky break in his career and capture the pirates, he would most likely never recover the money. The pirates would be hung and that would be the end of it.

Anelis took a deep breath and knocked on the door.

"Who's there?" called Amos.

"It's me, Anelis."

"Corporal Anelis, I expected you sooner." Amos opened the door.

The whole right side of his face was swollen like a melon. He was purple and black and looked hideous. Anelis could not help but pull away from him.

"Yes, hideous, I know. Please come in, Corporal. We've been expecting you."

"Yes, I'm sorry for the delay. There's been more than one crime committed last night, I'm afraid."

"More? Who else was robbed?"

"Not robbed, killed."

"Oh, no!" Amos sat down and took a deep breath.

There was little justice left in the world they lived in and the law protected the crooks more often than the honest man. Amos and Tamael had used the pirates' cover for bringing some justice to the world and, sometimes, it had been necessary to exterminate certain criminals in order for the greater good to live on.

"Yes, pirates. What I don't understand is that the pirates never attacked the imperial guard before."

"The imperial guard! What has the world come to?" Amos didn't know who those men were and didn't care. They had stolen the money and they were guilty. They had worked for Titlis and deserved to be exterminated. Titlis was too bold and had used his own guard to perpetrate the crime.

"Yes, indeed. It would seem that the pirates were followed by the guards and ambushed, but the pirates, approximately ten, I was told, attacked and killed Anis and Iklis. They let Teris live to tell of their exploit; a sad day, indeed. The pirates only used to attack rogues, but now it's become more serious."

"Yes, it has. What shall we do?"

"I'm afraid that your money is lost and that even if I arrest the criminals, the only justice you would get is their death."

"Justice, indeed!!"

"I'm sorry, Master Amos." Anelis truly was. He had joined the guards to be of service, to help the victims and the orphans to live in a better world, but most times he had very little consolation to offer.

"Corporal Anelis, please keep in touch and let me know if you make any progress. As for me, I will take the week off and go home to my wife. My friends and I need some time to figure out what we will do now that we have lost an entire five year's wages."

"I'm very sorry. If I ever find your money, I'll get it back to you...."

"It's alright, my good man. I am aware of the new justice system, just like you. Even if you were to find my money tomorrow, it could take years before I could set my eyes on it again. Good day to you, sir."

"Good day." Anelis looked at the door as it closed behind him. He was sad for Amos and his friends. Anelis was determined to get to the bottom of this crime.

Ohuru, Atleos, and Amos walked to the boat with some provisions and a few changes of clothes.

Tamael was sleeping with Raphael in his arms when he heard a noise outside and woke up. He let go of Raphael and walked to the door. Grabbing his knife, he waited in the shadows.

"Tamael might still be sleeping. Let's not wake him up," whispered Amos.

The door creaked open and Amos felt a particularly sharp edge on his neck. "It's me, Amos," he said with his hands in the air.

"Since when are you so quiet?" Tamael was flustered. He could have killed his best friend.

"Since we've all had a long night. The minute we're out of the harbor, you'll take my place at the wheel while Amos and I get some sleep," shot back Ohuru.

"Very well. Did you bring a change of clothes?" asked Tamael.

"For you, yes, not for the boy. There was no time to make more than one."

Turning to Ohuru, Tamael said, "Ohuru, you smell good. Did you shower already?"

"Had a bath. I'll get breakfast ready while you wash."

"Indeed." Tamael went for the shower while Amos set sail for Isifilmos.

When he was finished, he put on the same colorful ensemble as Amos, ate breakfast, and went up on deck to replace Amos.

"Your turn to wash and eat."

"Can't wash here, but I'll eat and sleep for sure."

"Are you okay about last night?"

"We did no less than when we were guards ourselves twenty years ago. We captured the guilty and executed a sentence. I just have been in the skin of a merchant for so long now, I find it hard to roll back into the routine."

Tamael silently agreed. "Rest well, my friend."

Suddenly, the two men heard thunderous steps coming down the stairs. Amos sat at the table and started to eat.

"No offense, Amos, but you might want to freshen up a bit. You're starting to smell," grimaced Ohuru.

"No offense taken, Ohuru. I admit, I smell, but even worse, I'm hungry and tired. In case you didn't notice, I don't fit in the shower anyway."

Ohuru had a surprised look on his face. He glanced back, measuring Amos' bulk and realized that Amos was far too large for the shower. Ohuru laughed, "Sorry, didn't notice that."

A silence crept upon the friends.

Finally Amos muttered between bites, "You're lucky to be such a good friend, Ohuru."

"Why is that?" asked Ohuru.

"Your cooking sucks," Amos said teasingly.

"Make fun, if you please, but it's better than nothing."

"I will have to agree, my friend." Amos went over to his bed, rolled Atleos over to make room for himself and fell asleep.

Ohuru went up on deck and asked Tamael when they would arrive.

"I expect it to take all day. When Amos wakes up, send him up so I can have a nap."

"What about me?" asked Raphael.

"You, you will catch supper. Get the fishing rod and let's see if we can make a real sailor out of you."

Amos slept until late afternoon. When Atleos got up and started to complain about Amos' smell, Amos figured he was better off on deck. Atleos was surprised to see Amos pass by the food and just walk straight to the deck.

"I'm sorry, I didn't mean to offend you," Atleos said, but his voice faded in the background as waves crashed against the boat.

Atleos was too hungry to worry and filled his stomach.

"What's up, mates?" called Amos.

"Look, Amos. Pa calls it food on a stick. Isn't it great?" Raphael waved a half-eaten fish on a stick.

"Who cooked that up?"

"I did," said Tamael, raising his hand to take a bite of his own fish.

"Ohuru, I'm glad you're giving others the chance to exert their talent," said Amos.

"You're welcome, but it's Raphael you should thank. He's the one who caught the fish in the first place."

"Really?"

"Yeah, and I got one for you and Atleos also. You want it?" asked Raphael.

"Of course. Bring it here."

Amos was glad to have company. He didn't want to be alone today. As he chewed his fish, which tasted great, he took over the wheel and let Tamael have a rest.

"Come here, mate, I'll teach you how to sail." Amos gestured to Raphael.

"Cool!" Raphael liked this trip more and more.

"Ohuru, come here, please," Tamael called from his room.

"Yes, what is it?" asked Ohuru once he got to the berth.

"Can you get a barge to bring us to your ship? I'm supposed to be on Essay by tonight."

"We'll be late for Essay, but as soon as we land, I can call a barge from the ship and have it pick us up on Isifilmos."

"Very well. I'll go catch some sleep. See you when we get there."

"Have a good rest." Ohuru turned to Atleos who was sitting on the bed. "What about you, Atleos? Care to join us on deck?"

"Yes, I guess I can after I shower and change."

The rest of the trip to Isifilmos was uncomplicated and the clear open sea made it a great day for sailing.

Amos pointed out an island, "There's home. Gentlemen, I present to you Isifilmos."

Amos was very proud of his island. He had bought it ages ago and loved the tranquility it procured. There was no one around to be concerned about and he could cloak the island when he didn't want to be disturbed. It was a great hideout.

"Come on, Raphael. Get your father up, I want him to be awake by the time we get there."

"Alright." Raphael walked out and into the room where he found the sleeping figure of his father.

"Pa, wake up, wake up. We've arrived!"

"Hmm, good, good. Just in time for supper," Tamael murmured.

"Now, you're talking like Amos," Raphael said giggling.

"Yes, Amos is a very good friend."

When Tamael got up on deck, he saw Romanichel, Amos' wife, standing on the dock, waving her hands. Seeing her there reminded Tamael of how much he missed his wife. He felt empty in his heart, but managed to wave back.

"Tamael, grab the sail!" Amos yelled orders to everyone, but Atleos and Raphael had no idea what he was saying.

Atleos was happy because landing meant that Amos was finally going to have a shower.

"Welcome, everyone. Welcome!"

Romanichel was a happy woman who had curly red hair that fell down her back. She wore a white blouse that exposed her shoulders, a wide green skirt that fell to her knees with a shawl wrapped around her waist and draped around her hips. A cape protected her from the windy sea while bracelets adorned her ankles and wrists. She tinkled as she walked.

Amos looked at her and smiled, "You are by far the most beautiful creature I've ever had the chance to set my eyes on." He jumped off the boat and ran to her. "I missed you."

"You stink. How long has it been since you had a bath?"

"Don't know, don't care. I missed you. Kiss me."

She kissed him on the nose, "Now, you go have a bath. There's one ready for you."

"I knew you were the best the day I set eyes on you."

"So did I, but I never expected you to be so…"

"Fat," Raphael spurted.

"No, so smelly. And who are you?" smiled Romanichel.

"I'm Raphael, Tamael's son."

"Welcome to Isifilmos, Raphael. Are you hungry?"

"We had fish on a stick this afternoon, but I could eat a little."

"Very well, let's go to my house. And you might be?" she asked Atleos.

"I'm sorry, I forgot my manners," Tamael said. "You know Ohuru, and this is his new partner, Atleos."

"Pleasure to meet you, Atleos. I missed you, Ohuru. You should come more often."

"Yes, my lady, but time is of the essence and I have to earn a living," Ohuru replied.

"There's no lady here, Ohuru. Call me Romanichel, like everyone else here does. You too, Atleos."

"Very well, it's a pleasure to finally meet you," Atleos said.

"How come you're not fat like Amos?" Raphael asked.

"Aren't you full of question, little Raphael?"

"At least he's honest..." Tamael blushed. He never realized how honest Raphael was.

"Honest and frank. Admirable qualities of the spirit. Only merchants are fat, Raphael. Me, I'm an artist."

"Like my mother?"

"Like your mother."

"Do you know my mother?"

"It was a long time ago, but I've met her. She was a remarkable artist. How is she doing, Tamael?"

"She's pregnant and about to give birth. I can't wait to go home."

"When must you leave?" asked Romanichel.

"Tonight, I'm afraid," Tamael said. "I told you, the barge will be here late. We will leave tomorrow." Ohuru didn't want much sleep, but he did want some.

"It's settled then. I'll have a maid prepare the beds."

"Maids?" Tamael asked.

"Yes, the baby was born 4 weeks ago and I needed help with Amos gone all the time."

"I see." Tamael started to think to himself. Poor Amos can't even remove the stupid extra body he's carrying all day after he gets home.

They walked together to the house that stood in the center of the island. It wasn't a big island but for the two of them, it was plenty. They all went inside and sat on the porch where the sea breeze blew gently. Ohuru sent the homing signal to the barge aboard the ship and sat back to enjoy the view. Romanichel went inside and checked on Amos.

"Well, how are you doing?" she asked Amos.

"I'm staying for the week. Something came up that I must tell you about. I want you to send the maid tomorrow to look after the shop."

"What happened, Amos?"

Amos told her the events of the previous evening and was nervous to see her reaction. Romanichel wasn't happy to see her husband playing pirate again, but she was glad the resistance would get the money they needed to survive. She brushed her husband's skin suit and showed him something new she had made: a flannel cover so his skin would not touch the rubber. Amos smiled. He just wished they could do away with the whole thing, but agreed that it would be an improvement.

Romanichel helped him get dressed and went to check on her guests.

"Supper is ready. Whoever is hungry, come and join us!"

She brought platters of food to the table and sat down with a smile on her face. She looked at Atleos and said, "Will you try to stomach everything my husband eats, or will you follow the voice of reason tonight?" She cradled her baby who looked as hungry as Amos.

"The voice of my stomach, telling my brain when to stop." They all burst out laughing.

After supper, Amos got the bongos out, took his guitar and asked Romanichel to dance for them. She gave the child to Tamael and got ready.

"There are many forms of art, Raphael, and my wife is the best dancer I ever saw."

"Can I dance, too?" Raphael asked.

"Of course. Come with me" Romanichel took Raphael by the hand and started to dance to the music. She was graceful and light as air. It was beautiful to see. Just then, the barge arrived and floated above the deck. Romanichel stopped dancing to go meet the barge. She caught up to Ohuru who was in the process of getting the barge to land.

"Ohuru, where were you planning to land this thing? On my house?"

"Sorry, where can I land the barge?"

"There's a clearing near here. I'll show you." Romanichel started to walk away.

Atleos sat still, mesmerized by her dance. She was beautiful.

"You shouldn't set your eyes on a prize that has already been taken," Tamael said nudging Atleos with his elbow.

"Maybe not, but she is so beautiful."

"Romanichel is at her best when she's dancing, that's her beauty. You must learn to see each woman that way, and when one is more beautiful than the others. She'll be the one."

"What is it you saw in Lilay?"

"Her music. She's the most beautiful when she plays."

"I'll remember that. I best go to sleep. Unlike Ohuru, I need more than five hours of sleep to be a happy fellow."

"Good night, Atleos. Come on, son, time for you to hit the sack as well."

"They have mattresses here, you know," said Raphael.

"Yes, and you'll be in one very soon. Amos, your baby is very sweet."

"Thank you, my friend. May yours be as healthy and beautiful."

Tamael passed the baby to Amos and retreated to his room. Tonight, he wouldn't have to share a bed. Amos had enough guest rooms for everyone.

Ohuru walked back with Romanichel. It gave them a chance to talk.

"How's Atleos doing?" she asked.

"He doesn't know much. Normally, this would be the year he would spend as a guard and I guess he is guarding someone, but I just don't know how trustworthy he really is. Amos and Tamael haven't revealed much of their plan to him. All he knows is that nothing happened at the store. We got drunk for nothing and Amos was just overly worried about the money."

"Shouldn't he know the truth?"

"We'll never say we gave the money to the resistance. We're to pretend it never happened."

"Too many secrets, Ohuru. It's not good."

"Just let me get close to him and decide for myself what his worth is. Then we'll let the elders tell him more."

"Does he know about Tinay?"

"Tinay doesn't know about Tinay."

"Good. That's our secret weapon. She must, at all cost, remain a secret."

They arrived at the house and went to bed quickly. Their sleep was good for the most part. Only Tamael and Amos needed a bit more time to fall asleep and convince themselves it had to be done.

The temperature was lovely on Isifilmos. It was a beautiful morning and Romanichel was up with the baby when Ohuru joined her for breakfast.

"When are you leaving?" she asked.

"As soon as they get up."

"Well, I had everyone woken up thirty minutes ago. They should just about be ready now."

"You didn't send anyone to my room?"

"No, I knew you'd be awake," teased Romanichel.

"Good morning." Amos bent over and kissed his wife and child, "Where is everyone?"

"We're right behind you." Tamael tapped his shoulders and sat down beside Romanichel.

"This is how it should always be; a table full of friends and a house full of guests," Romanichel smiled.

"Time will come, sweetheart, time will come," said Amos.

"Yeah, now my father will be living on Kyr and he'll be able to visit more often, I'm sure. He promised to visit me."

"Yes, Raphael. Soon we'll all be living together again." Romanichel patted his head and smiled.

After a succulent breakfast, they walked to the shuttle and said their good-byes. They boarded the shuttle and left for their ship docked in space. They made way for Essay and, not to attract too much attention, they used their regular speed. While Ohuru was driving, Tamael melted the couplings into bars of solid metal. At least they could sell them and make some money.

It took all day to reach Essay again, and Raphael wanted to spend time with his dad before he was left behind.

"Why are you so clingy, Raph?"

"I'll miss you"

"No, you won't."

"Yes, I will." His eyes filled up with tears.

"Raphael, it's only for a few days while Ohuru and I go to El and visit some old friends. Then I'll be right back with you."

"I get to stay with you?"

"You'll come home and help us move. Next trip is when you'll start your work on Essay. I just thought it would be good for you to meet Merdaine before I left you here."

"That's a great idea. I love you so much, Pa!" He jumped into his father's arms and hugged him.

"I love you too, son, very much."

Back in the control room, Atleos saw ESSAY appear on the screen and turned to Ohuru and said, "What is it with you guys? You always time everything with a meal?"

"If you had been friends with Amos long enough, you would have come to realize a good meal is very important to maintain the proper function of the body and brain."

"Shall we park for the night then?"

"No, we'll take the shuttle to Merdaine's house right away. We're behind schedule."

"Schedule for what?"

"It's a surprise for Tamael. I don't want to spoil it for him."

"Alright then, keep your secrets. Won't be the first time."

"Now, that hurts…"

"What hurts?" asked Tamael, freshly washed and clothed.

"Nothing. We're here. Let's get to the shuttle and get down to meet Merdaine. He'll wonder what took us so long."

They took the shuttle down to the village of Elne to meet Merdaine.

"I hope he has food for us, I'm starving," said Raphael.

"I have to say that now that I've survived a meal with Amos, I'm starting to feel hungry myself."

"Just listen to your stomach this time," warned Ohuru with a grin.

They landed in the clearing by Merdaine's house. The door opened and Raphael could not believe his eyes. A man stood in front of him who was the size of a giant. He was all muscle and wore a silly straw hat on his bald head. The man had no shirt on and carried a long fork.

"Merdaine, my friend, long time no see." Tamael moved forward and embraced Merdaine.

"Yeah, you couldn't have called to say you'd be a day late?" asked Merdaine.

"Oh! Now don't be a crybaby," Ohuru teased. "The only reason we make plans is for life to undo them. You know that." Ohuru moved towards him with his arms wide open and gave him a big hug.

"Well, I'm happy to see you all alive. How long are you staying?" Merdaine asked.

"We have to leave tonight for El, right after supper," Ohuru replied.

"Where's the boy?" Merdaine asked.

"Raphael, come over here and say hello." Tamael motioned for Raphael to join them.

"Hello..." Raphael said hesitantly.

"Well, he doesn't talk much," said Merdaine.

"No, it's quite the opposite normally," said Ohuru.

"That's because he's put his foot in his mouth so much lately there's no more room for words," joked Atleos.

Everyone laughed except Raphael who turned red.

Instead of staying quiet, Raphael ventured another comment. "You're big," he said to Merdaine.

"Yes, that I am." Merdaine picked Raphael up from the ground and sat him on his shoulder, "and you'll make a fine friend for Elaine."

"A girl?!?"

"Yes, my girl. My son is a little too old to play with you."

"Oh man, that sucks," Raphael sulked.

"You haven't even met her yet, how can you say that?" Tamael definitely preferred his son quiet.

"But, Pa, she's a girl."

"She'll teach you how to ride a horse," said Merdaine.

"Um, maybe I spoke too soon."

"And another foot gets stuck into his mouth. Aha aha aha!" said Atleos and everyone burst out laughing.

They settled by the fire and ate their meal in peace. Raphael felt scared, happy, unsure, and anxious. And yet, what an adventure this had been so far.

"You should meditate tomorrow and take care of those negative feelings that are plaguing you. This is going to be very good, you'll see," Tamael said reassuringly.

"Hmm." Raphael hugged his father and closed his eyes. He hoped to fall asleep in his father's arms once more. But it was not meant to happen tonight. Ohuru and Tamael boarded the ship and immediately left for El.

Atleos stayed behind to try and locate a Healer, and Raphael waved courageously at his father's shuttle as it left.

Chapter 8

THE PYRAMID

Once the dust settled, Tinay could no longer see any light coming from the tunnel. A small ray of light hit the ground, but it was not enough to bounce off the crystals on the walls. A ray of light meant air was filtering through, but the hole was not big enough to get out. She was trapped. She looked at the entrance. *Maybe I can move the rocks out of the way,* she thought. She wobbled over to the entrance and saw stones too large to be moved. Even if she could move one or two, there was no way to know how wide the cave-in was. She started to feel her stomach turn. Her head started to spin, breathing was becoming more difficult, and her heart was pounding in her chest.

"MOTHER!" she screamed.

Idiot, she can't hear you. Let's try a mind link. For a mind link, she had to calm down and control her breathing. This was no easy task as she was scared like never before in her life. Life on Sasgorg was uneventful, only the last few days had proven to be more excitement then her whole life. But this was too much. She is stuck in a cave. There was a volcano about to erupt, and half of her family was missing. She lay down on her back and started to breath normally, then she slowed it down and the queasiness started to go away. She slowly calmed her heart rate and was able to focus her mind on her mother, *Mother, are you there?* she asked in her mind.

Yes, dear, what is it? Does your ankle hurt you?

It's worst than that, Mom. The last tremor created a cave-in and I'm stuck. I can't get out!

Do you have enough oxygen?

Yes, but...

Do you have any light?

Yes, but...

I can't go and help you. You'll have to help yourself. I'll try to contact your father and ask him to come back to help us both. It's too late for the lithil now, I'm going to have this child soon. My fall and all this exertion saw to it. You have air and light. You can use one of your crystals to light up the cavern. Align it properly and you'll have no problems. Once there's light, look for a source of food.

Mom, someone decorated the walls with the stories of Atlanti and Apotheleme. What does it mean?

It means that while you are in that cave, you will receive your calling and you will know what you will apprentice in. You have to pass the challenge of the cave. This cave, just like the one we live in, was a pyramid. When the star went nova, everything dried up, burnt and turned to sand. Sand took over everything and covered the land. This was the center of a large city. Our residence used to be the residence of the Meji and Mount Ardel was the temple. The only real mountain around here was Mount Galgamel. The pyramids were beautiful works of art and stood royally in the center of the city. Now everything is gone and all that is left is the most important of all: the history. Argg!

Mom! Mom! Are you alright? Tinay was worried.

It's another contraction. I must leave you for now, but I'll be back. Look for food and continue to read what the walls have to teach you. I must be ready for when the baby comes.

How can I get out of here, Mother? Tinay waited for the answer, but it was too late: her mother had severed the connection. Labor was hard, long and complicated. Her mother needed to keep in touch with her baby and would not be able to help her. She had to rely on herself. For the first time in her life, she felt alone and disconnected.

Meanwhile, Lilay was in pain, "I could really use that lithil now. Ohhh!" Lilay couldn't concentrate long enough to make the pain go away. "I must warn Tamael. I must."

Once the contraction receded, she was able to concentrate and visualize her baby. The baby was a beautiful soul, a girl. She would have the ability to tell history and history was now in the making. Maybe this was why she wanted to come early, or maybe she was just adventurous. Nevertheless, the child was in a hurry and Lilay was not ready.

Loni, my child, why the hurry? Lilay asked and a faint reply came forward.

Manyr sends me. I must come now. We will not be protected on Sasgorg much longer and we most relocate soon. Since you won't relocate before I'm born, I must come now.

Lilay wondered what a difference two weeks would make, but apparently it meant freedom and survival. She had given birth to other children before, she could do this again, but this would be the first time she would have to do it alone. This was not going to be easy. She was the keeper of time, the teller of stories. She wrote books and repeated history, but it was never her place to make it. She never understood much of the medical books she kept. She didn't have the intuition.

It was time for her to contact her husband. She went into the bath she had prepared for herself and concentrated her energy. Her soul was connected to each of her children and she had a special bond with her husband. She escaped her body and let her soul float to outer space. She followed the line that looked like a ribbon and magically passed through dozens of star systems. She arrived at Merdaine's village and located Raphael. He was meditating while Alzabar watched over him. Lilay's soul changed color. She was astonished that after so long her father would come back and help one of her children.

Father.

Alzabar looked at her. In his eyes she found the love she had been missing and the glory and grandness that belonged to her father. She had missed him for so long now, and without a body, she could not feel the comforting sensation of a hug or a kiss that had been denied to her. But she still had emotions.

What are you doing here? Don't you know your mother is searching for you and your child? She needs a healer.

Yes, I know, but Tinay is in great danger. She's stuck in a cave and the cave fell in. Father, I must warn Tamael.

He's not here and I cannot let you jeopardize his location. Leave the message with me and when Raphael sees his father again, he'll tell him to hurry back. Is that all you want said?

She was never able to lie to her father, but she couldn't risk saying that she was having the baby or even that she was pregnant. If her mother found out, she would intensify the search.

No, Father. Just tell him to hurry and come back. We need him to help Tinay.

Tinay is of age to find her calling. If this is her initiation, you know very well that Tamael won't be able to help her.

Yes, but. . .

There are no 'buts'. She must face the initiation alone. It's the only way she will succeed. If she fails, all will be lost. Our last chance to reinstate the order will be lost. No, I will not pass on the message. You will be fine. They'll be back soon enough.

Lilay knew it was no use to argue with her father. He protected Raphael from any intrusion on his meditation, so she wouldn't be able to contact him either.

She left the area and knew that the only way to contact her husband would be to call him by his real name, something she had not done for twenty years. The name would stir echoes and would wake her mother's sense and draw unwanted attention.

She couldn't do that either. She returned to her father once more.

Father, you must listen, she said.

I will listen, but I will not change my mind. Tamael and Raphael will remain safe and the Order will not be disclosed to your mother or her allies.

I understand. I have spent twenty years of my life on a desert planet preparing my children for their destiny. I have followed the rules and regulations of the Meji order and I have upheld history and truth forever. Now I need you to warn Tamael of a danger and make him return home. Please.

But the initiation, darling.

I will not jeopardize the initiation, but you must help me.

Alzabar had been a strong and proud man when he was alive. He had not made beggars out of his children. There was something his child was not telling him. He understood the urgency, but he didn't have the whole truth.

Child, if I refuse to alert Tamael, what will you do?

Stir the echoes. Lilay said with fear in her voice. She knew what she would accomplish by this, but what she didn't know weighed even more heavily.

My child! Alzabar didn't know what to say. *The Stir of Echoes? You can't be serious.*

Yes, Father, if I must.

Very well. If you promise that the initiation will be completed as tasked and that there is no other way, I will do it.

Thank you, Father. I must go now. Softly, Lilay left and retraced her steps.

She woke up in her bath at the house. Her hands cradled her large belly. The water was getting cold. "Hummargg!" Another contraction took her by surprise. She breathed quickly at first and then started to slow down. The contraction eased away. She needed warm water to keep the contractions slow and painless. She got up and went outside to see the sundial. It was already seven p.m. She had been gone much longer than she thought. She was hungry and knew she was going to need all the strength she could muster if she was going to do this alone.

Back at Ardel, Tinay had managed to hang her pendant on a stalactite and create a rainbow that fed light to the crystals on the walls of the cavern. This allowed her to look around. She could not find any stairs like the ones at her house. This was an enclosed area with an altar in the center: a dead end. There was no way out. Again, the feeling of dizziness invaded her and she fell unconscious. When she woke up, the light of the sun had been replaced by the reflection of the moon. The cave had an allure of fantasy. All the colors refracted off the crystal and onto the wall. Her crystal pendant that dangled from the stalactite twirled, sending the light in an ever-changing arc across the walls. Tinay realized she was hungry. She opened her pouch and ate some of the food she had packed with her. The air seemed easier to breath now that the dust was all on the ground. She moved slowly as her ankle hurt worse than before. It had swelled until she could no longer stand on it. She wondered if her mother had contacted her while she was unconscious. She couldn't recall anything, as it had been a dreamless sleep.

She looked around and could not find her ferret. Draco was trained to hunt for anything alive, be it plant or animal, to feed himself. If he was gone, he must have been hunting. Maybe there was an escape after all. Tinay looked around the cave closely and found many cracks and small holes, but unless she was a ferret herself, she could not get beyond the floor she was on.

"Let's see," she said. "At our house, the cave gets bigger as it goes deeper into the ground. This one should too if they were of similar architecture. There must be a hole in the floor somewhere."

As she said this, she saw Draco emerge from the floor dragging behind him a dried up piece of meat. Tinay got closer and looked. She could not see anything because it was too dark, but obviously something was there.

"There must be a way to get in there," she said. "Let's see."

Draco came to her and chewed on the piece of beef. She figured that if he was able to find it, and eat it, there had to be more and she could feed herself. How could she get under the floor and see?

"Of course," she said. "I'll take an astral trip and see if there's a lever."

She lay down on the floor and closed her eyes. She forced herself to breathe slowly to calm herself. She transferred the air from her lower lungs up and exhaled the air from her mouth, breathing out all thoughts of anxiety and fear. This took much longer than usual. For the first time, she realized how scared she really was and how this had affected her. Her mind was not clear. Maybe that was why she couldn't concentrate on finding the answer; she was too worried. She finally had the energy flowing through her like the wind moved the sand on the plains of Landel. She realized her ankle was absorbing a lot more energy than the rest of her body, but in doing so, the pain was slowly leaving her body and a sense of warmth enveloped her ankle. Hmm, that's much better. She decided to try sending more energy to her ankle. Slowly, her ankle shrank to its normal size.

Then she went to the next temple, but although she could picture the red circle of energy, it was weak and dark. At first she wondered if this had to do with the cave and the lack of light in it. Then she realized it couldn't be, since she was on the spiritual plane and energy provided the light, nothing else. In the darkest place she could have light, all she had to do was to control the energy.

No matter what she tried, she couldn't and her frustration made her concentrate on her breathing again because she was upsetting her balance. She decided to try her mother.

Mother?

Yes, dear? Her mother sounded far and distant like in a dream.

I can't focus the energy; I can't get past the red temple.

It's time for you to learn the meaning of the temples. The red one represents your security and safety. Your basic needs must be dealt with before you can continue. Once you can achieve peace and balance of your basic needs, you'll be able to move on to the next stage.

Why haven't you told me this before?

Because I didn't want you to get past your third eye. My fear stopped you. There was a lot of risk involved. Now the time has come that some risk must be taken, so I'll walk you through what I can. Why are you meditating?

I want to try to project my body in an astral plane and go see what lies beyond the floor and how I can get to it.

Excellent! Very good! Lilay was impressed. *That is excellent! You are progressing very well. Align all the energy you can and then go out and see. Oh-oh, another contraction is coming. I must go.*

That was it. Tinay was on her own again. At least she knew she was on the right track and she could focus her efforts. She concentrated once again on her red circle of energy. She asked herself, *What is bothering me?*

Out of the depth of her mind came the answer, *I'm afraid I won't find food.* And thus a dialogue with herself began.

I don't have to be afraid of not having food. I won't be here forever. I don't need to eat much and I can be frugal with the reserves I have. Once I find a way to get the trap door open, I will be able to access more food.

What else am I afraid of?

You're afraid of another cave in; you don't feel safe here.

Hmm, that's true, but if the rest of the mountain was going to cave in, it would have done so by now.

You're hurt. You're in pain!

Come to think of it, I'm not in pain anymore. My ankle feels fine. Things aren't so bad; I'm separated from Mom, but she doesn't seem worried. I'll be fine. This is just like a puzzle that needs to be solved.

As she exhaled the last bit of doubt left in her body, she saw her red circle not only shine and grow, but also spin. She was ecstatic. She moved on to the next temple of energy and found that she could bring up the orange circle quickly and with less effort. She wondered what this temple represented and why she had no trouble balancing it, but she was happy to move on to the next one. This one was yellow; this one she didn't understand. It was a challenge to make the sun shine, so she decided to ask, *What am I afraid of?*

This time no answer came. Why wasn't she getting an answer? Why did it work before, but not now? What would the third temple represent? She was full of questions and she was not getting any answers. What could she do? What was she feeling? Finally the answers came: she was afraid. She was afraid her parents didn't care about her because she felt abandoned. She was afraid because she had no clue where she would live. She was afraid because she would not be with her family anymore. She felt scared and alone. She wanted to feel loved. *I miss my parents. I want to continue to teach Raphael. I don't want him to go. Wow*, she thought. *Some of the stuff that I heard I didn't even know I felt.*

Then a calm voice rang above the tumult.

That's why you must meditate everyday and find what is holding you back. You must deal with it and reassure yourself that things will be fine and that the greater good will be served.

Yes, it all made sense. It seemed that the third temple had to do with the center of emotions. Why didn't any of it this come up before? *Because I was not challenged before. My life has always been quiet and uneventful. Never has anything of consequence ever happened. That is why the last few days have been so draining and tiresome, because so much has happened, so many difficult moments, decisions, and fear. For the first time in my life I have felt fear.* The sun began to rise and float freely above her chest. She felt that although not all was all right, she knew inside it would be. Although her parents weren't sharing all the information with her, she knew exactly what to do and, therefore, she could trust that everything would be fine. Her sun began to brighten. Her mother didn't seem too concerned for her safety; Lilay wasn't abandoning her, Lilay was letting Tinay figure it out on her own. That meant she was supposed to do this. She didn't have to be afraid. Yes, that's it. She would be fine.

The sun shone brightly. She could move on to the next temple with the green band around her chest, close to her heart. When she meditated on this temple she would see herself and then her family. That's all that was in the circle most of the time, but she remembered her mother had told her that as Tinay grew older and met other people, she would put them in her heart, too. She had no difficulty in seeing her family there with her. It made her feel much better and calmer. She knew she would never be completely alone; she would always have her family in her heart. Her spirit felt elevated. Moving on to the throat, she pictured a blue crystal shimmering. She couldn't tell what this temple was about, but it lit up easily. It became brilliant and bright. All of a sudden, she felt a tremendous pressure on her body. The whole cavern was pushing against her. Her breathe caught in her throat, but she couldn't understand why she was panicking. She was doing fine and the cave couldn't have shrunk to this size. What was going on? She remained calm and tried to breath normally again. When she opened her eyes, she saw her spirit slowly lift through her skin. She was doing it! She was free.

The cave was no longer dark, so she could see much better. Moving closer to the hole that Draco had come out of, Tinay filtered herself through it to see what was on the other side. She saw a mechanism that would move the stone and make it into steps. From there, she could access the room below. A sarcophagus was there, made of a brilliant metal, and more drawings adorned the walls. Now she needed to know how she could get in there to change the stone into a staircase. She looked at the mechanism and saw that it led straight to the altar. She would need to explore the altar to find the answers.

She went back to her body and slowly brought it back to life. She wiggled her toes and moved her legs. She felt the blood flow to her fingers and back into her arms. She opened her eyes and was surprised to realize how dark the cavern really was. Slowly getting to her feet, she was surprised to find that her ankle seemed to have healed. She felt much better now. She walked to the altar and started to blow the dust away. A lot of time had gone by since this cavern had been looked after, but surprisingly, the cavern's altar was still clean, other than the recent dust settlement from the cave in. She saw something she had not noticed before. There were ridges and markings on the altar. She tried to read it, but it didn't make sense.

It said, "To a moving ladder came grace and to a lever came the first step.

To descend through the spirit, to transcend through Ages,

To find the questions that will answer the quest,

One must weigh their indecision on the balance of truth."

What could this mean, she asked herself. As she looked at the image of the balance, she tried to clean some of the dust that had fallen. The receptacle lowered into the altar.

She quickly removed her hand. What could this mean? Now that she looked carefully, the other receptacle of the balance was a little lower yet. What if she pushed both of them together? She tried it and the ticking of a clock was heard. The sound of stone against stone followed and, as she turned around, the floor behind her moved to show a set of stairs. Now that she could see down, it wasn't as dark. She gathered everything she had with her and collected Draco, who had fallen asleep against the rocks, and descended the stairs. She found strange things staggered around the sarcophagus. She didn't know what a sarcophagus was for, but more importantly, she spotted something she did recognize: food!

She quickly walked over to the table, and grabbed some fruit and meat and ate. Everything was amazingly fresh and tasted great. She did not understand why until she looked at the bottom of the plate and found Alenor crystals. That was what had been keeping the food fresh: Alenor crystals. They had the capability to keep the air clean and to revive stale and corrupted water, and keep food supplies fresh forever. This was what her father had discovered and dedicated his life to harvesting and selling these rare crystals, which were found abundantly on Sasgorg. She quickly put the rest of the food and the crystals in her pouch. This would keep her plants alive.

She knelt on the floor and looked at Draco, who was still asleep. She decided that it would be better to pass the time by sleeping. It had been an exhausting day, after all.

Chapter 9

KAPLARA

Raphael woke up feeling tired. He did not have a very good night's sleep. He tried to do as his father had said and meditate for a little while. He found that, although he felt a little scared, his fear was overwhelmed by his curiosity. He wanted to know what Essay looked like. He wanted to see this new world. Maybe he wasn't afraid because this was all so new for him. The past few days had taught him so much. His lonely world of Sasgorg was far behind him and he would be able to make friends, play outside on the grass, and eat a variety of foods. Not that his mother's food wasn't good, but variety was not a common word on Sasgorg. This was turning out to be better than he'd imagined. Instead of looking at it pessimistically, he looked at it with a smile. He was a bit disappointed that his only friend would be a girl, but she wasn't the only kid around, there were lots of kids here on Essay to play with.

He went to the kitchen wondering if it was time for breakfast yet. At home, he was always considered the early riser because everyone else did their meditation in the morning and he did his in the afternoon. He was surprised to find that Merdaine's wife was already cleaning the kitchen table.

"Hello, sleepy head. Remember me?" she smiled.

"Yes, you're Merdaine's wife. I'm sorry, I forgot your name," said Raphael, blushing.

"I'm Giselle, a miner's daughter from El."

"How did you meet Merdaine?" Raphael was curious.

"To make a long story short, we met at the market on Os and it was love at first sight."

"My mother would call that romantic."

"And what would you call it?"

"Just luck, I guess. I'm not ready for anything like that, so I'll avoid girls until I'm ready."

"Ah ha ha! Only a master can control his emotion that well! But I think that you're a little young to worry about things like that," grinned Giselle.

"So, you think it's safe for me to play with Elaine then?"

"Yes, Elaine thinks it's great she's getting a step-brother to help her with her chores."

"I knew this was too perfect to last!"

Giselle laughed. "Well, part of your training here on Essay is to learn how to work."

"But I thought I was going to have to read a lot of books and stuff."

"Read? Very few people actually know how to read. When you become an apprentice, you learn first-hand by the master. None of it is written in textbooks."

"So why did you pick me?" Raphael was curious.

"Your father is a friend of Amos, and Merdaine employs Amos to sell his crops. They had a mutual acquaintance. My husband needs a boy to help him around the farm. To take you on an apprentice was the ideal thing for us. Your father knew how much time mining took away from family and did not want that type of life for you. Since I was the daughter of a miner, I figured I was in a great position to help you adapt to your new world. What do you say?"

"I'm surprise how well this has been organized. Elaine is my age, then?"

"Not exactly. She's only four, but she already feeds the chicken and the pigs and looks after weeding the garden with me and...."

"Four years old! But she's just a baby!" cried Raphael.

"She's growing up. She's lonely. We thought that it would be a good idea for her to have someone around."

"Well, at least she won't be bossing me around."

"That's the way to look at it, always find the silver lining to each situation. Your father taught you well," she said sarcastically.

"It was Mother, actually. Pa was away during the day. He rarely stayed home unless there was a sandstorm. Then we got to spend some time together. That's why I miss him so much."

"That's why he doesn't want you to have that life. You know, on Essay, during the winter months, life is terribly quiet. That's when you care for the animals, go hunting and learn a musical instrument, but I'm sure we could spare you for a week or two to you visit your family," offered Giselle.

"Really?"

"Yes, your father will have time to come for visits as well," she reassured him. "Your mother will have to earn money for your family now, so your father won't be as busy."

"Fantastic!"

"Now, would you like some breakfast?"

"Would I ever. Has Atleos eaten?"

"No, he's sleeping."

"Then I better wake him up and make him come to the table. Then we can clean up the kitchen together."

"Yes, we'll clean up only to start making lunch. Life here is a lot of hard work and everyone needs a full stomach to keep their strength."

"Do you need any help?" he asked.

"That's the spirit, Raphael, but I think that Merdaine wants to take you on a tour of the farm and show you what we do around here."

"Very well then. I'll go wake up Atleos." He turned, but stopped as Atleos walked into the room.

"No need, I'm up." Atleos stretched and yawned. "I thought I was the early riser, but it looks like I was beaten to it."

"I would say so. Here we get up at five in the morning and in the fields by six. There's a lot of work around here and we must all contribute," said Giselle.

"Five in the morning? That's really early!" said Raphael.

"So, what will it be?" asked Giselle.

"We have a choice?" Raphael was so excited. On Sasgorg, it was always the same old thing. This was absolutely great.

"What is there?" asked Atleos.

"Eggs, bacon, toast, omelet, pancakes, cereals."

"No cereals, please." Raphael wanted to taste something new. "I'll have pancakes, if that's alright."

"Me too. Pancakes sound delicious." Atleos put on an apron.

"What are you doing, Atleos?" Raphael asked.

"Well, since Madam Giselle will prepare the breakfast, we can help clean up the rest of the kitchen, and that way she won't be the only one left to do all the work."

"Thank you, Atleos, I appreciate your help." Giselle was glad to have such a helpful guest at her table.

Raphael started to dry the dishes as Atleos passed them to him. He remembered that, since this was preparation time, it was also his time to pray for the food he was about to receive. He could not understand what was so wrong about praying and thanking the Overseer and the Goddess for their gifts. Raphael turned around to Giselle and asked her, "Giselle?"

"Yes, Raphael?"

"Do you pray?"

"I used to, but ever since Paletis banned prayers to the Overseer and the Goddess, I stopped. You see, she feels the prayers should be addressed to her," she explained.

"And you pray to Paletis then?"

"No, I have only one God and one Goddess. She's simply a fairy with an inflated ego..."

"And that's the type of talk that is going to bring the inquisition to our house and have you burned at the stake, Giselle," a deep voice interrupted.

Raphael was startled. He didn't hear Merdaine walk in even though Merdaine was a big man. Raphael thought that Merdaine would have been noisy. Raphael was in awe of Merdaine the night before, but now he felt a chill down his spine. Merdaine had a look on his face that would have scared any wild animal to death. Raphael held his breath.

"But Raphael wanted to know..." Giselle started.

"Never mind what the boy wanted to know. The neighbors are somewhat sympathetic to Paletis cause and for the ransom she offers for witches. They would turn you in, in an instant. Raphael?" Merdaine turned his attention to Raphael.

Raphael gulped. The last thing he wanted was to be in trouble. "Yes?" he whispered.

"Your father taught you well, but now that you are among other people unlike on Sasgorg. You will have to learn that your religion is forbidden in the new world Paletis created. She is queen and wants all the power for herself. I will continue your father's teachings, but you must wait for the appropriate time and place. Do you understand?" Merdaine stared sternly at Raphael.

"Yes, sir," Raphael gulped.

"Very well. Now that you've eaten, let's get to work!"

"I'm making them breakfast now. . ." Giselle cut in.

Merdaine loved his wife, but he wished she wasn't so timid. She had let the guests sleep in when he had asked her to wake them up an hour ago. He had work to do and wanted to show Raphael what his life would be like here. He needed an apprentice, not a slacker.

"I can go with you now, if you wish, sir," offered Raphael.

"No, it's alright. I'll clean the stables until you're ready to join us." Merdaine sighed.

"Very well, sir."

"You can call me Merdaine, Raph, it's alright."

"Of course, sir. And my name is Raphael." Raphael hated being called Raph by anyone but his parents.

"I see. Meet me at the stables when you are ready." Merdaine left for the barn. He walked steadily and, unlike Amos, stealthily.

"I'm sorry for getting you in trouble, Raphael," said Giselle

"It's alright. It's better I learn now instead of when it's too late."

Giselle smiled. She was a short woman with flame-red hair. She wore glasses and had a voluptuous form, but she was a bit skinny. She was a hard worker and loved her husband. But she wished she had Raphael's wisdom. Even now at twenty-seven years old, she never knew when to be quiet. She knew her husband was only being protective of her, but he found it hard to relegate her beliefs to the dungeon when what the world needed most was conviction in the old ways.

For almost twelve thousand years the Atlanteans had lived in relative peace, found a corner of space that wasn't inhabited, and grew into a large society. Giselle was still baffled about how one woman could overthrow an entire government and take precedence over all the colonies.

"Um, Madame Giselle, the pancakes..." Atleos reminded Giselle.

"Ohh!" Giselle, thinking deeply, had forgotten all about the pancakes and burned them.

"I'm sorry, I'm afraid I'll have to start all over again," she sighed.

"No, it's alright. We'll have cereal today," said Raphael in a defeated tone of voice. He didn't know what was worse, to eat the same thing every day or to be given a choice and still end up eating cereal.

Giselle prepared the food quickly and set out to finish cleaning the kitchen. She still had to prepare the sandwiches for the lunch Raphael and Atleos were to bring with them.

Raphael and Atleos ate their breakfast quickly, not wanting to take too long and make Merdaine angrier. Atleos had stayed behind for a single purpose, he needed to find a healer. Ohuru had assured him, this family might be able to help him, but now he wasn't sure what to do. He liked Giselle and did not want her to be in any more trouble.

Raphael got up and walked towards the sink to bring his plate to Giselle.

"Do you want any help?" he offered.

"I think that you should brush your teeth and get ready to go. I'm almost finished the sandwiches. I'll take care of the dishes on my own, don't worry." She smiled as Raphael rushed upstairs.

Atleos looked down at his feet and had an idea. "Madame Giselle?"

"Yes, Atleos?"

"I burnt my shins on Sasgorg and Tamael gave me a cream to put on there, but I'm running out. I was wondering if I could find a healer near here to..."

"Healers are long gone," She interrupted. "Merdaine might have something to help you, but I can assure you there are no healers left on Essay."

"I see." Atleos looked down at his feet once more and felt a great emptiness inside him. He wondered if he would ever find a healer.

Even if he did, would she have found a cure for the poison Paletis had created?

Raphael ran back into the kitchen, ready to leave, "Are you staying here, Atleos?"

"No, I'll go with you. Maybe we can make up for sleeping in."

They grabbed the sandwiches and headed for the barn. Elaine was getting her pony ready for training in the arena.

Elaine looked up, "Father, they are coming."

"Yes, I see that."

"Is he always going to get up this late?"

Merdaine frowned, "No, but for the next few days, he's here to see what we do, so let's not push him too hard."

"He's already missed half the day as it is. How much more of a break is he going to need?" Elaine complained.

"Oh, be kind," chided her father. "He comes from a different world. He could teach you a thing or two. Now, off you go. I'll show them the farm." Merdaine pushed her gently.

Elaine ran off to her pony and took him into the arena where she was going to practice jumping.

Merdaine walked to the door and waited for them to join him. His dog started to bark as they got closer.

"Easy, Sherry, easy. They're coming with us." He patted the dog's head as she sat down beside him.

"Here we are, sir!" Raphael was grinning from ear to ear.

"Very good. Have you ever ridden a horse before, boy?"

"No, sir."

"Well, let's get you started." Merdaine had prepared three horses to ride the farm circumference. He quickly lifted Raphael up onto the smallest horse.

"Maggy here is old and won't give you trouble. She'll follow my lead. For you, Atleos, I have prepared Pistachio. He's a bit bigger and will require a bit more control, but you can handle him." Merdaine motioned to a large dark haired horse which stood proudly by the fence. It had a long tail and mane. It was a majestic animal.

Atleos moved towards the horse and took a swing to get on him. As he was struggling to get on, he talked to Merdaine, "Merdaine, sir, I have burnt my shins on Sasgorg and I was wondering if I could find a healer nearby that could help me."

"Healers have been gone from Essay for a long time, but I'm sure I can find something that could help you. We put it on the hooves of the horses and cows. It should do the trick."

"I heard a rumor that Kaplara was here and was working on…"

Merdaine cut him off, "Master Atleos! I would not know if Kaplara was here or not! I will certainly not have you wandering around asking such questions and have my life here destroyed. I will help you with your shins, but they'll be no more mention of healers, Kaplara or any other witch."

"I'm sorry. Kaplara was a renowned healer and she had been spotted here. I need a healer to help me and that's why I stopped here." Atleos was practically begging.

"Your stop was in vain. There has been no sign of a healer in ages, or else I would have five children and not just one. I would not have scars on my legs and I wouldn't be losing any animals each year to disease and complicated births. Paletis has provided us with some engineers to help, but they are too expensive. We cannot afford them on this farm. That will be the end of it, young man, or I'll have you shipped on the barge to Os where you can spend time with Amos until Ohuru returns."

"No need, sir, I apologize. I never meant to …"

"Apology accepted. Now, let's ride and see what Essay has given me."

They galloped through the land as Merdaine proudly showed his cereal fields, and his forest that circled the north of his estate. For a man of little means he certainly had a lot of land.

"The problem is I have no help from friends here and Giselle's family cannot help either. I swallow all my profits by hiring helpers. We're hoping that Raphael is going to help us free up some money and make a profit next year." Merdaine winked at Raphael.

"I'll do my best," said Raphael.

"What's going on over there?" Atleos pointed to the horizon.

"I don't know. That's where my horses are running."

They rode to the group of horses and the few hired hands that Merdaine had hired. Once they arrived one of the four men came towards Merdaine.

"We'll be losing both mother and baby again. The foal is coming in by the back. There's no way for us to pull him out," the worker frowned.

"I can't afford to lose another one. Raphael, your father said you're a capable knife handler?"

Raphael nodded, "Yes, sir."

"Time to put you to work! Atleos, go home and get the suture kit. Tell Giselle I need it for the horse." Merdaine grabbed Atleo's horse's head and whispered, "I need you to ride fast, as fast as you can to save these two here."

Atleos rode hard towards Merdaine's residence and wondered what they would do.

Merdaine shot into action, "Okay, Raphael, have you ever gutted an animal before?"

"Yes, I did some hunting on Sasgorg with Pa."

"Very well, I'll let you cut the skin and I'll guide you during the procedure. All you men, hold the mare down. Now, Raphael, you have to shave the skin before you cut her stomach."

"Alright." Raphael had no idea what he was doing, but he closely shaved the horse. "Sir, maybe it would help if you told me what we're about to do. I doubt that shaving her will help her give birth."

"I have lost many mares and foals. Last year, we paid for an engineer to come and save one of them. He cut open her stomach and the uterus, and got the foal out. Then he tried to suture the mare, but he had taken too long because of the hair and she died. I can't lose both of them, I need to save the foal at least."

"Ok." Raphael started to sweat. Opening the carcass of an animal was quite different from opening a live one. He finished shaving her and looked up intently. "Are we ready?"

"Yes, it's now or never."

Raphael cut through the thick hide of the horse, and Merdaine helped him grab the placenta.

"Now be careful, Raphael. We want to try and sew her up after, and we don't want to cut the foal."

"Of course, I've done this many times, no need to worry," Raphael said with half a smile.

There was little bleeding, which was a good sign. Raphael was doing well. Now he wished he had read a book about operations somewhere in his mother's library. He slowly cut the placenta and two legs popped through. The mare let out a cry and passed out.

"Oh no! She's dying," said Raphael.

In the distance, Atleos rode back, having a hard time keeping up with the horse. "Easy, Pistachio. I can't afford to fall, old buddy."

The horse felt the urgency, but seemed to understand that if he arrived without his cavalier, he would be useless to help the mare. He slowed down a bit but kept on galloping.

Merdaine checked Ella, the mare. He could still feel a heartbeat and she was breathing slowly.

"No, she's just passed out. If we move quickly, we might be able to save her." Merdaine pulled the foal out and cleaned the foal's face so he could breath.

"What do I do now?" asked Raphael.

"Now you look after the foal while I sew the stomach of my horse."

Atleos jumped to the ground and handed the basket to Merdaine. Then he turned around and tried to keep his breakfast in.

Merdaine shook his head. He went straight to work and sutured the mare's belly back together. He was used to caring for his helpers and himself. He always left a scar, but at least the mare would live.

The mare came to and raised her head slowly. She started to lick the brownish foal.

"Job well done, Raphael. Thanks for your help, gentlemen." Merdaine nodded to his workers and Atleos. "It's time to bring her back in now. Raphael, I think you should have the honor of naming the foal."

Raphael smiled and went over to Ella and said, "I think we should call him Brownie. What do you say, Ella?"

The mare licked his face and went back to her foal.

"Brownie it is then. I'll get the horse carriage and get her and Brownie to climb on it. We don't want her to exert herself. You stay here, Raphael, and look after them." Merdaine jumped on his horse and went down to the farm.

The sun was setting when Merdaine returned with a carriage. They let the mare and the foal get in, then they drove them back to the barn where they could rest. Merdaine gave instructions to have her wound looked after and went home for supper.

"Did you save the mare?" Giselle asked.

"Yes, the mare and foal are doing fine for now and with some luck they'll both survive the operation and live long happy lives."

Giselle gave her husband a big hug and kiss.

"Well, supper is ready. Let's eat."

Raphael had not realized how hungry he was. The day had gone by so fast. Maybe his father was right, he would be too busy for the hours to drag. After supper, he helped Giselle clean the kitchen under the approving eye of Merdaine and finally got to meet Elaine. She was not so bad, but she was taller than he thought she would be. He wished she had been a few years older, not just a baby.

Raphael went to sleep. Unbeknown to him, Aznebar was keeping a watchful eye on him.

Atleos couldn't sleep and went to the kitchen for a glass of milk. On his trip there, he overheard a conversation between Giselle and Merdaine who were standing by the fire.

"He was asking for a Healer. I told him to talk to you," Giselle was saying.

"He's not just looking for a Healer, he's looking for Kaplara herself."

"Kaplara? But no one knows where Kaplara is. She went into hiding."

"Some people know, and if he is instructed by Amos, he might be able to find some trace of her."

"But he's really hurt, his legs were badly burnt. You can see the scarring beginning to form," Giselle fretted.

"Yes, the burns are there, but he could still be a spy. Tamael and Amos did not entrust him with the knowledge of a warrior. They simply said he had a mission and Ohuru got him from the Elder. He's young. He could be from the imperial guard. He could be trying to infiltrate us."

"Don't you think the elders would have sensed a spy?" she questioned.

"If the elders were that good to start off with, they wouldn't have been forced into exile and most of the fairies would still be alive. After twelve thousand years, everyone is starting to have a little bit of their blood mixed up. If the elders knew what happened, they would have found a cure by now. If the elders …"

"How long have you been there, Atleos?"

Atleos bit his lip. How she felt his presence he did not know, but now he had to come up with answers he didn't want to give.

"Not long, I was just coming to get a glass of milk and ..." she began.

"And you spied on us!" Merdaine was getting angry, and he didn't look like a man you wanted to have angry at you.

"No, no, really, I just heard you talk about Kaplara and I was hoping..."

"You were spying on us!" Merdaine walked towards Atleos and grabbed him by the neck and brought him close to the fire.

"You tell your secrets!" Merdaine lifted Atleos up in the air and brought Atleos' head against his. *Now!*

Merdaine saw, like a movie, that Atleos had been raised on the far away moon by an old man. Atleos never knew his real father. He had been adopted. Raised in the ancient ways, he had joined the resistance. On the insistence of the old man, the elders had given him the training of a guard and recently assigned him a mission.

That's all you need to know, Atleos assured him.

I want all the truth, Merdaine was insistent.

I'm afraid you'd have to kill me first. I cannot reveal anymore other than part of my mission is to locate Kaplara and give her something.

I can make you tell me, boy, threatened Merdaine.

No, I wouldn't let you. So far you saw what I wanted you to see. I have nothing to hide about my past, but my mission is mine alone to bear.

Merdaine tried to get the information but only saw a giant brick wall on top of which sat Atleos.

You cannot force the wall, or I'll fall, and if I fall, I die. I have been trained in the arts just as well as you, Merdainesar of the order of Kanilan.

Merdaine growled, *Insolent. You have been trained well. What will you do with your knowledge?*

I will keep it a secret. I was entrusted to Ohuru for my mission and I already accepted the fact that anyone associating with him must have a part to play in the resistance. I do not know what yours is, and I will not look to find out. I will keep your secret safe with me. I swear upon my death.

Your death will not be necessary, but you must leave when Ohuru arrives.

It shall be done.

Who told you that Kaplara was on Essay? demanded Merdaine.

Ohuru had heard the rumor of her being here some years ago.

Very well, you must learn to be more careful of the questions you ask and who is around hearing the answer, Atleos. You have put my family in danger.

I'm sorry, I never meant to.

Let Ohuru guide you and you might find Kaplara through him. We shall speak no more of this.

Merdaine let go of Atleos. As Atleos gasped for breath, Merdaine turned to Giselle. "He seems to be true."

"He shall live then?" she asked nervously.

"For now...."

Atleos looked up and could not believe Merdaine still doubted him. Frankly, Atleos was happy to be touching the ground again. He got up and decided he would fall asleep without milk tonight, and went back to his room.

On his way out, he heard Merdaine say to his wife, "And tomorrow, they all get up at five o'clock."

Five o'clock came quickly. Merdaine and Giselle woke up with the rooster singing his praise to the sun. Giselle decided that it would be best if Merdaine took care to wake their guests up while she went and prepared breakfast. Merdaine had little patience for this sort of thing. He walked into the room where Atleos was staying and pulled the covers off of Atleos.

Merdaine grabbed him by the leg, "Get up, lazy head. Breakfast is served."

Atleos, still trying to catch his breath, managed to answer. "Yes, sir."

Merdaine dropped him on the bed and walked out. Atleos realized he shouldn't have pried into Merdaine's thoughts. He realized now that Merdaine was right to fear him. If Atleos was ever discovered, he put everyone he knew at risk. He regretted his foolish action of the night before, but it was too late. From now on, he would to remember to never again call Merdaine by his true name.

Merdaine walked towards Raphael's room and knocked on the door. No answer came. He walked in, lifted the blind, and sat on the edge of the bed.

"Time to wake up, little man," Merdaine shook Raphael gently.

Raphael groaned, "All right, I'm awake."

Merdaine laughed. Raphael was working so hard to please, and yet he was going to have to learn to go to bed early if he wanted to survive the week.

"I have an important task for you," said Merdaine.

"What is it?" Raphael asked curiously.

"My men worked all night watching the mare and the foal. Now I shall teach you what you need to do and leave you to it."

"Really?" Raphael said excitedly.

"Yes, you brought him into this world, you look after him. The mare will need her rest. It will be up to you to keep him busy."

"Oh, this is so great! Do I have time to meditate? My pa said I had to keep on meditating while I was here."

"Of course, I'll give you half an hour and then you'll have to come down to eat breakfast. How does that sound?"

"Very fair."

Merdaine patted his head and left the room. Raphael got into position right away and he did well. He was no longer worried and he didn't miss his family as much. There, in the shadows, he saw Aznebar. Raphael extended his hand and welcomed his grandfather in his circle of light.

I must give you a message that came from your mother while you were asleep last night, Aznebar said.

Ok.

Your sister has been trapped in a cave and your mother needs help from your father to get her out.

Questions streamed from Raphael's mind, *Oh no! Tinay is trapped? Is she hurt? Is she going to live?*

Your mother only said she needed help to get her out. It seems that Tinay is all right. You must give the message to your father.

But my father is gone for another two days, not including today. I have no way of reaching him.

It will have to wait. Who else could help you?

Merdaine, maybe.

Ask him when you are alone with him.

Very well.

Now go and get ready for breakfast. That's enough for today.

Raphael came down the stairs and walked slowly to the table. He ate little because he was worried about his sister. He loved her so much, and now she was in danger and he couldn't help.

"I think you better eat well, Raphael. A long day is ahead of you," Giselle warned.

"I'm not hungry, Madame Giselle, but the pancakes are delicious."

"What do you have in store for me, Merdaine?" asked Atleos.

"You, Atleos, will be weeding the garden and the herb patch. Beware not to pull anything worthwhile. My wife spent hours preparing this."

"Of course." Atleos bowed his head.

"It will be a long and hard day for you, Atleos, but I shall help you." said Giselle.

"You will do nothing of the sort," Merdaine banged the table with his fist. "He must earn his keep. You'll be busy enough with the cooking and the cleaning in here."

Giselle bowed to her husband and knew that the weeding was more of a punishment than a chore. Whatever had happened between Atleos and Merdaine the night before had kept Merdaine from sleeping as well as he usually did.

After breakfast, Raphael walked to the barn with Merdaine and took the opportunity to ask for his help, "I spoke to Aznebar this morning."

"Who?" Merdaine was puzzled. No one had arrived at the planet lately.

"Aznebar, a friend of my family."

"And where was this Aznebar?"

"In my meditation."

"In your..." Merdaine was amazed at how well trained Raphael was; to receive a visitor in his meditation meant he had reached a high level of meditation.

"Can you tell me when you reached the third eye?" Merdaine needed to know.

"The what?"

"The sixth temple."

"Oh no, I've only just mastered the sun in the plexus. Aznebar is helping and..."

"Who is Aznebar?"

"A protector of sorts. Ma said he was all right."

"Okay then, and what message did Aznebar have for you?"

"My father must return to Sasgorg to help my sister out of a cave." Raphael said all in one breath, but the words hurt him.

"Your sister? That's troublesome, but I cannot reach your father until he gets back. I'm sorry, little man."

"Aznebar said she isn't hurt but Mother can't get her out. I'm worried for her."

"There are many ways your mother could have contacted your father. She did it the safest way, which means it wasn't that urgent. When your father gets home, we'll give him the message. Everything will be fine. Don't worry, little man. Let's go see that foal of yours, what do you say?"

"Hmm hmm." Raphael was not completely convinced that what Merdaine said was true, but he couldn't worry about it for three days either. He had work to do. He rolled up his sleeves and followed Merdaine into the barn.

Chapter 10

THE TOURNAMENT

The flight plan for El was simple. Once Ohuru avoided the black hole, he was on a straight line to El. It was an isolated system with plenty of moons. The planet El was not a beautiful planet by any means. It was just a series of mine shafts and deep caves. Everything that could be excavated was. There were a few colonies dispersed on the planet, but most of the miners had moved on to distant star systems and pursued their careers there. El was grassy with a few trees. No real mountains populated El, mostly just hills and lakes. It was a quiet planet with very little traffic except once every two years when the miners got together and reunited under a single banner to celebrate their craft.

Tamael knew that Ohuru was taking him there because it was part of the deception, but he had no interest in joining anyone for a celebration. He wanted to sell his metal blocks and leave. He knew nobody there and wasn't planning on making friends. He missed his wife and wondered how she was doing on Sasgorg with the baby so close to arrival. The good thing was that Tinay was there and helping. Lilay wouldn't exhaust herself.

Ohuru let Tamael drive during the evening while he took a nap. The reunion was the best time to sell the metal. There would be plenty of miners interested in their mixture. The new form of metal Ohuru had created was greatly appreciated among the other miners. Amos' advice to find the one thing everybody wanted and that would never get out of date was taken seriously by Ohuru. Creating this metal that had been radiated for five years by the Alenor crystal made it strong, light, and easily malleable.

It took thirty-six hours to get to El and, on the morning of their eighth day of travel, they finally arrived. Ohuru was glad that he was there and was going to get some rest. Even though his idea was the one being sold, he was going to sleep while Tamael arrived at a decent deal. Amos had helped them, too. After all, it was his area of expertise. Ohuru wanted to be rested for his surprise for Tamael. He headed for his quarters and met Tamael on the way out.

"My friend, she's all yours. I think you should leave us in orbit and take the barge down with the bars. They're all stored in there already," Ohuru patted Tamael on the shoulder.

"Great idea. You're not coming?"

"No, I trust you'll do great even without me. Just remember what Amos taught you and make me smile when you get back here."

"It's a deal," Tamael shook Ohuru's hand.

Tamael walked to the cargo bay and embarked aboard the shuttle. He didn't like to fly and preferred that Ohuru take care of that aspect of the job. He had made good contacts the last time he was there, ten years ago. He was hoping to meet some of his old contacts there. Not that he could easily remember their names, but he knew one thing, their occupation as miners would have them interested in his product.

He landed near the front entrance and got out to reserve a space for his ship.

"I need a table space big enough to park the barge. What do you have?" Tamael asked the port assistant.

"Nothing. Everything has been sold out for months. Are you new here?" the man asked.

"I've been here twice, but my friend always manages to get us a space for our material."

"Well, maybe your friend did. What's his name?"

"Ohuru from the Armada," Tamael replied.

"Ohuru, of course. I've been wondering when he would get here. You were expected yesterday."

"I'm sorry, we've been delayed."

"Sorry won't do, I'm afraid. I kept the spot because it was Ohuru and he always paid well, so it'll be a hundred and fifty roublons a night."

"Oh, sure. How much is that in gold leaves?"

"Twenty five a night. Ohuru only reserved it for two days."

"That's all we'll need then. Here you go." Tamael handed him a hundred gold leaves and waited for his change. The cashier handed him a hundred and fifty roublons back.

"Here you go. There's your location on the map. Arrive from the north so as not to disturb everyone. Some people have been asking for you. Hopefully they're still around."

"Who would leave before the celebration tonight?"

"Hmm, maybe lucky for you then. Next!"

Tamael walked away with his map and went to the north to set up. He made a large arc and settled down at his site. It was easy to spot where he was to park. There was little room elsewhere, and his spot was guarded by rope. He slowly landed the ship backwards and popped open the back door. Ohuru had prepared a banner to hang on the door lift and Tamael was busy trying to hang it up when he heard some noise behind him. He looked over his shoulder and saw three people lining up.

"Can I help you?" he asked a slim young miner wearing dark blue overalls, who was covered in dirt from head to toe.

"My father has been waiting for you to pull up since last night. He wanted me to get in line while he got his money ready."

"Yeah, well I was here first, so I want to see your best mixture," demanded a fat muscular man. He was short, but appeared to be as strong as an ox. Tamael remembered him from a previous visit. His name was Anaël.

"There's plenty to go around. Just let me hang this up and I'll be right with you," assured Tamael. The man scoffed at him impatiently.

Tamael brought forth three blocks and let the customers examine them. He went back inside to get a table and set it up by the edge of his parcel of land while five more people arrived. It had never been very busy before, but then again, they had never been this late either.

"I am ready to bargain," said a tall skinny man.

"Just a moment, I'll get my cash float." Tamael ran back inside and when he returned, he found seven more people waiting to see what he had to offer. "Wow!" he said, amazed by the reputation Ohuru had build up over the years.

"Is this the shipment for the arcanium?" asked the man, using the name that Ohuru had given the metal, a name from the book of fables, Arcanium.

"Yes it is," answered Tamael.

"Can I see a sample?"

"Just a moment. Let me finish with these people. They were here first. Now, sir, it's a hundred gold leaf per blocks," Tamael said, turning towards Anaël, the short man.

"I'll give you fifty," Anaël said.

"I'm afraid, it's a hundred or nothing. There's a large demand and it takes us five years to produce them. We can't give them away. We have families to feed," argued Tamael.

"Hmm, that's no way to barter, young man!" Anaël exclaimed.

"Very well, you want to barter? The price is a hundred and twenty five. Now, what's your offer?"

"Don't make fun of me!" protested the man. "I am Anaël, a Master miner and a Master smith!"

"I'm not making fun of you. Just look behind you, there are already twenty people waiting to buy some of this and they'll gladly pay the hundred gold leaves I'm asking for. Now, sir, do you want it or not?" Tamael was getting exasperated.

"What if I buy more than one?"

"Same deal as usual. You buy ten, and get one free."

"Ah, that's more like it," Anaël said with a satisfied smile. "Give me fifty."

"Fif... sure, right away. Where should I put them, sir?"

"Here's my son coming over with the lift. We'll just stack them up on there."

"Alright, fifty-five arcanium blocks for five thousand gold leafs."

It only took a few hours before Tamael's stock was mostly depleted. He went inside and put most of the gold leaves inside the safe. His barge looked empty. A girl approached the table where he had placed a few samples.

"Can I help you, miss?" he asked.

"Yes, is it only gold leaf you take?"

"Yes, we travel everywhere and we cannot afford to have only roublons," he explained.

"Could I pay you with roublons, sir?"

"Hmm, how many did you wish to acquire?"

"Three."

"That would be a lot of roublons, eighteen hundred, in fact. Do you have that much?"

"No deals here?" she smiled.

"No, same price for everyone. But if you buy ten you do get one free."

"No, no, too many. I have roublons here, but nothing else. Still no deals?"

Tamael looked back and decided that the faster he was out of here, the faster he could get some rest. He only had one hundred and twenty-five more to sell, so he decided Ohuru could do with more roublons.

"Fine, but don't tell anyone I accepted roublons or else no one will pay me in gold leaf ever again."

The young girl giggled, "My father was right when he said you always had a soft spot for young women and that I would get a better deal if I came alone."

"Who are you?"

"I am Isabella, the daughter of Margos."

Tamael's face broke into a grin, "Isabella, is that you? Wow, you've grown so much!" He hugged her.

"It's been ten years. My father has a letter for Ohuru. Could you pass it on?" She handed him a small envelope.

"Of course. Will I see the old man before we go?"

"He hopes to see you tonight." Isabella bowed and left.

Tamael noticed how graceful she was. A big difference from the tomboy he remembered. He was hoping to sell his merchandise quickly to bring the good news to Ohuru. They were all good friends. It would be nice to see a friend after being isolated for so long. Tamael was getting the feeling Ohuru had this planned all along. It took Tamael another three hours to liquidate all of his stock.

He got into the barge and called Ohuru over the intercom that linked the barge to the ship. Ohuru was ready and waiting.

"Slept well?" Tamael asked.

"Yes, it was very welcome. Just lock up the barge and I'll pick you up at the end of the south field in the parking lot. I've been dying to try my new shuttle."

"Why not take the barge?"

"I want people to think that we are still on the ground visiting and shopping. Just put the sign 'out of stock' on the wall and then meet me at the lot."

"We're not going to shop at all?" Tamael said sarcastically.

Ohuru laughed, "Don't worry, you're not missing anything. We have a date."

"Yeah, your surprise is ruined," chuckled Tamael.

"What?" sputtered Ohuru.

"Isabella came to the counter today and told me we're meeting her and her father tonight. Sorry."

"Oh well, I guess at least you're happy about it, right?"

"Yes," Tamael assured him. "She also left a letter for you."

"Ah! Good, good. I was wondering about that. Meet you in twenty minutes?"

"Yeah, it'll give me a chance to look around."

Tamael bought some food and trinkets for souvenirs to give to his wife, daughter, and son. And something special for the new baby. He met Ohuru in the lot and jumped in the empty seat next to him.

"Pretty cozy little thing," commented Tamael.

"Yeah. It's made to travel fast, light and in tight spaces."

"Ok. But it's old. Where did you get it?"

"Actually, my friend, it's brand new. I built it. But to avoid the new technology falling into the wrong hands, I disguised it under old stuff. Functional old stuff, but I can switch it to this," and with the touch of a button. The panels flipped 180 degrees.

Tamael looked at the buttons he had flashing in front of him. "Impressive, my friend."

"Yeah. The whole ship is build out of arcanium. Now, the letter, please, my good sir." Ohuru extended his hand and waited for Tamael to hand it out.

Tamael reached into his pocket, then started to pat down all his pockets, "Oh-oh!"

"What do you mean 'oh-oh'?"

"Relax, Ohuru, I was just teasing you."

"Not funny. Hurry up, I don't want to be late."

"Late for what?"

"You'll see."

The letter was a series of coordinates to enter into the computer board and the ship started its voyage into the core of El. It only took thirty minutes and they were there.

Tamael got out of the shuttle and could not believe his eyes. All of his old friends from the guard were there chatting. He had missed them so much.

"Some elders are here also, but most importantly, they prepared a tournament!" Ohuru pointed happily.

"Tournament?"

"Yeah, I entered you in the sword competition."

"Sword?" Tamael hesitated. "I don't have my sword."

"Ah! But you do." Ohuru dragged out a box from the shuttle. "I took the liberty."

"Hmm, maybe this would be fun. I don't think I can remember fun."

"Absolutely! Let's get you ready."

As they walked past the caves, Tamael saw that there was more than just swordsmanship being fought here. There was a knife throw, najar fights, hand-to-hand combat, and even archery. It was all here. If he had more time, he would have entered more than one competition. He had been rehearsing his arts for ages now, but only for protection and survival. This was a great treat.

He grabbed Ohuru by the shoulders and kissed him on the forehead, "Thank you, my friend."

Ohuru saw the smile on his friend's face. Ohuru had missed that smile.

They walked toward the end of the cavern and saw the council there. Tamael recognized someone he had not seen in a long time:

Lord Andemar. He ran towards the council, but before he could reach them, he tripped and landed on the ground.

Lord Andemar started to laugh, "For a master, you did poorly on the hundred meter dash, Tamael," he teased.

"My lord, always a pleasure to see you," Tamael ginned.

"Always a pleasure."

"And a little painful."

"Come. Let's eat and talk."

Tamael got up and looked around to see Ohuru walk past him, smiling.

Tamael brushed the dust from his tunic and went over to eat with Lord Andemar. They had a delicacy of seafood and fish, which was very rare on El. They didn't talk about business until after they had eaten.

"I hear you have a little financial help for the resistance, Tamael," Lord Andemar said as he looked at Tamael.

"I'll need to have a little of it. Whatever my lord can spare, and then I'll return to Sasgorg and get my wife a decent house."

"Indeed, your sacrifice for the resistance is well noted. I will leave you with seventy-five thousand. Enough for you to get by, I hope." Lord Andemar smiled.

Tamael was speechless, "Seventy five thou...that's much too much, my lord."

"No, I insist. We'll leave Ohuru with the same. Amos is donating his share to the resistance, stating his position had been so lucrative over the past twenty years that he is not in need. So I'm splitting his share between you and Ohuru. Actually, I'll split it up as soon as you give it to me. You do have the gold leaves that the 'pirates' stole?"

"Of course, my lord," Said Tamael with a grin.

"I'll take care of that, my lord," Ohuru interrupted. "I was hoping Tamael could enter the sword competition and see if he still has it."

"That promises to be interesting. Do you still possess the dexterity and strength, Tamael?" challenged Lord Andemar.

"We shall see, my lord, we shall see."

"Have you seen Okapi yet?"

"No, I have not. Is he here?" Tamael hoped that he was.

"Yes, I always travel with him by my side. He's the best guardian around. Couldn't ask for better."

Tamael shook his head, "I'm afraid there's no time. The competition is about to begin and I want to watch some knife throwing before we get there. Maybe later at the reception?"

"At the reception Margos has asked for you to be seated at his side. What do you say, Tamael?"

He was pleased, "I can't wait to see Margos."

"It's set then. We'll see you tonight and maybe you can cross paths with Master Okapi later."

"Yes, my lord," Tamael said as he and Ohuru got up to leave.

Tamael and Ohuru bowed down and left for the knife-throwing arena.

A lot of young men were out to prove themselves. Tamael wondered why Ohuru had entered him in the sword and not the knife-throwing contest.

"It's simple," Ohuru explained. "You're the best with knives. It's no fun. Swords could get interesting. There you have an opponent that is unpredictable. More interesting."

"In other words, I'm your guinea pig," Tamael laughed.

"No, but you are an experiment in motion," Ohuru laughed.

The knife-throwers were all good. They had to hit different targets in sequence within a time limit. Many were excellent, but no one struck Tamael as particularly exceptional.

"You're right, I would have beaten them hands down," Tamael decided.

"Let's get you warmed up. Might even end up with a trophy," said Ohuru good-naturedly.

"Might?" Tamael raised his eyebrows.

"Don't be too full of yourself. There are a lot of young lads here. You're getting up there."

"I'm only forty-seven, and in the full force of my means."

"We'll see."

They walked over to the arena. Tamael took off his tunic but kept his pants on. He had seven tattoos over his back. The biggest was of a unicorn swimming out of a mist that was in the center of his back. He started to warm up and stretch while Ohuru polished Tamael's sword.

"How many opponents am I to face?" Tamael asked.

"Well, assuming you make it to the final, just five. They have not changed the rules since the last time you did this. First draw of blood," Ohuru assured him.

"Very well. I don't intend on adding any scars to my body today."

Tamael approached the ring and prepared himself. His opponent was much younger than he and full of prowess. Tamael was never much of a showman. He went straight for his opponent and carved a half moon on his opponent's shoulder as he spun with his sword above his head. The sound of a whistle was heard and Tamael walked back to Ohuru.

"You could have made it interesting," Ohuru pouted.

"Nope. In real life there's no room for flowers and show-offs. You have to nip them in the bud."

They waited for the first heats to be finished and for his turn to come up again. Lord Andemar was now seated and watching the performance. When Tamael looked at him, Lord Andemar gave him a wink. Tamael was ready to defeat anyone, but if there was one man he would not take on, it was Lord Andemar. He was past a hundred and, yet, Tamael feared the man if he had a sword in his hand.

Tamael was not impressed with the men he had to fight for the next two rounds. He defeated them easily. But Issar proved to be more challenging when Tamael arrived at the semi-finals.

Issar was a tall man, ten years younger than Tamael, who had done away with the showmanship and proved to be a better opponent.

While Tamael blocked his opponent, he looked for a weak spot. Issar was well trained. They shuffled inside the arena, and a crowd gathered around to watch. Tamael was stuck in the defensive mode and needed to change his position, so he decided to resort to a more eccentric maneuver. He jumped, flipped through the air, cut Issar on the shoulder blade, and landed behind him teetering on the line of the arena. Issar had succeeded in cutting Tamael's pants but never made it to the skin. For Tamael, this meant that he was moving to the finals and would most likely face a challenging opponent, but he could not believe his eyes when Margos walked towards the arena.

"I guess it's between you and me. Maybe this time I can beat you," said Margos, his cousin.

"I know my opponent well. It is a disadvantage for you, but I also know how good you are. This will not be easy."

"I don't intend to make it that way," Margos said, grinning. "Looks like you're out of practice."

Tamael followed Margos' gaze to the cut in his own pants. Tamael had no time to reply as the referee was already calling them to the center of the arena.

"Ready your places, gentlemen," the referee said as he entered the center arena. "Fair play and honor is expected. You must stay inside the ring. To the first cut."

"To the first cut," said both Tamael and Margos as they bowed to the referee.

They turned to Lord Andemar who was now sitting on the edge of his seat, eager to see this fight.

"Ohuru, who do you think will win this one?" asked Okapi.

"I don't know, Master Okapi, but if Tamael sees you here, he might get nervous."

"Then I shall retire. I wouldn't want to be blamed for his loss."

"No one will believe their eyes, that's for sure."

Tamael started to circle the arena, wondering what his cousin was planning, "How long have you two planned this?"

"When Ohuru picked up Atleos, he informed me you would be coming here. I informed him we would have a tournament with a meeting of the council. He proposed we fight again."

"Well, I have missed our training sessions. Ready?" Tamael was excited.

"Ready."

Tamael approached the center of the ring and the battle started. It was a clash of strength and energy. Every part of their bodies was used for balance and fighting. It looked like they were dancing a well choreographed ballet. Their agility and accuracy were amazing. Margos succeeded in entering Tamael's defense, but was pushed away. Tamael rolled on the ground and brought his sword within a millimeter from Margos's calves. The fight was one of endurance and required quick movement and energy. Margos jumped in the air and brought his sword down on Tamael and cut a chunk of his hair. The fight was harsh, and Tamael didn't appreciate getting his hair cut off. He backed away from Margos and calculated what maneuver would most likely land him a victory. The hard thing about these combats was to control one's sword to only cut slightly and not harm or kill the opponent. After all, they were friends. He realized that although his cousin knew him well, he did not know his newer moves. Tamael jumped. Margos, thinking he was bold enough to try the same move as before, aimed high, but Tamael pirouetted at waist height and cut Margos on the stomach, a slight cut that barely shed a tear of blood. Tamael landed on the ground, but he knew he had won.

He got up and saw Margos wipe his stomach. Yes, he had been cut but this one would not leave a scar.

"Well, it looks like you got me again," Margos admitted.

"Yes, it would look like it indeed."

Margos shook Tamael's hand and said, "Congratulation, Master. Once again you'll bring a trophy home."

Tamael wiped the sweat from his brow, "My last trophies were melted. I'm afraid this one deserves the same fate."

"Not likely. It's a beautiful tapestry for the new house. You'll love it."

"Nice, very nice."

Tamael and Margos embraced each other and left the arena.

"Ohuru, I'm all sweaty now. Anywhere I can clean up and change?"

"Yes, Master, right over there. I have a change of clothes in the shuttle for you. I'll get it."

"Margos, I'll clean up and see you at supper tonight."

"I'll be waiting."

Ohuru hurried to the shuttle and brought back a change of clothes for both Tamael and himself. Then they headed for the showers.

Chapter 11

THE CELEBRATION

The ceremony was warmed by the large fire pits. The cave was lit by the fires and candles on the tables. With plenty of food for everyone, meats were roasting on the fire, and salads and fruits were set on the tables. There were hundreds of guests seated all over the cave. Laughter and lively conversation filled the air. It was a rare gathering of the old guard. Paletis would have killed to know this information. She was bent on killing any remnants of the old Order. In order for her to obtain supremacy, she needed to change twelve thousand years of tradition -- not easily done. She had succeeded in over-throwing the fairies and in poisoning most of the Meji, but some survived. No matter what she tried, some always managed to survive. Paletis had visions, but they were often obscure and dark. She could have guessed there would be a reunion, but without some informants to explain her vision, the old guard was safe for one more night.

Tamael walked towards the entrance. He was dressed in the original green cape of the old guard. He had a white shirt with large sleeves tucked into leather bands around his wrists. He had a green vest, hand-sewn with silk trimming and decorations of three-dimensional mystical beasts, a dragon, a phoenix, a unicorn, a winged stallion, a golden dolphin, a gryphon, and a cockatrice. He wore a large black silk belt, and green pants that hung loosely over his leather boots. Tamael had not worn his uniform since the overthrow of the Meji Order. He couldn't believe it still fit him. He was proud to once more wear his family colors and honor his ancestors. The hostess bowed to him and asked for his name.

"I'm to be seated with Margos," he replied.

"Very well. I still need your name, sir."

"Tamael."

"Right this way."

"Oh. I'm waiting for a friend to join me."

"He is. . .?" her voice trailed off.

"Ohuru."

"He's already been seated."

"Very well, then." Tamael followed the young girl through the alley and recognized a number of faces: Ilsimar, Elliot, Merlot, Cretion, Cartel, and Mineus. All were too busy to recognize him. Tamael wondered if his face had changed that much.

She showed him to his seat, "There you are, sir, your table."

"Thank you."

"Welcome, my friend. You look splendid," said Ohuru.

"Thanks to Ohuru. Where did you get that?"

"Lord Andemar asks that you wear the traditional outfit while you're here. You'll have to change before we go," said Ohuru.

"Well, it's nice to be wearing it again. It brings back fond memories. I wish Lilay could see it."

"Well, she'll have to wait a little longer," said Margos. "Eat my friend. Tonight is a celebration."

"Have there been many reunions like this?" Tamael asked.

"Once a year, when we are to take on a new apprentice, free one from his mentor, or issue guarding duty," replied Margos.

Tamael was surprised, "I was never invited to any."

"Because you didn't have an apprentice to take or release and you already have your duties assigned to you," said Margos.

"It still would have been nice to see some of you," Tamael said.

Margos smiled, "You were isolated for a reason. That's the way it had to be, but Lord Andemar was happy to know you would be coming to El just in time for this reunion. That way it doesn't look suspicious for you to travel here."

"Thank you, Margos, for allowing us to sit at your table," Tamael said gratefully.

"I've missed you too, cousin. I'm glad to have you here."

"How's the cut?"

Margos' hand went immediately to the scrape, "You nearly missed, or your skills have grown immensely since we last saw each other. Which one is it?"

"I don't know." Tamael was used to being evasive. He found it hard to be completely open with his cousin, "I have seen improvement on your side of the sword. You did well."

"Thank you."

"And now, for the prizes, Lord Andemar will issue to the winners of each category," announced the Master of Ceremonies.

There were no women seated at the table of honor. In order to deflect the power of Paletis they had separated the elders from their loved one to make it easier for them to hide. If solitude weighed heavily on Tamael, at least he still had his wife to go home to. He looked up as Andemar stood up and walked to the left of the head table.

"For the best hand-to-hand defense combat, the beautiful ore sculpture goes to Ilsimar."

There was a standing ovation. Ilismar's strength was as well known to the Order as the oak which stays in the ground. He walked over and accepted the statue of a sphinx.

"For the best najar manipulation and demonstration, this amazing tapa of a centaur goes to Merlot."

The crowd cheered. Merlot was a hero to most of the young men present. The more renowned the competitors had been in their past, the more secluded they had been. It was a luxury to see so many masters present for this competition. Merlot was an agile man that could bend as easily as the wheat in the field under the wind. He had shown that he had remained alert and flexible through the years.

"For the most accurate aim with the bow, the beautiful painting of the mermaid goes to Mineus."

The crowd was wild. Mineus was younger than Ilsimar and Merlot, but he had proven today that he was a master of his art. Tamael wondered how he would have fared if Merdaine had competed. Mineus was a strong athlete, muscular and ambidextrous, and made a wonderful archer.

"For the swords competition, where a drop of blood must be drawn from the opponent in order to advance in the competition, but where an injury or death disqualifies you, the winner of this tapestry depicting a satyr goes to Tamael."

Tamael expected some hands clapping, but instead everyone stared at him. He did not know what to do. He had won fair and square, why was the crowd so unrewarding? Margos stood up and shook his hand.

"Your visit here is a surprise to many. Not a lot of people have actually recognized you today. They are simply in shock to see you here," Margos reassured him.

"Why?"

"Because the time is pressing and everyone is preparing the resistance to attack. No one really expected you to leave your hiding spot until the moment of attack."

"Maybe they are right. It might not have been wise to extend my trip," doubt flooded back to Tamael.

"Take no notice. It was good to see you fare so well."

Ilsimar walked over to him and embraced him, "Margos is right, my friend. I had heard the rumor of a Tamael winning at the swords. Now that I see it was you, I'm disappointed that I missed the match. It's good to see you, old friend."

Behind Ilsimar was a line of his friends gathering to shake his hand and hold him tight to their chests. They were there, happy to see him: Elliot, Merlot, Cretion, Cartel and Mineus.

"Ahem! The tapestry?" Lord Andemar was still standing at the podium with the prize.

"Ohh!" Tamael started to run towards the podium.

"Make sure you don't run into me, now," joked Lord Andemar.

The comment broke the spell the crowd had been under and they all started to laugh and applaud their champion.

"It's beautiful. Thank you." Tamael took his prize and went back to his seat.

"And now, for the first time in our tournament, a surprise contestant has won the knife throw. For the winner of agility and aim, I call Isabella."

The girls in the crowd went wild, but the masters, although applauding, weren't so sure this was a great idea.

Tamael was shocked. Never before had a woman been allowed to enter the tournament. He watched as Isabella got up and went to get her prize.

"Here you are, Isabella, it's a music box made out of wood." Lord Andemar presented her with her gift.

"Thank you," she said and opened the box. A woman with the body of a serpent played a soft melody on a lyre as Isabella reached her seat.

"Margos, what is the meaning of this?" asked Tamael.

"Paletis is counting on us to remain true to tradition, but by doing so we're telling her what we are doing. A few of us have trained our daughters to become guards and infiltrate the palace. When the resistance is ready to attack, we'll have informants and soldiers already in place. We have innovated a little on the old principle," Margos replied.

"But is your daughter willing to give up the hope of children?"

"The prophecy states there are only a few more years before the future is set. She'll play her position until then and if evil wins, she is better not to bring children into the world. If good triumphs, there will be time for her to become a mother yet."

"It's a hard sacrifice to make, Margos."

"We all make sacrifices, Tamael. To each of us, the price to pay is enormous, but liberty and freedom are worth the cost."

"As you say, my friend, as you say."

"And now," Lord Andemar took over the assembly, "let's begin the festivities."

Musicians began to play and people got up to dance. Tamael needed to see that there was still good in the world.

Margos looked at him and smiled, "I have one more surprise for you, my friend."

"Really? And what would that be?"

"A guitar."

"No way! Where did you get this?" Tamael was shocked.

"You'll have to thank Lord Andemar. He wanted to hear you play tonight."

"I haven't practiced in years. I can't go and play for him."

"He wants you to play for all of us."

"You have got to be kidding."

"No, I'm serious, my friend. See, he's waving at you." Margos pointed.

Tamael looked up and saw Lord Andemar standing by his chair, calling him forward.

Tamael walked up to him with guitar in hand, trying desperately to remember what he used to play.

"I'm afraid, young man, that I've put you on the spot," Lord Andemar apologized.

"My Lord, it's been so long..."

"Yes, it has, but now you will need things to keep you busy in your new home."

"Well, I figured the baby..." Tamael's voice trailed off.

"Ah! Yes, the baby will distract you somewhat, but you'll need time to brush up on some skills. Have you figured out a way to practice your training away from prying eyes?"

"No, my lord but…"

"Well, then, you could go and practice your guitar and bring a few knives and a sword with you, couldn't you?" Lord Andemar suggested.

"I guess so, now that you mention it."

"I won't ask you to play tonight, but dance, my friend, and enjoy."

"Thank you, my lord." Tamael bowed to him and walked back to his chair.

He was playing a few notes when a breathless Isabella came over to him.

"Let's dance!" she panted.

"I'm not that good without my wife."

"Oh, please! My father tells me if you had entered the knives competition I wouldn't have won so easily."

"But he still thinks you would have won?"

"Yes, I'm good, you know."

"It would seem so. I'll join you later," he promised.

"But later there will be dancers and a play. We won't be able to dance," she pouted.

"Very well, young lady, let's dance." Tamael deposited his guitar by his chair.

As they walked over to the dance floor, gay music was being played. Tamael knew the moves, but his heart was not in it. Isabella was a fine dancer, but dancing made him miss his wife very much. A young man came over and asked to take over. Tamael acted as if he wanted to continue, but gave way to the boy. He walked back to his table and sat down. The faces around him were smiling and happy. It was hard to believe how repressed the people of the Order had been and for so long. But they had managed to survive and were still able to smile and have a good time. Paletis, in her quest for supremacy, had destroyed the very heart of what the order had stood for: peace. But she had not killed hope.

There would be no peace until Paletis was destroyed. Tamael knew that better than anyone now. His family deserved better than to live on a planet made of ashes and sand. His baby deserved to smile and learn where she was from and to honor her ancestors. His son should not have to be separated from his parents. It was unfair that in order to survive they had to be separated in such a fashion.

He looked at the time. It was ten o'clock at night and the dancers were just entering the stage. The festivities would, no doubt, continue late into the night. Tamael wanted to return home. He had not planned to be away for more than seven days and now he would not get home until thirteen had gone by. He wanted to go home.

He walked over to where Ohuru was standing and asked him, "My friend, are you enjoying yourself?"

Tamael hoped that Ohuru would understand that he wanted to leave early, but he was mistaken.

"I'm having fun, Tamael. This is a great reunion. Look at those dancers. I'm starting to regret never having a wife. Do you think that I still have what it takes?"

"My friend, you are still young and these are hard times. There's still a chance for you to meet the right woman."

"I hope so. Margos says that there's a widow on Falafel that I should take the time to get to know."

"So what's stopping you?"

"She has six kids…"

"I see. Not an ideal honeymoon, but since you can't have any, it's not like you'll end up with many more."

"Maybe not, but I got used to the idea of not having children, so I'll need time to get used to the idea of six."

"Maybe so, but if you wait too long, you might find someone else is going to take the widow away from you."

"Margos described her as pleasurable, funny, and beautiful."

"Well, after you're done here, you should take a trip down to Falafel and have a good look," Tamael offered. "See if she is as beautiful as they say."

"Um, maybe, but there are plenty of beautiful women for me to look at right here."

"Have you seen who is Master Andemar's protector?" Tamael asked.

"It's Master Okapi."

"Okapi is here? Where is he?"

"I don't know now. I saw him retire. I think he was tired."

"That's too bad. I would have loved to talk to him." Tamael turned his attention back to the dancers.

The dancers were vivacious and agile. Their dresses floated in the wind and the colorful outfits could have competed with the rainbow. The music was light and happy. Tamael decided to stay and enjoy the show. Ohuru was lonelier than he would ever be. It felt unfair to pull him away from something he enjoyed so much.

After the dancers were done, Tamael and Ohuru regained their seats. The play was about to start.

It was an old legend of a half-human, half-beast. The Atlantis scientists had developed slaves with super strength by enhancing their DNA with that of animals. They had made different beasts, such as a sphinx that had the body of a lion and the head of a human, a centaur, that had the body of a horse and instead of the horse's head was a human upper torso and head. There was also the mermaid who had the head and torso of a human and the tail of a fish, the Harpy which had the body of a bird and the head of a human. The Satyr had two goat legs and the torso and head of a human. The snake-headed Mera had the torso and head of a human but instead of legs it had a snake's body and her hair was covered with small serpents. The last they had created was the werewolf, the only one that could change from the shape of a wolf to that of a human. The play reminded the viewers that power unrestrained and led by greed and lust could amount to no good. Those beasts had existed and perished with Atlantis. Their servitude had accomplished nothing more than a decadent era for Atlantis. It marked the beginning of the end. The moral of the story was that Atlantis was lost because a number of people were lost, and that the Order could save their society if they stopped the madness from spreading.

Tamael loved the parable and was surprised to find the script had been written by children. The five children walked on the stage and received a standing ovation. Although simple, the story brought back hope that all was not lost.

The night was advancing and Tamael was tired. He found Margos and bid him farewell.

"Don't leave yet. There's more food coming," Ohuru protested.

"Tell you what, you stay as long as you want. I'll go to sleep in the shuttle and wait for you there," suggested Tamael.

"Alright, see you in the morning."

"Morning? But I want to leave in the morning."

"And we will, I'll catch some sleep before we head off. How does nine o'clock sound?"

"It's sounds all right. What time will we arrive at Essay?"

"If all goes well, we'll be there the day after tomorrow for supper."

"And then we'll make our way to Sasgorg?"

"I'll have to refuel and do a maintenance check, so we'll leave the next morning. How's that?"

"Very well."

Tamael walked back to the shuttle. The noise from the celebration echoed through the tunnels. He had his guitar back and that would be a great way to put the baby to sleep. He arrived at the shuttle and found Lord Andemar waiting for him.

"I had the liberty of having new clothes made for you. Yours looked a bit tattered," Lord Andemar said.

"Thank you, my lord, but I am just a miner now."

"Not anymore. You are the husband of an artist. You must dress accordingly. The gift comes from Manyr. She wanted to be part of the celebration."

"Manyr? Is she here?" Tamael looked around.

"No, we barely see each other anymore. A sad way to live in our old age, but I don't want her associated with anyone that could bring her down. She's away, safe from the world."

"Thank you."

"Don't thank me yet. I still have to get your uniform from you."

"Oh, yes. I forgot I was still wearing it. I felt closer to home with it on."

"Lilay did do beautiful work on the vest. It's a shame you cannot wear it more often," Lord Andemar sighed.

"She's been making new things for our move to Kyr. She wanted it to be a surprise, so I have yet to see what she has been hiding from me."

"You have a good wife. She'll provide well for you on Kyr."

"I wish she could have the life she deserves."

"I don't think she minds the life you chose. She found peace on Sasgorg. That was no easy task. You fared well, Tamael. Your father would be proud of you."

Tamael bowed and went inside to change his clothes. He found the cedar box the uniform had come in and deposited all of it carefully for Lord Andemar to take with him. He walked back outside and handed the wooden box to his lord.

"Will I ever see those again?" Tamael asked.

"Yes, in the final battle. We shall all display who we are. But the time has not come. Don't worry, it'll be safe with me." Lord Andemar handed him a coffer that contained Ohuru and Tamael's share of the gold leaf.

Lord Andemar walked away slowly and disappeared in the corridors of the cavern. Tamael walked back inside the shuttle and went to sleep on a bunk.

The sun was rising on El as Tamael was awakened by Ohuru, who had taken a shower and was on his way to take command of the shuttle.

"We're on our way to get the barge. You'll need to get up and pilot it. I thought I should give you a few minutes to wake up," Ohuru said.

"What time is it?" muttered Tamael.

"Five in the morning."

"And how much have you slept?"

"I went to bed at one this morning. I'll take a nap later on. As for you, you can go back to sleep after the barge is in the ship. I won't need you around."

"Thank you. I'm tired from all this traveling."

They took off from a new flight plan that Margos had given them. Everyone was to leave in the next half hour by different routes to avoid detection.

Tamael walked back to the barge after Ohuru had dropped him off and saw the remnants of the party that had occurred on the surface. When he got to the barge, he had to remove two men who were sleeping on the side of the barge. Tamael thought to himself, *It must have been a good party up here, too*, when he spotted the two empty bottles of wine. He shook his head. That was an invention that the ancestors should have left behind. He pushed each man outside the field and took off for the main ship anchored at the space dock. He landed without any trouble and joined Ohuru on the main deck.

"What's your flight plan?" Tamael asked.

"Straight ahead, around the black hole and straight until sunset. We're right on time."

"Actually, I told Lilay I would be back within ten days."

"I told her to expect some delays."

"I better go to bed. Wake me up when you want me to take over."

"Will do. Should be around noon. We'll eat together and I'll sleep so as to be ready for the night shift."

Tamael went to sleep and dreamed of his new home on Kyr.

It would be a quiet trip for Tamael and Ohuru until they finally reach Essay.

* * * * *

Slowly, one by one, the lights in the atrium came on. Again, Mani was done for the night. The eyes of her guests slowly adapted to the lights, returning to normal for the first time in hours. Mani wished she had more time, but six chapters were all she could do in one night. Not only would her guests be tired and fall asleep in the middle of this story but she was also getting tired herself. The children and their guardians stretched and hugged each other. Mani looked over at the table still full of baked goods. She knew her story had been entertaining if no one had gotten up to eat. They would eat now. She looked at John and Brett who were talking in the corner. She walked over to hear what they had to say.

"That was good. I liked it. There's a bit of humor hidden in there. I laughed," said Brett.

"I wonder if I would be any good at manipulating swords. What do you think, Brett?"

"I think, young apprentice, you would need much practice to master the sword," Brett spoke in a low voice, then he went back to his normal voice. "I think I want to be an archer. Bows are beautiful, slim, and flexible."

"I like the risk that goes with the sword. Can you imagine the guy that always ends up losing? He's got cuts all over his body," John chuckled.

"Might be. There weren't many contestants to start with. I would stick to bows. They're safer," Brett was adamant.

"Indeed, bows are safe," interrupted Mani, "but a good sword has no equivalent in close combat."

"I guess. But I would be wise and stay as far away as possible," said Brett, and both the boys laughed.

Mani was happy to see that she had touched the imagination of the boys. It was hard to keep both boys and girls entertained. Tinay's story had some for girls and boys, but it took time to tell it all.

She saw Marcus eating a muffin in a corner. He didn't look happy. She went over to talk to him.

"Marcus, what is it? You look disturbed," she asked worriedly.

"I'm a bit disappointed. There was hardly anything about Tinay tonight. This is the story of Tinay, is it not?" he frowned.

Mani smiled, "Why yes, but Tinay didn't become a warrior princess overnight. To understand the transformation that's going to take place, you must understand where she came from, what she did and why she makes the decision she does that starts her on her path."

"What about next week? Will we hear more about Tinay?"

"Next week, we will have four chapters on Tinay and one on her father's and brother's adventure. Is that going to be better?"

"Yes, I want to hear what happens to her," Marcus said stubbornly.

"No doubt so does everyone else in this room, but you'll see in chapter four that Tinay and her mother lived through eight days. We needed to catch up to her father and her brother for those eight days. Now that we've caught up with them, the story will be more uniform."

"Thank you, Mani. My son loves your story, but as he grows older he's becoming a bit of a critic." Marcus's mom, Andrea, was a regular customer and she was glad that her son had taken an interest in her storytelling so she had an excuse to come back and enjoy the stories of her youth all over again.

"Are there any new paintings?" she asked.

"Yes, Romanichel is new. I captured her dancing by the fire while Amos plays the guitar while they were still young." Mani pointed to the painting.

"It's beautiful. Where do you get the inspiration, Mani?" Andrea asked.

"I have those people living in my head. Sometimes I see what their past was like and why they decided to join the resistance. They, too, have been free-spirited people who loved life, and shared their joy. That's when I paint them, when the spark of life illuminates them."

"You've done well, Mani. It's a shame we cannot buy the paintings."

"They are there for everyone to see. If I start putting them in the book, what would bring people here? I have to have something more to offer."

"Just something that Amos would have suggested," grinned Andrea.

"Yes, indeed. Have a good night, Andrea and Marcus. See you next week."

Mani surveyed the room. As time went by, it always took longer for people to leave. They were making friends, talking about the story, and making plans for the following week. Mani saw Alayana on her way to put her cushion in the closet. Mani wondered if Alayana enjoyed the night.

For the first time since she had heard the story, Alayana could not see Atleos' face the way her grandmother described him. Not that she did a better job the previous time, but this time she kept seeing Jeremyah. She couldn't brush his image away from her mind. He was so handsome. She put her cushion down and turned around and bumped into a red cushion.

"Oh, I'm sorry," she said.

"My fault, I wasn't looking where I was going," said Jeremyah. "Tell me, do you work here day and night?"

"I work here from Tuesday to Saturday. I usually take Monday to read." Alayana felt relaxed talking to him. She wondered if this was because the initial shock had passed or if she was becoming accustomed to talking to him.

"So you spend your whole life with books?" Jeremyah teased.

"I don't live here. I'm from the city, but in the summer I work with my grandmother. I like it here, but I don't have many friends."

"I decided to come to live at the bed-and-breakfast here in town. My parents are busy and I needed to be away from the city for a while, but I don't know anyone here. I was wondering if you would mind showing me around." Jeremyah looked at her hopefully.

"I can certainly put my books aside this Monday and show you what there is for activities around here. If the weather permits, there's a lake in the forest that is great to swim in."

"Is it alright if I bring my dogs with me?" he grinned.

"Dogs? How many do you have?"

"Just two, Howler and Kintut."

"Funny names. They should be in one of Mani's story. What kind of dogs are they?"

"Mutts. Their dad was a Samoyed and their mother was a terrier. They turned out to be very obedient, loyal companions."

"I'm sure they run all they want around here."

"What about a job? Does your grandmother need an extra pair of hands?"

"I don't think so, but maybe you should ask her. She's right over there." Alayana pointed across the room.

"I will. See you on Monday at ten."

"Ten is fine. I live here, so just come in the store when you're ready."

"All right. Goodnight."

Jeremyah walked over to Mani hoping to find some work for the summer. Mani was talking to Lyauria when he approached them.

"Mother, I'm tired," Lyauria was saying.

"Lyauria, you're about to have a baby, I understand. Just go lay down and you can drive home tomorrow. I'll clean up with Alayana."

"Are you sure?" Lyauria furrowed her eyebrows.

"Of course I am, don't worry. Good-night." Mani kissed her daughter on the cheek and sent her to bed. Jeremyah waited nearby.

"Yes, Jeremyah, what can I do for you?" Mani finally asked.

"I was just wondering if perhaps you would be in need of a helper around here."

"I have Alayana for the summer. I'll be fine. Besides, wouldn't it be a long drive to come to work?"

"I'll be staying at the Blue Cauldron for the summer. I wanted to keep busy," Jeremyah explained.

"Well, in that case, I can phone Gerard and ask him if he wouldn't like help at the store. Nothing fancy, but he usually pays fair wages."

"What kind of store?"

"Clothing, dear."

"I have no experience…"

Mani interrupted him, "He'll teach you, if you want."

"I do. Where can I find him?"

"Here, let me write it down for you." Mani wrote on a small piece of paper the full name and contact number for Gerard. She handed the paper to Jeremyah and he left after bowing to her. She was beginning to like the young man and his manners. She just wasn't sure about the way he looked at Alayana.

By now, everyone had gone except Alayana who was beginning to clean up. Mani stood by the door to say a final goodnight to her guest and locked up behind them.

Chapter 12

THE HISTORY OF ATLANTEUS

Alayana loved Sundays because she could sleep in, but this week she didn't get to sleep in at all. She was awakened by her grandmother at six in the morning.

"Wake up, Alayana, wake up."

"What is it, Mani? What time is it?"

"Your mother. She started her contractions last night. It's time we move her to the city. She'll need to go to the hospital."

"What about me?"

"You'll come with us and help her out. She wants you to be present when the baby is born."

"What about Dad?"

"It's not like we can bring him in from his peace-keeping mission. We'll send him a video of the whole thing."

"A video?!"

"That's where you come in."

"Oh, yeurk! That's gross."

"Come on, get up and get dressed."

They took Mani's car to the city. It was four hours away and Lyauria was well advanced in her labor. The drive was smooth and Alayana was able to figure out all the buttons on the camera.

"Alayana, have you figured it out yet?"

"Yeah, do you want special effects and everything or can I just capture it and you play with it when you have time?"

"Just tape me having the baby and Dad will feel like he was there with us."

"Why did he have to go on a peace-keeping mission anyway? Couldn't he have stayed home?"

"It's his job, honey, and he loves it. I knew that when I married him."

"I miss him. He shouldn't be missing his child's birth."

"It's not his fault. Don't be mad at him." Lyauria gave her daughter a kiss, "We're almost there. Can you start filming?"

"What? You want him to see you puff like a dog every 15 minutes?"

"Funny, Aly, very funny."

Alayana started filming the rest of the drive and their arrival at the hospital. She was excited and, yet, she missed her father terribly. She wondered what it would be. A girl? A boy? They went up to the tenth floor, into the maternity ward, and there, the long walks in the corridor began. Lyauria was now having contractions every five minutes. The doctor checked her. She would be ready to begin pushing in approximately thirty minutes.

"Now is a good time to make sure you have enough film, Aly."

"Yeah, well maybe you shouldn't be taking so long."

"Aly, I have no choice in the matter."

"But, Mom, it's been hours already."

"It took longer to have you and you didn't hear me complain."

"That's not what I heard." Alayana smiled and winked at her grandmother.

"Whatever. What time is it, anyway?"

"It's three in the afternoon."

"It's been fourteen hours already. Hurg! I want this kid out."

"Well, that's good because we'll prepare you to push." said the doctor as he walked in.

Lyauria pushed and pushed. Finally, she gave birth to a beautiful boy.

"What will you call him?" the doctor asked

"Slug would be a good name. Look at him," Alayana said.

"Oh, he's gorgeous. I'll call him Anthony."

"Is that the best you could come up with?" Alayana was not impressed.

"Well, what do you suggest?"

"You mean other than Slug?"

"Aly!"

"Ok, okay. Um. . . Let me look at him. How does Matthew sound?"

"I like it."

"Me, too," said Mani.

"Welcome to our world, Matthew."

Alayana put the camera on a table and aimed it at her mother and quietly left the room.

"Hungry?" Mani asked

"Starved," replied Alayana.

"Let's go eat and let them rest."

"Should we call anyone?"

"Let your mother tell them. It's part of the joy of having a baby, you know."

"All right."

They spent the afternoon at the hospital and when visitors started to pour in, they left.

"Aren't you going to stay?"

"No, Mani, I have a date tomorrow. I can't cancel it."

"So you like that boy."

"I think he's gorgeous, but I don't know him well. Tomorrow will change that."

"Well, you saw where a relationship can take you."

"What are you talking about?"

"A baby..."

"Oh! No, I'm not going there, no worries."

"Good. I want you a virgin as long as you're unmarried."

"My mother already gave me the speech. Many times..."

"It doesn't matter how many times you hear it, it's about remembering it when temptation comes."

"How about I talk to you when I get tempted?"

"It's a deal."

Mani took the wheel while Alayana laid back on her seat and stared at the ceiling for most of the ride back. They both went to bed early, feeling they had been cheated out of their sleep to witness a miracle.

Monday came and Alayana wished she could have gotten more sleep. She was still tired, but she remembered that today she was to meet with Jeremyah. That made her jump out of bed and run to the shower. She was ready in no time. She went to the kitchen and sat down to eat some cereal. Mani was already up having her grapefruit.

"How did you sleep, honey?"

"I slept well, but I'm still tired. What about you?"

"Me too. Getting up with your mother in the middle of night was a little much for me in my old age."

"What do you think I should do with Jeremyah today?"

"Why don't you borrow my bicycles and go for a ride in the forest? You could have lunch by the beach."

"That's a great idea. I'll get lunch ready."

"When is he coming?"

"He's supposed to be here at ten."

"Well, make a light lunch, just in case you don't end up using it."

"Yeah, but if I do? I better make it perfect, just in case."

"Okay then, I'll go open up the store. See you down there."

"Okay."

Alayana prepared a lunch with a salad, some fruit, a baked chicken, and a pasta dish left over from two nights ago. She was almost ready. She just needed to add some juice and water and it would be complete.

"Alayana, Jeremyah is here."

"Okay."

"Hello, I made us ... lunch."

"Me too, since I didn't know if we were going to have lunch together or not, so I prepared for the worst." Jeremyah smiled as Alayana laughed.

"I can leave mine behind, if you want."

"No, bring it and we'll have a feast!"

"That sounds good. Do you want to go for a bike ride and then we could eat on the beach?"

"That's a good idea. I will leave the dogs in the yard. Let's go."

"See you later, Mani!"

"Good-bye, kiddo!"

Alayana and Jeremyah went to the shed and took the bikes. They went on the bike trails and were gone for most of the morning. They had many things in common, and Alayana felt comfortable in his presence. Jeremyah told her how he had found work at Gerard's, the clothing store, and was going to start the next day. They arrived at the beach, and although they weren't alone, they could still be themselves. They played Frisbee and volleyball with other kids there and the day flew by. The sun was low on the horizon when Alayana realized it was time for them to go back.

"I really enjoyed the day. I hope you had fun also."

"Yes, I did. Your grandmother has a wonderful place here. I was wondering if maybe we could go for a walk tomorrow."

"I'm working all day."

"Oh, it's alright, I just..."

"I was going to say that if you were free at seven, then I could go with you for a short walk."

"That would be nice. Maybe I could bring the dogs?"

"Sure, that would be great! Have a good night."

"Yeah, you too." Jeremyah waved, got his dogs, and walked away toward the village.

Alayana waved and went inside to find Mani on the phone.

"Yes, she was gone all day, but I have met the boy, nothing to worry about. Ah! Here she is. Alayana, come, it's your father..."

Alayana ran towards the phone and took the receiver from Mani's hand.

"Hi, Dad. Where are you?"

"I'm still on my mission, but I received a telegram from your grandmother telling me I was a proud father of a boy. I also realized how much I miss you. Where have you been?"

"Oh, the trails, then the beach for a picnic and a few games."

"All day?"

"Yes, we left at ten this morning."

"So, who is this young boy I keep hearing about?"

"Jeremyah. He's a nice guy. He's here for the summer working at Gerard's. We both don't really know anyone here so, you know, we're just spending time together."

"No kissing."

"Dad!"

"Okay, okay. I'm just worried my little girl is growing up too fast."

"Don't worry, Mani is keeping a close eye on me."

"Very well, Darling. I have to go. Just remember I love you and miss you terribly."

"Me too, Dad. I love you and miss you."

"Oh, by the way, nice name. I like it. Matt."

"Not Matt, Matthew. You know mother doesn't really like nick names."

"Sure, that's why she calls you Aly."

"Yeah, okay, you win."

"Okay, I have to go. Other guys are waiting to talk to their family, too. I jumped line because of Matthew, but now I have to let them have a chance at this before it's too late."

"All right. Miss you, Dad. Goodnight."

Alayana felt warm inside. She was happy that she got to talk to her father. She couldn't wait for him to come home, but that would probably take another year.

"Want something to eat, Alayana?"

"Nope. I ate like a pig at the beach. I think I'll just settle in for the night, I'm really tired."

"Very well, I'll wake you up tomorrow."

Tuesday morning, Alayana woke up rested and happy. She sang in the shower and when Mani heard her, she couldn't help but think Alayana had been bitten hard. She was happy for her granddaughter, but she hoped that if it didn't work out she wouldn't end up being too hurt.

Alayana had a smile on her face all day. She chatted with the customers and made great sales. She even managed to refer three customers to Gerard's shop for trinkets. Mani was starting to think maybe she should buy shares in Gerard's shop. His sales were bound to go up.

At the end of the day, Alayana hurried upstairs and started to make supper.

"What's the rush?" Mani asked.

"Oh, I guess with Father's phone call yesterday I forgot to tell you I was going for a walk with Jeremyah tonight."

"You have work tomorrow and you know I don't like you out after dark."

"We're only walking his dogs, and maybe play catch with them at the park. I'll be gone for an hour at the max, don't worry."

"One hour. No more, or else I won't let you out for the rest of the week."

"All right. Can I borrow your watch?"

"I guess so, if it's the only way I can be sure you'll be responsible."

"I don't see what the big deal is."

"Babies, babies, babies...."

"Would you cut that out? We haven't even kissed yet."

"Good. Keep it that way for a while. He seems nice, but make sure you get to know him better before you get too involved."

"I will. What do you think this walk is all about?"

"Okay, okay. I'll make supper while you get ready."

"Why? What's wrong with me?"

"Nothing. Sometimes girls want to double check to make sure everything is fine."

"Um, maybe you're right. You do the salad, I'll put some meat on the grill."

Alayana ran upstairs and could not find anything wrong with the way she looked. She had clean clothes on and since she didn't have many, there was no point in changing.

She returned to the kitchen, "I'll be fine this way."

"Yes, I think you will."

"Where are the apples?"

"None left."

"Why couldn't you have found him a job at the market instead of a clothing store?"

"What difference would it have made?"

"I could go to the market every time we ran out of something and see him."

"No, because then you wouldn't get any work done. And don't forget that tomorrow we're receiving a new shipment and I need your help."

"I won't."

They sat down and ate. Alayana was just finishing her desert when the doorbell rang.

"Oh, he's here," Alayana squealed. "Bye. Love ya. See ya."

"One hour!"

"Yes, I promise."

Alayana ran out the door and got jumped on by two big mutts. She laughed.

"This is Howler, and the brown and white one is Kintut. I've been telling them about you."

"Really?" Alayana bent down to pet the dogs, "And what did you say?"

"Well," Jeremyah said as pink crept into his cheeks, "I said I've been spending time with this nice girl and she had agreed to meet them, if they behave."

Alayana laughed. "Wonderful! Let's go to the park. Did you bring a toy for them?"

"Yes, but what's the rush?"

"I only have an hour, then I have to be home."

"All right, catch me if you can then," Jeremyah called over his shoulder as he started to run.

"That's the wrong way!" Alayana yelled and waited for him to get back to her door.

"Where is it, then?"

"That way!" Alayana started to run in the direction Jeremyah had gone before. "I tricked you!"

"I'll catch you!" and off Jeremyah went after her.

They threw a ball for the dogs to retrieve. Time went by quicker than Alayana wanted to admit.

"I guess I better get going. If I'm late, I'm not allowed out for the rest of the week."

"I'll walk you."

"That's very gentleman-like of you. Thank you."

"Want to do this again tomorrow?"

"I can't. I have to unpack the new order of books coming in. What about Thursday?"

"I'm working late on Thursday, but I'm free on Friday night."

"Friday night I spend baking for the story time."

"Well, I guess I'll see you on Saturday night for the story then."

"I guess so. Maybe we can plan it better next week."

"Is your schedule going to change?"

"No, not really."

"Well, I'll see if I can work late on Friday instead of Thursday. We could see each other then."

"Well, if you feel like baking, you could come and bake with me on Friday. I could ask Mani if she minds."

"Sounds good. I'll see you Saturday. Come on, boys, let's go home. Good-night."

Alayana started to want a kiss. A kiss would have been nice. She opened the door and went upstairs. Mani was painting a new scene.

"Who's this?"

"The guardian."

"He looks good."

"How was your night?"

"Good. And I'm on time."

"I know. I didn't say anything. You just look bummed out."

"When do you know it's time for a kiss?"

"When both people are looking each other in the eyes and they're in love. Then sometimes, you get a kiss out of it."

"Do you have to be in love?"

"Yes, I would think so, or else there would be no magic."

Alayana grabbed her book and started reading thoughtfully.

For the rest of the week, Alayana kept busy with the store and read her book. In no time, it was Saturday again. Her mother was out of the hospital, but she would be missing this week's part. She didn't want to take the drive with the baby.

Six o'clock came and Alayana was at the door, greeting the group.

"Welcome. Get ready. Have a seat. Nice to see you, Brett and John."

Alayana was on her toes looking for Jeremyah, but she could not see him anywhere. Marcus arrived and everyone was there except Jeremyah. She walked to the atrium and set her cushion to the floor.

Mani walked by her and whispered, "He called to say he'd be late, but he is coming and to wait for him if we could."

Alayana smiled

"We are only missing one guest. We'll wait for him..."

"I'm here," Jeremyah walked in and in his hand he held a stuffed dog and a bigger cushion. He sat down by Alayana and smiled.

"Why are you late?"

"I went to get a new cushion and I got caught in traffic."

"What's that?" Alayana said pointing to the stuffed animal he held in his hands.

"I just thought you might like to have something to hold on to when I'm not around. What do you say?"

"Thank you. My lord, this is a very fitting gift," Alayana giggled.

"Quiet now. Let us return to Tinay's story. Lights, please. We'll start with these paintings. Who can tell me where we're at?" Mani asked. Mani pointed to Marcus who had raised his hand, "Yes, Marcus?"

"Tinay is asleep in the cave and Lilay is having contractions. The boys are on their way back to Essay after the ceremony."

"Very well, Marcus. We'll continue our story with Tinay."

* * * * *

It was a perfectly beautiful sunrise on Sasgorg. The sky was pink with streaks of purple, but no one was there to see it.

A spotlight lit the picture of the desert on Sasgorg, close to Mont Ardel.

Tinay woke up. Sleeping on the rock surface had done more harm than good. She thought to herself, *I thought I had a hard mattress. Ouch!*

She normally began the morning meditating, but she wanted to find a way out. She concentrated and called her mother.

Mother, are you there?

Yes, dear. I woke up a little while ago. The contractions stopped for a few hours so I rested well. I'm making some chamomile. Unfortunately, it's old and not as powerful as the fresh leaves, but every little bit helps.

I'm glad to hear it, Mother. What do you suggest I do now?

What do you think you should do?

Well, get out of here and be with you when the contractions start again.

Good. How are you going to do that?

Find out as much as I can about this place?

That's a sound idea. Where will you find the information?

I was hoping you could help me with that.

I'm afraid I can't. You'll have to find the answers on your own. The temple was meant to answer all questions. It was meant to be traveled alone. You must use what your father and I have taught you all these years. Keep in mind that you are traveling the wrong way and that the entrance is buried in sand.

So you know about this place?

Yes, I do. It was meant to be traveled from the base up. Now that the planet has been abandoned, it does not matter which way you travel through the Pyramid, as long as you travel through it.

What's the point in trying to get out that way? I should start removing the rocks and try to make a hole and escape.

I wish it was that easy. You must go through the pyramid for your initiation. I left a message for your dad to come home. He'll be here and get you out. In the meantime, you must continue your initiation. Even though you're traveling the wrong way, you must read and learn about the history of Atlantis that is written on the walls. The rest must come from your training.

Ok, Mom, I'll do it.

Tinay opened her eyes and now that the light of day was filtering through, she saw the walls and their message. She started to read:

The Colony settled on Sasgorg. It took the ship over one thousand years to travel to Sasgorg. There never seemed to be a perfect planet to satisfy the needs of the human body and all the different guilds. There were so many things to consider: a source of water, food, shelter and raw materials. But mostly, they were searching for a specific element: the Alenor crystal. The crystal was indigenous to Earth and its properties were so numerous that it could not be overlooked. The society of Atlantis was built on it and to change that would be to change their way of life. The crystal was given to every child born and presented at the temple. It protected them from sickness, purified their water, and kept their food fresh. There was a supply in the ship that replenished the air and helped the growth of the plants in the agroponic bay, but the supply was not sufficient for a new civilization. The Atlantis they knew had changed. The crystal was no longer given but sold, and this led to disharmony between the castes and the King. Greed had taken its hold and was not ready to give up. By finding a planet rich in Alenor crystal, they could re-establish equality. Everyone had a part in the system and each was dependant on one another.

It was important that they settle where there was something for everyone. It didn't matter how long it took to get there. When they finally arrived at the planetary system of Sasgorg, they found what they were looking for. They knew the ice age would last several centuries and there was no rush to return to Earth right away. They needed to be sure that those left behind survived were kept alive by the colonists. It was important to settle and meet the needs of the new community. The Temples of Ardel, Landel, Zuel, Ecumel, Galgamel, Anamel and Manerv each had a special function to perform and each was under the guidance of a different guild.

The temple of Ardel was designated for the Meji and the Fairies. The Overseer and the Goddess were worshiped and ascensions took place there. The temple was the first one constructed. To help the spirits and souls find their way, the walls were incrusted with Alenor crystals, which were found in abundance on Sasgorg. It was a beautiful temple ornamented with gold sculptures and rock architecture.

The second temple was Galgamel. It was the source of all the water in the area, which was distributed throughout the city through tunnels to a well in each temple and in the center of town. Galgamel's care was given to the guild of Merchants. Merchants, through time, had remained fond of water and their ports, where they did most of their exchange and business.

The next temple was built for the Farmer's guild. They needed a place to store the products of their harvest for the next season. The temple was decorated with wood sculptures and other beautiful artworks donated by the Artisan's guild, which didn't have a temple at that point. The name of that temple was Ecumel.

The Temple of Anamel was the next temple built. Anamel was taken care of by the engineers. It was a research center and a hospital. All new technology was centered there and adapted to the new environment. The temple was also a place where research was done to advance the use of space travel.

Landel was the next temple, built near the landing strip where the administrator could supervise the whole valley. The building was inspiring and beautiful. By now, the Artisans were using potteries and materials to decorate the temple. Since they didn't have their own temple to decorate, they had plenty of time to make Landel gorgeous and welcoming. Landel was used to welcome others species living close to that area of space, which they had met during their thousand-year voyage. Landel was a multi-cultural port used for many encounters and exchanges.

The guild of the Miners needed a place to store their gems and metals they had found. This temple was kept simple, since most miners were always away and there was never anybody around to care for it. But the Miners left a testament to their talent as carvers in Temple Manerv. The temple was a place of acceptance where guests were invited to stay. The beauty of the surroundings inspired even the most modest of visitors. Unconditionally, the miners welcomed anyone who would demonstrate an open mind and accept his neighbor.

The final temple to be built was Zuel. It became the center of the community on Sasgorg. The artisans were well practiced in many shapes and forms of art, transforming the temple into a work of art. Zuel displayed the true soul of the community. Through their art, the world could see beauty. The art there represented more than the Atlanteans, which was shown in all the other temples, but a touch of all the other races they had met through their journey. They honored their friends and displayed their own character in paintings, carvings and sculptures. They borrowed the techniques of their friends and compatriots to achieve the most beautiful works of art.

It was then decided that any children called to apprentice in the arts should start at Ardel. Their calling needed to be confirmed by the ancestor. Then they could be guided by the beauty they saw. When they moved on to Galgamel, the art became fluid, and fountains ornamented every floor with crisp and fresh water. Afterward, they would continue their journey to Ecumel and decorate the hall of the granary, to learn how to find beauty even in necessity. Their training would then lead them to Anamel. This was probably the most rewarding place since their service was used to brighten the morale of the sick. Most of the gifts were given to the patients. The teachers would leave their art to decorate the walls and healing room. Then they would be sent to Landel. It was an honor to be at the door to the galaxy. There they saw firsthand the wonders from other worlds and helped to make better communication. They would inspire the newly arrived strangers and make them feel welcomed. In Manerv, they learned to work with stones, gems and metals. The learned to make jewelry and ornaments. Finally, they would finish their training at Zuel where, in their own form of art, they would illustrate their passion with one final piece.

Each temple required a year to complete, and once the training was done, they were free to choose where their work was most suited and where it would reward the public most. They also chose which medium suited them the best.

Each guild was awarded seven years to form their apprentices into skilled workers, based on the system the artisans had developed. Each guild developed a book of learning to make sure each of their students would encompass all the knowledge they needed to be the best at what they could do.

Tinay sat back, amazed by all that she had read. She knew from what her mother had said that she was to be an artist. Now she knew what she would be doing for the next seven years. She would have the privilege to travel from one planet to another and visit each world, helping to make it more beautiful. She would then have the advantage of choosing where she wanted to live and maybe become a mentor, like her mother had been, inspiring others.

Tinay was hungry. She found some food in her pouch and shared it with Draco. She couldn't tell what time it was, but the darkness had made her strain her eyes more than usual and she had a headache. She decided she should meditate and try to make it go away like she had done with her sprained ankle.

Lilay's contractions had receded and she was able to prepare for the inevitable birth of her baby. She had been watching over her daughter, Tinay, making sure she understood the messages she was getting, but since Tinay was reading it in reverse, it was bound to make less sense than if she had started the beginning. Normally, she would have an ancestor watching over her and now there was no telling if she would ever achieve this stage. Time passed by quickly as Lilay wondered if Tamael would be there in time for the birth of their child.

She had not sensed him coming yet, which meant he was far away. It also meant he was not in any danger and, therefore, he remained safe.

What could he be thinking at this moment? She heard the slight sound of a voice resonate in her mind, "I love you," and she smiled.

Nothing was happening in the cave. It was quiet. Lilay moved as little as she could so that she would not induce labor again. She guarded her strength and slept.

Chapter 13

THE SEVEN TEMPLES

After a few hours of sleep, Tinay woke feeling disoriented. Although there was light in the pyramid, her crystal broke the light into a rainbow and she could not tell if it was day or night. Tinay had no idea how long she had slept. She looked around and saw the books of each temple under some dust and rubble. She stretched and realized how much she missed her bed. She had a quick look over the books she had found: The Way of the Engineers, The Way of the Farmers, The Way of the Miners, The Way of the Merchants, and The Way of the Administration. She put them into her pouch. This information might become useful when she traveled to foreign planets to develop her skills. There wasn't much more for her to find here, except a way to go down. She explored all the nooks and crannies of the level she was on, but could not see anything that indicated a lever.

Hmm, she thought, *I guess I'll have to be more imaginative*. She looked closely at the relic on the floor and noticed small urns. Some had sand in them and some were put aside empty. *Wonder what this means?* She looked at the urns and removed some debris that blocked her way, and saw a loose stone in the floor. *Maybe that's it?* She removed the stone and found a funnel. The only thing she had at her disposal was sand, so she started emptying the urns in the hole. She felt this would take forever. Maybe the sand was just piling up below her and was not doing anything after all.

She was empting an urn when, all of a sudden, she started heard a mechanism slowly moving. The center of the room started to lower itself, but no stairs appeared. She would have to jump or go now. She quickly emptied the last urn into the funnel and dashed for the center of the room. Then she saw Draco sleeping on her bag. *My bag!* She rushed over to the bag and grabbed it along with the ferret and ran for the opening in the floor. The slate was already down halfway so she would have to jump. She closed her eyes and jumped. Not her most brilliant idea!

She landed on her feet, but lost her balance, finishing the ride on her butt. She looked around. This new room was bigger than the former. And although the walls were marvelously decorated, there was no writing on them.

In the room, she found a pile of books, smaller ones underneath a larger one, which sat on a small desk along with an oil lamp. She wondered how much more reading she would have to do. This was interesting, but a bit much. She sat down and looked at the table. As she reached for the large book, it tumbled and revealed the smaller ones underneath. The first one she picked up was called, *The Power of the Number Seven*. That sounded interesting enough. She opened the book and started to read.

The number seven is revered as holy because it is the number of days it took for The Overseer to build the original earth, and, therefore, the secret society had been built to honour the number seven. Because it is impossible for a human to achieve anything in seven days, it was decided that seven years would be the right amount of years to learn about a profession. Each guild set up a meditation center that was to be associated with their duty, reinforcing the number seven all throughout their way of living.

The number seven is also in accordance with the principle of meditation that was taught by the Ancestor. They taught that the number seven took more significance than other numbers, which helped the person meditating to balance his life and live in harmony, not just with others, but with himself. It is an important part of a healthy body and a healthy mind. Each individual learned from a young age to differentiate between and master the energies that surrounded him, instead of stealing the energies from others by fighting them, bullying them, or ignoring them. Each meditation helped the energy circulate throughout their body. The energy is visualized as a white current floating in the body. When pain is present, the energy stops flowing and concentrates in one particular spot. By breathing deeply, the energy can be made to travel once more and allows the body to obtain complete relaxation. At this point, a person should be able to visualize a reflection of himself floating slightly higher than his actual body.

The first temple of meditation built was Ecumel. Ecumel represents basic needs like food, shelter, and safety for oneself and for one's family.

The first temple is where anxiety and fear is expelled out of the body and the mind. Bad energy must be controlled and eliminated before continuing to the next temple. The first temple is where the instinct resides and is the center of force, vigor and energy.

Once in meditation in the first temple, a person is to rid himself of doubts and insecurities, and assure himself in the present. The best way to meditate on this center is to picture an image that is red in color and spins on itself as it becomes increasingly pure. For children, it is easy to picture an apple or a ball. A person whose aura is red indicates aggression and conquest. It's the sign of an ambitious personality, who is vigorous and opinionated. The red aura is not necessarily bad as it is also a sign of an optimistic, outgoing and impulsive attitude. It fits quite well for a person who is full of the force of life, sex drive and creativity, but a negative aura also means the person will turn to himself and indulge in acts that benefit him only.

Once a solid base has been established, the person can move on to the next temple, Anamel. Anamel was built in remembrance of the second meditative stage. It represents the body's internal organs, sexuality and healing. The color orange represents thoughtfulness and consideration, two important qualities in keeping our body, mind, and relationships healthy. This is where an individual will spend time thinking of each organ in the body and activate them, make them come to life and meditate on their sexuality. This is also the stage where the assimilation of knowledge and food will be further assisted. Here, a person wants to visualize an orange floating over his belly button and, as the energy floats more freely and becomes vibrant, the orange will spin on itself. The orange aura reveals a person who is sociable and likes to help others. These first two temples are the base of the pyramid and must be solid in order to build upon them.

The next center is higher up on the body at the solar plexus and, like the sun, the center is yellow. Galgamel was built in memory of that mediation center. The solar plexus is the center of emotions, and is associated with breathing. The color yellow affects the nervous systems and the digestive functions. It also regulates the skin. This is where a person needs to explore his emotions and get rid of anything negative. It's okay to have anger. Anger should not be ignored. It should be focused on realigning the energy into something constructive. It can be interpreted as the center of friendliness and well-being. If a person keeps anger and resentment inside, it will build up and disturb the bodily functions to a point where the person will be sick and need treatment. When a person is meditating at this center, he will find it easy to focus on a sun radiating on top of his sternum. As the sun becomes bigger, the warmth from its rays flows down to the extremities. One will know when one has achieved peace of mind when one's whole body feels warm and embraced. The yellow aura at this temple represents an intelligent person who is wise and open to new ideas. He is creative and confident. The person with a yellow aura has firm convictions emanating from strength of character. The down side of this aura represents a person who is selfish.

The fourth meditation center is represented by Manerv. Manerv was built for the Heart, the center of unconditional love. It is love that encompasses everyone we know and meet. Unconditional love for everyone is the respect for Mother Nature and all living things, and the appreciation for the beauty of the world that surrounds us. If one can find beauty, one can find the love. The main color of this center is green and it is easy for the beginner to picture a green belt surrounding the chest. As the belt turns around the body, the beginner will picture those he loves at first and then those he knows, but does not have a particular affinity for and, finally, he will picture his enemies and those who have offended him. This step is particularly hard and requires time for it is the step to forgiveness. Green is the color of nature, abundance, and the renewing force that brings strength and harmony. This will provide a better circulation of the blood and a healthier heart. Green is healing and helpful to the individual and the community. The green aura represents a person who has hope, harmony, and balance. It is an indication of trustworthiness and openness in a person. To have a green aura, a person must be filled with joy, sincerity, frankness and thankfulness. This kind of individual prefers a quiet and peaceful life. The negative side of this aura is an opinionated person who likes to be in control.

The next center of meditation is represented by Landel, the center of communication. It is conveniently located in the throat. It represents not only daily conversation, but things that also remain unsaid. It is the center that helps to communicate and interpret the meaning of the message that must be transmitted. The color of this center is blue. To meditate, a person can focus on a star that emanates rays of blue light, which touch all the other centers and emanates from the body, reaching out to others. This will help the person connect and talk with an interlocutor and express himself favorably. This is the center where one must practice and review what one has said and what one intends to say. Words can do immense damage and hurt people and, therefore, should be used accordingly. Blue symbolizes serenity, spirituality and peace. It is soothing to the nervous system and helps reduce agitation. It also helps defeat insomnia and nervousness and it stimulates creativity and artistic talent. The blue aura reveals a person with an introspective temperament who is seeking spiritual answers and who takes responsibilities seriously. This makes the person faithful and steadfast, but, when taken to the extreme, becomes rigid and introverted.

As one continues higher up in the body, the temple of Zuel is next. The functions associated with it are most important. This meditation center is the third eye, the eye of the spirit. The eye is closed until opened by an elder. The spirit can then, from that moment on, see the truth around it and be a better judge of character. It enables the person to see the truth, the beauty and the true nature of the world that surrounds him. The individual here should work on his everyday actions and examine if he has been non-judgmental, seeing the beauty and valor underneath the surface. This center of meditation is a center of reflections and openness. The third eye's color is indigo. This color is associated with religion and the search for the truth. This is the center for mental disorders. It has a spiritual influence on the soul of the individual. It expands the mind and makes it think clearly and openly without limiting itself. An indigo aura individual is high minded and idealist: an intellectual. He has wondrous powers of concentration and discernment, and he will, therefore, be a very good communicator and intuitive person with a logical mind. If he falls into the negative realm, he will become argumentative and self-important.

Tinay stopped and reflected on what she had just read. She finally understood why she had never been able to open her third eye. There was no elder around. Tinay felt cheated. All the time she believed it was her fault because she was not concentrating well enough. She sat in the lotus position and tried to mentally connect with her mother.

Mother? she said. *Are you there?*

Lilay was sleeping, but was awakened by the soft echo that floated in her mind, *Tinay?*

Yes, Mother, it's me. I was reading a book about the number seven and all the temples. It was quite interesting.

Did you learn anything new?

Well, I just read that the reason why I can't open my third eye is because I need an elder to help me to do so. Why didn't you ever say that to me?

I guess your dad and I didn't bring it up because it was not safe to call an elder to come here.

How am I ever going to get my third eye opened then?

There's another way to contact an elder than to have one present with you.

Oh, what is it?

The elder can come and visit you in the astral form to open your third eye. But she won't come until you have answered the guardian's riddle.

What riddle? What guardian?

This pyramid was built from bottom to the top. The first level has a well and a giant staircase. You left your family behind and then went up a giant staircase alone. On the second floor, you will meet the guardian who will ask you a riddle. On the walls are carvings with the oldest and wisest philosopher's works. Once you have successfully completed the tasks, the guardian will offer you an Alenor crystal to wear. Then you must proceed by levitation to the next level. It is where the mysteries of the fairies and the Meji are revealed. This is an important step in your journey. Not everyone was allowed in the temple of Ara. Just the initiate who would become a part of that temple is allowed.

Why am I here then?

You are more than an artisan, Tinay. I cannot reveal the complete truth to you, not yet. The next level is opened by completing a puzzle, but since you are going another way, you'll have to manually activate the mechanism like you have been doing so far. You will end up where you are now except in the prophecies room. An extensive amount of time is spent here, but there's no need for you to read the prophecies for now. You'll run out of food and I need you to get back here soon. Then you would have ascended to the next level to learn about the relevance of the number seven and how our society is based on the number and how we reach balance. Each guild must complete seven years of training and distribute their work in the apprentice system. Did you find all of the books?

Yes, I have them in my bag.

Keep them. They'll be of use to you in the future.

Mother, I thought I was going through this because I was going to apprentice on Kyr and I was going to travel to each planet and learn the art for each temple and...

In a way, you will be an artisan. You will travel to each temple and you will learn the way of life for each guild. All I'm saying is that you will be much more.

How come there aren't seven levels in the pyramid?

The top was destroyed. The sixth level had the regular exit where you met your mentor and where you were greeted by your family again and the last level was reserved for the ascension ceremony.

Ascension ceremony?

You don't need to worry yourself with that. Only fairies and Meji ascend, not artisans.

Oh! For a minute it sounded scary.

Don't worry, it was perfectly safe.

How are the contractions, Mother?

They've stopped for now, but my time is fast approaching.

What time of the day is it?

Your father has been gone for ten days and it's eleven p.m. at night. You should get some sleep.

I had a nap earlier. I had better press on if I want to get to you soon. I still have no idea how I will get out.

All right then, I'll go back to sleep.

Goodnight, Mother. See you soon.

Tinay realized that she should eat some more if she was to continue that night. Draco had been patiently waiting by the bag. Not much for him to do here. She looked in her bag. It was getting full, but she had less food than she thought.

She eyed the ferret again, "No wonder you're so quiet. You've been eating like a pig, haven't you?"

The ferret was quite content with himself, almost smiling. He climbed on her and licked her cheek for forgiveness.

"Well, at least you didn't chew the herbs."

She opened up the book and started to read the last bit that was left.

The last temple is the crown. The crown is represented by the temple Ardel. It represents the union with the Overseer, the meeting of the ancestors and the recognition of the spirit. It is where the soul finds its purpose in the material world and finds its inspiration. It is the center of the search for the purpose of life and its meaning. It is the religious icon of society. Its color is violet. It reflects the highest power of healing, the energy of the red, and the spiritual healing of the blue. It brings regeneration to the soul. It cures brain damage and relieves neurosis, nervous systems inflammation and eye injuries. The person with a violet aura reflects judgment and understanding. He is broad-minded and generous in his influence. He is sensitive to others and possesses a firm sense of integrity and character with a generous nature. If the soul is handicapped with negativity, the person becomes overbearing and self-centered.

Tinay closed the book and took a deep breath. She sure had a lot left to learn, but for now she would put the book away and look for the next door that would lead her to the fairies and Meji prophetic room.

After the conversation with Tinay, Lilay did not go back to sleep. She entered into a deeper trance and exited her body. She went looking for Mani the elder. Mani was the only one who could help her daughter progress past the third eye. She had no idea where Mani had gone into hiding, so she would have them find a guardian and hope for luck. She knew where the Ara congregation had gone into hiding, so she went there directly.

She hated to travel through space for long periods of time. She always had the impression that she was losing herself between the stars when long amounts of time passed. She went past many planets, and then systems. There were so many of them. She passed through Us, then Essay. She admired Os for a few minutes and moved on to Ara, which was unrecognizable. Then she passed Is, which had completely changed since she had last seen it. She moved passed Kyr, her future home, and left with a heavy heart. Finally, she arrived at El. She might have hated traveling through space, but she found travel through matter to be more intrusive and violating to her soul. She found that matter was too condensed and hard to travel through. She arrived at a cavern. She didn't need a body to tell her it was hot and probably smelled like sulfur. The guardian lived there and sensed her.

Who goes there? he asked, probing her mind.

The probing hurt Lilay, even though her body was on Sasgorg.

It is I, Alilayria. I must seek your help.

Alilayria, it is not safe for you to travel at such a precarious time.

I must. The time has come. Tinay needs to open her third eye.

Time goes by so fast for you humans. I had kept this event in the back of my mind for a while now.

Do you think Manyr, the elder, will be able to come and help us?

I will locate an elder for you. I can't promise who will show up.

Guardian, you know what is at stake here. I must have someone that has not been corrupted.

Understood. I will search immediately. When will you require my services?

Henceforth.

I will immediately prepare to attend with the elder.

Thank you, Guardian. Lilay bowed to the guardian and left.

When Lilay returned to her home, she found she was able to sleep properly for the first time in days.   The guardian didn't wait long before he set out to locate Manyr, the Elder. He located her gardening under the harsh sun of Kyr. She was an old lady, with a full head of white hair. She was small, but powerful. She was happily singing a song to accompany a bird in a tree nearby.

The guardian whispered in her mind, *Manyr, we must speak at once.*
There there, Okapi, I can hear you.
The time has come.
Not a moment too soon.
She needs her third eye opened and I must test her.
This will be accomplished. We'll leave tonight and hope she will be ready by next morning. I must return, so as not to awaken any suspicion.
Very well. I'll make arrangements, so I won't be leaving the order unguarded.

The guardian returned to his hiding, re-entered his body, and went to the council.

He walked into the great room, as always, grumbling, "No place to live, no honor, no decorations. Never should have given up the temple."

He approached the great council and addressed the Great priest. "Lord Andemar, I must request relief of duty, for I must attend the eye opening ceremony of ..."

"Yes, Okapi. No name, please. There's only one that would cause you to leave your post. I'm glad the ceremony will take place. Time is running short. We will need all the help we can get."

"Yes, my lord. I'll leave tonight and be back by morning."

"As you wish. You must report to me then. We'll have guards posted at the entrance and at all access centers."

"Very well, my Lord."

They both bowed to each other in respect for their old age and wisdom.

"Oh, and Okapi?"

"Yes, my lord?"

"What riddle have you prepared for our young subject?"

Okapi smiled, "Now, my Lord. It's up to me to know and for you to find out."

They both smiled at each other. Okapi turned around and left the great hall. He must prepare for the night ahead of him.

Manyr had to work in the garden and go about her day in a normal fashion, so that no one would notice anything different. She knew she would be extra tired in the end. She would be in a trance all night as there was much distance to be traveled. No one must suspect her. To everyone else, she was just a retired woman who gardened slowly every day. She had not used her powers for many years, for fear of being detected, but now the time had come where she would have to oversee the training of Tinay. Now the time had come to take chances and teach her to become all that she could be.

Lilay woke up not long after returning. She didn't like leaving her body when she was pregnant, but there was no other way. She went to her bed and realized how lonely she felt. She missed her husband and her children. She wiped a tear off her face, put her head on the pillow and fell back asleep.

Tinay could not find a way to exit the room. The floor was covered in dust that had accumulated over the years and had never been disturbed. No matter where she looked, she could not find a possible opening. She sat back frustrated. What now?

Draco seemed bored. He was running along the south wall, back and forth, and would not stop. It was turning into an obsession.

"What is it, Draco?"

She got up and went over to him, "What have you got there, boy?"

The ferret stopped and stood on his back legs reaching for the sky.

"You want up?"

The ferret started to jump all over the place. Obviously he knew something she didn't.

"What is it?" she asked.

Draco started to climb up her clothes and went straight to her shoulder. He started to paw at the wall.

"You sure are acting strange today! What do you want me to do? I can see you want the wall, but what of it?"

Draco was an old ferret, tame and very domesticated. This was a strange way for him to act.

She put her hand on the wall. Draco ran down her arm and tried to go higher up. This was strange behavior indeed.

"So, you want to go higher up? We came from there. We're supposed to go down."

She let out a big sigh and lifted the ferret as high as she could. He jumped out of her arms and landed on a beam that was stretched across the room.

"Now what?" said Tinay.

The ferret ran along the beam and, a quarter of the way across, stopped and seemed to dig some dust and dirt out of a hole in the beam. It was clear to her now. Draco had been here before and he knew what was expected of him. All he had to do was push a lever and then he would get a treat.

Tinay was perplexed. How on earth did Draco ever learn this trick? Not that it mattered anymore because the door on the north wall opened.

"No wonder the floor didn't look like it had moved in years. Duh! It was in the wall."

She started to walk over to the wall and saw Draco aim for her. "Come on, boy, get down here!"

Draco jumped and landed in her arms and then went straight for her bag.

"Hang on, you! We have to see how much longer we're stuck down here. You can't eat everything!"

Draco didn't look happy at all. He went to her shoulder and lay down.

Tinay walked toward the entrance in the wall, and started to go down the stairs.

Chapter 14

THE GIFTS OF THE FAIRIES

Tinay walked down the stairs. Everything became dark. Even though there were Alenor crystals once embedded in the walls, the light could not be refracted any longer. The crystal was missing. She continued down the steps and found a large room. Lit with a soft light, she realized this time it was the moon shining. She looked at the far corner of the room and saw a tunnel that made its way to the sky. The tunnel supplied a welcome breath of fresh air.

Tinay felt she could relax and wait for morning to discover what new marvels lay hidden here. She curled up on the floor and went to sleep.

The first ray of sunshine woke Tinay. The room was brightly lit and she had no difficulty looking around at the walls. Beautiful works of art had been made and preserved here: statues, obelisks, urns, carpets, and other artifacts. This was a room full of treasures. Tinay could not believe her eyes.

She looked at the far end of the room opposite the tunnel, and saw the hole she had to levitate through. She didn't worry about anything now. She didn't have to look for another trap door or mechanism. She tried to levitate, but she could only jump. She ran over to the hole only to realize that the creators of the pyramid were smarter than she thought. The floor was twenty feet below. It was impossible for her to jump. She had to levitate. But how?

"Hun, more reading" she said out loud.

Her voice resonated inside the four walls. It was suddenly very creepy to be here alone. She felt a shudder run down her spine. She shook it off.

She didn't know where to start. She looked in her pouch for some food. Although she hadn't made a sound, Draco seemed to have heard someone yell, "Breakfast!" because he ran over to have his share.

"You know, Draco, I never realized how much you actually eat. Here's your share, buddy. We better find the information I need or else we'll have no food left."

Draco ignored her and continued to chew on the bits she had given him.

Tinay looked around and, although she knew what she had to do, she was overwhelmed by the work ahead of her. She would have to move everything in the room, find the starting point and keep moving everything until she was done. This would take hours.

Her attention suddenly focused on a book from the previous room that was sticking out of her bag. It was smaller than the prophecies book, but a little bigger than the previous one she had read. It looked much newer than the other works she had read. She didn't recognize the handwriting, so it wasn't her mother's either. She looked around and saw the writing on the wall. It talked about the gift of the fairies. She turned to the book cover and was happily surprised to find that the book was a transcription of the wall's story. She wouldn't have to move the whole room after all.

The fairies are regular human beings that have been genetically modified to produce only four children, so they have enough time to train them and see to their up-bringing. They produce three daughters and one son. All four children remain in the hierarchy of the Order.

The Order was created as the nucleus of the new society. It wasn't based on power, but on knowledge. The caste system was set aside and doors were opened to anyone who wanted to live a new way and who was able to accept a more rudimental way of life, a life based on the ancestors' knowledge which had been passed from one generation to the next.

The fairies were gifted with a sixth sense. There are three categories of fairies: the medium, the historian, and the healer. Together they form the force of three: the sum of their parts is much larger than the three of them alone. Together they can accomplish miracles. On their own, the fairies are built to work together, and their protection is provided by the Meji. The Meji are pure blood descendants and recruit two outsiders for each trilogy of fairies born. The Order assigns one Meji to each fairy. The Meji and one of the fairies most often ended up marrying each other.

The fairies have rudimentary teachings to go through. Their first year is spent learning about Meditation and all the different centers. Great emphasis is put upon this first year, as meditation is the basis of balance and equilibrium. The second year is spent learning about the history of their people and how they arrived at their destination. Their third year is spent learning about plants and their use in medicine and cooking. The fourth year is spent learning about what a medium can do and how endless the possibilities are to see through time. Their fifth year is spent learning about the healing process. During the sixth year, the fairies learn their specialty. During their final year, they experience their practicum. They are joined with an experienced fairy and learn all they can before their twenty-first birthday, when they begin their ascension.

The medium's specific lessons are based on recognizing the aura and its meaning, knowing how to differentiate between ghost and spirits, knowing how to communicate with ghosts and spirits, reading from cards, leaves, crystal balls and lines of a hand, and finally recalling their visions in details.

The historian learns the process of the lessons and becomes an expert in past history and studies the book of prophecies. Her job is to match old prophecies with present day events and to help interpret prophecies about the future. She is also an artist who takes care of tattooing her initiate with her family's emblem so the lineage will be preserved.

The healer learns how to make potions to heal the sick. She uses her hands to manipulate the body and its energy to heal the body and the soul. She learns how to counsel tortured spirits and help the dying and dead move on to the next plane. She also serves as a veterinarian and a gardener, using non-intrusive technology to heal all forms of life.

The Meji Order has a similar form of training: The Million and One Ways to Defend and Protect Yourself and/or a Loved One. The first four years are spent studying meditation to control any negative energy that might weaken them. Then three years are spent studying philosophy and the wisdom of old. During the following five years, hand-to-hand combat is learned, as well as how to use a bamboo stick, knife manipulation and combat, sword fighting, and how to shoot bows and cross-bows. After a heavy five years of weapon training, they must complete three years of peace-keeping duties in different planet systems. Then they become a mentor for two years, teaching what they have learned and what their experience has brought to them and their community. In the last two years of their training, they are assigned to a fairy, who they get to know, and eventually join the fairy in ascension.

During the initiation, a newcomer will be given a chance to prove her ingenuity and wisdom by challenging the guardian. A series of riddles will be asked of one to another. The initiate has two possible ways to win: either she can come up with a riddle that the guardian cannot solve or she can solve all of the riddles by sunset. A wrong answer will terminate the initiation and the initiate will not be allowed to pursue her training.

Once the challenge has been completed, the guardian will issue the initiate her own Alenor crystal, which was removed from Earth in a space ship and kept for centuries by the guardian. Due to its rarity, it cannot be replaced if lost, and since no one needs more than one, it is useless to steal one. The Alenor crystal properties extend to a variety of uses such as purifying water, air and metals. It also keeps food and plants fresh and alive until used again. The crystal can help focus the healing energy and ward off bad spirits. It has awesome powers that can be used to focus light and harvest energy. Because it was misused on Earth, only small crystals could be issued and the reserve remained heavily guarded so that no one could attempt to create new weapons.

It was decreed that after the second cataclysm, the Order would not allow any technological weapons to be created, since it was that loss of control on the newly created technology that caused the lost of Atlantis. Without advanced weapons and a balance of the ying and yang, the Order remained stable for millennia. Peace was acquired at too great a price to risk losing everything again.

The initiated fairy has seven years to complete her practicum and face the great council in her ascension. The ascension remains a sacred rite and will not be described here. It suffices to say that the ascension involves a great deal of energy and that the person who successfully graduates from the ceremony will come out forever changed and improved by the powers involved.

The essential criteria for the ascension are that both the fairy and the Meji must be virgins and love each other. Failure of either of those two requirements leaves the couple unable to unite and successfully pledge to each other for their present lifetime.

The future couple meets when the fairy is nineteen years old. The Meji is assigned to her, the fairy, as she must travel often into the unknown. The Meji also provides support to the fairy when she transfigures herself and departs from her physical form to travel through time and space. The fairy's body cannot be left unattended. The Meji is there to see that nothing disturbs the fairy or hurts her physical form.

The Meji is a peacekeeper, not a soldier. Although he is trained in the many ways to hurt and kill an opponent, he is only to use his strength to control a subject and bring him forth. The Order has no power to judge a felon, it can only help to rehabilitate him and teach him a better way of acting, thinking and living. The Meji also believes in Karma, the force that circulates through us all and regulates our actions.

The ether of the second plane records all of an individual's actions, reactions, and thoughts. At the end of life on the first plane, the soul is shown all that it has done during its period on the first plane and is presented with the opportunity to weigh in its good and bad actions. The sum of good or bad does not cancel each other out.

The soul must measure to what degree it has understood the lesson it came to learn and to see if it has mastered the lesson. The soul then determines what it needs to work on and prepares a life-plan for its future reincarnation. From one life to the next, the soul travels through the physical plane hoping to reach perfection in its mastery of life. Life is an ongoing process to eliminate imperfections and to ultimately join the third plane and become an ancestor.

The council of the elders is comprised of a group of individuals who are on their last plane on earth. They are recognizable by the violet aura and their infinite wisdom. The council looks and oversees the progress of the Order and helps make society a better and more peaceful place. It negotiates with alien species and draws up treaties for exchange and barter.

In the same way, the Council of the Ancestors is comprised of a group that has ascended to the third plane and guides the souls in their planning for a new journey on Earth. They help facilitate the transition from one plane to the next. They are the followers of peace. The Ancestors help guide the soul toward achievement of self. It is a conscious plane where the physical aspect does not influence their lives and, therefore, has no temptation. In order for a soul to grow it must be tempted and provoked. It is based on the question: What is a choice if no choice exists? The notion of free will was given to humans because their soul allowed them to experience joy and sorrow; a meter for good and bad. The soul is to test its limits by new experiences and then use its wisdom to make the right choices. If, however, a soul should become lost on Earth, it has a chance to see its poor choices, learn from them, and try again.

To keep the soul from losing its way, seven guides are assigned to it. Each guide presides over a source of pleasure. There are no ranks among the seven guides and they work together in cooperation for the good of the soul they supervise. The group of seven never changes. They follow each other one lifetime after another, taking turns on the physical plane. They are the little voices in the back of one's mind, one's conscience, one's chill in the spine, a little subtle change to push the soul one way or the other. There's a guide to oversee the body, a second guide to oversee spiritual growth, a third guide to help with relations with the family, a fourth guide to help with relationships made outside the home, a guide to supervise the health of the mind, and finally a guide for one's life purpose. The final guide oversees the others. The Overseer makes sure that no one guide takes precedence over the other and maintains harmony between the different goals that each guide is assigned by the entity.

It is ultimately up to the individual how much she wishes to learn and how hard her life will be. She can learn lessons from the experiences of others, but sometimes this is not enough and the soul needs to experience firsthand what the incident and the lesson have to offer. The benefit of the continuum is that once a lesson is learned, it doesn't have to be relearned again. Once an individual has learned not to steal, he won't go from being honest to evil. However, to make sure the lesson has been retained, there will be temptation along the way to reaffirm the character of the person. The individual or the entity must suffer or feel some pain and discomfort in order to grow, or else the entity will lay inactive and not make any gains in a lifetime. Standing still may, in fact, lead the individual backwards so that they do not attain greatness.

Well, this is all very interesting, but it doesn't say anything about levitation, Tinay thought.

Mother, I need your help.

Yes, dear, what is it?

How are you doing, Mother?

I'm great, actually. I haven't felt better in weeks. I'm totally rested.

I'm glad to hear you are doing so well.

I wouldn't be, if it weren't for you. The labor will most likely start today, and this time it won't stop.

But you just said...

I said I felt great, which is when the body usually decides to go into labor because it's rested and ready for the shock of labor and the trauma it causes to the body.

Well, I'm in the fairies and Meji room now.

Wonderful! You're almost there!

Yes, but I don't know where to find the information to help levitate. Where should I look, Mother?

Of course. That information is on the level below you. You won't have any access to it. Did your dad leave the ladder behind?

My dad? What do you mean 'your dad'?

Your dad. Your father. Tamael.

I knew that. I meant both of you knew about this cave all along?

Of course we did. Your father stashed all of our belongings in that room. Did you find the book of the fairies?

Yes.

Well, your father and I did that together, some twenty years ago.

I didn't recognize your handwriting.

No, I improved the book with the pictures. Your father was doing the writing then.

I see. What am I to do with the levitation part?

That's a hard one to explain. You will have to assume the lotus position, and concentrate on your breathing. You must slow your breathing and your heart rate until time seems to slow down. Then you will look inside yourself and see what you are made of, literally. You will see all the atoms that compose you and make your organs and skin. You will see the constellations inside yourself and see the intricateness of it all. Then you will no longer feel as a mass but light as the stars of which you are made. Instead of lifting your whole body, concentrate on lifting the atoms in the air and slowly making them float. You'll go over the edge and continue slowly down to the next floor. Like a feather, you will hardly feel the gravity sucking you down and you will be transported lightly to the next stage. If I were you, I'd drop a few cushions down the hole just in case you drop out of the trance too soon.

Gee! Thanks for the vote of confidence."

Honey, it's a hard thing to do, but remember each time you meditate, you are able to lift small objects. It's not really all that different, just bigger, really.

I didn't think about that.

Well, let's go then, I don't have all day.

It's not you who's risking your neck."

Tinay got in the lotus position.

Tinay, you forgot the cushions.

No, mother, I just want to try first over here.

There's no need, I'll walk you through. You'll be fine.

Tinay got up reluctantly and grabbed some large cushions. She dragged them across the room to the hole in the ground, and dropped them to the bottom. She looked down and felt her stomach move to her throat.

"Yeurk!" she said.

Don't let fear overcome you. I know you can do this, her mother said.

"Alright, here goes nothing!"

Tinay assumed the lotus position once more and concentrated on her breathing. She slowly moved the air from her chest all the way down to her diaphragm. Then she moved the air around in her lungs and slowly exhaled, starting from her diaphragm until she had no air left in her lungs. Then she started again. She lost track of time because her mother didn't disturb her. Tinay was relaxed and didn't know if she was still breathing at all, everything was so peaceful and quiet. She didn't feel the need to rush anymore. She was calm. She then realized how light she was, and pictured all the tiny balls that made her. At first she was all white, but as she looked closer, she saw that there were indeed constellations inside of her. This was fantastic, simply amazing. She paused and looked deeper inside herself. She felt as if she was swimming with the stars in the night sky. Her mother was impressed. Lilay could see Tinay floating above the floor.

Now, just blow on the stars and make them move to the left, her mother said.

Tinay smiled. She blew softly on the stars and her whole sky moved gently to the left. She laughed. *This is great.*

Now, imagine you're laying on the ground and the sky is coming to touch you, Lilay said.

Tinay pictured that she was now under the sky and it was coming towards her without touching her. She was coming down slowly eighteen feet, sixteen feet, thirteen feet, nine feet.

That's very good, honey.

Should we try to move soon?

ARGGG! Lilay screamed as a contraction took her by surprise.

By yelling, Lilay had disturbed Tinay and Tinay fell the last five feet to the ground, her body hitting the cushions while her head hit the floor.

"Ouch!" she said, rubbing her head with the palm of her hand. So much for a feathery descent!

Mother, are you all right?

Yes, sweetheart. Sorry I startled you. It took me by surprise. How's the head?

I'll be fine. I'm just glad I had some cushions to break the fall.

Tinay looked up and let out a curdling scream that could have awakened the dead. Then, she passed out.

Lilay turned around and was startled herself. There was the Guardian and Manyr.

"Manyr, Okapi, I'm so glad you are here."

"I will take it from here," said Manyr.

"My labor has started. I must get everything ready."

"Very well. Best of luck to you," said Okapi.

"I love you, honey. We'll have Tinay on her way as soon as we're done," said Manyr.

"Very well, Manyr."

Lilay returned to her home and started to prepare for her new baby. From the looks of things, her husband would not make it after all.

Chapter 15

THE CENTAUR

Raphael woke up and looked at the clock. It was four o'clock in the morning on his clock. He could not understand why he felt so rested. He got up and went to the window. Everything was quiet. Not a thing moved. He decided to use this time for meditation and, hopefully, be done by the time five a.m. arrived. He hated when his father caught him sleeping in the afternoon after he meditated. Now he would have an excuse to stay alert. Merdaine would find him dressed and ready. He changed into his clothes and lay on the floor where he would be less comfortable and less likely to fall back asleep. He closed his eyes and slowed down his breathing. He had told his mother about Aznebar but did not mention how much help he had been in just a few sessions. Aznebar had done a lot of explaining and everything made more sense to him now. He no longer liked imagining apples and oranges. He preferred to see each temple beautifully decorated. He could concentrate on his fears and control his flow of energy better. Today he wondered what new wonders he would experience.

Ah, son, I see you've used your time well today.

I woke up rested and I wanted to meet with you before breakfast. I am used to waking up early on Sasgorg, but I have never awakened so early before.

That's because you're in a different star system. Not all the planets have the same rotation and take the same amount of time to revolve around their sun.

What does that mean?

Earth revolves upon itself about every 24 hours and takes 365.25 days to revolve around the sun. Sasgorg is very similar with its 22 hours rotation and takes 398.5 days to revolve around the main sun. So a year on Sasgorg is the equivalent of a year on Earth. Essay is a bit different in that respect. The days here are 30 hours long so there's a 16 hour day's work and still plenty of time to rest. It also takes 438.33 days to rotate. For every year on Essay, one and a half goes by on Sasgorg. All the planets have been adjusted to follow regular Earth years to keep in mind the aging and growth of the body and the mind.

Wow! So how will it affect me?

You will age three years instead of two every other year. And you should have plenty of time to do your chores, your meditation, and your training.

Very well. What shall we to do today?

I will open your third eye. You will reach the sixth temple today.

But even Tinay can't do that!

She will, soon enough. You cannot be permitted to waste time. Your sister has learned of things in a different order, but she will eventually reach her elevation on time. You have started your timeline early because much is expected of you, and your progress has been because of your great work and your father's amazing teaching. The love he shares for you has created fantastic bonds, which will allow you to apprentice well. Your isolation on Sasgorg prevented the distraction that you will now have to face. So don't be surprised to move in certain areas quickly.

Aznebar continued, *Now the temple of Zuel is where you will see your own aura and find who you are. Your aura will change color as time goes by. It will describe your present state. You are young and there is time for your soul to mature. Shall we?*

Yes, I want to see the world with a different eye!

Slowly, Aznebar drew an eye on Raphael's forehead. Raphael saw the light penetrate his skull. It was as bright as the sun at midday on Essay and was warm and invigorating. He gently felt himself float through his third eye and saw that he was swimming in a sea of golden light.

Yellow. Yellow is good. Aznebar smiled. He hoped for a higher color, but was happy with what he found.

What does yellow mean? I can only tell when people are angry or lying or being dishonest. I have not seen a yellow aura before.

All the auras have a positive and a negative side. Your ability to see the aura is when it gets denser and, therefore, materializes better in the physical world. You only saw the negative side of the aura. The color red and orange have good meanings also, and we will learn those at a later time. Suffice it to say, for now, that your aura reflects an intelligent person who is wise and open to new ideas. You are creative and confident. And eventually, I expect you to develop firm convictions coming from your strength of character. Apprenticing here on Essay is part of building that strong character of yours.

Is this the last temple then?

No, there is one more, but you can only get there when your ascension takes place. There's plenty of time for that.

Very well. Anything else?

Have you given the message to your father yet?

No, he's not back yet.

Hmm, he's late. He should have been here by now.

Raphael heard footsteps coming and he ended his session with Aznebar. He wiggled his toes and fingers and opened his eyes to find Merdaine staring at him on the floor.

"Are you all right?"

"Oh yes! I was just finishing up my meditation with Aznebar."

"Who?"

"Aznebar. Don't worry. Mom said it was okay. He opened my temple of Zuel today. I have a yellow Aura."

"You....Zuel... You saw your..." Merdaine was confused. How could such a young child be making such progress? He was too young, but obviously he had been in contact with an elder. How could this be? "You are sure Aznebar is ok?"

"Yes. He's my grandpa and he wants me to be my best when the time comes. He says there will be plenty of time for me to do my chores, my training, and my meditating because the days here on Essay are longer."

"Yes, I guess I should have told you about that."

"When is my dad coming back? I have a message for him."

"Well, let's see. He's flying on Sasgorg time and it takes thirty-six hours to get there and thirty-six hours to come back. He should not spend more than a day on El, so that means he should be back.... sometime tomorrow morning, which will be suppertime for them. A bit confusing really, but for us, only two and a half days will go by while your father will have spent four days away."

"How do we keep track once we're all on different planets?"

"Engineers sell clocks that keep the Atlanti calendar and a conversion to the planet you're on. We could ask Ohuru for one if you wish."

"Yes, I think that would be wise."

"Now that you know about our different systems, you'll soon realize it will be hard on your body at first, but once you get used to the change, you will be able to stay awake for longer periods of time than people on Is, for example."

"How long is their day over there?"

"Eighteen hours and a rotation is exactly four hundred and eighty-seven days. The perfect planet. It matches Earth perfectly and there are no carry-over days necessary. Since her reign to power, Paletis has changed the Atlanti calendar to her own because she said it was perfect, like her."

"Full of herself, isn't she?"

"Yes, well, let's not share that opinion of her too loudly, ok?"

"No problem."

"Time for breakfast, little man."

Raphael followed Merdaine down the stairs. He was happy because he only had to wait for another day until his father arrived. The smell of bacon floated in the air as he reached the kitchen. He saw the table was already set. He had no time to say a blessing before he ate, so he did it while munching on the food set before him. Giselle was a great cook. He was amazed that Merdaine was not more like Amos.

"What am I to do today, Merdaine?" he asked.

"Well, that foal needs looking after, the stables need to be cleaned, and the horses given food and water. I think you'll spend the day in the stable with Elaine."

"Good." Raphael turned and smiled at Elaine. "It's about time we got to know each other."

Elaine smiled back, "And if we work quickly there should be time for us to ride the horses before night fall."

"Well, I better get some sandwiches ready for you," said Giselle who was already cleaning the table.

"What about me?" asked Atleos.

"There's more weeding needed. Ask Giselle, she'll have plenty of work for you."

Atleos looked at his hands. One was dirty and green, and the other was still bandaged. Despite his effort to use it as little as he could, the ride on the horse the day before had made the wound open again. Giselle felt sorry for him. He was in pain and was in need of a healer, or at the very least, a doctor. After they all left, she went to the garden and gave Atleos a little stool to sit on.

"This will help you to stay low to the ground without spending all your energy trying to keep your balance. I brought some cream for your hand and a clean bandage. The wound must be kept clean."

"It looks worse than it feels," Atleos began, but stopped after she touched his hand.

"How did this happen?"

"I cut myself."

"Really? From one side to the other?"

"Yes. I was walking with the knife. I tripped and then the knife fell back down and cut right through my hand."

"I see...." Giselle didn't know what to think, but if his story were true, he would never help her in the kitchen nor come close to anything sharp.

"There, it's looking much better now. Maybe I should lend you a hand so you can be done quickly today."

"No, it doesn't matter. I should be done soon enough. It just would be faster with two hands, but I can't, so Merdaine will have to be happy with me and what I can do."

"He expects all of us to work really hard, and he has no patience for slackers. But he is aware your hand is injured so that's maybe why he keeps you here with me."

"Yes, probably..." Atleos knew better. It was because he had entered Merdaine's private thoughts and he was being punished. But he didn't care much about that. He deserved to be humiliated a bit. Giselle walked away and went to her routine making lunch and a snack for the late afternoon for all the hands on the ranch.

Raphael was on the top of the barn throwing down clean bales of hay for the stalls. It was hard work, but he was enjoying the task. Elaine was a hard worker for her young age. She had the job of giving grain and water to the horses. Raphael loved the smell of horses, but it didn't make the cleaning of the stalls any nicer. It took hours to look after everyone. He changed Brownie's mother's bandages. Although the resulting scar would remain visible, the wound was healing nicely. He looked out the window and saw the pasture grass undulating in the wind. It was a perfect day for a ride. He loved to ride. He couldn't wait for his training to remain around the animals. He had been around plants all his life, but horses were impressive. He heard a whimpering coming from a corner of the barn where the apples were stored. He walked over and saw a little brown lab puppy walking to the barrels.

"Elaine, come and see the puppies!"

Elaine came running. Panting, she asked what was wrong.

"Nothing, he's just... I didn't know you had puppies."

She shrugged her shoulders indifferently, "Yeah, they were born 3 weeks ago. We'll be selling most of them in the spring."

"Do you think I could keep one?"

"You would have to ask my dad. Everything on a farm is done for a purpose. Every new foal, puppy, or calf has a destination."

"I like him." The adventurous puppy had made his way to Raphael. "We could call him Chestnut. What do you think?"

"You shouldn't name him until he's yours. That's what my dad says."

"He let me name Brownie."

"Whatever. Just talk to my dad."

The end of the morning came slowly, and, after a quick lunch, Elaine and Raphael went horseback riding in the woods. There was a beautiful mixture of trees.

"Isn't it strange that your father has such a sizeable forest on his land since he could make more money if he were to cultivate it?" Ralph asked Elaine.

"My father and his employees can only do so much. There's no need to be rich but to be able to earn a decent living out of the land. He doesn't turn a large profit, but we don't exert ourselves either."

Ralph stared at Elaine. "You don't sound like a four year old."

"Didn't anybody tell you how the time changes from one planet to the next?"

"This morning, actually, my..."

"Well then, I'm four on Essay, but on your world I would be somewhere around six nearing seven."

"That makes more sense. So we're not so far apart in age, are we?"

"No, we're not."

"When is your birthday?"

"I was born here on the solstice of the sun in the spring. So we celebrate my birthday according to Essay's calendar. When's yours?"

"I was born on the 30th day of Mars of the Atlanti calendar."

"You won't be able to keep that here. We'll have my friend Adriaine look up your birthday on her converter and see what your birthday would be here."

"Sure, I guess since I'll be here for a long time. I should adapt to your calendar."

They changed their course once more and ended up by a lake. Raphael and Elaine got off the horse and led them to the water. Raphael stretched and yawned.

"Are you tired already?"

"I'm not used to such long days. Your father said it would take me some time to get used to it."

"I guess so. Maybe I can go see Adriaine now and you can have a nap here in the shade. Can you make your way back alone?"

"Yes, I can. On Sasgorg I guided myself with the stars at night, so I would not get lost in the sand. I'm sure I can do the same here."

"Well, don't sleep too long or you'll miss supper."

"I won't."

Elaine got up on her horse and galloped away from the clearing. Raphael took the saddle off his horse, laid it on the ground, and closed his eyes. He loved sleeping in the afternoon. He was so used to it on Sasgorg. Even though it angered his father, he would always sleep after meditating. That way he could always stay up a little longer with his father at night. He closed his eyes and had no trouble falling asleep.

Raphael didn't know how long he slept, but the clearing was dark. He felt someone near him and looked around suspiciously. His sister always loved to scare him when he was alone by the well on Sasgorg. But it couldn't be her; she was stuck on another planet. Maybe it was Elaine. She had returned from her friend's and was ready to tell him what his new birthday would be. He stood up and looked at the sky. It was still clear. He couldn't see the stars yet, so it couldn't be that late. He heard a ruffle of leaves and wondered if maybe it was an animal that was observing him. What kind of wild animals were here on Essay? He didn't remember reading that chapter in the book. He started to worry. He looked around and saw a man standing in the bush with a cross bow on his shoulder.

"Hello. I'm Raphael. I'm here, uh, sleeping... Um, I thought I was on Merdaine's land. I'm sorry if..."

"No, youngling, you are on Merdaine's land, but at dusk, we take care of the forest, making it safe for his livestock."

"Yes, I was wondering what kind of animal might live here. Elaine left me here so I was not too worried, you see."

"Elaine never comes to the woods after dusk, she knows better. She told you not to sleep too long, did she not?"

"Yes, um, as a matter of fact."

"It is time for you to go home now."

"Yes, um, of course." Raphael walked over to his horse and put the saddle on him. He gently spoke to him, "You're a good boy. You were watching over me, weren't you?"

"You are kind to animals. I heard you saved a foal and a mare yesterday. Is that true?"

"Yes, well, Merdaine told me what to do. I think he could have done it himself, really..."

"No, he could not have."

"Well, I thought that since I..."

"You thought wrong. It is very difficult to do what you did. You must be very good at manipulating a knife."

"My dad taught me, but Merdaine had a knife also and..."

"He is a great bow and crossbow archer, but his knife is not very agile. You saved two lives yesterday and my clan wanted to say thank you."

"Who are you? Who is your clan? Was the foal destined to be yours?"

"My clan does not believe in property. In Atlantis, we were once the property of the king and at the mercy of soldiers. We fared poorly and a few of my clan escaped with the order. We resettled on different planets, where there were no humans."

"I see."

"We colonized our world, but when Paletis overthrew the order, we all went into hiding to protect ourselves and our young ones from becoming slaves again."

"Why would your clan be a slave more than any other family?"

"I am Yehudi of the Menuhin tribe. I am a centaur." As he said those words, he walked in the clearing and showed his lower half of his body. He was half man and half horse.

"I thought you were just a legend!" Raphael was so surprised he didn't know if he should be scared or in awe of the sight before his eyes.

"We are a genetic manipulation of mad scientists who were looking for intelligent, yet very strong slaves that could not escape. They transformed us, without pity or wisdom. We are what we are and have learned to accept what we have become. But we refuse to be slaves anymore."

"I don't blame you." Raphael was unsure if he should bow to the creature or actually mount his horse. "Do you mind that we ride horses then?"

"I would mind if you were to mistreat them. And there is no one to ride us now. We put ourselves at the service of no man."

"But you protect the woods for Merdaine."

"Because we worked together when Sasgorg faced eminent destruction, we allowed humans to settle here. Again, we join forces to defeat the Evil Queen. Once peace has been restored, we will return to our planet and leave your world behind."

"It's too bad. I'm sure there's lots we could learn from you. You have not been slaves for thousands of years, so you must have evolved into a complex society."

"Wise words you have spoken, youngling. Indeed, we have learned to read from the clouds, the mountain currents, and the wind what is to come. We live peacefully with our clan and wait for the next run in the hills. But a society, we are not. We live as free as the wind and play music when not at war."

"Music?"

"Yes, I play the violin."

Raphael was surprised, yet he didn't know why. He should be in shock; he just met a legend who played the violin. His mind was not making sense of it all just yet.

"Well, it is an honor to have met you, sir. Um, well, will I see you again?"

"When you return, I shall be here. I would love to talk about your procedure that saved the mare and the foal."

"That would be a great pleasure for me."

"We shall then see you on your return. Follow the northern path. It will lead you to the farm."

"Thank you." Raphael waved and left galloping through the woods. His heart thumped harder than the horse's hooves on the ground. He had met a centaur and he lived to tell the tale. This would make such a great story. He saw a shadow growing near him. The sun had set a while ago and the prairie was growing dark, but he could see on the horizon the fire made by Merdaine's men. He finally was able to make out the shadow of Merdaine himself coming towards him.

"Little boy!"

"Yes, sir." Raphael was starting to think not a day would go by without angering Merdaine.

"Are you safe? Are you all right?"

"Yes, why shouldn't I ..."

"The woods are not safe after dusk. You shouldn't have slept this long," Merdaine said gruffly.

"I'm sorry. I didn't mean to but, uh, Youdini was watching after me."

"Who?"

"Youdini of the Menini tribe?" Raphael realized he was not so good with names to start with and the centaur had been so impressive, he hardly took mention of his name.

"You met Yehudi of Menuhin?"

"Yeah, that's it. Yeahoudi of Men-ouhhan..."

"And you lived?"

"Why shouldn't I?"

"He doesn't like strangers and trusts no one except me, and he tolerates Elaine just because she is so young and pure."

"Well, he not only let me live, but he guarded me from harm."

"Wha...?"

"Yes, he even invited me again to talk about how I saved Brownie."

"I see. He knows already."

"Yes. Is that ok? I mean, if I go back?"

"Yes, but not today. And tomorrow, your father will be here so it'll have to wait until you come back."

"Okay." Raphael was happy. This would give him time to read more about centaurs in his books at home and be better prepared the next time.

"Merdaine, I saw the puppy in the barn today."

"Yes." Merdaine raised his eyebrows.

"Well, I was wondering, can I have Chestnut?"

"Chestnut? Which one is he?"

"He's the curious one."

"You two would fare well together. I think that can be arranged. You'll need a dog for the hunt. Chestnut is as good as any."

They rode silently towards the fire. The days had already started to get shorter and fall colors were starting to replace the green of the summer. Raphael was happy to see reds, oranges, and yellows, and not just purple, white, and black. He was not very sleepy and sat by the fire after supper and started to read more from his book on plants. There was nothing new there. His mother had apparently taught him well. He wouldn't have to study much, at least for his first year. He would be able to exercise his hand at the knife and, hopefully, the crossbow. Raphael stayed up after everyone went to sleep, his body unaccustomed to the rotation of Essay. It was not until early that morning that he finally fell asleep.

Merdaine was up a few hours later and saw that Raphael must have been up most of the night since he had almost finished reading the book he had only started the night before. Merdaine decided to let him sleep.

It was about five p.m. aboard the ship when Tamael and Ohuru caught sight of Essay.

"I'm looking forward to a nice supper at Merdaine's. I hope his wife made lamb," Ohuru said.

"I hate to disappoint you, but it's morning on Merdaine's farm, not evening, and therefore you might end up with porridge or cold cereal." Tamael was also disappointed, but hid it well. He wanted a taste of something different.

"You know, maybe there will be leftovers?" said Ohuru, half asking, half stating.

"Maybe." Tamael was unsure there would be with all the men she had to feed.

The landing went well and they took the small shuttle to go pick up Atleos and Raphael. They arrived just in time for breakfast. Merdaine, who always loved to see outside when he ate, saw them arrive and met them outside.

"Hello, men. Had yourselves a good time?" he said, motioning them inside.

"It was amazing. Sold everything and the celebration was fantastic," said Ohuru.

"Yes, I must say, it was our best trip ever."

"Really? Met some old friends?" Merdaine smiled.

"Yes, I guess you could say that." And in a whisper Tamael added, "You knew?"

"Yes, but I couldn't go. Not this time. How was the competition?"

"Oh, well, you know…" Tamael blushed.

"He won, but he could have been more dramatic about it," said Ohuru as he reached the door. "What's for breakfast?"

"Giselle prepared your favorite dish last night and made sure there would be some left for you two this morning," said Merdaine.

"Favorite…?" Ohuru hoped Merdaine wasn't taunting.

"Yes, my dear, lamb in mushroom sauce. It is your favorite, Ohuru, is it not?" Giselle asked as they entered into the kitchen.

"Oh, may you be blessed." Ohuru sat down and started to eat immediately.

"Where's my boy? Do you already have him put to work?" Tamael asked.

"Actually, he'll make a good worker. First, he'll need time to adjust to our different time and length of days. Then we'll be fine."

"Yeah, I keep forgetting about that. Where is he?"

"Sleeping on the couch. Eat, you can wake him up later."

Tamael agreed. The food smelled delicious, who could resist?

It was nearly seven in the morning when Raphael woke up. He was completely disoriented and couldn't tell which day it was or what part of the day this was. All he knew was that he was hungry again. He looked at the kitchen and saw his father sitting there. He rubbed his hands over his eyes, thinking he was still dreaming, but then realized he was awake. He ran to the kitchen, "Pa!"

He jumped on his father and they lost their balance on the chair and ended on the floor hugging each other.

"I missed you so much and I have tons to tell you about horses and puppies and ..."

"The forest is to remain out of conversation, little man."

Raphael understood that he would not be discussing centaurs anytime soon, but he still had tons of stuff to say.

"How can you have so much to say if you missed me so much?"

"Huh?"

"I thought you would have been too distraught to do anything or to have any time to explore and enjoy yourself," Tamael said, grinning widely.

"Yes, well, Merdaine kept me busy. Right, Merdaine?" Raphael sent a pleading look towards Merdaine. He had missed his father, he didn't realize just how much until he saw him. That should count. He didn't mean to forget about his family, but he was so busy here, time just flew by.

"Yes, no time to play or to sleep. We kept him very busy."

"Rightly so," said a smiling Tamael. He, too, felt guilty. He had so much fun on El, he forgot all about the dark time, even for a few hours. That was a blessing and gave him hope that life could return to normal.

"Oh, I almost forgot, father!"

"What is it, Raph?"

"I have a message from Azn..."

"Yes." Tamael couldn't remember if he had told his son to never pronounce this name. This was something he would have to correct very fast. "What news of your imaginary friend, Aznel?"

"My... who... oh...yeah...well we were in a dream together and we saw that mother was calling for you and wanted you to come home right away." Raphael hoped that he had done well on this one, but everyone at the table looked perplexed. As long as his dad understood, that was all that mattered.

"Well, son, I think your dream is right about one thing, your mother would probably rather have us come home sooner than later. We are a few days late already, so we best move on. Merdaine, Giselle, thank you for your hospitality, but we must be off."

Merdaine did not know what was going on, but he knew if his friend was in a rush. It was best to help them on their way. He went upstairs and dragged Atleos out of bed.

Ohuru, who was still eating, did not understand what had just happened, "No rush, my friends. I need to do a check up and fuel up the cargo and, you know, see if anything is needed."

"That won't do. We must leave immediately." Tamael became more authoritative.

"Well, I was not planning to depart until tomorrow morning, to tell you the truth. I'm a bit tired and…"

"I'll fly. We're going now."

Ohuru knew he was missing something because his friend had never talked to him that way. He got up, kissed Giselle on the cheek, shook Merdaine's large hands, and went to the shuttle. Atleos, still half asleep, walked quietly a few steps behind them. Raphael waved at Elaine and started running to his father's side.

"I'm sorry that we must leave so soon. We'll have more time to visit next time."

"Yes, of course. Is everything ok? Can I help?" Ohuru was confused.

"I hope not, and no, you can't help unless you can make us go faster."

"I'll do what I can. I'll call the landing platform and tell them to fuel the ship now."

"Thank you, my friend. Thank you."

When they reached the shuttle, all four of them climbed aboard and Ohuru departed immediately. Ohuru did not say a word.

Tamael turned to Raphael and said, "I'm sorry, but you cannot talk about Aznebar in public. From now on he'll be your imaginary friend. What is it that he said exactly?"

"Mom needs your help and you have to go home immediately."

"When was this?"

"Yesterday morning."

Tamael murmured a curse under his breath. If his wife had taken a risk to ask for his help then it had to be serious.

"We need to get to Sasgorg quickly. Ohuru, I apologize to you, but I need your help."

"No need to worry. I was surprised by your behavior, nevertheless. I imagined I was missing something. I guess we'll have to go the shorter but more dangerous way."

"Dangerous?" Atleos did not like the sound of that. He was collecting scars faster than he wished and had no desire to acquire more.

"We'll fly into the asteroid field, which means very little sleep for anyone tonight. I'll need eyes everywhere. We might come out a little dented, but we'll only need 25 hours to get there," said Ohuru.

"I need to get there now!"

"Tamael, I can understand this, but what do you suppose I am to do?"

"Light speed after the asteroid field."

Ohuru's mouth hung open and he swore his heart skipped a beat. "No," he said simply. After twenty years in exile, he would bring forth all this attention to the Armada and put all his family in one tight pinch. He could not believe it.

"Then what?"

"I can travel a little faster on manual in the asteroid field, but that increases the danger of us getting hit."

Again, they heard Atleos squeak, "Danger?"

"But on the outside we'll have to resume our speed, if we make it out alive."

"Alive?" Atleos turned green. Maybe he wasn't cut out for this kind of stuff.

"Atleos, get a grip," Raphael whispered.

"How much time?" asked Tamael.

"Depends. I can't say until we've gone through the asteroid field, but I can give you an estimate on the other side."

"That's the best you can do?"

"Yes, for now."

"Very well, then." Tamael stared at the window outside and started to pray fervently for the safety of his wife and daughter.

Chapter 16

THE GUARDIAN

Tinay laid on the comfortable cushion and had no idea how long it had been since she had the scare of her life. She kept her eyes closed, and tried to make sense of it all. Her dad had been in here, a few times by the looks of it, and he never had mentioned any skeletons, monsters, or anything scary for that matter. She, as a matter of fact, didn't recall ever being scared. Her fingers were still tingling and her head still felt light and the room still spun a bit.

Maybe, some of it has to do with that lump. Ouch!

She must have been tired, and it was only a hallucination she had. It just wasn't real. It was plainly impossible. She sat up and slowly opened her eyes. No, it was still there. No hallucination, it was real. What was that anyway? She stood up and slowly walked over. Whatever this thing was, it was huge. If the roof of this room was twenty feet high, the beast would hardly be able to stand up. Its tail was about twenty feet long and finished with a large spike that looked like an arrow. It must have been forty-five feet long. It had an impressive wing span. Alive, it must have been an unbelievable beast. All along the spine were spikes. On the tip of its toes were claws that looked like they could tear through any flesh or scales. The tip of its head had horns and the mouth was filled with large teeth. A scary skeleton, but he would be even scarier if he was alive. A net covered most of its form and, on the center of the head, a single Alenor crystal hung from the net. It had a clarity that reflected pure light. She took a few steps back and looked at the majesty of the beast. *A dragon, here, on Sasgorg?* Then a voice answered her mind's question.

Yes, my child.

Startled, Tinay asked, "Who are you?"

I am known as Manyr, but your mother always preferred to call me Mamili.

"Great grand-mother?"

Yes, dear child, it is I. Can I show myself to you?

"Yes, of course!"

Slowly, Tinay saw a violet silhouette build up in front of her. She looked three-dimensional, but she was only composed of violet highlights and shadows. Tinay could tell she was beautiful. Manyr's traits were soft and her hair flowed gently around her.

This is the essence of me. I may look slightly different in person, but if you were to look into my eyes, you would always recognize me.

"I see you. How old are you?"

My, what a curious nature you have. I'm ninety-eight years old.

"You don't look a day over fifty."

Thank you, child. Kyr preserved me well.

"Is that where you're from?"

Yes, I'm an elder. I'm here to help you achieve the sixth step in your meditation, the third eye.

"That's great! I was kind of stuck there. What about this dragon? What does he represent?"

He is the Guardian. He is the one you must face before I can help you open your eye. May I introduce him to you?

"Introduce him? How could he fit in here without me noticing?"

Just like me, he couldn't come here in flesh and blood, but his spirit can fill the skeleton and bring it to life again. He is scary to look at, however, he is a protector and would not harm you in any way.

"Well, I guess a spirit can't hurt me."

I wouldn't be so sure about that, darling, but for today, I think you'll be safe.

Tinay didn't know what to make of Manyr's last comment, but she didn't have to linger very long on that thought. Before her eyes, a greenish glow appeared inside the dragon's body. He was magnificent and large, very large. Tinay started to feel dizzy. She realized she had stopped breathing. She gasped for air. The dragon was incredible. She had no idea what to do next. He stood calmly smiling at her, waiting.

"Welcome to Sasgorg," she blurted.

"Thank you. Now, it is traditional that you should bow to me," the dragon said.

Tinay quickly bowed and took a moment to catch her breath. This beat all the books she had read so far.

"Very well now, stand up," he said gravely.

"Why can I hear your voice with my ears, but only hear my grandmother's in my head?"

"Your grand-mother is human, I'm a Knucker dragon. I have abilities that humans do not possess."

"My apology. I have never seen a dragon other than in picture books and they do not do you justice. I thought you were a figment of the writers' imagination."

"Very well, shall we proceed?"

"Proceed?"

"I am here to test your cunning and wisdom. I am here to challenge you and see if I can either be beaten or drawn out before sunrise. My sunrise, that is. I cannot be absent for more than that. I'm afraid and your grandmother does not have the time to stay much longer than I."

"Very well, let's begin."

Tinay sat in front of the dragon and even though only his spirit lit the skeleton up, it was an amazing sight. The Alenor crystal shone brightly on his head. She could only imagine what he would look like if he was covered with them.

"I can read your mind, child. I would look fantastic, and I did once, but the Alenor crystals had to be moved so only a carcass remains, but..."

"How is this going to be fair, if you can read my mind?"

"I won't do it while we play."

"What guarantees do I have?"

"YOU HAVE MY WORDS, SILLY HUMAN!" Okapi growled, offended.

"I'm sorry, I was just...."

"You will have to trust me. You have no other choice."

Tinay thought to herself. She did have a choice, she could just walk away. But somehow this seemed a little bit more important than winning an argument with an ancient dragon.

"Very well. What should I call you?"

"You can call me Master Okapi. Ready?"

"Yes, I am," Tinay said with conviction in her voice. After all, she had played riddles with her mom since she was a toddler.

"Let's start with an easy one:
> What goes on four legs in the morning, two in the afternoon, and three in the evening?"

"Hmm, let's see. What kind of marvelous creature would grow four legs to start with and not need them by lunch, but by the end of the day would require three and this on a daily basis? That would be ridiculous. Unless it only lives one day. Then, perhaps, it would learn to walk on four and then gradually end up on two, but why revert back to three? And what lives only one day other than insects? But insects have more than four legs. Is this something I know?"

"Yes, it is. It would be unfair to question you about something you are not aware of. But it could be something you learned from a book, and have not necessarily seen with your eyes."

Tinay thought that although she knew lots about plants, potion and books, she had very little experience with the rest of the world. So what on her planet could walk on four legs rather than two and finish on three legs?

Could it be?

"A baby walks on all four when it's born, then as he grows up he learns to stand on two legs. I never saw an elder before today, but I know that a crutch can be made to help the injured walk and so that would be three legs. So when the human is old and has difficulty walking, he uses a cane. The answer would be a human."

"Well done, a human."

"But a human takes a lifetime to evolve into each stage. Why say it was only in a day?"

"In the dawn of its life, the human crawls as a child. In the afternoon of its life, a human walks as an adult. At the eve of its life, the human uses a stick, crutch, or cane to help him or herself."

"I see how this game is to be played."

"It's now your turn to ask me a riddle."

"All right then:

> Only one color,
> but not one size,
> stuck at the bottom,
> yet easily flies,
> present in the sun but not in the rain,
> doing no harm, and feeling no pain."

"Very well, no pain, so it cannot be alive. Something that could easily be a kite. It could be stuck at the bottom for the lack of wind, but it would be present rain or shine. If it disappears when it's wet, it could be because it's wet itself and would lose form like a tear or a drop of water. Or it would have something to do with the sun. What is present at day and not at night? Hmm, I see a shadow would be there. It would be of one color, but would vary immensely in size or shape, for that matter. It would be stuck at the bottom, unless the shadow is projected onto a wall. My answer is a shadow."

"Well done."

"Now what?"

"We continue:

> What force and strength cannot get through,
> I, with a gentle touch, can do,
> and many in the street would stand,
> were I not a friend at hand."

"It cannot get through, so the idea is to get through something. Something that would leave you outside if it was not for the item we're looking for. So we are trying to get inside. Is this a literal one or is it another figurative thing? Could the strong come from mother nature and the soft from a human hand?"

Tinay looked over at the dragon and tried to look deep into his eyes, but found only a twinkle for her trouble.

"Here on Sasgorg we have no need to lock our doors for fear of strangers, but we do try to prevent the wind from invading us with sand and we need to hold to doors closed. The key to the lock only needs a gentle touch and it does fit in your hand. I will say it's a key."

"Hmm, you are better at this than you let on."

Okapi was disappointed. This was going so fast. Although he knew many riddles, it would cost him all his knowledge to keep the game going for hours if she continued to do so well.

"Very well:

> Round like an apple,
> deep like a cup,
> yet all the king's horses can't pull it up."

"Ahh! Child you must beware of the clues that you give."

Tinay was startled. She didn't give him much to go on and, yet, he still thought this was easy.

"There are no kings on your planet and you have never before been anywhere else. You have taken this riddle from a book. A book on knights and king Atlantis. Not many things were round except the island itself and the well where the water came from. Only the ocean knows no bound, so therefore, it leaves us with only a well."

Tinay could not believe her ears. He smiled as he looked at her getting ready for another riddle. His were by no means easy to figure out, but she thought she was a bit more of a challenge to him than this.

"How can I win this again?"

"You must find a riddle I can't answer or keep playing until sun up."

"Right, this might turn out to be more challenging than I thought."

"We're moving right on to the next one:

> Old mother Twichet had one eye,
> and a long tail that she let fly,
> and every time she went through a gap,
> She left a bit of her tail in the trap."

"Wow! These are not easy. Now, let's see. I don't know an old mother Twichet and I've never heard about her before. I have certainly never heard of a woman with one eye. So this must mean it's figuratively speaking. Something with one eye? A snake doesn't have one eye. What else could have a tail that they could let fly? A bird and a dragon have two eyes. So it's not someone that lives. What has something that has a tail that flies? A kite maybe. It has a tail but not one eye. And what of the gap that became a trap. It either doesn't know about the trap or voluntarily goes there. This is hard. I must be looking in the wrong direction. If it's an inanimate object, what could only have one eye? Could it be a telescope? It has one eye, but no tail. Hang on, what about a needle? It has one eye. The thread could be its tail and as you sew the thread stays behind."

Tinay looked at Okapi and waited for a sign.

"What?" asked Okapi.

"Is that the answer? A needle?"

"It cannot be a guess. You must tell me your answer. You're allowed to guess all you want, but you must give me a final answer."

"Then my final answer is a needle with thread."

"Very well, it is the right answer. You are doing well, Initiate."

"So it's my turn now? Right?"

"Indeed."

"Here goes:

> It has long legs,
> bandy thighs,
> a little head,
> and no eyes."

"It would indeed make an interesting animal. Some animals do manage without eyes, but they're fishes, not really an animal. What about some vegetable? A green onion, perhaps. It has a long stem and a little head and no eyes. But bandy thighs? Could be a stool. It has long legs and a little head and no eyes, but bandy thighs? That's hard. What about a shower? Nope, no legs. Maybe a fork or a spoon. It has the head and no eyes, but only one leg."

Okapi noticed Tinay raise an eyebrow. He knew he was on the right track.

"What other utensils have two legs? Thongs? Yes, it is a thong."
"I can see why they call you Master. You're very good at this."
"Indeed, let's see if you can complete this one:

> In marble walls as white as milk,
> lined with skin as soft as silk,
> within a fountain crystal clear,
> a golden apple did appear.
> No doors are there to this stronghold,
> yet thieves break in and steal the gold."

"All right, before we continue, can I eat something?"
"No, water only."
Tinay got up to go towards her gourd when it slowly moved towards her, floating in the air. She looked back and saw the dragon grinning.
"Simple levitation, Tinay, simple levitation."
"Right."
She took the gourd from mid-air and swallowed a big gulp. She needed time to think of a better riddle for herself. Not to mention she had to solve this new puzzle.
"Ah, let's see. It has a skin of some sort, so it could be a human and the gold could be an organ. But who would want to steal anything inside a human body? Maybe not human then. An animal? Their skin can be strong. Its skin is white, the soft hair could be compared to silk, but what would be golden about an animal's insides? It's the fur that someone would want. Maybe a vegetable? Corn could be the gold, but it's not wrapped in white. Its envelope is green. What about an onion? No, it's the reverse. The outside is gold and the inside is white."
Tinay looked to the dragon for some hint and she got no help there. His face was stone cold, just his eyes were sparkling.
"What else is white? Oh, I see it! An egg. It's an egg. It's white and it's got a lining. The inside is clear matter that surrounds the center, the golden apple. It's an egg. Ha ha ha!"
"Hmm, I guess you're better at this than you readily admit."
"I believe this one will give you a run for your money. Are you ready?"
"Yes, I'm always ready for a good riddle."

"Then let's try this one for size:

> Black we are, and much admired,
> men seek for us if they're tired,
> we tire the horse, but comfort man,
> tell me this riddle if you can."

"Dear child, I'm a dragon. I know man well for I have cohabitated with them for millennia, but most of all, I, myself, like warmth and comfort. Coal is black, yet it is admired for its properties. Men seek it to warm their stoves and furnaces and the warmth comforts them and the poor horse has to pull it from the cargo bay to their dwelling. And it is one of the few forms of heat you possess here on Sasgorg. The answer is coal."

Tinay's shoulder's dropped. What else could she think of that was not from her world?

"At this rate, we will be continuing this until morning."

Tinay wasn't sure if she was looking at this positively. How many more riddles from the Master could she solve? They were not easy and she considered herself lucky she had come this far. What was next?

"Here's an easy one for you:

> As I was going to St. Ives,
> I met a man with seven wives,
> each wife had seven sacks,
> each sack had seven cats,
> each cat had seven kits.
> Kits, cats, sacks and wives,
> how many were going to St-Ives?

"Master Okapi, I don't think it is that easy. Now, there's the man, so that's one and he has seven wives, so that makes eight. That would be too easy. Each wife is carrying seven cats in sacks, I don't count the sacks but I could count the cats, so that would make fifty and with the kittens that would make three hundred and ninety-three. Hmm, not very hard math involved, but easy. I don't believe you would simply give it to me. What is it you asked me again? How many were going to St. Ives? So let's go over this again. You were going to St-Ives. Should I be counting you then? Where's the catch? You met a man who had seven wives. Oh! Ha ha ha! One, only one is going to St. Ives. You met only the man. It doesn't matter how many wives he has. He's alone. You met one man! AH!"

Okapi smiled. For a minute, he thought he had fooled her and it would be the end of this ritual. But it looked like they were going for another round.

"Yes, you're right, only one man. What do you have for me now?"

"I wish I had a bit more time to think or a bit more experience with life so I could make it a little harder for you to go through this. But here goes:

> A hill full,
> a hole full,
> you cannot catch a bowl full."

"Nice rhyming. Now let's see, what could cover a hill or fill a hole without being caught in a bowl? It couldn't be earth or rain because that could be contained in a bowl. What else is there on a hill? The sky is above it and the air is part of the sky, so are the clouds, which physically could actually be put in a bowl. So what's left? It would have to be something without substance like smoke. What could be rolling on the hills? Ah yes, the mist rolled in. Interesting one and you even made it rhyme. Good effort, the answer is mist."

Tinay was absorbed in her thoughts. She had not been listening to the rambling of the dragon, as she was getting ready for another riddle instead, the better one, the one he wouldn't find.

"Huh?"

"I said the answer is mist."

"Oh yeah, mist or fog. I would have accepted both answers. I guess it's my turn now?"

"Indeed, here we go:

> Little Nancy Etticoat,
> in a white petticoat,
> and a red nose,
> the longer she stands,
> the shorter she grows."

"A red nose? What, a clown? I guess not, but that was a funny image. Hmm, so something that shortens over time. Maybe a shadow, but we've done that already so that would be very unoriginal from a Master."

Tinay looked up at Okapi. He smiled.

"So what else has a red nose? A thermometer. It has a red nose. It sort of stands, but the mercury goes up and down, not just down. What else is white with a red nose? Hmm, the longer it stands, the more it shortens. An old lady who is getting smaller and has a drinking problem? Ah aha. Oh! Come on! It's funny."

Okapi didn't laugh.

"Where have you learned about alcoholism?"

"It's in one of mother's books. It's a disease, but it can be cured and one of the side effects is a red nose. I just thought it was funny next to a clown, you know."

Master Okapi had a serious look on his face. He clearly didn't think there was any humor in this.

"Okay then, it's probably not a person. This is just like old mother Twichet. I'm looking for a thing. Oh, what about a candle? It's long at first, but when it burns, it's red and it shrinks with time. Yeah, it's a burning candle."

"Very well, you've succeeded again, but you must remember this is no laughing matter. Your initiation is the beginning of seven years of intensive training. This is your future you hold in your hands."

"I apologize, Master Okapi. I'm tired and I'm hungry. My mother needs me and my father is away and she needs him as well."

"I can reassure you he is on his way. He will be here soon. You need not worry about him. Now, do you have a riddle for me?" Tinay bowed her head.

"Yes, Master, I do.

> Black within and red without,
> with four corners round about."

"You keep your riddles short in hopes not to give too many hints. However, this also means your answers are simple and cannot be described in an intricate manner. I put myself in your shoes and can see the truth come to me. Something is surrounded by a square.

On your world, hardly anything is square, for it to have four corners is special and would hold a significant place in your life, and if it's black inside, in this planet of light and brightness then it must be inside your home. What in your home is square? The table? A bed? A dresser? What would be red without?" Okapi breathed fire and watched as the red flames lingered for a moment in the air.

"What else is inside a home and, if not contained, would turn everything into a blaze? And where is the fire kept so it won't set ablaze the home and its content? The chimney, of course. Your answer is the chimney."

"Right again you are, Master Okapi, and your riddles are not getting any easier. Let's hope I can resolve this one."

"There are but a few hours left, my child. You have a good chance of passing."

Tinay could keep creating simple riddles all night, she was not worried about this. But she was concerned about her own power to solve the Master's riddle. She could not count on luck much longer.

"Let's move on, shall we?

> Thoughts of red,
> goes to your head,
> when you think of me,
> I warm you up,
> but I can't be held in a cup,
> I have nowhere to go but up,
> when you let me flee,
> unless you imprison me."

"Warm, what could keep you or me warm? Fire keeps you warm, but you can't imprison a fire, so maybe it could be vapor. It goes up and when it's vapor, it's warm. It could even burn. But it's not red. What could flee and go up? A bird? It could be red, but why would it warm me up? I'm not sure I can take much more of this. Warmth means heat. That's it, isn't it? Heat. When you think of heat, you think of fire, red and warm. It can't be held in a cup and tends to go up and it is kept under a blanket. Yes, it must be heat."

Tinay was physically and mentally exhausted. She needed this to stop so she could eat and regain some strength. Master Okapi bowed his head.

"Yes, indeed, heat. Something not missing from your planet, but that I miss dearly on mine."

"Well, one last round, then, and let's hope I can end this now."

"Don't despair, my child. The morning on my planet will be here soon. Your trial is almost over."

"All right, I have been preparing this one. Listen well:

> Building blocks to the temple,
> the key to the mysteries of life
> dependant on each other
> united they stand, divided they fall
> the three that explain it all,
> two in the present, one in the future,
> it explains the past trials
> and the success of our survival
> over all that is evil
> and the decaying house they live in."

"This one is much better thought out. I can see the planning involved, which is why the other riddles were so easy. Now let's see, there are three. A trinity? The three fairies, perhaps? But you wouldn't have them fight evil and overcome it in time. You wouldn't know that just yet. Or maybe it's their abilities that I should focus on: the experience, the learning or the imagination or knowledge. Hmm. . . There are so many. I think that the decaying house is a body and, therefore, it probably represents the mother, the father, and the future is the child. Together, they defeat the body by procreating and, over time, overcome evil with learning, and what is more mysterious than the birth of a child? And the temple would be the family they are building. Yes, a mother and a father expecting a child, that is my answer."

Tinay smiled. She clapped and wanted to shout, and then she figured, why not?

"Hurrah! You lost! I win! This is over! I get food! Ahahahaha!"

"What do you mean I have lost? What is the answer to the riddle then?" Master Okapi had always solved any riddles given to him. The initiation always lasted until morning and the initiate was allowed to move on.

"The temple is life. We are looking for the mystery of life. There's more than one thing, there are three. Only together can they defeat evil, and apart they are worth nothing. They are lodged in the body that does decay over time. The two in the present are unconditional love and faith, which in turn give birth to hope, and with hope, everything can be defeated."

Tinay beamed. She got up and went towards her bag for food, but suddenly she was immobilized by a force she could not see.

"You may have won and it may be a rare feat among humans, a very rare feat. But you still owe me respect and honor."

"Of course, I'm sorry. I only read about legends and myths. I have no protocol on how to behave in this instance, I'm deeply sorry. What am I supposed to do?"

"You should keep the festivities for later and maintain control of your emotions."

I knew I shouldn't have shouted, she thought.

"Next, you will bow to me and await there for me to grant you your Alenor crystal."

Tinay lowered herself to the ground, kneeled down and bowed her head.

"Good. I hereby grant you the title of apprentice and pledge you with the house of the ..."

"*Dragon! Master Okapi! Dragon!*" Manyr interrupted.

She had been patiently waiting for the game to finish. Tinay's real descendants and heritage had to remain sealed for a little longer. Not the whole truth could be revealed.

"Uh, Dragon," Tinay said, calling Okapi's attention back to her.

Okapi continued as if nothing had happened, "Here's your Alenor crystal. You must be careful. You will only receive one. It will help guide you, focus your energy, and help you accomplish things. There are many powers inside such a simple gem and, just like you, its power will grow and assist you. Throughout your apprenticeship, you will learn how to use the crystal."

Master Okapi levitated the crystal and deposited it around Tinay's neck. It had a fine chain of gold that was beautifully intricate. The crystal that lay on her chest emanated a bright yellow light.

"Congratulations. Now I must return. My work is done here."

"Thank you, Master Okapi. I understand there was some risk involved in your journey. I am deeply honored and thankful for your visit. It means a lot to me, and my family will be so pleased to see I have found my way."

"The honor was all mine, Tinay, all mine."

The great dragon flapped its astral wings and left through the light shaft. He was still majestic even though he was only in the astral form. He was beautiful to watch.

I guess it's just you and me now, child, said Manyr.

Tinay turned around and looked at Manyr. Manyr was soft and quiet. This should be a nice change. Now that she passed the test, it would get a little easier, she thought.

Actually, child, your life has just been sent into turmoil for the next seven years. You will live one adventure after another: meeting people, and making friends, and maybe some enemies along the way.

Enemies?

Eventually you will meet someone you can't please. They'll envy you and hate you. It's inevitable.

Tinay looked perplexed, *What are we going to do?*

Well, I'll let you eat a quick bite and then we'll lay down for a meditation and open up your third eye. How does that sound?

Scary, why would I need help if it wasn't dangerous?

It's not dangerous, it's just that once you open your third eye, you can see others, but it also allows them to see you. You are not guarded anymore and you need to learn the different ways not to let anyone invade your mind at will. They can do so at a distance.

Master Okapi could.

Yes, he could, but he's a dragon. Dragons have a code of honour. They would never use it against you or your family.

What about Mother?

Your mother has been in contact with you since you were first conceived. The bond you share is a bit different.

I see. Will you teach me everything I need to know?

I'll take you on a special astral trip. I'll be there with you and then I'll come and teach you a little more as you meditate in the morning. It's important that you continue your meditation every day before you start your work. When I can, I'll be there to teach you. How does that sound?

Like Mother said, there's no need to learn too much at once. You'll get an overload, she has always said. I am beginning to understand what she meant now.

Let's move over to the cushion and let you eat a bit, shall we?

Together they moved towards the cushion and sat down. Tinay started to eat. Draco, who had been asleep all night, woke up at the sound of the rustling and came over for his share.

"Right, you sleep in and get to eat. Do you actually think that's fair?"

The ferret stared at her.

"Of course you don't care. You just want food."

Tinay broke off a piece of jerky for him to chew and continued eating.

* * * * *

As the lights in the atrium lit up, Alayana saw her surroundings take shape again. She was so eager for the end of the story. She could not believe she would have to wait for another week to hear the story. That was the advantage of having a book; at least she could read until she was done.

Brett and John were talking about the dragon. They could not believe their ears. Marcus was satisfied that Tinay was involved in some adventures and was not just reading a book the whole time.

He came towards Mani and asked her, "Where do you find those riddles, Mani?"

"I read many books on dragons and sphinxes. Many of the riddles came from the creatures themselves, for they were very intelligent creatures because they lived so long. They liked games of the mind. They could always defeat any opponent from their strength and magic, so to make it fair they would allow their minds to battle instead. But like Tinay, there was always a fair price to pay if you could not measure yourself to them."

Marcus nodded his head in approval and walked to join his mother.

Mani looked around and saw Alayana and Jeremyah talking together. They were talking in low voices. Mani wondered what good would come of the two. She felt that Alayana was much too young for romance, and yet Mani remembered the first time she set eyes on the man she fell in love with. There was no hesitation in her heart. There was music in her ears, and there was nothing anyone could have said to make her change her mind. She had been happily married for years, and wished the same fate would be with her children and grandchildren.

She hoped the story pleased everyone and that they would come for the rest of the story next week. It was quite a commitment to make, and she was not sure her crowd would stay with her to hear all seven installments of the story. What a shame it would be if they missed the endings and didn't hear the new beginning evolve.

She shook hands and helped everyone get their jackets, then stayed on the porch until everyone was gone. She locked the door behind her and walked back to the atrium and heard someone laughing. She thought everyone had already left. Wondering who was still there, she peeked inside and saw Alayana and Jeremyah cleaning up together and putting away the paintings.

"Dear, there's no need to do that tonight. It's late. Jeremyah should be on his way."

"No problem, I'm glad to help. It gives me a chance to see the paintings more closely. They are a work of genius. I just love the way they come to life in your stories." Jeremyah had a wide grin on his face and spoke with genuineness.

Mani was tired, but didn't feel it would be proper to head off to bed and leave the two lovebirds alone.

"I guess you're right. Better they be put away before they collect too much dust."

Alayana tided up the cushions, used the broom, and collected the dishes and leftovers from her cooking.

"I don't know why I bother," she said. "No one really eats until the end."

"Maybe if you put some vegetables and stuff that don't need a fork to be eaten, they could munch on them before story time," Jeremyah suggested.

"Yeah, maybe. Worth a try. What do you think, Mani?" Alayana turned around and saw Mani yawn. "Jeremyah, thank you for your help. I think this is good for now." She winked at him and pointed to Mani.

"Okay, if you say so." He started to walk towards the door and bowed to Mani. "To the pleasure of seeing you soon."

"How soon?" Mani asked. The boy was polite but if he kept coming back, the two of them would need a chaperone.

"Uh, well, I don't know. We haven't discussed it yet."

"Tomorrow is the blessing of baby Matthew. I'm afraid we'll leave early and come back late," said Mani.

"Monday would be a nice day to catch up," said Alayana.

"Yes, and I'll have a surprise for you then."

Mani looked up at the boy and wondered what the surprise would be.

"I'll escort him to the door, Mani. I'll be right back."

Mani was too tired to fight back and let them go to the door without a chaperone.

"What's with Mani?" Jeremyah asked.

"She's afraid I'll kiss you or something."

"Oh, I see." Jeremyah blushed and was glad he was standing in the darkness. It didn't show as much. "Well, have a good day tomorrow. I'll see you Monday."

"When?" asked Alayana.

"Monday, this Monday."

"No, I meant when on Monday, so I can be ready on time."

"Oh. About ten o'clock. And wear jeans and boots. I'll bring the rest."

"Boots? What kind of boots?"

"Just boots and jeans, nothing fancy. See ya." Jeremyah waved and left on foot toward a trail in the field.

Alayana closed the door behind her and walked to the stairs with her head in the clouds. Mani heard the door close and she came to the stairs.

"No kiss tonight?" she asked.

"Not yet, but when I mentioned you were worried we would, he blushed," Alayana giggled good-humoredly.

"Hmm, just as I thought. The boy likes you. He will try to kiss you soon. Beware," Mani teased.

"I will, but I can't imagine what it's like. What is it like, Mani?"

"Oh, the first kiss is different than all the rest. It's the first kiss. It's unsure, timid. Your heart beats quickly and your hands sweat.

You don't know if he'll kiss you back. Should you close your eyes or not? And it seems to take forever for your lips to finally touch. And when your lips touch, you feel as if you are melting. Your eyes close automatically and you feel as light as a feather. It's unique." Mani had a dreamy smile on her face. It didn't matter how old she got, she still remembered her first kiss. "Of course that's what I experienced. Maybe your first kiss will be different."

"I'll tell you all about it when it happens, I promise."

Mani smiled. The inevitable would happen, but Alayana was still so young. Mani was afraid she would end up having her heart broken like many other girls she had known.

Mani lay down in her bed, happy to go to sleep. She had a long day ahead of her tomorrow.

Chapter 17

THE THIRD EYE

Sunday morning came quickly. Mani and Alayana woke up and got ready for their trip to the city. Alayana didn't like the trip, but she missed the baby very much. She wanted to see him more than anything. The baby was sleeping in his mother's arms when they arrived at the hospital. The ceremony would be a lively one, but since she was alone to prepare it all, Lyauria decided to have the main ceremony today and to have the celebration when her husband returned home. Lyauria felt stretched with her family spread all over. She wanted cohesion and to hold them like she was holding her new baby.

The Elder that was present prepared the bath water and called the three women over to him, "My friends, we gather today to give thanks to our creator for the blessing of this new life in our family. As our ancestors held their children over the water, so will we now bless the baby, together as a family. Each by their action will accept the responsibility to bring up this child in the world. Each will accept to play the role of mentor, and lead by example..."

Alayana stopped listening. She gently touched the baby's hair as he smiled back at her. He was so soft. She just wanted to cuddle him, to hold him close to her heart. He was so precious and patient. The room was warm and Matthew seemed to enjoy his surroundings. He didn't look like a slug anymore. He was so pretty. He had no neck and his limbs had yet to find some control. He had a birthmark on his bottom, a family mark by the looks of it. Alayana had it also. She looked up and realized she had missed the entire ceremony.

"Oh, I'm sorry. I was enjoying it so much I stopped paying attention."

"It's all right. I can see everything will be all right." Her mother approached Alayana and gave her a hug. Mani handed her a towel, and she got to hold her little brother. He was so light and cuddly. She thought to herself, *If he was covered with hair, he would feel like a teddy bear.*

They stayed in the city for lunch and then packed her mother's bag. Lyauria was now going to take a year's leave from her work in the city to take care of the baby. She didn't think she would go to work afterward unless their father returned home. She wanted to spend time with her child before he grew up and became a teenager like Alayana. She already felt guilty for being gone so often.

They returned to the store in the late afternoon. Alayana prepared the bedroom for her mother and the baby. It was going to be nice to see the baby grow every day. In a week's time, he had already changed so much.

Mani came into the room with a cradle and some blankets.

"How long is Mother staying?" asked Alayana.

"Until your father gets back."

"Wha...? That could be months!"

"Yes, did we forget to mention to you that you're going to school here this year?"

"Oh, Mani! This is great!"

Alayana ran to her grandmother and hugged her. Then she ran out of the room to her mother, but stopped when she realized that Lyauria was asleep on the couch with the baby. She ran back to the room and could not hold still. "This is great! It's wonderful!"

"Yes, indeed it is. There's more, but you can't talk to anyone about it just yet."

"Well, if I'm not supposed to know maybe it would be best...."

"Nonsense! You're a big girl and you have a right to know what is going to happen."

"Well?" asked Alayana curiously.

"Your mother is planning on living here. She's going to supervise the renovations at the old house and then she wants to open up her own practice here in town. Your dad wants some peace when he gets back and they agreed this would be a great place to spend some time."

"Really?" Alayana was so excited that she couldn't stand still. "This is such a good thing. Why are they keeping it a secret?"

"Because Doctor Zola has not retired yet. She'll be waiting for your mother to resume her work, and therefore, they don't have an exact date. But it's in the works. The renovations will start in a few months. They'll take a while."

"And we'll be living here until then?"

"Yes, we'll be crowded for a bit, but ..."

"Never mind. It's going to be so great. I have to tell someone."

"No, no, no. You said you'd keep this to yourself."

"Jeremyah? Just him? Please."

"I guess that couldn't do any harm. As long as he doesn't talk."

"No problem. By the way, I'm seeing him tomorrow. You'll be fine without me?"

"Yes, dear, I'll be fine," Mani reassured.

The rest of the day went by faster than Alayana expected and to make sure she would be rested for her surprise the next day, she went to bed early.

When Monday morning came, Alayana realized she had woken up way too early and could not decide what to do. She was too excited to go back to sleep, so she had a long bath. Then she curled her hair and even put a touch of perfume on her wrist. She took hours, it seemed, to select the right blouse to go with her jeans. She wondered where she and Jeremyah would go. The terrace, maybe, for an ice cream cone or to the movies. She hoped he would notice her hair. When she was finally ready, she went downstairs and realized she still had another two hours to wait for him. She slumped into the chair and stared at the sky.

"Are you hungry, Alayana?" Mani asked.

"Not really, but I guess I should eat something."

"How about a banana sandwich?"

"Yeah, sure."

"When is he going to be here?" asked Mani.

"Ten."

"Maybe you should read a book until he gets here," suggested Mani.

"Yeah, maybe. Which house did mom and dad get?"

"The yellow one."

"Really?" Alayana said with excitement.

"Yes."

"There must be, like, ten rooms in that house!"

"Yes, but some of them she will use for her practice, but it will be definitely bigger than the condo."

"Cool!"

Alayana sat at the counter and ate her sandwich and then looked at a book with old houses, dreaming what her new room would look like. She wanted her room to be in the tower. She wanted to be on top of the world. Her daydreaming made the two hours go by fast, and before she realized it, she was tapped on the shoulder by her mom.

"He's here," she said.

"Who's here?" asked Alayana, disoriented.

"Jeremyah, I believe he said."

"Oh." She looked at her watch and saw it was indeed ten o'clock. She went down the stairs and met him outside. She was surprised to find him leaning on a motorcycle.

"What's this?" asked Alayana.

"Um, a motorcycle."

"Yes, I know that, but whose is it?"

"Mine. My employer decided that he wanted a newer one and sold this one to me for a very fair price."

"Really. And you know how to ride one of those?"

"Yes, I grew up on one! I just love the feeling of the wind in my hair," he said, grinning like a fool.

"Well, here it's mandatory you wear a helmet," Alayana said, refusing to allow his mood to make her forget herself.

"Yeah, I know, we will."

"We...."

"Yeah, that's the surprise. I'm taking you on a bike ride. I have to work at two o'clock today, so I'll need to be back. But I thought I could show you a nice spot Gerard recommended to me."

"Oh, all right. But I don't have a helmet."

"Got one here, just for you." Jeremyah got a helmet from behind him and handed it to her. Alayana took the helmet and put it on thinking what a waste of time doing her hair had been. Not only had he not noticed, but now it was squished under the helmet.

She hopped on the bike and realized how little room there was for her to hang on to. Jeremyah started the bike and told her over the noise of the engine that she would have to hold onto him by his waist. Once she grabbed hold, she realized how close she was to him. They had not even held hands yet and there she was embracing his whole body, clamping her leg on each side of him. He felt warm. She liked it and yet she was a little uncomfortable being so close to him. She sat leaving a space between Jeremyah and herself but her butt hung over the guard of the seat.

Jeremyah, on the other hand, was grinning from ear to ear. He had thought this might help break the ice and initiate contact, but this was much better than he had hoped. He was enjoying himself. They took off on the side road and went up river. She wondered where he would take her. And after an hour, he slowed down and came to a natural dam. Surrounded by trees, the place was gorgeous. There was mist on the ground and the water cascaded down the rough slope and ended up in a whirlpool in a picture perfect setting.

"This is amazing," Alayana said breathlessly.

"I thought you might like it. I took the liberty of checking it out first." Jeremyah was pleased, "You really like it."

"This is really beautiful. Thank you."

"Want to go for a swim?"

"Um, I don't have a bathing suit."

"Right, that would have ruined the surprise. Well, I guess we should get going then?"

"You look disappointed."

"Well, I just thought we could spend more time here."

"We can. Just not swimming."

"Would you mind if I did?"

"No, I guess not. I'll just sit there on that rock."

"Good, the water is really good here." Jeremyah started to undress himself and left his boxers on and started to climb down to the pool. "Coming?"

"Um, yeah, sure." Alayana couldn't believe her eyes. There he was, almost naked in front of her, and he was completely okay with it. She had seen him in shorts at the beach, but still these were boxers. She gave a frail smile and started to follow him. As Alayana sat on the rock, Jeremyah jumped in the water and came up with a smile, looking like an overgrown fish. She loved to see him smile. His whole face lit right up.

"Are you missing your family?" she asked.

"No, I grew up with one brother and two step-brothers and it always felt too crowded. I like to travel and discover new places."

"Going back to Germany in the fall?"

"Yeah, I'll be back for Christmas. I'm hoping to convince Mani to tell chapter three during the Christmas break. What do you think my chances are?"

"Oh, I don't know. That's up to her. I usually go back to the city in the fall, so I don't know what she usually does. I'm about to find out about it myself."

"What do you mean?"

"We're moving here, into the yellow house in the village. It will be great."

"I guess we'll continue to see each other when I get back here."

"Yes, I guess so."

Jeremyah smiled as he got out of the water and lay down beside her. He looked at the clouds floating by. She could not keep her eyes off of him. The water slipped off his skin in crystal droplets and the sun reflected off his chest. She wanted to touch him again.

"This one looks like a shoe," Jeremyah said, interrupting her thoughts.

"Huh?"

"That cloud, it looks like a shoe."

"Oh, yeah." Alayana turned her head to the sky and looked up. The cloud did look like a shoe. "What about this one over there? I think it's a little lamb."

"No, maybe a large dog."

"What? No way! Look, it sounds like it's baaing right now. Baa baa."

They laughed. Their hands touched and Alayana's heart leaped in her chest. Yes, she liked him a lot. She just hoped he liked her just as much. Jeremyah waited until he was dry and got back into his clothes and they headed out. This time, Alayana had no intention of getting her butt vibrated to death, so she sat closer to him. She was close now, real close. It felt good to hold onto him, to feel the heat emanating from him. She was on cloud nine, the one in the shape of a heart.

They headed back and she stood there as he talked to her through the front of the helmet. Alayana figured quickly enough that she wouldn't be getting a kiss this time either.

"So what about tomorrow night?" he asked.

"I was thinking about staying home and spending time with my new little brother. Would you mind?"

"No, of course not. I'll put in a few more hours at the store, and maybe wash some clothes, you know."

"Yeah, I was going to mention it, but..." Alayana smiled.

"Yeah." He laughed. "You're so funny," Jeremyah said sarcastically. "I better go."

"Why?"

Jeremyah gave his head a shake and pointed at the window. Alayana looked up and saw Mani staring at her in the window, and her mother sitting on the porch of the third floor. She realized she was being watched, not the best moment for magic and a first kiss moment.

"Okay, well, I'll see you on Thursday then?" Alayana asked hopefully.

"No, I had to work this Thursday, but I thought I could actually take you up on your offer and bake with you on Friday."

"Sure, okay. I'll see you at seven then?"

"Seven sounds good." Jeremyah revved up his bike and left in a cloud of dust. Alayana waved the dust out of the air and walked back to the store. She walked by Mani, waved, and went upstairs. Her mother came in and looked at her with her funny smile.

"So, who is he?" Lyauria questioned.

"Would you believe me if I said he's just some guy I met?"

"No," Lyauria replied smiling knowingly.

"Okay, well, we better sit down and I'll tell you all about him."

Tuesday, Wednesday, and Thursday came and went. Alayana kept busy and played with her new brother and visited with her mom. She loved the way the summer was turning out.

Friday night came with birds singing and kids laughing. The night sky had pink and purple tones and the sun was slowly descending on the ocean. Alayana breathed in the ocean air and smiled. Life was good.

Jeremyah pulled into the parking lot on his new bike and waved at Alayana. He was on time, which was something she really liked about him. How he managed it, she didn't know, but she loved this about him.

He came up the stairs and saw Mani. He went over to her.

"Mani," he looked at his feet, "is it okay with you if I see Alayana?"

"Yes, I suppose," she replied.

"It's just you don't look too pleased about it."

"No, I just hope you are the gentlemen you seem to be and that you will keep some distance."

"Um, how much distance?"

"Gentlemen-like distance," she said with raised eyebrows.

"I see. Of course. I have a lot of respect for Alayana. We're just starting to know each other. There's so much I don't know about her," he said.

"Yes, take your time and get to know her. Be wise in your choices," Mani warned subtly.

"Yes, um, so you disprove about...?"

"The motorcycle. Much too close to each other. It does not allow for proper. . .distance…"

"The bike is gone. No more rides on the bike," Jeremyah promised.

"I can understand you are young and there are many beautiful girls everywhere, not just here. This is maybe just a fling until the next beautiful girl comes around, and Aly could get hurt. I don't want that."

"No, I wouldn't, never. I don't think… I understand what you are saying."

"Jeremyah, are you coming?" called Alayana from the kitchen.

"Yup, be right up." Jeremyah turned around and looked at Mani. "I also wanted to ask you when you could give volumes three through seven."

"When can you be back?"

"I wouldn't presume you would do this for me, but..."

"Andemar asked me if you could continue to hear the story from me. I'm ready to accommodate to a certain extent."

"Wow! What if I came back at Christmas? Maybe we could do it then?"

"Yes, I can arrange it. I'll send the schedule to Andemar. Just make sure you free your schedule for me."

"Oh, I will. I can also come back for spring break for volume four."

"Very well, it can be arranged."

"That only leaves volumes five, six, and seven...."

"Let's not jump too far ahead, but I imagine that we can do volume five and six during the summer and move on to volume seven at Christmas. That is a long way from here. Let's just get through volume one first. I'll keep in touch with Andemar and make sure you can attend the sessions."

"Thank you, thank you so much." Jeremyah took Mani's hand and shook it vigorously. He planted a kiss on her cheek.

"Oh my, boy, control yourself," Mani teased.

Jeremyah ran up the stairs two by two and joined Alayana in the kitchen.

Alayana quickly realized Jeremyah wasn't much of a cook, so she let him try out his own ideas by peeling cucumbers and carrots and cutting the celery for a veggie platter. Lyauria watched them and smiled knowingly. She liked him because of what Alayana had said about him, but seeing the two together she could see the chemistry. She just hoped it would take them a while to figure it out. But somehow it felt already too late for that.

Saturday night came and Alayana took her usual spot, and this time Jeremyah was early and they sat beside one another for the next installment of the story. The paintings were up and Alayana was pointing to the ones that were new and explaining what they meant.

Mani walked in the room and went straight to her seat.

"This is the most exciting part of the story yet and there's a lot of ground to cover, so we may as well get to it right away. Who can remember where we were?"

A young girl raised her hand and looked eager to answer the question.

"Yes, Amy?"

"Um, Tinay met the guardian and she's about to have her third eye opened and that means she's almost finished the initiation. Her mother still hasn't had the baby yet, which, by the way, is the longest labor I've ever heard of...."

Lyauria laughed. She wished she could tell the little girl how bad it could get sometimes.   Amy continued, "Tamael is on his way back and hopefully he'll get there in time to help because, like my mother said, it's his..."

"Yes, very well. Amy, thank you," Mani interrupted. "Yes, let's focus on the portrait of Manyr and Tinay in the cave eating."

* * * * *

As they sat there, Tinay stared at her elder. She wasn't quite sure what she was seeing. Was it a ghost or a spirit? There was no way she could tell, but what she was looking at was, nevertheless, beautiful and quite pleasing to the eye. She had a beautiful violet aura that seemed to shine in the darkness of the cave. The fine highlights made soft details stand out on her body and fine lines ornamenting her face. She looked middle aged, but felt much older. The calm and peace she felt was the same as when her mother would comfort her as a child. The whole world ceased to exist and she was wrapped in a bubble against time and the world. It felt as if nothing could touch her or harm her. She certainly did not have that security earlier on when she had met the guardian. The dragon had looked fierce and savage. He had been scary at first, but had inspired respect after. She wondered what feelings would replace peace after she got to know Manyr better.

Is something troubling you, child? asked Manyr.

Who are you? asked Tinay.

I am Manyr to you. I am known by many names and I serve many functions in my life.

What is your function now?

To become your teacher in the spirit world.

Is that what you are then? A spirit?

No, Manyr smiled. *I'm a human, a very old human. I am a retired artist who lives on Kyr and tends her garden, until recently. Now I will be your guide.*

Oh! I'm sorry, I thought you had to be a ghost or something to be a guide.

No, I'm a living being. I will try and teach you about spirits and ghosts. What you see is my soul. Not a perfect representation of my physical body. I am frailer and older in real life. But what I lost in physical strength, I gained in wisdom and knowledge. If you, too, are wise you will learn from me and others instead of experiencing everything by yourself.

For now, it's more adventure than I have ever had.

How do you like it?

It's interesting, yet dangerous, but my mother really does need me. She'll have her baby soon.

Yes, it is time. It will be easier if you lay down for this. It's better when you do this lying down in a safe place where you are most likely to be alone and quiet so you will not be startled or woken up before your time.

Very well.

Tinay laid down and looked intensely at Manyr, *What comes next?*

We will use our mental voices to talk to one another and you'll close your eyes.

Tinay rested uneasily on the cushion wondering what would happen now. What new horizon would open before her? Where and when would she be doing this meditation session and what else would she learn?

I know you have been meditating for many years now, but I will walk you through it and make a good review of what you know and what you have recently learned.

Tinay took a deep breath and slowly started to breathe like her mother had taught her.

What you have learned in the last few days was knowledge only for the fairies. They were the only ones allowed to know all the truth. It was decided by the Order that it should not be common knowledge because it holds so much power and could potentially be destructive. Your mother and father moved here to harvest the Alenor crystals and found the caves. They became aware of the knowledge and shared it with everyone they could. After years of practice, they both became very good at what they do. Your mother is an awesome teacher. She teaches others through the books she and your father wrote. They share the knowledge with selected individuals that are willing to use it for the greater good. *You must understand that right now in the imperial city they are looking for ways to learn about the great mystery and they will torture anyone who has that knowledge to use it against each other. That's one of the reasons your third eye was not opened sooner, those who have the knowledge must remain hidden from the imperial guard and learn as much as they can. You are not considered well learned or wise enough to start sharing what you have learned. You must keep anything you have learned about meditation and potions secret from the world you're about to enter into. You have much more to learn. Your parents have affiliates on the different worlds you'll be visiting and these individuals will help further your knowledge.*

There are many other properties of the fairies that you will learn. Your heart was judged by the guardian to be true or you would not have been given the Alenor crystal. I share this further knowledge with you in hopes that you will use it for the good of humanity.

I will, Manyr, I will. Tinay was now intrigued. *But how did Okapi know my heart?*

Manyr smiled, *The riddles are a portal entrance to your thinking pattern. Evil can easily be revealed through this process.*

Now, let us continue, shall we? Manyr began without waiting for an answer. *Very well. I see you have slowed your breathing by moving the air from your lungs down to your diaphragm and expelling the air in a slower fashion. While you do that, I want you to picture the air coming in as a current or water flowing freely around your body and, just like waves moves the sand, it will slowly move all your body. You will feel the current running through you. Once it has reached the extremities, it will amass together all the negative energy and push it back out as you exhale. Each time you exhale, you will feel lighter. Your body will fill with energy and you will be able to see your astral body floating above you.*

I don't feel light whatsoever. I feel like there are ten people pushing down on me. I can hardly breathe.

Tinay was almost in a panic now.

It's all right, dear. It's just your skin and your organs.

Why are they so heavy?

Your astral body is trying to get out and it must pass through your body in order to do so. At first, you will find that it's hard to go through any hard surfaces, but as you understand the concept it will become easier, but will never be without an effort.

Okay, so what do I do?

You must picture your body as a constellation of stars, each organ composed of tiny stars, millions of them, everywhere.

Like I did for the levitation?

Yes, like you did before, and then your astral body doesn't have to go through solid matter anymore but simply go through the tiny energy line that connects all the dots together.

I see them. They're easier to see now that I have seen them before, but why will I not levitate now?

Because you won't be blowing on them to make them float, but you will be letting your astral body simply go through the maze of energy fragments and free itself.

Tinay's body no longer opposed her and she could feel herself breathe normally again. She pictured her astral body cutting through the tiny energy lines and slowly forming on top of her. She really felt like she weighed nothing.

Now that you see your astral body, you will focus the energy of each temple inside your astral body. We will start with the temple of Ecumel, the red energy. Now that you know what it stands for, you can analyze your feelings, your fears and your anxieties better. The simplest way to look at it is to see what your terrestrial body needs: food, shelter, clothing, and warmth.

I haven't been too concerned about food since I was imprisoned here. I found some in the previous stage, but now there isn't much left. I'm afraid it won't last more than a day at most. Since I reached the bottom of the cavern, I should be able to find an exit soon. My father will arrive soon and free me and I can go help my mother.

Shelter?

I have a home. I will always have a safe place to go to. It doesn't really matter to me now that I will be traveling because as long as I know where my family is, I will be able to come home. I will miss Sasgorg and our cave, but meeting new people and discovering new ways of doing things should be fascinating. I'm not too worried. Like you said, my parents will help me find somewhere to settle on the other planets as well. I'll be safe.

Clothing?

I am not concerned about my clothing. This would be so trivial. I'm comfortable, I'm covered from the sun and I have a change of clothes at home. I need for nothing here and my clothes are heavy enough to keep me warm in the cave.

Very well, I admire your confidence. You might encounter more difficulties in your travels. This stage might not always seem this easy, but I can see your energy ball is well focused and vivacious and active, and that you are not lying to me. But remember this when difficulties arise. Let's move on to the next temple, Anamel, the orange entity. The entity of organs, health and sexuality.

I normally focus on an orange. Should I have a more appropriate image?

The orange is fine, as long as it's inside your astral body and that you can concentrate on it to make it spin on itself. Do you have any worries or anxieties at this stage?"

No, my organs are fine. My stomach could probably do with more food and water, but I'm fine. I'm a healthy person, so I don't worry much about those things.

When you find you have no worries, before skipping ahead too soon, you might want to take time to thank the Overseer and the Goddess for all your blessings.

Oh, Dad thanks them at every meal. I did not know how to thank them otherwise.

Together, they created the heavens and the earth. They saved a select few from extermination and helped us stay alive through a very long journey in space. They helped us settle on a new planet and thrive until it was time to move again. They both gave the fairies the ability to foresee the future and helped to prepare us for another exile. There are many things to be thankful for. For Ecumel, you are to be thankful for the food and your shelter and your clothes, the harvest, the blanket on your bed. . .

I miss my bed, Tinay said, remembering that, for the first time, she might wake up from this without a sore back.

Exactly. Your father was very good at observing the thanks as a family at every meal, but you can also take some time as an individual and say thanks. For Anamel, you must be thankful for your health, if you have it, or pray for health to return if you are sick. It's not going to be just about a ball of light anymore. It won't be just to be at peace with yourself. It will be about praying and giving thanks.

Tinay was smiling, *What am I supposed to do with the sexuality? I don't have anything related to sex around here.*

Maybe not here, but soon you will see a lot more of people. Invariably, sexuality will surround you. You'll be thankful that you are protected.

You mean I will see a lot more people.

Yes, Especially on Os. The heat, the water, and the beaches cause people not to cover themselves up as much. They use every excuse to expose themselves. Your sexuality might suddenly awaken and cause you to be troubled.

What do you mean?

Well, you will meet a boy, maybe your age or a few years older than you, and when you'll look at him, he'll be beautiful. You'll only see his good qualities. In your eyes, he will be perfect.

What's wrong with that?

Nothing, but nobody is perfect. The problem is that it's not because they're beautiful that they are well intentioned. Some of them will have no honor and will have no problem with lying to you about how they feel about you so as to have sex.

I'm not ready to bear children. What could I possibly offer to him? Tinay was confused.

Maybe not, but he will. You must protect yourself and wait for the proper one to come along. You must not give away your gift of virginity to anyone. This should be reserved for your husband.

I don't disagree with you, but what is so important about my virginity?

It can only be given once. I have often heard women complaining that they gave themselves away at the first promise of love and were left alone and ignored and sometimes pregnant. Others complained that once they found their true love, they could no longer offer any valid gift to them, the one of saving themselves for their true love was lost. True love will come once you have been tested. Once you have time to look around and meet different people. True love will mean that you will be able to build trust and respect. You will share your inner-most thoughts and will be there for each other. It also means that you will be ready for a family of your own. It's not just about virginity, it's also about the chances of having a baby. What would you do with a child alone in this world? Your parents would help you, I'm sure, but in the end, that child would grow up without a father figure. How good could that be? That's not the way it was meant to be.

What about kissing?

Aha ha ha! Yes, you can kiss. But beware of men's real intentions. You can go out with people. You can see what you like in someone. Take your time to be his friend first, then once you are ready to know them better, take that step. Just take it slowly. You are a very beautiful young lady, Tinay. Many will pay attention to you, bring you gifts, take you out, try to kiss you even, but many will lie about their true intentions and some will not be ready to make any sort of commitment. The latter won't know the difference between love and friendship. Many won't show any respect.

I'm not ready for boys, Manyr. I haven't even bothered to think about them yet.

No, maybe not now, but a year from now, remember we had this discussion. Remember it when you meet someone that makes you feel special, for whom you will do your hair up and wear perfume and make sure you're wearing new clothes. The people you live and study with will influence you, whether you want them to or not. Everything will be different and you'll want to try new things. Always remember to stay true to yourself.

Really?

Oh yes, dear, you'll see. It just might not be the one. Your feelings might be true, but he may not be the one to which you will share those feelings forever.

I'll be careful, and I'll remember our conversation.

Very well, let's move on to Galgamel, the center of emotion. Surely you must have had a whirlwind of emotions in the past few days. What does your sun look like?

Yes, that I have, but the meal we shared together calmed me. Your presence is extremely soothing. You calmed me. My sun is as usual after a good day: big and bright, warming up my body.

I'm glad I have that effect on you. You'll realize that some people will infuriate you, others will infuriate you and some will disgust you. You cannot always let those feelings get in the way and affect your inner being. But those feelings will be your guide to let you know if you should continue to see that person or be more aware of the vibrations they are sending you. They will create an imbalance and will steal your energy if they can.

But I never felt that before I met you. What makes you think it will happen again?

After your third eye is opened, you will notice a few changes in your life. Among them, you will see people's aura and you will get certain feelings when you shake their hand or are in their presence.

Like what happened with you?

Yes, you will use the aura of a person as a guide. It will be helpful to know what drives them and what their motivation is. It will be easier to know what they need or what they are looking for. When you meet Amos, the best merchant on Os, you will soon realize that he can read auras very well and that he uses his gift to help people feel better about themselves.

Amos. I'll try and remember that.

So if your center of emotions is clear, let's move to the love circle.

Love circle, I like that.

It comes from the band encircling your body and your heart. It's the temple of Manerv, the center of love and acceptance. You will picture everyone you love there. Who do you see?

That's easy. I see Mom, Pa, Raphael, Ohuru, and that's strange, I see Atleos there. Why is he there?

He should be there. This is the center of not just love, but unconditional love. Everyone you know should be there. There should be a place for Draco in there and the guardian and even me.

Really? That could get busy in the next few years.

Not just busy, but hard. You will also have to put people there who aren't being nice or polite to you. Some will neglect you, but you will have to find a place for them in your heart.

Why?

Because that's where you can truly forgive someone and make peace with their inappropriate actions. It's in your heart that you will find the strength to forgive and forget, so you can finally move on.

I don't know anyone who has meant me any harm before. It feels strange to think that a perfect stranger would intentionally want to hurt me.

Unfortunately, the world has not been the best these last few years. Morality and spirituality have not been a priority. You will see things that I hope you will find are horrors and you will not try to join their group. Perhaps it will sound tempting at first. You will try to belong, but I hope that you are strong enough to resist certain urges.

Like sexuality?

That and other things. Just keep your soul open. Don't believe everything you hear and think before making some choices, explore your options.

Okay, I'll try.

Don't try. If you try, you will fail.

But...

No 'but'. You must do this. Believe you can do.

I will. Tinay tried to sound more convincing this time. She really did want to please the elder. She was just so new at this.

Tinay, I understand your desire, but you must understand. The evil in this world will play on your uncertainties and make you waiver and finally lead you into temptation. For that reason, you must be strong and remember your teaching.

All right.

Now, who do you see in your circle?

Mom, Pa, Raphael, Draco, Ohuru, Atleos, Okapi the guardian, and you. Tinay was so proud of herself. She could picture all of them dancing around her smiling.

What about yourself?

Huh?

You must, above all else, love yourself.

Of course I love myself!

Then why are you not in the circle of love?

Well, I'm there, they're dancing around me.

Why can't they dance with you?

I don't know.

You must not isolate yourself. All of the temples are about you; how you feel, how you cope with your emotions, anxieties, doubts and fears. Love should also be about you. Make sure you include you.

It's strange, I feel more love now than before, as if I can not only love them but they can also love me.

Well done! Manyr was proud to see Tinay progress so well. She had little time left so she had to move on quickly.

The next step is the temple Landel. It is the center of inspiration and communication. I encourage you to truly concentrate on this one while you complete your apprenticing. This is where ideas flow into your hands and transform what your hands hold into fabulous works of art. This is where, when you get in a fight and you must apologize, you will find the words and the actions that will bring peace between you and your friends. This is where you can defeat an opponent. Sometimes you will find that the pen is mightier than the sword.

I'm good with a sword, Tinay said, finally glad she knew something.

Yes, and you can kill a person with a sword. With your words you can cure, help, and provide much needed comfort for a person in need. Your sword would not be any help there.

Yes, I know that's when a potion or a soup has better use.

Exactly. Are you able to communicate well with your family?

Yes, we talk a lot. I miss my mom. Pa is often away so we talk to him when he comes home. We tell him all about our day and everything that goes on in our minds. With mom it's different, she'll pass her hand through your hair and we know she loves us. There are fewer words expressed, but they say just as much. Sometimes she'll be busy knitting and she'll look up and send us a kiss. I know I'm always in her mind. It feels great.

Good, then you understand that you are not alone with words. You can communicate worlds with your body and facial expression, and you must always keep that in mind when you meet new people. Their first impression of you will come as much from what you have to say as from the way you behave yourself. Just remember that the diamond in your throat has many angles and the rays of light emitting out of it go in all directions and touch the small and big, human, animal, or even vegetable. You must take the time to talk and express your feelings to all beings that breathe and grow. Now we are pressed with time, we must move on to the third eye.

Tinay felt a shiver go up her spine. She suddenly felt all the excitement all at once.

The temple of Zuel, the mirror of the soul, the barer of truth, and the inner beauty, are all concentrated here. The eye is of an indigo color and will be different for each and every one of us, so I can't really describe it for you. Let's see what yours looks like.

Tinay concentrated hard on her forehead.

Relax, let me do the work. Manyr put her finger on Tinay's forehead and drew an eye.

At first, there was only the line of the upper lid, then the eyelashes appeared and the eye slowly blinked. The lower lid and its eyelashes appeared. The inside of the line seem littered with small stars and there was a glimmer inside the eye. It was the most beautiful and amazing thing Tinay had ever seen. As she looked in the eye it seemed to open into space. She could now see her grandmother floating in front of her, and she had her hand stretched out, inviting Tinay to join her.

You will meet a lot of people this way. Your seven guides will be glad to take you on journeys to help you learn more about yourself and what your goals are. They will never force you, but always invite you to join them like I am now. What do you say?

Oh! Yes, take me with you.

Slowly, Tinay pulled her astral body inside her third eye and exited her body that way. She was light as air. No, even lighter than that, she was air. She no longer felt any confinement at all.

Your astral body has joined your soul. This is what an out-of-body experience is. This is how you will communicate with me or your mother in the next few years. This is your new school.

Tinay looked around and saw the reflection of her astral body on the wall. It looked like she had a light inside her and the astral body was made of water and the light reflected in ripples. It made her feel like she was floating in a vast water reservoir. She was in the middle of the sky in a bubble of water. She had never felt this way before. Her aura was green.

Now that your eye is open, it will never close again unless you do that yourself. I have little left, but I will teach you a small lesson on spirits and ghosts. Ghost are souls that have departed their mortal body and do not accept their deaths, or wanted to leave a message behind for a loved one, or simply insisted on waiting for the loved one to join them before they go on to the next plane. They appear as smoke and have no real physical form. They can often haunt our dreams which is the only place that their spirit will allow them to have a complete form, the one they had when they were last alive. Most of them are of no consequence, but they might insist that you help them before they leave you alone. If feasible, receive their message, but sometimes you might have to say no to them. There are evil souls that do not make it to the light and seek to do harm. Beware of those souls that will not hesitate to take your place and conduct their misdeeds in your name. That is why you must always protect yourself when you go to sleep. Say your prayers and envelop yourself in a golden egg. See your room brightly lit by positive energy. That will keep them a safe distance away. If you find yourself in a room with one of them, you will know and feel their presence. Burn a piece of cedar and pray to Archangel Gabriel this way: Archangel Gabriel, come to my aid. Bring here with you into the light those present here that have lost their way. Protect me against any harm and remove those that are present in this room that mean harm and plan on hurting me or anyone else. Close the portal behind you and keep me safe, Argor.

I will remember. Tinay felt relieved that the reason she needed protection wasn't present. There were probably not many ghosts here on Sasgorg, but when she traveled the galaxy, this would come in handy.

Next are the spirits. There will be mainly seven around you at all times. Those are the ones you will see. They are here to help guide you and show you the way. They talk in images. It will take some time before you understand their messages well, but in time, they'll get clearer and you will understand their way of communicating with you. Would you like to meet them?

Can I?

Yes, here they are. Jeanne is your guide for the health of your body. If you get sick pray to her, she'll help guide you to find what is wrong with you.

Jeanne was a frail woman, with long hair in a bun. She wore a long dress with frills that Tinay had never seen before. She had an umbrella and a small purse. She bowed.

Barbara will be your spiritual guide. She will keep you on the right path and help you.

Barbara was a middle-aged woman, with a rounder body. Long brown hair rested on her shoulders. She wore pants and a T-shirt. Tinay had never seen a woman wear pants before, so this looked funny to her. Barbara smiled back at her.

Your family guide will be Jean-Pierre.

He was a lean fellow, with long hair and a beard. He was warm and friendly. He was also tall and imposing in a way. Tinay liked him already.

Your friends guide will be Julie.

Julie was short with glasses on her head. She also had long, dark brown hair that rested on her shoulders, but she was petite compare to everyone else. She was neither lean nor fat, just well balanced. She wore a knee-high skirt and a blouse.

Your mind and its health will be supervised by Deirdre.

Deirdre was blond with curly hair. She was curvy and wore longer shorts and a T-shirt with a collar. She was very bright and waved her hand gently. Tinay wanted to wave back, but couldn't see the point since she was in her astral form.

You may not see it, Tinay, but you have a form for them to see. It's okay to wave to them.

Tinay smiled and waved. She hadn't realized she still had a form. She didn't feel like she had one. She felt so light and free.

Your career or life plan will be guided by Joynarae. She is a kind and patient woman. She'll be of great help to you.

Joynarae seemed older than the rest of them. She was about fifty, Tinay thought. She had a large belly, grey hair, and glasses. Her hair was curled in large rolls and surrounded her face, smoothing out the lines on her face making her look soft.

Your overseer will be MaryJean. She's the eldest of the group and has been an overseer for a few of your guides already. She's really good.

MaryJean was oldest and had a white head of hair pulled back in a bun. She wore a simple dress with flowers on it. She was rounded off. Tinay thought it was weird that they had body shape so distinctive and such a unique appearance. She was also glad this was the case. This would help her understand the messages they would have to transmit to her.

That's it for now, Tinay. I must go. It's already morning on my planet and I must be off before anyone becomes suspicious.

Why would it matter to anyone?

Because being an elder of the spiritual world is not safe anymore. I don't use my real name with you or your mother so nobody can trace me back. Be safe and I'll see you soon. Don't forget to cloak yourself in the golden egg from now on.

I won't.

Manyr departed the room and went upward, just like Okapi the Guardian had done. Tinay guessed that even Manyr didn't like moving through solid rock. She wondered how far she had come from to be here and how much distance was separating her from her home. She looked back at her guides. They seemed to be talking to each other, but she could not hear what they were saying. They turned back and came toward her, then each one gave her a hug. Tinay didn't realize how much she needed them and how comforting they were. Then she saw the golden egg, which they all stepped into and then it lowered itself to her body. Yes, they were right, she was tired and she would welcome sleep now. She lowered herself back into her body and went to sleep inside the golden egg.

Manyr could not go home just yet without stopping by the cave and checking on Lilay. She loved Lilay with all her heart and she had missed her so much over the last twenty years. Their visits were so far between that she could not miss this opportunity.

When she entered the cave, she was pleasantly surprised to see Okapi.

Master Okapi, I didn't know you would also pay her a visit.

Well, she was so close by and I wanted to tell her how her daughter had finished the challenge early by posing such a good riddle.

I was surprised indeed. I could not answer the riddle myself when master Okapi challenged me to answer it.

Lilay beamed. She looked rested and happy. Her daughter had passed the initiation and had obtained her Alenor crystal in her own right.

Master Okapi looked at her and raised his eyes, *How many riddles did you teach her?*

Lilay blushed. She knew she could not lie to the master, *Hundreds, all the ones ever recorded. I want her to be prepared, but I never knew what you would be asking, so I felt she was never really ready.*

Now that Manyr is here, I shall leave you with her. Master Okapi bowed and left the cave.

Lilay took a deep breath. She was sad to see him go. Maybe it was the pregnancy making her more emotional, or maybe it was just the time she had been away. She was tired of being so isolated. She wanted more visitors. She turned to Manyr and wanted to hug her, but without a physical form, it was like hugging air.

I miss you so much, Manyr. Lilay wiped a tear off her cheek.

I miss you, too, dear child. I miss you, too. Manyr approached her and gave her a hug. Lilay could feel a tingling all over her body. Peace came over her.

How are the contractions, dear?

They haven't started yet, but she is sure moving a lot. And I'm out of tea. I had my last cup while I was talking to Master Okapi. I'm afraid if Tamael doesn't get here soon, he'll miss all the action. Lilay tried to smile but the last thing she wanted was to be alone while giving birth to her child. Manyr understood her fear, but her fear made the baby nervous and her moving so much close to birth didn't present a good omen.

You must not try to stop the labor anymore. The baby is ready to come. No matter what happens now, you must deliver this baby, alone if you must.

Yes, Manyr, I understand. How did Tinay do with you? Lilay was trying to change the conversation away from her and the baby.

She did very well. Her aura is green, bright as day, and it emanates light like a star in the sky. It is beautiful to see. She also had a chance to meet with her guides. She's on the right path. I must go now, darling. Time for me to get home.

Of course, Manyr, I love you. I'll see you soon.

Yes, indeed, we'll be reunited soon.

Manyr left, floating away like a feather in the wind. Lilay was alone once more. It was early, eight o'clock at night, but she knew the baby would arrive in the next day or so. It was time for her to get to bed and hope for the best. She laid down and rubbed her belly, praying hard for her loved ones to be safe.

Chapter 18

THE CROWN

Tinay felt safe and her body didn't ache as much, in part because she had cushions to thank. She was tired. The food she had eaten had sustained her, but she needed more than those frugal portions. She had to be in top shape. She also knew that there was another step to her meditation: the crown. Not a real crown, but an energy crown that was her link with the rest of the world. It would link her to the Goddess and the Overseer. It was the link to all creation, all life. It was too bad Manyr could not stick around a little longer. Tinay had questions now that she'd had time to rest and think. She had no idea when she would have the chance to see Manyr again. She wondered about her mother, but she didn't want to disturb Lilay in case she was sleeping. Lilay needed her rest right now because the baby would come soon.

Tinay felt a presence in the cave before she saw the person. She opened her eyes and looked around, but saw nothing. She closed her eyes again. She tried to go back to sleep, but she felt a strong presence beside her. When she opened her eyes, she saw a ghost sitting beside her on a cushion. The ghost silently shook her head.

Tinay was surprised. The ghost understood Tinay's thoughts and was indicating that Tinay was wrong, she wasn't a ghost. Tinay was still groggy from her sleep. When she turned around, she saw her own body. She looked around again. She was still in the pyramid. She was, however, still asleep and apparently still in her astral form. Tinay looked back at her body. She recognized the spirit now. It was Joynarae. The career guide wanted to speak to her. Joynarae nodded her head.

Joynarae extended her hand towards Tinay, very much the same way that Manyr had done before. Tinay extended her own hand in return and was transported somewhere she had never seen before. She was inside a building with lots of metal doors. The doors had little windows in them but they were too high for Tinay to be able to see through. There were many people around. It seemed chaotic. Tinay was not used to having so many people around her. She had no idea where she was. She was there, if she really was anywhere and if this wasn't taking place in her head.

All of a sudden all the lights went out and someone grabbed her and started to run. She ran up the stairs.

Thinking aloud, Tinay said: "Where are we going? We're not in a basement. Why are we running?"

She couldn't tell if she was talking or just communicating with her mind, but all this seemed so real she felt she was running. She felt she was out of breath and she definitely felt like the person next to her could hear her speak even though whomever it was that was pulling her was definitely not listening.

"If we need to get out, why are we going up the stairs? Where are you taking me? Please talk to me."

They finally arrived at a door that opened. Tinay found herself outside with the person who she felt was still Joynarae, in some form or another. Tinay tried to catch her breath. How could she be a spirit and need to catch her breath? This did not make any sense. Where was she?

She looked around and found herself on the tar roof of the building she had been in. There was nowhere to go. A large figure over by the facade of the building looked toward her. She walked towards him. She had never seen a human like him before. He was fat and his large, pain-filled eyes were close together.

"What is it? Tell me what's going on. I don't understand all this. What is happening? Who turned off the lights? Why are you so scared? Please talk to me."

The boy looked more like a child now than an adult. She looked into his eyes and saw fear. He was mortified by the actions of others around him. He knew the quickest way out was out the door and not up the stairs, but there was something else he wanted to show her. Either he could not speak or the fear prevented him from speaking, Tinay couldn't tell which, but telepathy did not work with him. He lifted his arm and extended his finger and pointed to his right. Tinay followed his finger and saw why he was so afraid. Hundreds of children were running away from the building in fear. She could not hear them screaming, everything was so quiet, but she saw many of them running for their lives. They ran straight ahead without thinking. On each side of the alley was fifty feet of grass, and then a forest started. Tinay realized what they were afraid of: men. Armed guards were chasing them, beating them with sticks and other weapons.

"My Overseer!" Tinay exclaimed. "They're only children."

Tinay could not understand the violence. She could not see why someone needed to mistreat them so. Why were the children running in plain sight? Why not hide in the woods and make it harder for them to find you? Struggling, each of the children were brought back to the building. Maybe it was because Tinay was so far from them that she still couldn't hear them scream, but she was certain they did not want to be back there. Whatever treatment they had just received in the field would be much worse inside.

"Tell me why?"

When she turned towards the boy, she saw no one left standing there. He had either escaped or returned inside. Tinay hoped that he wouldn't get treated so badly since he hadn't tried to escape. And now she was alone and afraid. She was becoming well acquainted with that feeling in the past few days. But this wasn't real. She wasn't really there, was she? Her body was on Sasgorg. How did she get here? How would she get away? How would she return home?

"Right, well, I'm on my own. I guess I better put my escape plan to the test and try to make a run for it. Staying on this roof will lead me nowhere."

She turned and saw the door that would lead her back inside, "Maybe that kid wanted help, but who does he think I am to defeat an army of guards by myself? I will help, but I can't let them capture me now. I need help. I need to tell other people what's going on here so they can help. They need to stop sending their children here and get the ones that are here out to a safe place, protected against those mercenaries."

Tinay walked around the top of the building looking for a way down and found a fire escape. Luckily for her, it was in the shade of the full moon. The moon would help her escape from this place later on, but for now it was a menace. She had to keep guarding herself from it.

Tinay climbed down the ladder and hit the ground in a soft thud. She walked crouched down to the edge of the woods, which was much closer on this side of the building and started to run as soon as she was near the woods. She kept looking back and saw no one behind her. She didn't feel anybody was left outside. She ran, but missed a step and went flying. She landed on the trunk of a tree and felt pain, sheer pain. She didn't scream, although she wanted to. She looked at her knee. It was cut open and bleeding. She was badly hurt and wouldn't be able to run anymore, but instead hopped like a rabbit. She tore her robe and wrapped her knee with the improvised bandage. It slowed the bleeding.

Tinay got back on her feet and started to hop along as quickly as she could. Even though her body was still in Sasgorg, she could still feel real pain in this dimension.

She came to a wall. It was too high for her to climb over. Now she knew why the kids were running straight ahead. They were running for the door. She looked over the bushes and could see the door in the distance. It was as high as the wall and, to her dismay, it was closed. There were two guards with dogs circling the door. She looked around her and saw a tree twenty meters away that hung over the wall. Quietly, she went to it and soon realized that this tree was her only chance. She would have to climb it and run once she was on the other side and try to find cover and heal her knee somehow.

She slowly but steadily climbed the tree. It looked like a giant oak tree that had been there for centuries. The branches were sturdy and solid. She laid down on the branch that leaned over the wall and pushed her weight along the branch. It was a slow and painful progress. All her body was aching now. She got to the wall and saw a problem she hadn't anticipated. Yes, the tree was leaning over the wall, but there was about a ten-foot drop on the other side and there was nothing to smooth out this ride.

Tinay started to cry. She couldn't go back. They would keep her. As a prisoner, no one would know where she was and no one would ever find her. She had to go on. She had no choice. Lowering her body from the branch, she heard a noise. CRACK! The branch broke. She was five feet closer to the ground, but the noise had alerted the guards. The dogs started to bark as they came closer. She let go of the branch and ran in a straight line away from the gate. She hobbled down the road as the dogs continued to bark. Once past the wall of the institution, she saw she was in a neighborhood with houses on both sides of the street. A town, she was in a town. There might be a chance for her to get some help after all.

"Wait, come back!" a woman yelled behind her.

Oh no! They know I'm here! Tinay's eyes filled with tears. She was running as fast as she could, but the woman was catching up to her.

"What do you want from me? Leave me alone!" Tinay yelled, hoping somehow to get some explanation.

"You made fun of my glasses. Come back!"

Tinay could not make sense of this. The woman was talking, but she was not making any sense.

"What glasses? Why would I make fun of your glasses? I don't know you. I have never seen you before!"

This was not getting easier and the woman was closing in. Tinay looked around and saw a yard with kids' toys lying on the grass. She grabbed a piece of wood with wheels on it, threw it on the ground, and hopped on. She kept her leg that was injured on it and pushed with the other. This would give her an edge.

Tinay decided there was no need to continue the conversation with the woman. The woman was slowing Tinay down and wasn't making any sense. Tinay saw a house with a porch light on the left corner of the street, but she figured if she knocked on the door, the other woman would probably catch her before Tinay could get anyone to come to the door. Tinay continued up the road, which turned right to an intersection. A road went left and continued to a wider road that continued on. She continued to look for shelter. Her knee really hurt and she knew she needed to hide and rest.

Meanwhile, the woman had stopped running and was calling on a radio for guards.

"She's bleeding. Bring the dogs and we'll find her easily. She's not going anywhere quickly now."

Tinay looked behind her, but couldn't see the woman. Maybe she gave up, she thought. She saw a large house that lay hidden in the trees. There she could find a hiding place. She walked by the house, but it was directly in the light of the moon so she continued on. All the lights in the house were turned off. Making sure she stayed quiet, Tinay reached the end of the wall but there was a nice yard that was pooled in moonlight. This was not what she had hoped for. She continued around the house until she reached a portion of the house that stuck out more than the rest where she found a receding wall, garden tools, and a pile of leaves. That was it; the answer to her prayer. She could hide in the leaves with a rake in her hands and if the woman came after her here, she would hit her. Not hard, just enough to stop the woman from pursuing her and then Tinay would return to the house with the porch light on and get some help.

Tinay only had time to sit down with the rake in her hands when she heard footsteps coming along the building. She got ready with the rake and waited. The bandage on her knee was soaked with blood slowly dripping down her knee.

As the sound of the footsteps got closer, Tinay raised the rake in the air and...

"Oh my!" she cried.

There were fifteen armed men accompanying the woman. Their weapons were pointed at her. They had lights and a dog that snarled at her and looked like he hadn't had lunch in a week. Tinay fell to the ground. She couldn't escape them now.

"Fine, I give up, I give up," she said, dropping the rake from her hand.

Tinay heard the clicking of the guns, sending a chill down her spine. She started to cry. They were not going to bring her back. This was an execution squad. They were here to kill.

"I don't understand. What have I done wrong?"

The woman leaned down on one knee and looked at her.

"If you're going to kill me, there's nothing I can do. I have no weapons, no way to hide and nowhere to run, but please tell me why. Why do you beat and abuse those children? They're only children."

The woman looked at her strangely and tilted her head to the side, "But what else are we supposed to do? They must learn to obey us, otherwise, they will run the place. It can't be done. They must learn discipline and obedience."

Tinay was crying so hard now that she could hardly breathe, "What about love?"

"Love? What do you mean love?"

"What about loving those children? Hugging them? Showing them the right way, instead of hating and hitting. What about kisses and forgiveness?"

It seemed so obvious to Tinay. "Children need love to grow and be the best they can be. If I was a child living in that institution, I would have tried to escape. You are right to want to kill me. I will not stop trying. This is wrong." Tinay looked down at her bloody knee. If she survived, she would never recover from her injury.

"I'm sorry," the woman said, touched by Tinay's tears and her willingness to die. "But this is all we know to do. Nobody ever taught us any differently. This is the way it's been for as long as can be remembered. Can you forgive us?"

Tinay cried harder than ever. "Yes, I forgive you. If no one ever told you a better way, how could you have known? Go and change your ways. I'm ready now." Tinay looked at her knee and the pain subsided. It stopped bleeding and the skin mended itself. Her knee looked as good as new. She looked up and everyone was gone, leaving her standing in the mist. She took a few steps and the pain was completely gone. What had just happened?

There was Joynarae, again, smiling, standing with her hand extended towards her.

"What? Where are you taking me now? I would like to go home and think about this. Isn't this enough action for one night?"

Clearly Joynarae believed the night was still young and she had more to show Tinay. Again, she extended her hand towards Tinay and waited for Tinay to put her hand in hers.

They didn't go very far. They were at the curve of the roads that Tinay had encountered earlier. Tinay felt different. She was not much older than she was originally. She wore a dress and she walked in daylight. She took the road that led to a field and saw no one. She continued to walk and saw an intersection with a much larger road going left and right. She decided to continue across that road and see what was on the other side. Once she reached the other side, she saw a bunch of stores lined up in a row down the street. She entered in hopes of finding out where she was and when this was. Tinay was confused. She felt she was in someone else's body. She didn't feel this was her life. She started to wonder if this was in the past or maybe the future or if it could be happening now, but somewhere else. There was no way to tell. She was at a loss. Her lack of knowledge of other planets did not help. Maybe if she had these visions after visiting all the home worlds of each guild, this would make more sense to her, but right now she was lost.

She was greeted by a shopkeeper who was busy with a customer. "Hello, I'll be with you in a moment," he said with a nice smile.

Tinay smiled back, *Good, this is good.*

Tinay looked outside and saw a crowd start to run in one direction, screaming and yelling.

"Oh no! Not again!"

Tinay felt like she was going to throw up.

"What's going on?" the shopkeeper asked.

"I don't know. Everyone is running from over there. They seem scared," answered a customer.

"Running from the mall? Maybe it's a robbery." The shopkeeper came over to the window and looked. "Oh no! Them!"

Tinay turned around and looked at him. She felt dizzy as she saw the fear in the shopkeeper's eyes. Whoever they were, whatever they were doing, they were bad news.

"I'm sorry, the shop is closed. Everyone out. Now!" The shopkeeper shooed everyone out and closed the door behind Tinay.

"So much for getting some help."

An old lady ran across the road yelled at Tinay, "Anna! Anna!"

Tinay was dumbfounded. So she wasn't Tinay here, she was someone else. She was Anna. Anna who? Tinay ran over to the woman.

"Yes?"

"What are you doing out here in the open? They'll catch you. Help me get home. We must pack and leave at once!"

The old woman was surprisingly agile and swift.

Tinay ran behind her. Either the woman was in great shape or her fear gave her wings.

"What is going on? Who is after me? What have I done?"

"Nothing, Anna, you have done nothing. But your gift of vision, Anna, is what they want. That's why we must hide. They want your gift."

Tinay now understood a little more. This was a fairy. She had the gift of vision and someone was going after the fairies to steal their gift. Could their gifts be stolen? Or could it be used against them? Tinay ran swiftly behind the old woman, happy that her knee was healed and allowed her to keep up with the woman. They cut across a field where the grass was hip high. Tinay looked sideways and saw mercenaries gather up young women, any women it seemed, and put them in a wagon to take them elsewhere.

They returned to a house in the neighborhood where Tinay had been hiding before. The house looked imposing in the neighborhood with its large trees and its brick facade. It was built to be strong, yet it was decorated with wood trimming that softened the look of severity it possessed. It had a name, Tinay saw, "The Drakar Hall." She went up the steps, and entered the house and saw a woman and a man packing suitcases.

"Thank the Overseer! Anna, you're safe!" The man, of middle age, came running down the stairs and hugged Tinay hard.

Tinay was surprised by the gesture. Not knowing who this person was, she lightly patted him on the back and was relieved when he finally let go. She watched him return to packing. He looked frantic trying to pack up his bag and get everyone somewhere else.

"Bella, are you done yet?"

"No, I have to pack Anna's things."

"Hurry up. There isn't much time. Someone will talk and point fingers at us," Jucaby, the maid, said.

Tinay looked as the whirlwind took everyone up and sent them spinning in one direction or another as she stood silently.

"Can someone just tell me what's going on?"

"Anna, the inquisition is here. They're in town. We must leave or they will have our heads cut off and impaled on poles at the entrance to the town and our bodies burned."

Tinay had read about shock in her mother's medical book and she knew she was starting to experience it. She pictured her dismantled body and her head on a spike. She, too, suddenly felt the urge to help pack her things, Anna's things.

"Never mind, Anna. I got your things," Bella said passing by, giving her a bag, and kissing her.

"But there's so much left." Tinay looked around and saw so many books, furniture, and clothes scattered over the place.

"Never mind that. Once the villagers talk, they will come here and burn it all. At least we'll escape with our lives. We'll start over again. We'll be fine. Come, Anna."

Bella put her arm around Tinay and lead her to the basement. They entered a crawl space and maneuvered their way through a long tunnel. Finally, they arrived at a wooden door that Jucaby opened and jumped down. It was another tunnel, but this one was high enough to stand in and there was room to run.

Jucaby helped Bella and the old lady jump down. When the two women were down, Tinay passed him the entire luggage they were carrying. With a pounding heart, Tinay jumped down and started running with the others. They ran for miles, it seemed, and finally another trap door opened up in the middle of a field.

Tinay looked around. They were miles from their previous location. They had escaped the city wall and were nearing a forest.

Jucaby and Bella helped the old lady pull herself up from the ground and run for the forest. There, they had a caravan with horses waiting for them. Tinay looked back and saw smoke rise from the city. They were burning the houses.

"I barely escaped this one," said the old lady.

"We all barely escaped," said Jucaby. "But we're safe for now. We'll just have to keep moving ahead of them from now on. We won't be able to stay in one place too long."

Tinay sat at the back of the caravan and looked sadly at the city they were leaving. She had a feeling she was leaving more than just a house and some books back there, much more.

The mist filled the forest and the caravan disappeared from under Tinay as Joynarae appeared again.

"I don't really understand what you are trying to say to me. What does this have to do with my career? You are my career guide, aren't you?" asked Tinay.

Joynarae nodded. She pointed her index finger into the sky and then extended her hand again.

"One more? You want to show me one more? What choice do I have? I have no idea how to return home without you. I will follow you for one more but, afterward, please let me rest."

Joynarae nodded. One more, and then Tinay could finally rest and maybe make sense of it all.

Tinay wondered if this was the same message sent to her in three different ways or if they were three different messages. Tinay was glad she would be with her mother soon because she hoped Lilay would be able to help Tinay make sense of it all.

The mist started to fade. This time when Tinay looked around, she saw a crowd around her. Everyone was saying how much fun this new jitterbug dance was, and that song from Benny was so great. Tinay had no idea where she was, but the sign was written in a language she did not understand. It was illuminated and pointed to two small windows in the wall. Everyone made a line while waiting for something. Someone held onto Tinay's hand; a seventeen-year-old girl, or maybe eighteen. A group walked away from the window with ice cream in cones.

"How is it?" the girl holding Tinay's hand asked.

"It's delicious, Isabelle," a boy answered as he took a lick from his melting ice cream.

"Did you hear that, Sophie?" Isabelle asked looking intently at Tinay.

"Yes, yes I did."

Tinay did not know what she was doing here, but for some reason she suspected things would go wrong very soon. She wanted to leave before she got caught. To take her mind off the feeling, Tinay studied Isabelle.

Isabelle was smaller and shorter than Tinay. Her long, black curly hair was pulled up in pigtails. As Tinay glanced behind Isabelle, she caught a reflection of herself in the window. She had long blond hair that hung freely over her shoulders. She wore a funny hat with a veil on it. She had very red lips and had blue eyelids. It almost looked like it was painted on. She looked at her feet. Wearing black and white flat shoes, she thought they went well with her flared skirt.

"Are you still thinking about Frederick?" Isabelle asked.

"Yes, that's it. I'm thinking about him." As Tinay said that, she turned around and saw a young man in a cap with a hoodie covering his head. She could only see his eyes, but his eyes were deep as the sky. Tinay looked deep into those eyes and saw something calling to her. Sophie had a deep feeling for this Fred and something was telling Tinay that this might just be the Fred in question.

"Fred?" she asked quietly.

"Shh!" he said. "Follow me quickly. The Gestapo is on its way."

Tinay looked at his clothes. He seemed to be wearing normal clothes just like everyone else. This being a spring evening, all around the streets were covered with water from a previous shower.

He grabbed Tinay by the hand and led her away from the ice cream store.

"Sophie, what are you doing? Our ice cream!" Isabelle protested as she saw Tinay being pulled away by the strange man.

"Quickly! Hurry up!" Fred said, his voice muffled by the crowd. He grabbed her by the other hand and pulled her away.

As the three of them made their way out of the crowd, a black car pulled around the corner and some guards came out and shouted for everyone to stay where they were. Fred started to run and the police opened fire and hit Isabelle. Tinay grabbed the young girl and started running with Fred. Fred took Isabelle away from Tinay and kept on running around the corner.

"Where are we going?" Tinay asked.

"Away from the Nazi. Follow me and don't get lost!" he said as he turned sharply to his left.

The guard that fired the shots scared the rest of the group of youths who panicked and started to run in all directions.

"IDIOT!!" the commander said. "We need them alive!"

The soldier looked back and could not see where they went. They had lost him once again.

Fred ran up and down the alleys, turning left and right and sometimes doubling back on his steps.

"Are you lost?" Tinay asked.

"No, I'm just trying to get the dogs confused if they decide to hunt us down. This way."

Fred turned and went straight down the alley and knocked on a wooden door and waited. Isabelle started to weigh more than she did before. Fred was sweating profusely. Someone came to the door and opened a small window high on the door.

"What is it?" he asked.

"The nightingales stopped singing. The redness of his pain covered his entire body."

"Come in, quickly," the man said.

Tinay followed Fred inside wondering what this riddle was about.

"She is hurt. She needs a doctor quickly," Fred said.

The man looked at her side and saw the blood. He ripped her shirt open. Surprised, he said, "Shot? She was shot?"

"Yes, the Gestapo at the ice cream parlor is rounding up the swing kids for camps."

"Have you been followed?" asked the man who suddenly looked older than he should.

"No, I made sure of that. This is Sophie. She'll need to stay here for the night."

"Very well, but if she stays, she helps."

Tinay had no idea what she would have to do, but she was glad that until morning, she was out of danger.

"Just tell me what to do," she said.

"Wash your hands and start ripping some cloth to make bandages."

Tinay followed the old man without hesitating and asked, "Where's the bathroom?"

"No bathroom, just the water pitcher over there," said the old man pointing to the end of the room.

Tinay moved over there, and Fred followed her. He put his arms around her and hugged her. Tinay could feel the love coming from him. She felt safe and secure in his arms.

"I knew it was dangerous for me to come out from underground, but I missed you so much. I needed to see you and hug you."

"I want to stay with you," Tinay said without thinking.

"You can't. It's too dangerous. If the Gestapo had found me tonight they would have tortured and killed me and anyone I cared for. I can't let that happen. I love you too much."

Tinay turned around. She needed to look in his eyes again. He kissed her.

"I must go, but I'll be back. I must find out if anyone was arrested and if the underground is in danger. I love you, Sophie."

Tinay held on to him. She had just met him, but she knew Sophie loved him with all her heart.

"Please, don't go," she pleaded.

"I must," he said and he kissed her again and left.

The room clouded with mist and the scene was over. Tinay had no idea what a Nazi was, or why there was a need for an underground anything. But, being inside Sophie without knowing what everything was, she could understand the Gestapo was like the imperial guards and that meant bad news. She didn't think that she was in her planetary system anymore because she had never seen that writing on the sign before. She had never seen those signs either for that matter.

She was tired and confused and couldn't make sense of it all. She looked around and saw Joynarae there smiling. Tinay smiled back. Tinay realized she never really was in any danger at all. She seemed to have witness an incident from someone else's point of view.

Joynarae came over to her and hugged her. Taking a step back, she made a ball with her hand, and another and another. She made the imaginary balls into one and pretended to put them into a bag that she threw over her shoulder.

Tinay understood that she was to take those three experiences with her and keep them for the journey. Tinay knew that, for now, none of this would make sense, but with time maybe these other experiences would help her understand more of the world around her. But she had learned a new feeling now on this journey. She couldn't quite name it yet, but it was fed by ignorance, vengeance and power.

She found herself in her golden cocoon in the cave and realized she had never really left it. She dissolved the cocoon and sat up on the cushion. She had been in a trance for a long time, which meant she had not really slept yet. Just as she was about to stand up she heard someone scream, "AAAAARGGGGGG!"

Chapter 19

LONI

"What on Sasgorg is going on?"

Tinay looked around ready to defend herself against an attacker. Nothing. She was alone. She had definitely heard someone scream. Where was that person now?

Think, Tinay, think. Who could there be? There's only you and your mother on this planet... Mother.

Tinay came back to reality with a rude awakening. But this was the only explanation. Her mother was having the baby, *Mother!*

I'm here, Tinay. Ooohh! That hurt, her mother said.

What happened, Mother?

The contractions have started. There's no stopping them now. They'll come every hour or so and then closer until they're only a few minutes apart. I will have to push her out. That leaves us with a few hours to go. Tinay, you must come to me. The initiation is finished, there's no need for you to stay behind. Lilay panted, trying to catch her breath.

Very well, but what do you propose I do? I'm stuck here, remember? I was waiting for Dad to come home.

I don't know what is delaying your father, but I can't wait any longer. You must come to me.

Okay okay, I'm coming. I don't know how much help I can be in the astral form, but I'll be there beside you.

No, Tinay. You will come to me body and all. Go down the stairs and find the well. My idea might work.

Tinay grabbed her bag and walked toward the stairwell. Her bag seemed heavier. She looked in it and found Draco asleep. She rummaged through the bag. There was no food left!

"You pig! You're no ferret! You're a pig in disguise!"

Draco didn't wake up at her yelling. He was comatose from so much food, but very happy, it seemed, in his dream.

What's wrong now? Lilay asked.

Draco ate all the food. There are only crumbs left. I have no choice but to leave the cave now. I'll die of starvation if I don't!

Are you at the well yet?

Getting there.

There were more stairs than Tinay had anticipated. She put Draco around her shoulders and started to eat the crumbs left behind. There wasn't much. How long had she been without sleep? What time was it? She had completely lost her bearings in this ordeal.

Okay, I reached the bottom. What is it I'm looking for? Tinay surveyed the entrance of the pyramid. It was huge, the biggest room of them all. It looked bland compared to the rest of the rooms that were so highly decorated. She pictured the cushions and the paintings and the curtains in this room. *Yes, that's probably where everything was. I wonder why they moved everything upstairs.*

Pa decided that they would do nicely in our new home on Kyr. We have little belongings and we must decorate when we get there. Since no one is using this, we figured we could use it. Do you see the well?

Yes, it's in the front of the room. I wish I could have seen it in its glory days. It must have been impressive to walk through those doors.

Yes, it was. Go check the water level in the well.

Tinay walked over to the well and saw that the floor was decorated with beautiful stones with intricate designs carved into them. She could recognize a dragon, a phoenix, a fish, and a tree. It was beautiful.

She approached the well and leaned over. The water was much lower than she expected. There was the line where it seemed to be regularly, but now it was twenty inches lower.

How is the water? her mother asked.

Well, it looks like it's about twenty inches lower than normal.

That's how it looks down here, too. That means that there's a flow of air in the tunnel and you'll be fine.

What do you mean, I'll be fine? What is it exactly that you intend on having me do?

Swim, of course!

Swim? In the well? Have you gone mad? It'll be half a day's walk to get here. I would have to swim for a half of day! I can't do that.

It's not that deep. You can probably stand up, but you won't be able to breathe because your head will be under water. You won't drown. I wouldn't risk your life. You'll be fine. If you leave now, you'll be here by morning.

Do you really think it's the only way?

Yes, I do. Now, please, hurry!

Tinay looked at herself and decided if she was going for a swim she had better take some clothes off to make traveling easier.

Mother, what about Draco?

You will have to let him swim and bring your bag with you. I will need painkillers by the time you get here.

Tinay left only her basic dress on and strapped a cord around Draco, so she could pull him when he got tired. She put her bag across her shoulder and jumped in the well. Draco was most unpleased with her. Her bag floated in the water. It was not going to drag her down.

She looked and saw two tunnels making a junction at Ardel. She had four ways to go, North, East, West or South. She had no clue where North was.

Mother, which way should I go?

Try to remember your steps and retrace your way down.

You've got to be kidding!

No, honey, I can't leave my body now so you'll have to do it. Or simply chance it.

I can't chance this, Mother. I could get lost down here.

She projected her mind to retrace her step. She had come in from the south of Ardel and walked north. She walked down the steps to the east, then the stair in the wall turned, and she came down the stairs and they turned also.

This is impossible! Tinay exclaimed in frustration.

It's not impossible. What else could I do to help you? Hunnn! Contraction. Be right back.

Tinay looked at the walls of the well. They were lined with Alenor crystals, which meant they could refract the light that found its way into the cavern. She waited for her mother to be done. Maybe Lilay could light the way for Tinay.

Mother?

Hang on, pff, pff, pff, not done.

How long are the contractions?

Just under 2 minutes, pff, pff, pff, pffffiou.

Mother, I have an idea. If you can find a light that will go under water, then I think we can light up the tunnel, and I'll know which one to take.

Marvelous idea, Tinay! Let's see what I can find.

Lilay rushed around. She could not think clearly because she was tired. What could go in the water? She looked at the lamp. She could not immerse it, but maybe with mirrors she could reflect just enough light for Tinay to know what tunnel to take. She brought the lamp over to the well and set the lamp on the mirror. She lowered the lamp into the well and let it float on the water.

Tinay, do you see anything?

No, Tinay turned around looking at each tunnel hoping for some light to show. *Yes, mother, I see a flicker of light. I know which one to swim down. Make sure you have a warm fire for me when I get there, and a blanket.*

I will, I will. Walk and I'll be there with you the whole way, Lilay said and stopped talking with Tinay.

"I love you, Tinay." Lilay whispered in hopes that her daughter would hear her. There was no reply. She bowed her head and started to pray to the ancestors for help.

Two inches of air existed above Tinay, which meant she had to swim on her back and keep her nose out of the water. She moved Draco onto her chest and tried to swim. She had not accounted for the ripples she was making with her arm and swallowed water. She started to panic and returned to the well entrance. Swimming would not work, so she went under water and touched the bottom. She could walk with her head sticking out of the water, which meant Draco could do the journey on her head and have no problem breathing, but it would be a challenge each time she needed to take a breath. Maybe a straw or a breathing mask would help. Maybe she had jumped into the well too soon. She was getting cold, she needed to start moving soon. She looked in her bag for her water bottle. She smiled when she found what she was looking for: her straw. She pulled it out and tried the straw as a breathing device. It worked! She could walk and breathe, but she would spend the most of her morning under water. All she had to do was walk straight ahead, but the confines of the tunnel made her feel queasy.

Oh no! Mother, the walls are closing in!

No, they're not. You're just feeling a little claustrophobic, which means you're not comfortable in small spaces, but you'll be fine. You can stand up. When you need to breathe real air just float on your back and breathe. Talk to Draco and me while you're underwater.

I think I'll concentrate on breathing and keeping Draco safe for the first little while.

Very well, honey, I love you. Once in a while I'll talk to you and see if you can hear my voice. That way you'll know you're getting close. How's that?

Yes, it would be nice to hear your voice.

Tinay looked ahead and figured if she didn't start moving ahead, she would never get home on time. It was more than a three hour walk she had to do. She had done this often. She could do it now even though the method was more challenging. She took a deep breath and went into the tunnel. She deposited Draco on her head. He knew better than to move. Tinay didn't know if he knew what she was trying to do, but he hung on to her head and would not move from there. She put the straw in her mouth and took a deep breath. It worked! She started to walk. Again, she swallowed some water. She panicked and returned to the well. The plan was a good one, but the straw was too flimsy to float. Tinay searched her bag once more and found a cork that kept nuts in a jar. She tied the straw to the cork and hoped that would leave the straw out of the water enough for her to breathe easily.

She gave it another try. She put the ferret back on her head and this time he knew what was coming and dug his claws into her flesh. He had no intention of being dislodged when she dove into the water. With the straw in her mouth, she tried to breathe again. This time it seemed to work. It had to work. She couldn't walk for fifteen minutes and then have it fall apart on her.

She decided this was the moment. She better start walking or else she would be stuck helplessly in the well for days. She took a few steps, but a little water seeped into the straw. This would have to do though. She started her trek under a hundred feet of dirt with no light and only water and walls to guide her step.

Lilay was unable to watch over her daughter like she had done over the past few days. She couldn't afford to leave her body now. Her body needed her. She wondered where her husband could have disappeared to. It wasn't like him to be gone for so long without getting in touch with her. She hoped he wasn't in trouble. She needed him to get through this. She missed him, too. She was not used to being alone anymore. She was used to having a child beside her the past fourteen years. Suddenly, she felt very lonely.

She rubbed her belly, and smiled. *I guess I'm not alone after all.*

I'm ready to come. Why have you delayed my arrival, Mother?

I'm alone, dear. I was hoping your father would be here or, at the very least, your sister would be here to help, but it looks like it's you and me now. Maybe your sister will be here for the birth, but she won't be here for the labor. It's you and me.

Yes, Mother, I am afraid I have moved too much. Are you sure we'll be okay?

Yes, of course. How far can you move?

I feel stuck.

"*It's normal, honey. You lowered yourself into the birth canal and now your head can't move as much, but everything will be fine.*"

Lilay rubbed her stomach and felt another contraction come on. They were getting closer together. It was going to be a long night. She breathed through it counting, "*One thousand and one, one thousand and two, one thousand and three.... One thousand and sixty, one thousand and sixty one, one thousand and sixty... ahh, that was harsh. And I have just a few more hours to go through this.*

I'm sorry, Mother, for putting you through this.

It's all right, it's not your fault.

Whose is it?

Lilay smiled, *Maybe I should blame your father for this.*

Could you?

No, I couldn't. I love all my children and I can't wait to meet you. I just have to get through the process. It's not just you, it was your sister and brother as well. It's the process, honey, just a biological process.

Tinay walked in the tunnel. She couldn't tell for how long or how much ground she had covered. Draco was still clawing her flesh and she knew unless her mother knew a secret recipe, he would leave scars for sure. Her straw system was working well. She just kept breathing. What she didn't see was that the cork had come undone and was slowly floating away. Tinay swallowed some water and started to panic. She couldn't breathe. Air, she needed air. She looked up and remembered that she could breathe if she laid on her back. She swam and put herself on her back and lay there motionless until she could breathe again. Draco had arranged himself so that he, too, could still breathe. She decided to see if she could swim on her back and make some time pass while she came up with another way of making it to the end of the tunnel.

Mother, are you there? Tinay asked.

Yes, dear. How are you?

I lost my cork, so I'm floating on my back now. I'm not moving as fast, but I have to come up with another way to breathe.

Your cork?

Yeah, I was breathing through a straw and I had attached a cork to it to make sure it would float above the water.

Can't you just hold it up with one hand?

I guess I could. I didn't think of that. I was using my hand to swim and walk faster. I'm getting tired, Mom. I didn't get any rest yesterday. I had three visions and. . . .

Visions?

Yes, things I know nothing about from somewhere else. I was walking in someone else's shoes and I was living intense moments in their lives.

We'll talk more about it when you get here. I will help you make sense of them.

Good, I was hoping you'd say that. I can't wait to hug you, Mom. I miss you so much.

Well, it's been two hours since I last spoke to you. You should be almost two-thirds of the way by now. Do you want me to try to talk to you down the well?

Oh yes, Mother, please try. Then I'll go back under water and finish walking the rest of the way. I'm just glad I'm past the halfway point.

Let me get down there. It may take a few minutes. I'm getting slow.

All right.

Lilay started walking down the stairs, but she came back up to the storage room. Tinay would need help getting out of the well. Lilay had better bring a rope with her. She grabbed a rope that was about sixty feet long, more than enough to pull her daughter out of the well. She left the room and started heading down the stairs.

"Oh oh, here comes another one." She sat down in the steps and started to breathe the only way she knew how. "Pfff, pfff, pfff, pfff, *one thousand and one, one thousand and two, one thousand and three... One thousand and sixty, one thousand and sixty one, one thousand and sixty two... One thousand and one hundred and ten, one thousand and one hundred and eleven, one thousand and one hundred... They're getting longer. The work is advancing well. Hopefully Tinay will be here soon."*

She quickly realized she forgot the blanket and a change of clothes for Tinay. She went back up and gathered the items she needed and started a fire, so there would be something there for Tinay to warm up to. She headed back down the stairs, but had a contraction before she reached the rope. She sat down again and decided there was no race and she better slow down the pace a bit.

Lilay continued down the stairs and arrived at the bottom and took a deep breath. This alone was more work then she was used to. She had stayed upstairs for a few days and now she was up the stairs three times in one night. She must be crazy, but at least now she had the rope and didn't need to get back up there until Tinay got back.

She anchored the rope at the base of the well and let the rope down into the well. She had been right; there was more than enough rope.

"Tinay, can you hear me?"

Her voice echoed down the well. The sound would have reverberated in the water and maybe allowed Tinay to hear the words.

"Mother! Mother! I hear you!" Tinay, in her excitement, swallowed some more water. *Good thing this is clean water.*

That's all right. You're close, honey. Maybe closer than we thought. You must push through and keep going.

I will, Mother. Tinay was invigorated with strength she didn't know she had. Hope, indeed, had been a powerful reinforcer of her faith. She was almost at the end of this journey and would see the sunlight again soon.

She decided to finish the rest of the trip underwater while blowing air in the straw to empty out the water and then take a breath. It was such a simple idea that she wondered why she hadn't thought of it.

Lilay sat beside the well and thanked the ancestors for their help and their ingenuity. She started to sing. She knew her daughter couldn't hear, but the music gave her courage. Hopefully, it would give courage to Tinay, too. She passed a good thirty minutes in this fashion and had two contractions. Indeed, the work was progressing well. She was unable to tell how far into the labor she was and when she would be ready to push, but Tinay was so close now.

Tinay continued, but now she was fighting a headache. She hoped that Draco would loosen his grip, but there was no chance, he wouldn't budge. She still couldn't see much. It was dark and, although the water was clear, she could not see through it without light. She thought she saw something ahead.

Come on, Tinay, let's not have your imagination play tricks on you. There's nothing down here, it's our drinking water. There's never anything down here. We've walked for hours now and everything has been empty and the walls clean.

As she thought this, she stepped on something. *Oh my! What the heck is that?* She looked down and swallowed water. She was starting to panic again, and she couldn't see anything, but she knew for sure she hadn't imagined stepping on something. Her head ached and she had lost Draco.

Oh no!

Forcing herself to calm down, Tinay took a deep breath from her straw. Then she let herself down and fought to find the string the ferret was attached to and pulled. He was stuck. *Oh no!* Something had a hold of him. She did see something. She did step on something. *Oh, gross!* She decided that Draco had not come this far to be served as food, so she yanked on the cord and then she felt a creature swim pass her.

"Oh! Really gross!"

She was unable to make the creature set Draco free. She would have to fight with it. She started to move in the direction of the string and grabbed the thing by the neck. She squeezed and pulled.

Wait a minute! Mother! I found a rope!

Lilay opened her eyes and saw Draco climbing out of the well.

Oh, dear, you made it. It's my rope I let down. Climb up!

I can't! I lost Draco. I can't find him.

It's okay. He's up here with me, trying to dry off. Hurry up!

Tinay surfaced from the water. "Mother!"

"Yes, I'm here!"

Tinay looked up and saw her mother. She never looked more beautiful. Tinay pulled herself up the well using her feet. She was cold and tired and that last effort she had to give was very demanding. As she squeezed the rope tightly in her hands, she couldn't believe that a few minutes before she thought she was fighting a giant snake. She smiled. "It's good to smell fresh air and breathe normally again, Mother."

"It's nice to have you here."

Tinay went over the side of the well and embraced her mother. She wouldn't have let go, but she was cold.

"Here, put some warm clothes on. Let's go sit by the fire."

Tinay changed her clothes and wrapped herself in the warm blanket. She hoped she would be able to sleep before her mother had the baby.

"Mother, do you think I could sleep a little?"

"Yes, dear, I can wake you up when it's time. Do you still have the spice and herbs with you?"

"Yes, they're in my bag."

"Then let's bring the bag upstairs. I'll replant them and make tea to ease the pain."

They walked up the stairs slowly. Lilay was wobbling and was glad that the next time she would go down those stairs she would be at least thirty pounds lighter. They arrived upstairs and Tinay went to get pots ready with fresh dirt for the seedlings. After all this time in the water, they had sprung nice roots. They were perfect to be replanted.

Tinay walked to the fire and put a bunch of wood on it and started to rock herself. She was finally home. The sun was just showing its first rays over the mountain as Tinay fell into a deep sleep.

Lilay made herself some tea to dull her pain. She was able to relax by the fire. She wanted to talk to Tinay when she realized her daughter was already asleep. Lilay got up and prepared some fruits and vegetables and put some soup over the fire to boil. It would be ready for lunch. Tinay would welcome real food compared to what she had been eating.

Tinay started to stir around lunchtime. The smell of the warm soup made her realize how hungry she was.

"I can't believe I fell asleep without eating. I was so hungry." She stretched in her chair, got up and moved towards the fire. Her mother smiled at her. Lilay, too, was hungry but she wasn't sure if it was wise to eat anymore. "We'll eat as soon as you have a look at the baby and tell me how open I am."

"Let's do it. I'm starving."

Tinay followed her mother to her bedroom and saw that her mother had kept busy and gotten the bedroom ready for the baby. Tinay checked her mother, but Lilay was not yet ready to push.

"You're about five fingers, mom. Half-way there."

"Very well, let's eat a little bit."

"Tell me about your visions."

Tinay explained her visions to her mother and awaited a simple answer.

"Tinay, I'm not sure, but it sounds to me that your guide showed you what took place on Earth, not here in our part of the galaxy."

"Earth was ages ago, mother."

"Yes, Earth was and still is. We have returned to Earth a number of times after the extinction of Atlantis. Some people escaped the cataclysm and continued the sacred teaching. They were in the highest peak of the mountains that covered certain areas on the earth. In the Andes, the Toltec survived. In the Himalayas, the Dalay survived. In Europe, the Celtics survived. And finally, Noah arrived in Egypt and started over in the Mediterranean Sea. To this day, the sacred teachings are being transmitted. But because of Atlantis and its demise, it's been kept secret from the general public so it can be protected against abuse and war. What you saw was the abuse of the power and greed. Your guide warned you against evil. When we left Atlantis, we lived without it for a long time, but it resurfaced again and it must be defeated. She told you three ways to defeat it. You can forgive the evil and be healed and move on with your life, the most complex thing to do, but just as you proved you could do it, you might have to do it again. Then she told you that sometimes it was okay to admit you're overcome by the enemy and to retreat to fight later. Finally, she showed you that love is the key and sometimes you will have to stop thinking about yourself and think about what's best for the community."

"How come it makes so much more sense now?"

"Your guide cannot talk to you."

"Why is that?"

"Because they would be tempted to talk to you all the time and it would take your free will away. There will be times when you'll hear a warning from them, but most of the time they will have images for you. Your guide must have been on one of the trips that returned to Earth to be able to link you that way."

"Why not return to Earth then, if it's still there?"

"Because it has changed a lot and they would see us as invaders. They have many of our gifts also, so their way of life has changed so much that the Elders don't feel like we belong anymore. But they keep tabs. Maybe one day our paths will meet again."

It was three in the afternoon and Lilay was eager to see what progress the baby was making. She and Tinay moved back to her room and Lilay asked Tinay to try and see the baby's position.

"Mother, I've got good and bad news."

"Give me the good first."

"You're opened at eight which means only a couple more hours and you'll be ready to push."

"Right, I'm ready to get it over with by now."

"But the problem is..." Tinay paused.

"Well, what's the problem?"

"The baby. She's not head or feet down, she's bum first."

"You've got to be mistaken!"

"No, Mother, she's seated. What are we going to do? I can't deliver you."

"I know. It's up to your father now. Either he comes or the baby and I both die."

Chapter 20

THE RETURN HOME

Raphael was glad he was finally able to give his father the message. He didn't think it was that urgent that they get home. The first few hours of flight were boring. Tamael decided that he better do the flying and let Ohuru rest so he would be in good shape for the asteroid field.

Raphael decided to practice his dagger throwing while Atleos decided to take it easy and read a book. The two of them, Raphael and Atleos, were well rested and hoped to be of help in the asteroid field.

Tamael was worried. It was not like his wife to ask for help. He wondered what could have gone wrong. He wished she could have left a bit more of a message, some explanation for his return. He knew he was late, but his wife was never bothered by this. There must have been something else. He could not understand what could have gone wrong. The baby wasn't due for another two weeks and Tinay had not yet discovered the cave when he left, which was amazing since she climbed that mountain so often to meditate on it. But she always remained on the north side of it to see the sun rise. She had never bothered exploring the south side of the mountain. It was much harder to do so because the rocks were jagged and sharp. He never pushed her, although he would have to soon if she didn't figure it out on her own.

After five hours of flying without any obstacles or even meeting another ship, they slowed down and stopped in front of the massive asteroid field. "Raphael," Tamael's voice echoed over the intercom, "wake up Ohuru for me. We're here."

"Okay, Pa." Raphael started to make his way to Ohuru's quarters. On his way there, he met Ohuru, who looked fresh and rested.

"Hey, I was on my way to wake you up."

"I know, but I set my alarm. I wanted us to lose as little time as possible. Your dad is worried."

"It happens a lot lately."

"These are hard times, Raphael, but I saw him smile just two days ago. He still knows how to do it."

"Good, that's good. I hope I'll see him smile again before I go back to Essay."

When they entered the control room, they saw Tamael observing the map and trying to see if there was a shorter way to get around the asteroid field.

"Ohuru, do you think…"

"No, my friend. By the time we go around the asteroid field at our present speed, so as not to alert anyone, then we will take just as long as if we would have gone the long way through Os. But I'm sure I can shave off a bit of time. I'll need help with the repairs afterwards, but I can help."

Ohuru sat confidently in his seat and took over the command. They departed and started their trek through one of the most dangerous parts of space. Ohuru knew that at normal speed this would take at least ten hours. A very tedious ten hours, but at fifty percent more power, he wouldn't save much time on the ride. Objects were coming at him that much faster and he needed his shield to be very close to the ship in order to avoid most of the debris. Two planets had collided here and their impact had destabilized the whole star system and eventually every planet had hit something on their trajectory. Some whispered that it had been an alien attack, but Ohuru's ancestors could not tell. All they knew was that it made it safe on Sasgorg because no one would come directly at them from that end of space. Just like the black hole protected Essay and Is. No one else in the galaxy was ready to live so close to the catastrophe between the planets.

Ohuru sent Tamael to bed reluctantly. Tamael lay in bed, tired but worried. He could not find peace. He wanted to talk to his wife. He was about to venture out when there was a knock on the door.

"Come in," he said.

Raphael walked in with a stern look on his face. "I want to know what is going on."

"Really!" Tamael said incredulously.

"I have a right to know. You cannot leave me in the dark. They're my mother and sister, you know."

"Maybe so, but I don't know more than you do."

Raphael's eyes welled up with tears. "Should I have tried to contact you sooner?"

"No, you did well. You couldn't have known I was going to be late. There was no way for us to know that we would be robbed by the guards and I had no idea about the reunion on El."

"Ohuru said you smiled there."

"I did."

"I..." Raphael stopped. "Why don't you smile with us?"

"Oh Raphael, I do. I'm just worried, with your mother expecting a baby, about us getting separated, and me having to be a full-time dad. I don't know if I'll be any good."

"Of course you are! You're a great dad."

"Thanks, Raphael. I'm glad you think so. I missed you."

"It was only two and half days."

"A bit more for me."

"Oh, right."

"Come, give me a hug and then let me have a nap."

Raphael hugged his father. He liked to feel his father's warmth envelope him. Space was cold. He was starting to figure out that he didn't have what it took to be a regular astronaut. He liked to have his feet planted firmly on the ground and have the sun warm his skin. He left his father's quarters and decided to do a bit of meditation.

Tamael, now alone, decided that he was better off sleeping than attempting anything. Ohuru would be exhausted when they finished going through the asteroid field and Tamael would have to take over for him.

Ohuru decided to start at regular speed through the asteroid field and see how rusty he was. He decided it wasn't so bad and started to accelerate. He was able to maintain his ship pretty smoothly when he got hit from behind. The asteroid sent him rolling sideways. He had to regain control, but another boulder quickly followed the first. He reestablished his flight plan, but his speed made it difficult to maintain the stability of his ship as he needed to keep veering to the right and left, sometimes upside down. It wasn't long before the rest of the crew met him on the bridge.

"Tamael, what are you doing here?" demanded Ohuru.

"I came to help," he said as he put his seatbelt on. "Fell out of bed about ten times before I decided that it was useless to try and sleep through this."

"I couldn't read the book. It was too chaotic back there. I decided to come and...." Atleos was interrupted when he went flying into the wall as Ohuru dodged a giant rock flying towards the ship.

"Are you all right?" Tamael sympathized with Atleos, who got up dizzy and walked to his seat.

"I'll be fine, really."

"Seatbelts! Seatbelts!" yelled Ohuru.

Atleos didn't have time to buckle up when, yet again, the ship went into a spiral and added numerous bruises to his poor body.

Atleos hurried to put the seat belt on and looked at the console.

"Couldn't we, like, blast our way through?"

"No, it would make more debris," replied Ohuru.

"Oh, hadn't thought about that."

"Has anyone seen Raphael?" asked Tamael.

"Nuh-uh," grunted Ohuru, trying so hard to concentrate. He remembered when he was young how much he loved flying in asteroid fields, but he never did the whole field at this speed. He would sometimes slow down, but there was no time now.

Tamael looked at the computer and located Raphael on the screen coming towards the bridge.

"He's on his way here. Can you keep it steady, Ohuru, until he's seated?"

"Pfff, right, and I'll make chocolate eggs while we're at it," scoffed Ohuru.

"It's just ..."

The ship went into another loop. Tamael kept looking at the screen and expected the little dot to go bouncing all over the place, but it remained steadily centered.

"I think he's got gravity boots on. He'll be okay."

"I should have thought of that too," whispered Atleos, rubbing his shoulder which no doubt would be bruised severely.

The door to the bridge opened up and let a sleeping Raphael float through.

"What the...?"

"What? What?" Ohuru wouldn't dare take his eyes off the screen and the monitor. "WHAT?!" he shouted.

"Raphael! He's sleep floating!"

"Huh?" Ohuru was surprised by Tamael's answer. Looking back for a second, Ohuru didn't see the moon-sized boulder that hit the ship's left wing. He had to maneuver quickly, but he wasn't quick enough. The boulder sent the ship flying between a tight row of smaller asteroids as the ship continued to bounce up and down on them.

"Ouch! That's gonna hurt." Ohuru didn't dare stop now, but he knew there would be some repairs needed before he could fly off Sasgorg.

Raphael continued to fly smoothly across the room toward a seat. When he was seated, the buckles attached themselves around him. Tamael looked and saw the fine outline of his son in yellow doing the work. He smiled. So, his son had made some huge progress with Aznebar. He had restrained Tinay for a long time, but it would seem that Raphael was to move a lot faster for some reason.

Your son will be extremely busy on Essay. He must progress while he can.

Master Aznebar, I trust your judgment.

Your son is brilliant, and will make an awesome Meji. I will train him well in the matters of the mind. Paletis will not undo him. My death has made me very strong. I have come back from the third plane to teach your son. Do you understand?

I do. I'm quite honored.

He will make you proud.

Master Aznebar bowed and disappeared from Tamael's view. At least his son was in very good hands. He wouldn't have to worry about him.

"Bumpy ride, Ohuru," said Raphael, stretching.

"Yeah, no kidding!"

Ohuru had sweat pouring from his brow. He concentrated so hard he was starting to get a headache. He loved Tamael like a brother, and that was the only reason he was risking his neck this way. Otherwise, he would simply have said no. He suddenly felt old.

It took them a tedious seven hours to get through the asteroid field when Ohuru finally passed over the command to Tamael.

"I need rest. Here, you take over."

Tamael nodded. He looked at the dial. Ohuru had successfully shaved three hours off their flight plan. Tamael would be there at around four in the afternoon, Sasgorg time.

On Sasgorg, time passed slowly. Lilay's labor was progressing well and she would be ready to push soon. If she didn't, there would be complications.

Tinay knew how to help her mother in normal circumstances, but these weren't normal. Helping her mother breathe and keeping her forehead cool didn't seem to be enough to keep her calm.

"What should I do, Mother?"

"I don't know, Tinay, I don't know. All will be well until it's time to push, and then I don't know."

Another hour of excruciating pain went by and the moment had come for her mother to push. It was two o'clock and her father wasn't close by. Her mother was trying not to push, but this created even more pain. Over her mother's scream, Tinay heard another voice calling Lilay's name. She thought she was delirious from the lack of food and sleep, but she looked around and saw the radio station.

"No, it can't be." She ran over to the radio and heard her father's voice repeat her mother's name.

"Lilay, are you there? This is the Armada calling. Answer me..."

"Father! Father, is that you?" Tinay said close to hysterics.

"Tinay? Are you all right?"

"I'm fine, but Mother is going to have the baby."

"Oh, is that all? You can..."

"No, I can't. The baby is backwards! I can't help her!"

"Oh, no! How long before she pushes?"

"She's ready now, Father, she's ready now!"

"Ooohhh!" Lilay let out a scream of pain.

"Mother!" Tinay ran to the bedroom and saw her mother had passed out with blood coming from between her legs.

On the ship, Tamael looked at his son and Atleos, and decided that he would go to light speed after all. He could not let his wife die now. He called for Ohuru, who was sleeping, and summoned him to the bridge.

A sleepy Ohuru walked onto the bridge, "Are we there yet?"

"No, but I contacted Tinay on the radio as soon as we were within range. Lilay is having the baby."

"Congratulations!"

"No, you don't understand. There are complications. The baby is breech. We have to go there now!"

"Man, we can't! Not after all the trouble we just went through to avoid detection."

"She'll die!"

Ohuru looked at his feet. He didn't have a wife, or children for that matter. Tamael was his family. He could not understand the pain Tamael was in, and Ohuru realized that without Lilay, this battle for the greater good would not mean anything to Tamael.

"All right," he said, walking decisively towards the commands. "Light speed it is. We'll be there in no time."

Tamael wiped tears off his face and went back to his seat. He couldn't wait to hold his wife in his arms.

Ohuru started to push some buttons on the console and calculated his jump to light speed. "Ready? Everyone's seatbelts are on?"

"Yes," they answered.

"Voila," Ohuru said and the ship made some weird sounds. It gurgled, sputtered, and shut down.

"Oops," Ohuru said.

"Oops? What do you mean 'Oops'?" demanded Tamael.

"Oops. The engine for light speed is shut down. We only have regular speed. I need to do the repairs from the outside. We won't have light speed for the rest of this trip."

Tamael put his hand over his face and started to cry. Raphael unbuckled himself and went over to his dad and hugged him. He had never seen his father cry before.

Tinay ran back to the radio. "Father! She's passed out and bleeding. I don't know what to do." Tinay was afraid and started to cry. This was supposed to be a joyous moment. Difficult perhaps, but nonetheless happy. Not like this.

"We'll be right over. Patience," Ohuru encouraged over the radio.

"Father, I need you now!"

Ohuru looked over his shoulder and saw a defeated man in the place of Tamael. He repeated in the radio, "We're only two hours away. Make sure your mother is well hydrated. We'll be right there."

"Two hours? She'll be dead by then."

"That's the best I can do."

"Go faster!"

"I can't. I would if I could, but the propulsion system for light speed has shut down. I can't go any faster. Keep your mother comfortable until we get there."

Tinay was crying hard now. Her mother was going to die. Two hours was too long. Lilay was already unconscious. What else could Tinay do?

Tinay looked around and saw the lilith. She decided that if she couldn't make her mother stop the contractions, she could at least ease her pain. She started to make a paste with chamomile and her tears joined the mixture involuntarily. She added her mocha cream and went back to the bedroom. She applied the cream on her mother's bulging stomach and heard her stir.

"Tinay?" Lilay said groggily.

"Yes, Mother?"

"What time is it?"

"It's almost three o'clock, Mother. Father will be here in two more hours. I talked to him on the radio. Just hold on."

"What are you doing, Tinay?"

"I'm trying to stop the pain, Mother. We'll be fine in an hour. Father will be here. Just hold on. Here, drink this."

"What is it?"

"Water, just water."

Lilay gulped the water, but most of it escaped her mouth. She looked exhausted and weak.

"Thank you, dear, thank you." Her mother returned to unconsciousness. Tinay didn't know what else to do. She cried for a moment and, too tired to remain awake, she fell asleep.

"What do you mean we can't land?" demanded Tamael.

"I can't open the landing gear."

"We need to get down there. Maybe it's not too late," Tamael said hopefully.

"Take the barge. I'll need the shuttle to do the repairs. I'll get to work on them right away," Ohuru ordered.

"Right, the barge, the barge. Come, Raphael, to the barge," Tamael said taking Raphael's hand.

"What about me?" Atleos asked.

"You stay here and help Ohuru," Tamael yelled as he and Raphael disappeared behind the door. They rushed to the barge and prepared to take off. The door opened with loud creaking noises and Tamael flew out of the center of the ship. He looked back and saw what his friend had put his ship through for him. He put his head down and prayed that his efforts and the price he had to pay was not in vain.

He decided he would land right by the house to avoid walking the distance between the landing strip and mount Ecumel. He landed in a whirlwind of sand and ran to the door with Raphael close on his heels.

They flew to the tunnels and rushed to the master bedroom where he found his wife motionless and Tinay crying.

"Noooo!" Tamael screamed. He grabbed his wife by the shoulders and shook her. "Wake up! You cannot die. Wake up!"

"Dead? She's dead?" Raphael walked dazed to his mother's side and could not believe his mother would be gone just like that. He grabbed her hand and felt a weak pulse. "She's not dead! She's still alive," he said relieved.

"She's been in and out of consciousness. She can't drink. Father, there's nothing I can do."

Tamael was at a loss. He didn't know what to do either. His wife was lost and so was his unborn child.

"Father, I can help. I'll need your suture kit," said Raphael.

"What...what for?" Tamael stuttered, secretly hoping Raphael could help.

"I'll cut mother's stomach open, take the baby out, and then sew her back together."

"What? That could kill your mom." Tamael shook his head.

"Maybe it's too late to save Mother, but I think I can still save the baby."

Tamael put his hand on his wife's belly and felt a little shudder. "Very well." He bowed his head and went to get his suture kit. He was back home, with his family and he had never felt so lonely in his life. He brought back the kit and watched as Raphael washed his mother's belly.

"Tinay, you'll have to hold her legs and you, Father, you'll have to hold her body." He said this as he started to shave the fine hair on her body.

"What are you going to do?" Tinay asked.

"I'll get the baby out. You'll see."

"How do you know what to do?" she asked tentatively.

"I did it to a horse on Essay already."

"A horse?"

"Yeah, but it's the same principle."

Tamael could not believe his eyes. His son had aged years in just a few days. He saw the blood come from the tiny cut Raphael had made and decided that he would look at his wife instead. There were things he did not need to see and watching his wife getting gutted like a pig was one of them.

Raphael worked quickly. In twenty minutes, he was holding the baby in his arms and was smiling. He cleaned the baby's mouth by sucking out the mucus and spitting it out on the ground. He heard Loni cry for the first time.

Tamael turned around, looked at his baby, and smiled. He was not going to lose everything after all. He looked at his wife. There was still hope. She looked white and pale, but she was still alive. Tamael took the baby and let Raphael cut the umbilical cord.

"Mom wants the placenta and the rest of the umbilical cord in here." Tinay passed a jar to Raphael.

"Yeah, just hold it there. That has to come out the right way. I just need to suture her well."

Raphael was shaking. He could not thread the needle.

"Normal suture?"

"Yeah," Raphael said wiping his forehead.

"I can do it, here."

He passed his sister the needle and the thread. He was happy to skip this step of the procedure.

"Dad, is this right?" Tinay asked as she started to suture her mother's uterus.

"Yes, you have it."

Once Tinay had completely sewn her mother up, Raphael bandaged her quietly.

"There, she'll be fine now," he said looking at his father.

"I hope you're right, Raphael, I hope you're right."

Tinay was busy cleaning everything up. "I should change her and let her rest."

"Yes, good idea. She should be moved as little as possible."

"I'll help you wash her. Raphael, can you hold the baby?" asked Tinay.

"Come here, Loni, come see Brother," cooed Raphael.

Loni slept peacefully. She, too, seemed exhausted from her ordeal. Raphael kissed her on the forehead and snuggled her in his arms.

"Watch her head," Tamael said as he walked out of the room.

"I will," and he closed the door behind him.

"Oh, Daddy, look at the wings and her hair! They're all full of blood," Tinay said.

"I know. We'll wash her carefully. It'll wash away."

"You think she'll be fine, Father?" Tinay said nodding her head towards her mother's bed.

"I don't know. I have never seen the procedure your brother did before. I just hope he knows it's not his fault if she dies."

"I see what you mean. She was in so much pain. It was so hard to watch her."

"I know. We needed a healer, Tinay. A healer could have helped her better than any of us."

"I wish I was a healer." Tinay put her hand over her mother's belly and accumulated energy there like she had done for her ankle.

"What are you doing?" Tamael asked looking at her.

"I'm doing something I did in the cave to heal my sprained ankle. It's all muscle, maybe it will help Mother."

"You found the cave?" Tamael asked.

"Yes, I did. I was stuck in it, too. There was a cave-in."

"I see. What did you do?"

"I went through it and then came back here by swimming through the well."

"The well? How did you manage that?"

Tinay told her father what had happened since they had been gone: of the guardian, the elder, the third eye and the visions.

"Visions? You had visions?" Tamael was surprised.

"More like weird dreams really. Intentional dreams. Mom says they're to help me understand things."

"Did you recognize any of the places there?"

"Not really. I studied geography of the main planets but I've never seen what they really look like. Mother said perhaps they were souvenirs from Earth from my guides."

"Is that what your mother said?"

"Uh-huh."

"Well, maybe the book of prophecies will help you. I left it in the cave before I left."

"Is it big and green and real heavy?"

"Yes," Tamael said suspiciously.

"It's by the well with my clothes."

"Oh, good. Well, that's it for your mother. Let's let her rest for now."

"I think I need some rest too," said Tamael.

"Very well, you go rest and I'll watch over her."

Raphael fell asleep in the rocking chair holding the baby close to his heart. Raphael, too, deserved to sleep.

Tamael walked over to his children and kissed them both on the forehead. He took the baby from Raphael and covered him with a blanket. He walked outside with the baby in his arms and looked up at the sky. It was dark purple and the stars shined brightly. He wondered if Ohuru would ever be able to repair his ship and fly properly again.

Then he heard a low scream. He ran back inside and found Raphael pushing his mother back to bed.

"You can't get up. You must remain in bed," ordered Raphael.

"The baby? Where's the baby?"

"I don't know. I fell asleep with her, but I..." started Raphael.

"Here, she's here." Tamael was crying again. This time his tears were tears of joy. His wife was alive, asking for the baby. "Here, she's right here." He deposited the little bundle beside his wife.

"Is she..." Lilay said, afraid of the answer.

"She's alive and well. Raphael saved you both."

"Raph, really? What did you do?" Lilay turned her head gratefully to her son.

It was Raphael's turn to explain what he had been doing and what he learned on Essay. He was so happy his mother was fine. During his story, the baby stirred and Lilay tried to lift her, but she soon realized she had no strength left in her.

"You won't be able to lift the baby for a few days. You must let the stitches heal. You have to stay in bed," said Raphael.

"I see. How am I supposed to feed her, Raphael?"

"Propped with cushion and pillows. You can't strain yourself."

"For how long?"

"A month I would say."

"A month? But how will we move to Kyr in that case?"

"There's time. Ohuru's ship has been severely damage by the asteroid field, so he can't fly anywhere for a while. He'll need to make repairs. Don't worry, we'll be fine." Tamael reassured.

"The asteroid field? Why..."

"We got your message late, so we tried to hurry up as much as we could."

"I'm glad you did. I love you."

"I love you, too. Here, let me change the baby and then we can try the cushion thing."

"Here," Raphael handed the baby over to his father. "I think I need a bath."

"I'll get supper ready after this. Don't fall asleep."

"I won't."

"What took you so long?"

"I had to stay longer on Os and then we went to El. There was a gathering of the old guard, a tournament, a celebration..."

"Did you have fun?"

"I did and now I feel so guilty." He turned around and went towards the bed. He propped his wife up on pillows and cushion. "I even won a prize."

"At what?"

"Sword fighting. It was such a good fight...." Tamael continued on his story while Lilay breast-fed her brand new baby. She smiled. She couldn't be angry. Everything had ended well and all her family was safe, but she hoped never to have to go through so much pain again.

Raphael washed and started supper. Tinay eventually got up and washed herself. She changed and met her brother in the kitchen. He was back in the rocking chair asleep. He had changed so much in so little time. She peeked in her parents' bedroom and saw them asleep. She ate some of the cabbage rolls that Raphael had made and decided she would get back to sleep also.

Chapter 21

THE BIRTHDAY

A week had gone by and everyone was still sharing their recent adventures. The repairs to the ship were advancing nicely. Ohuru was not pleased with the amount of work he had to do, but he figured the more battered his ship looked the greater the chance he would have to slip past the authorities unnoticed.

Unless, of course, they decide to pull my license because I'm a complete idiot for flying like that, he thought as he got back to work. He wanted to get as much work done before he met Tamael on the planet for Tinay's birthday and the blessing of Loni.

Tinay had started the day on Ardel. When she meditated, she was able to do so much more now. Her confidence had grown so much in the past few weeks. She couldn't wait to see Os, the world her brother described as voluptuous and luxurious. She could imagine the many markets and the food, such a diversity of food. Thinking about food made her think about returning to the cave to join her brother and her father to help empty their home. They were moving to Kyr ahead of schedule. Since Ohuru was stuck orbiting around Sasgorg anyway, they decided to load up the barge and make their way to Kyr early.

Tamael and Raphael were carrying tapestries and cushions to the barge when Tinay met them at the door. It had taken a few days to clear out the entrance of the cave.

"Ah, Tinay, could you get the ladder, please? I want to get those cushions you dropped on the second level," called her father.

"No need, Father."

Tinay was glad she could levitate things now. All she had to do was to picture the stars every object was made of and lift them in the air by an invisible string. She went down the stairs and got the cushions. She was happy all the marvelous stuff was being put to good use. Her family would have a lovely house on Kyr. She would have very little with her since she was going to travel so much, but she was glad all the plants she had grown were going with her mother.

Raphael and Tamael ate sparingly and continued their work until the evening. Together, they took the barge to Ohuru's ship and picked him up.

"Ohuru, my friend, are you ready?" Tamael asked.

"Yes, showered and smelling fresh."

"We'll have to empty the barge first, but..."

"No need. Let's just take the shuttle and then we can unload the barge tomorrow. I decided to take a break tonight."

"How are the repairs coming along?" Raphael asked.

"Well, it's faster when Atleos is not around. He asks too many questions. Besides, I have the old shell around the ship, but the actual ship is mostly intact. I only had to do major repairs to the light speed motor. I do have to make all the pieces myself so it's time consuming, but it'll be ready to move when you folks are."

"Tinay's at the house. She'll help Atleos with supper. Do you have everything ready here?" asked Tamael.

"Yes, I have the cake and the presents all loaded. Shall we?"

They boarded the shuttle and headed down to the planet. The sky was spectacular with rays of pink and violet. It would be a perfect evening for a birthday party.

Atleos had been helping Lilay with the baby and also took care of the meals. He didn't like Sasgorg much because of the scar it had left on his legs, but he grew tired of being in space. He was no mechanic. He was trained as a merchant. He could not wait for their departure and to go to live with Amos again. At least there he would be useful and he could look for a Healer. Lilay could manage to walk slowly if someone helped her up, but she couldn't carry the baby yet. He liked to take care of the baby. She was sweet and quiet and perfectly content to be there in his arms.

It was almost suppertime when Ohuru, Tamael and Raphael walked in the door where Tinay, Atleos, and Lilay were.

"What's for supper?" asked

"Stew," replied Atleos.

"Again?" Raphael said dismayed.

"It's lizard stew. Catch something else and I'll make something else," said Atleos offended.

"Touchy," said Ohuru with a smile. "I almost feel like I'm back home."

"Well, you shouldn't sound ungrateful. We all play our part here. I, for myself, don't see why I have to do the cooking when Tinay is the one helping at the cave. It should be..."

"I'm sorry to interrupt your rambling but I have been stuck underground for a while and I need fresh air now," sputtered Tinay angrily.

"Now children, let's not quarrel, let's eat," said Tamael. "Dear Overseer, Father of all, grant us the blessing of peace and see that my family remains safe over time. Dear ancestors, see to it that our strength is preserved and that our knowledge is not lost. Dear Mother Goddess, see to it that my wife and children are guarded in my absence and be fruitful in your blessing to our table. We are thankful for all our blessings, our health, and our house. Bless this meal we are about to have and bless this family which is about to eat it. Argor." Tamael lowered his head and seemed to continue on in his mind, while the rest of the family replied, "Argor."

Tamael brushed his hands together and started to help himself to the stew. He didn't know why Ohuru was complaining. Personally, it was his favorite meal. Even Atleos had learned to eat without wincing. Supper was good, and it didn't take long before they were all seated and laughing. After some time, Tamael stood up. "I have a surprise for all of you. Trinkets from El. I got them at the fair."

"Oh cool." Raphael sat up in his chair. "I'll go get them." Raphael got up and went to the hallway where he and Ohuru had left a few boxes. He came back with a pile.

"Oh, all that!" Tinay's eyes shimmered with excitement.

"Let's start with your mother. Lilay, this is for you," Tamael said handing her a box covered in paper.

Lilay had not expected presents for everyone. She was pleased to get something. She tore away the paper and opened the box. Everyone let out a collective sigh. It was a beautiful silk dress in red hues.

"You found that on El?" Lilay asked.

"No, not really. That I found in Amos's shop," Tamael smiled. He knew his wife had wanted one like that for years.

"Thank you, my love." She hugged him and gave him a kiss.

"Now, for my son!" Tamael turned and gave Raphael a square box.

"What is it?" He opened it quickly and saw nothing but a silver box.

"Ohh! You've got to open it here." Ohuru bent over and opened the silver box for him.

"It's a time converter. It can tell you what time it is on any habited planet and it can convert your birthday on Sasgorg to the date on any planet. It's real practical and..."

"Expensive!" finished Lilay. She could not believe her husband was giving such a present to a seven-year-old boy.

"He'll need it. Time is most confusing when you start living on different planets. At least he'll be able to keep track." Tamael took a small box from the pile beside him. "For little Loni, I got this."

Tamael opened the box and pulled out a fine chain made of a silvery metal with three birds entwined together.

"Oh, it's beautiful. Where did you get that?" Tinay asked.

"I ordered it a long time ago from a jeweler. He does great work."

"Indeed," said Lilay. She knew these gifts were expensive. "How can we afford this?"

"We've been able to afford lots of things for a long time, but there's never been any market to get it from or any need for such things. But now we are moving up in the world and we all need a little more."

Tinay knew her turn would be next. She wondered what her gift would be.

"For you, I got this."

She looked at the wooden box her father held out to her. It was strangely shaped and she wondered what it was.

"Open it. Go on," her father encouraged.

She opened the box and saw paint a brush, paint, paper, pastels and crayons. "Oh, thank you, Pa."

"You're welcome. And I figure you could use my old bag to travel with." Tamael went to his room and got a large weathered bag.

"Thank you, Pa."

"Maybe you should have emptied it before you gave it to her, Tamael," his wife said.

"That's okay, Ma, it's good. I don't need it right away," said Tinay.

"No, your mother is right. Atleos, Raphael, clear the table please."

Raphael and Atleos knew what was coming. They jumped to their feet and the table was cleared in no time.

"Now let's see what's in here. Hey! Wait a minute, that's not my bag! That's not my stuff!" Tamael said with a gleam in his eyes.

Tinay was surprised. Whose bag could it be?

"Look, Tinay, look for yourself," Tamael said grinning widely.

Tinay looked in the bag and saw a beautiful dress. As she removed it, she saw more clothes in beautiful colors with lots of green, her favorite color. She continued to look into the bag and found equipment for carving and sculpting, and so many more treasures. At last, she opened the last box, a jewelry box by the looks of it.

"What is this?" asked Tinay.

"Open it, you'll see." Tamael was smiling broadly. He had waited for so long before he could offer his family such presents. He was quite pleased with himself.

Tinay opened the box and saw a ring and a bracelet attached together with a titanium chain. A large emerald sat in the center of the ring. The rest of the bracelet was covered with little emeralds and shone brightly against the candlelight of the cave.

"It's beautiful!" Raphael said.

Tinay, however, could not speak.

"Put it on, come on now," said Tamael impatiently.

"Where did you get that, Tamael?" Ohuru asked.

"I made it. It took me a long time, but I made it. Beautiful, isn't it?"

Tinay still could not speak. It was beautiful, indeed. She had no idea her father was so talented.

"Why didn't you make jewelry instead of mining? You could have made a fortune with products like these," Atleos said.

"No, that one was special. Besides, that's what I plan to do when we get to Kyr, jewelry."

Lilay rubbed her husband's back. It was not what he really wanted, but there was beauty in his work and that in and of itself would satisfy him for a while.

"Why am I getting so many presents?" Tinay had finally recovered her voice.

They all started to sing a happy birthday song to her. When they had finished, they all applauded and each gave her a kiss, including Atleos. It was a happy birthday indeed.

It was Ohuru's turn to give her a present. "Here, you'll need this when you go away."

Tinay opened the box. Inside were two silvery metal boxes, much like her brother had received earlier. "What is this?"

"It's to write letters to your parents. They'll have one and you'll have the other. It works much like a radio but it's like a letter, and it's quick. It can be intercepted though, so no big secrets on there. But you know, it's good for keeping in touch and the messages can reach other planets. The messages are received immediately, without someone being there to receive them."

"Thank you, Ohuru." Tinay gave him a big hug.

"I have something also," said Atleos. He reached into his pocket and pulled out a small package. "Here."

"Thank you, Atleos." Tinay was curious. What could Atleos have given her? She ripped open the paper and found a beautiful square of silk. "Oh, how beautiful."

"I found that on Os. Even there it will be good for you to keep your face protected from the sun. I figured you could find use for it there."

"Thank you, Atleos, thank you very much. It's beautiful."

"Here's mine." Raphael gave her a little box.

"What's this, little brother?"

"I got that on Os, from Romanichel."

"Romani-who?" Lilay wondered who this new person was.

"Amos' wife, dear." Tamael patted her on the shoulder.

"Oh yes, I had forgotten her name." Lilay blushed.

Tinay opened the box and found several circular bracelets all silvery in color. "Why so many, Raphael?"

"It's to wear around your ankle. Let me show you. It makes music when you dance."

Raphael took the ten bracelets and put them around Tinay's ankle. Tinay made a tingling sound when she walked.

"I love it. I think I'm going to like Os!" Tinay said, beaming.

"Indeed, you will," said Ohuru, patting his stomach. "Indeed, you will."

"Well, I guess it's my turn. Tamael, can you go get it for me?" Lilay asked happily.

"Yes, dear." Tamael got up and went to the tool room and came back with a number of canvasses.

"I'm sorry they're not wrapped, but there are a few to get you started," Lilay said with great pleasure.

"Thank you, Ma. You didn't have to."

"It's my pleasure. Consider it from Loni as well."

Tinay smiled and kissed Loni and her mother on the head. This was a great birthday; the best ever.

Ohuru opened the last box and removed a sumptuous cake. They feasted on the cake and went to bed late that night celebrating Tinay's fifteenth birthday.

The next day, Tinay stayed at the cave with her mother.

"You must find an image for yourself that I can tattoo on you. You have completed your initiation. You deserve a reward. What would you like?" Lilay asked her daughter.

"A dragon."

"A dragon? Why?"

"For Master Okapi. He was so beautiful and he said I was pledged to the house of the Dragon."

"Very well. Will you design him for me or would you prefer that I do it?"

"We'll both make one and we'll see."

Tinay grabbed her easel and started drawing. All her ideas were scary. She could not make him look majestic without the look of fierceness and respect he inspired. She looked at her mother's drawings and saw that she was also sketching more than one image. Tinay needed to choose wisely because the tattoo would be on her skin forever.

"Mom..."

"Yes"

"What have you drawn?"

"Here have a look."

Lilay passed the board to her daughter. She looked at what her daughter had made. She hoped her daughter would choose one of her creations because Tinay's ideas would be painful to tattoo on her and would look vicious.

"This one." Tinay pointed to a beautiful sketch of a dragon made like a mosaic. It wasn't too vicious nor was it too scary and yet it still inspired respect.

"Good choice. I like that one too. Let's get to work."

Tinay decided she wanted it to be on her shoulder blade. Her mother cautioned her that the closer it was to a bone, the more it would hurt. But Tinay insisted that she wanted it there, so her mother started the work.

Tinay was happy she had chosen a relatively small dragon because the tattoo was more painful than she had expected. It took hours for her mother to finish and Tinay welcomed the interruption when Loni cried to be fed. Now she could have relief from the pain. It took most of the day and Tinay was happy when Lilay was done.

"Here. We must keep it covered for now. It'll be ready to see in a few weeks," said Lilay as she bandaged Tinay's new tattoo.

"Thanks, Ma. How many tattoos do you have?"

"Seven. One for each year spent at each temple."

"I see. Will they all hurt just as much as this one?" Tinay asked, worried.

"No. It depends on where you put it. I put all mine on my back, but it's your choice."

Tinay nodded. Her shoulder was itchy and uncomfortable. She decided that the next time, her tattoo would be in a spot where there was more flesh and less bone.

When Tinay got up the next morning, she found her father seated at the door reading a book with Loni sleeping in his arms.

"Hello, Pa."

"Hello, Love. I think maybe your mother was hasty in giving you the meaning of your dream."

"How so?" Tinay asked, confused.

"Well, I've read the book of prophecies and I found out that one vision can have more than one meaning, and being that you are not a medium, your vision was probably incomplete. You see, for a prophesy to be properly explained, you need a medium to see it, a historian to put it in context, and a healer to join the mind of the two, otherwise..."

"Pa, it was a dream, not a prophecy."

"No, you're right, but nevertheless, I think you should ponder more on what you saw, what you felt and what was said."

"Well, Mom said the visions were three ways to defeat evil by learning from what had happened on Earth. The first vision was about forgiving, the second was about admitting when you're beaten and leave and come back later. The third one was about love being the key."

"Yes, well, I'm not a historian or a medium for that matter, but the evil on Earth is the same evil that we face now. Human nature has often tortured itself in the sinuous ways of hell. I don't know why we must kill evil to win, to forgive or to love, but I know it's dangerous and people will get hurt in the process. Some already have, and it will be hard to forgive an enemy that hurts your loved one."

"I never had an enemy before. I'm not quite sure how I would react if I met our common enemy."

"Maybe then your vision was just a test to see how you would fare," proposed Tamael.

"You think so?" Tinay said uncertainly.

"Without a trinity, it might be impossible to know. Just keep your mind open, you might get to see those visions of yours in the lifetime."

"But Mom said..."

"Your mother has been trapped here on Sasgorg for twenty years. There's a lot of the world that has changed since she came here. Maybe she didn't recognize the places you saw, but it might still exist on our side of the galaxy."

Loni was starting to fuss in Tamael's arms. "Oh, time for a clean diaper and a fresh supply of milk." He rose to his feet.

"How's Mom doing?"

"She's healing quite well. The scar will be better than if I had done the sutures myself, and she's better at getting around already.

Soon she'll be back to her old self." Tamael smiled and went back inside.

There was little left to do on Sasgorg. Their departure was scheduled for the next morning. Only a few things remained to be packed away. It was going to be hard to leave this planet behind, although from what Raphael had been saying about Os, it was not going to be boring anymore. Tinay wondered how she would like life on Os, being so busy and eccentric. She heard some strange whispers coming from inside. She wondered what it could be. She went in and realized it was Ohuru on the radio to Tamael.

"Tamael? Anyone? Answer... Armada calling..."

"Here, here, I'm here....Shh... What is it, Ohuru?" Tamael answered.

"A letter from Amos. We missed a beautiful parade on Os. The guard seems to be moving, but he assures me that he might still have a chance to see it tomorrow."

"What?"

"Yeah, apparently they're going after some renegade in our region. Can you believe it? Renegades, here?"

"How ridiculous!" Tamael rubbed his hand over his chin. "Too bad we're going to miss it."

"Roger that."

"Send the barge. I'll have everything ready."

"Roger."

Tamael turned to Tinay, "Tinay, we're leaving. Everything must be gone except the dust. Do you understand me? There's no time. Paletis has found us. We must be gone. Actually, we must be out of sensor range in a few hours or else they will find us. Get your brother and gather the rest of our belongings. Now, Tinay!"

"Yes... right away." Tinay took off running to wake her brother whose biological clock was not set for time on Sasgorg yet.

"Raphael, wake up. We've got to pack and go now."

"Huh? What? Oh, ok. Five more minutes, ok?" Raphael turned around and pulled the cover over his head.

"No, now. Dad said NOW!" Tinay grabbed the covers and wrapped them quickly in a bundle.

"What's your problem anyway?" demanded Raphael.

"Paletis knows where we are!"

"Oh no!" Raphael got to his feet and started to pack the last of his things. Very little was left because he had done most of his room the night before.

"What about the plants?" asked Raphael.

"Don't know. We can't teleport because then they would be able to tell. We'll have to do it by hand."

"Yeurk! Do you realize how much work that will be?"

"I know, hurry up," said Tinay as they ran outside.

Ohuru landed the barge at the entrance of the house and lowered an automated platform to the door.

"I've been working on this for a while. It should help for the plants. Get the rest of the stuff in the barge. Atleos, come quick!"

"How did she find us, Ohuru?" Tamael asked.

"I don't know."

"I do," replied Lilay. "She was in my head when I was unconscious. She saw all of the sand. I'm sorry, I couldn't stop her." Lilay started to cry. "There was so much pain and I was so afraid. I hoped it was just a bad dream."

"It's ok, Love. We're ready, or we will be soon," comforted Tamael.

"What is your plan, Tamael?" Ohuru asked.

"The asteroid field. I don't care if we spend two days there, but now we can take our time getting around."

"That's what I was afraid of. If I had known, I wouldn't have spent so much time fixing the ship. Come on now, let's get to work. These boxes aren't going to move themselves."

"No, but I can move them faster," Lilay said. "Raphael, get over here." She handed the baby to him and started to move the boxes with telekinesis. "Tinay, you too, dear."

"Yes, Mom."

"Maybe you can leave the boxes to us and take care of the plants. With the stairs, they will be the most challenging."

"Very well. Tinay, go to the bottom of the stairs and I'll be at the top. Drop everything on the mid platform and I'll take it from there."

Tamael was glad to have his wife back, commanding and strong. She had brushed against death so closely, he was afraid she would never be the same again. He was wrong.

It still took a few hours before everything was loaded on the barge, and it had to be emptied a few times. Lilay was tired and so was Tinay.

Their talents had made everything go much faster. Tinay looked back at the empty cave and saw nothing but bare rock. It looked like an abandoned residence that never belonged to her family. It wasn't her home anymore. It made it easier for her to leave it behind.

Her father removed the door as Ohuru removed the cloth. No trace of civilization would remain, nothing but rock and sand. Tinay wiped a tear from her face and walked to her mother who was resting.

"What now, Mom?"

"There's sand everywhere. We must float sand inside, all the way down."

"Okay. How are we going to do that?"

"A storm will do nicely."

"A storm? Can you do a storm?" Tinay was intrigued.

"Yes, I can. We'll move to Landel, and together, we'll raise a storm."

"This I want to see," said Raphael.

"Is everyone ready?" Lilay asked.

"Yes, nothing is left, nothing at all. All the caves have been emptied. I checked twice. There's nothing left."

"Except maybe Nazar's skeleton in the main temple."

"Nazar can stay. All aboard then," Lilay commanded. She looked like she had grown a few inches. To Ohuru, she was the woman he knew from a long time ago.

Of course! I'm a few inches taller, Ohuru. I don't have to bend under the extra thirty pounds I had.

I think it's more than that, he thought. Ohuru was not well versed in conversing in telepathy, but he knew he could say a word here and there and she would understand.

They floated in the upper atmosphere where, with the help of Tinay, Lilay created a storm of gigantic proportion. It seemed there was no sand left on the ground. The winds made it hard for Ohuru to keep the ship stable, even though he was high up in the atmosphere. It didn't take her long to erase all traces of them. She let the sand fall back down and rest where it wished. She, too, had tears on her face. It was hard to leave a place she called home for so long. She sat back and let Ohuru take them to the ship.

"We must hurry," he said. "We'll be within range of Us within eight hours. I'll push the ship as fast as it can go on impulse engine.

But that will still put us just in the beginning of the asteroids in eight hours and twenty minutes. There will be a twenty minute window where she might detect us, so let's pray to the ancestors that they'll be looking the other way."

Lilay and Tinay decided to go to sleep. All their reserves of energy were exhausted. Tamael took Loni to the ship's garden and played with her there.

Ohuru knew that it was easy to speed up a little from here to the asteroid belt, but he had to remain within the limits or else all their hard work would be in vain. He engaged the ship's engines and headed for the asteroid field.

On the main ship, Paletis was raging. Her ship could not travel fast enough. She was trying to block all communications to make sure nothing would warn the rebels of her arrival. She thought she had seen the base of the rebels; a sandy planet. For months now she had seen sand. She had explored all the desolated planets until she finally had a glimpse of the sky. Why had she not thought of it before? Sasgorg was perfect! A bit too much out of the way for a base, but that might be why it was so perfect. She wasn't sure, but now she wanted to be there. Her incapable pilots had refused to pass through the black hole, and preferred the safest way around. For her majesty's safety they had said. *Ha! Vermin! They all are incapable! No one can touch me*! she thought to herself. But she was going to hit the rebels now. She was going to crush them! Hours, she was only hours away. They would pay! They would pay!

Ohuru had flown for eight hours, keeping a continuous sensor sweep on his long-range instruments. As long as he couldn't see them, they couldn't see him.

"Just another twenty minutes, Betsy." He patted the sensors gently.

"Who's Betsy?" Raphael asked from behind Ohuru.

"Argh! Don't you make noise when you walk anymore? You scared me!"

"Sorry. I had a nap and I thought I'd come check on you."

"Well, Betsy is my radar here. She and I are very good friends."

"Oh... okay."

"Raphael," Ohuru explained, "my ship is my wife and my inventions are my children. It gets lonely in space, so I name my inventions and ... uh oh!"

"What?"

"Tell your dad to get up here, now!" Ohuru said urgently.

"Okay," Raphael turned towards the intercom and called his father. "Pa, can you..."

"No, no, no. I could have done that! Shhhh, stay quiet. Physically go get your dad, please." Ohuru sweated profusely. He had detected the Guard lead vessel. A scout ship, no doubt. They were so close. He didn't want to be discovered now.

Raphael ran as fast as he could. He was out of breath when he joined his father in the garden.

"Must... go... to... the... bridge... hurry!" Raphael pointed back to the bridge.

Tamael could be a man of very few words when he wanted to. He left Loni with Raphael who was still trying to catch his breath and started to run.

The pilot of the avant guard was bored. There was nothing going on and, when the whole guard was moving, people didn't even bother to cross their path. They stayed behind the lines and waited for them to cross space. There was nothing to scan and he kept his scanning within attack range. His sensor had picked up the Armada, but not within the perimeter of its search. Therefore, it did not display on the screen.

"What is it?" Tamael asked out of breath when he reached the bridge.

"The avant guard. I detected the avant guard. They can see us now!" Ohuru was close to panic.

"How will you know when they do?"

"They'll send a few ships to inspect us."

"Why would they do that? We're a bit out of their way."

"Everybody gets searched now. No exceptions."

"I see. Make your way into the field as soon as you can."

"I can't go any faster."

"I know, I know. How much longer?"

"About ten minutes."

"Anelis, can you see that object on your radar?" asked the guard from on board the avant guard ship.

"Huh? What object? There are hundreds of them?"

"The one about to enter the asteroid field?"

"No, we're not configured for that far."

"Well, configure now. We need confirmation. We can't tell if it's an asteroid or a ship."

"Right away, sir!" Anelis hated his job. It was so mindless. So what if there was a ship near the asteroid field? Who cared? It's not like the queen was in any danger.

Aboard the main ship, the commodore hailed the Queen.

"My dear Queen Paletis, we might have a ship about to enter the asteroid field."

"What do you mean 'might have'?"

"We are not sure yet if it is a boulder or a ship. We're awaiting confirmation from the scout ship."

"If he is the scout ship why has he not himself already confirmed this information?"

"Huh, well ..." The commodore hesitated.

"Answer me, incapable idiot!"

"Malfunction, my queen, a malfunction. He's fixing it now."

"I'm on my way!" Paletis left her desk and stormed down to the command center.

Ohuru decided that maybe there was a chance to evade detection if only he had a few more minutes.

Paletis stormed into the room, making everyone stand up and salute. "As you were. Commodore, confirmation, now!" she ordered briskly.

"Yes, my lady." The commodore turned to his counsel and hailed the scout ship. "Scout ship, we require confirmation. Have you repaired the malfunction?"

"Malfunction? Why yes. It's fixed, but it's hard to get a straight answer. Lots of interference, almost there... yes... um..."

"Well?" Paletis was not a patient woman by any means, but this was too important to lose.

"Commodore, it's a ..."

* * * * *

The lights came on in the atrium and everyone looked shocked.

"What do you mean 'it's a ...' and then nothing?" Brett could not believe she would stop there.

"Now that's not fair! How can you leave us hanging like this?" John was irritated and disappointed at the same time.

"I've already started volume two. I must stop now. Next week we will continue the story of Tinay the warrior princess."

"But…" Marcus tried to say something.

"No 'buts'. I will now take orders from those of you who want to get a copy of the book, but first I will draw a name out of my hat to see who will win a free copy handwritten by me. Alayana, if you please."

Alayana came over to her and drew a name from the hat, "The winner is …"

All the participants made a drum roll on the floor. "Amelys."

A young girl got up and ran to Mani to embrace her. "Thank you," she said.

Reluctantly, everyone left. Most of the children ordered a copy of the book.

"Don't forget, the book was finished when they finished celebrating Tinay's birthday. The rest of the story goes into volume two," Mani said to everyone who ordered a book.

Alayana was left cleaning the atrium with Jeremyah who had already ordered his book.

"So if you heard the story before, why listen to it again?" he asked.

"I only know what happened in volume one and two. This will be the first time I hear the story from the beginning to end."

"You never read the books?"

"No, I always wanted to hear it from Mani first."

She put away the last of the paintings and said goodnight to Jeremyah who left, waving to her from the door.

"You like him, don't you?" Mani asked quietly.

"Very much, Mani, very much."

Mani put her arm around her granddaughter and walked upstairs with her. It had been a long and exciting day.

I was born in 1972 in St-Constant, Quebec in a family 8 children. I developed a joy for reading and specially Fantasy and Science Fiction. I attended University of Montreal and got a psychology degree and I worked as a police woman for the past 17 years. I wrote the first book of this series "The initiation" published in 2008. Over the past 25 years, I developed my gifts as a medium, Master Holistic Healer and Shamanic Practionner to heal those around me. Now, I teach and share my knowledge with the world.

CPSIA information can be obtained at www.ICGtesting.com
Printed in the USA
BVOW04s1950260215

389530BV00002B/8/P